Jefferson Randall Stanley Winston. The name didn't fit him at all. He ought to be called something like Gorilla Man.

Or Jungle Gia... She snorted. *Or Savanna...* Aloud, she asked, "Di... th... Rebe...

He frowned a... ...ow to answer that.

She rephrased. ..."Did the... ...ture you?"

"In a manner of speaking."

What the heck did that mean? "Care to elaborate?"

"Nope."

She tried a different tack. "Your grandfather arranged for your release. He's been very worried about you."

That elicited a completely indecipherable grunt from him. Could be disgust, could be gratitude. No way to tell. Sheesh, talking to this guy was like conversing with a brick wall. She gave up. If he wanted to talk, he would clearly do it in his own time and on his own terms.

She watched him through slitted eyes as he leaned back in his seat once more and seemed to all but pass out. Exhaustion, maybe? Except it looked more as if he was bearing incredible pain in stoic silence. What was up with that?

What was up with everything about this man? What in the *hell* had happened to him?

Dear Reader,

It's always fun to write a story for (and hopefully to read about) a character who's shown up in a number of previous books. I don't know about you, but it gives me a deep sense of relief to make some poor, unloved soul happy at last. Hence, it is with great joy that I present you Jennifer Blackfoot's story. She's had to watch most of her colleagues run off and find their happily ever after, but now it's her turn. And might I add, she finds love in a most unexpected place!

For his part, Jeff Winston is fully yummy enough to deserve a woman as awesome as Jennifer. Furthermore, as I close down H.O.T. Watch Ops for now—and in rather spectacular fashion if I do say so myself—it's really exciting to let Jeff introduce you to a whole new set of heroes and heroines who will sweep us off our feet, whisk us off to exotic locations and plunge us into love and danger.

I hope you enjoy reading the climax of the H.O.T. Watch series as much as I enjoyed writing it. Buckle your seat belts and hang on tight because the adventure continues…

Warmly,

Cindy Dees

HER HERO
AFTER DARK

BY
CINDY DEES

products and made from wood grown in sustainable forests.
nd manufacturing processes conform to the legal environmental
s of the country of origin.

Printed and bound in Spain
rint CPI, Barcelona

First published in Great Britain 2012
by Mills & Boon, an imprint of Harlequin (UK) Limited,
Eton House, 18-24 Paradise Road, Richmond, Surrey TW9 1SR

© Cynthia Dees 2012

ISBN: 978 0 263 89550 6
ebook ISBN: 978 1 408 97244 1

46-0812

Harlequin (UK) policy is to use papers that are natural, renewable and recyclable

logging a

regulation

Printed a

by Black

Cindy Dees started flying airplanes while sitting in her dad's lap at the age of three and got a pilot's license before she got a driver's license. At age fifteen, she dropped out of high school and left the horse farm in Michigan, where she grew up, to attend the University of Michigan. After earning a degree in Russian and East European Studies, she joined the US Air Force and became the youngest female pilot in its history. She flew supersonic jets, VIP airlift and the C-5 Galaxy, the world's largest airplane. During her military career, she traveled to forty countries on five continents, was detained by the KGB and East German secret police, got shot at, flew in the first Gulf War and amassed a lifetime's worth of war stories.

Her hobbies include medieval re-enacting, professional Middle Eastern dancing and Japanese gardening.

This RITA® Award-winning author's first book was published in 2002 and since then she has published more than twenty-five bestselling and award-winning novels. She loves to hear from readers and can be contacted at www.cindydees.com.

Chapter 1

Jennifer Blackfoot climbed out of the air-conditioned Land Rover into a muggy night echoing with the maniacal laughter of hyenas. She jumped as something screamed in the dark nearby. Whether it was a howler monkey or maybe a big cat, she couldn't tell. Nuwazi, Ethiopia, was about as far removed from the New Mexico homeland of her people as a person could get.

The African mercenaries with her were nervous, swinging their AK-47s from side to side like they expected a lion to leap out of the bush at any second. It was not reassuring that even the natives were unsettled.

A broad strip of dirt road stretched before her, thick with underbrush on both sides. "You're sure this is the place?" she asked her driver.

"Aye, Missy. 'Dis de place."

She glanced at her watch. Ten minutes till midnight. Her

counterparts from the Ethiopian government still had a few minutes before they'd be late for this clandestine rendezvous.

American entrepreneur Leland Winston was one of the wealthiest men on the planet if the rumors were true. His fortune supposedly extended into the hundreds of billions of dollars. She snorted. It was enough, apparently, to buy her personal services as a CIA field agent.

Winston's grandson, some kid named Jefferson Randall Stanley Winston, was in trouble with the Ethiopian government and needed extraction from the East African nation. Why Leland couldn't have just bullied the State Department into collecting the kid was beyond her. Repatriating American citizens fell under the State's formal auspices, not the CIA's. Although this wasn't exactly a normal repatriation. In point of fact, it had turned into a prisoner trade.

To that end, she gestured at the hired muscle with her to remove her prisoner from the backseat of the Land Rover. He was an Ethiopian national who went only by the moniker, *El Mari*. Big surprise, it meant *The Leader* in Ethiopia's primary language, Amharic. The guy looked and acted like a warlord of some kind. Although he'd been mostly silent on the ride here, an annoying gloating quality clung to him.

Whatever. Her job was to get Winston's grandson and bring him home. She seriously doubted Rich Boy was worth turning loose the man now standing beside her on the good citizens of Ethiopia. But it wasn't her call to make.

Headlights came around a bend in the road at the other end of the long clearing. A big flatbed truck with bare metal ribs arching over the cargo bed came into view. The mercenaries arrayed across the road at her side tensed, pointing their weapons at the vehicle.

"Stand down, gentlemen," she murmured.

They relaxed only fractionally, as if they knew something she didn't. Her tension climbed another notch.

The truck stopped about a hundred yards from her Land Rover. Green-camouflage-clad Ethiopian Army soldiers swarmed from the truck in a flurry of activity. She watched, perplexed, as they used a motorized lift on the back of the truck to lower a large wooden crate to the ground. Its side was pried open with crowbars and a dozen machine guns pointed at its contents.

Jennifer gasped as a tall, muscular man staggered out of the box. He was filthy, bearded and long-haired, and looked more like a wild animal than a human being. What in the world had they done to Rich Boy?

As the American stepped away from the crate, her shock intensified. He was wearing some kind of heavy leather collar around his neck, and four soldiers wielded what looked like long broomsticks attached to the collar. They wrestled him forward between them toward her. The American's hands were cuffed with metal bracelets to a chain around his waist, and his ankles were shackled. Just how dangerous *was* Rich Boy?

Unaccountably, the prisoner beside Jennifer laughed. It was a deep, full-throated thing that resonated with cruelty.

"It's not funny," Jennifer hissed. "How would you like it if we'd done that to you?"

He scowled over at her. "I am not crazy son-of-bitch." He lifted his chin toward his American counterpart and muttered in disgust, *"Mwac arämamäd."*

The hired guns around her surreptitiously held up their hands, making tribal warning signs against evil. *Mwac arä-mamäd?* Dead Man Walking? Her Amharic was rudimentary at best, but she was fairly sure that was what it meant. She glanced back at Rich Boy as one of his guards warily unshackled his ankles. Greasy strings of hair obscured his face as he staggered forward. He did look pretty close to dead at the moment. Or at least pretty savage. Nothing that a shower and a shave wouldn't correct, though. No one had told her Jefferson Winston was that huge and strong. The guy was over six feet tall and looked like a walking muscle. Alarm skittered across her skin. Was she taking custody of some sort of violent psychopath?

"Let's go," she ordered her prisoner.

She walked forward slowly with *El Mari* beside her. The closer they got to the American prisoner, the more appalled she was by his condition. His eyes were unfocused, and his lips drew back from his teeth in a feral snarl. Even the man beside her seemed to cringe a little at the sight of Rich Boy. Dead Man Walking, indeed.

The cluster of soldiers around Jefferson Winston stopped not quite halfway between the two vehicles. At a nod from the Ethiopian Army officer who appeared to be in charge of his side of the swap, she turned to her prisoner. *El Mari* held out his wrists and she unlocked his handcuffs. They fell away and she stuffed them in her pocket. Oddly, though, the Ethiopians didn't turn Rich Boy loose. Rather they gestured for her men to come and take positions on the collar poles.

Her men moved forward hesitantly.

Not interested in waiting for the handoff of the wild American, *El Mari* strode toward his own people, passing up her hired mercenaries and sneering at the American prisoner.

As the warlord drew even with the American, all hell broke loose. Rich Boy yanked his fists sharply and the chain around his waist snapped. With a single, violent twist of his torso, he wrenched the poles free from all four guards, leaped forward and pounced on *El Mari*. His attack was vicious and efficient. In a single shockingly swift move, he knocked the Ethiopian man to the ground and broke his target's neck with his bare hands, all but tearing the warlord's head off. There was no question that *El Mari* was dead as his body fell at a grotesquely unnatural angle.

Jennifer watched in stunned horror, uncharacteristically frozen in place as the crouching American unclipped the poles from his collar and flung them away. His limbs bunched. He sprang, charging her in a half crouch like a raging silverback gorilla.

He shouted something incoherent and took a flying leap at her, slamming into her just as a barrage of gunfire erupted. He barely knocked her out of the way of the flying bullets in time. Had he intentionally saved her life, or had that just been luck? The American was unbelievably heavy and smashed her flat, his large body completely covering hers. No air could enter her lungs, squashed as she was by his massive weight.

He pressed up and away from her into a bestial hunch. Galvanized into motion, she snatched her pistol out of its holster. Rich Boy's eyes flashed in chagrin as she scrambled to her knees and pointed the weapon at him.

But then she yanked his shoulder down with her free hand and fired past him at his captors, emptying her clip rapidly, and providing much-needed return fire for her men to reload their weapons and resume, effectively if not intentionally, covering their retreat.

The dismay in Winston's eyes turned to gratitude. She shrugged. One good turn deserved another, right?

He nodded briefly in thanks and then growled hoarsely, "Let's go."

"Right." *So. There was a man inside the beast.*

They sprinted for the Land Rover. A quick glance behind her revealed wholesale carnage on both sides of the firefight. The American shoved her at the passenger door and raced around to the driver's side. They jumped in simultaneously, and he slammed the car into gear without bothering to close his door. Gunfire aimed at them erupted. She ducked as the rear window shattered. The tires spun on the gravel as the Land Rover did a fish-tailing one-eighty and peeled out.

"My men!" she shouted at him.

"Paid to die," he retorted as he horsed the Land Rover around the first bend. The vehicle careened forward wildly for several miles before he finally eased his foot off the accelerator a little.

Terrified, she risked a look at the killer beside her. He truly did look more beast than man with hair hanging in his eyes and most of his face obscured by a heavy beard. What skin was visible was filthy, which only lent to the whole ape-man look. She rapidly rethought her childhood attraction to Tarzan. Jane could have him.

"Where's your plane?" His voice was guttural. Frightening, frankly. She ought to be terrified of him, but that brief glimpse of humanity in his eyes back on the road had reassured her just enough that she didn't bail out of the moving vehicle. Maybe she was stupid to trust him based on a single look, but her gut instinct was rarely wrong about people.

"Akimbe Airport," she replied, her mind racing. How much trouble was the United States in for letting *El Mari* be killed? What would the diplomatic ramifications be? And what on God's green earth was she supposed to do with Rich Boy *now*?

He drove on grimly. Since he didn't ask her for directions, she gathered he was familiar with the local area. The intelligence analyst within her duly noted it.

The Land Rover pulled up next to a sleek, unmarked business jet on the tarmac at Akimbe. Hmm, interesting. He knew which plane was the U.S. government bird without being told.

"Get on," he ordered, pointing at the plane.

Was she his prisoner? Was he planning to use her as a hostage to assure landing permission somewhere? Did he plan to kill her when they got wherever he was going? The trick in playing a game of cat and mouse was to make the other guy think he was the cat when he was the mouse all along. But she sensed this man was going to be very tricky, indeed, to manipulate. Where did a savage murderer flee to, anyway?

Jeff scowled as the beautiful, raven-haired CIA officer huddled in her airplane seat, hugging herself. He poked his head into the cockpit long enough to snarl a destination at the pilots, and then he fell into the seat across the aisle from his rescuer.

He couldn't believe she'd shot at the Ethiopian Army on his behalf. He'd been sure when she'd pulled out her gun it was with the intent to kill him. He would never forget grim determination in her eyes as she had shoved him out of harm's way. As if she could actually protect him from anything. It was laughable, really. But her impulse sent a ripple of warmth through his gut, nonetheless.

Bad idea to think about his gut. He became aware of the pain ripping through it until he was nearly crazed with the hellish agony consuming him. It took every ounce of will-power he possessed not to scream aloud.

"Buckle up," he gritted out at the woman.

Her hands shaking so badly she could barely follow his command, she managed to get the seat belt fastened around her lap. He followed suit, although he highly doubted it was necessary in his case. Probably not worth finding out the hard way, though.

He threw his head back, closed his eyes and gave himself up to the ever lurking, ever patient pain. Just a little while longer. He'd almost made it home. *Soon.* Soon he'd be able to give his body what it so desperately craved—what every last cell was begging for, and would keep begging for, until the pain drove him mad…or killed him.

Doc Jones would fix him up, though. He'd finally get some relief from the beast consuming him from within. And then maybe the beautiful woman beside him would quit looking at him like he was some kind of monster.

A groan escaped his throat.

Jennifer watched surreptitiously as the man across from her moaned in what sounded like tortured agony. He thrashed about, and she prayed he didn't accidentally stick his fist through the window beside him. He looked strong enough to do it.

Under normal circumstances, she might try to assist him. To hold his limbs down gently so he didn't hurt himself in his apparent delirium. But the idea of laying her hands on the monster across the aisle was repellent, not to mention terrifying. She had no intention of coming within arm's length of him. At least not without a taser on its highest setting in her hand.

She eased her cell phone out of her pants pocket and dialed a phone number quickly. She spoke in a bare murmur, "I have the American prisoner, but *El Mari* is dead."

Navy Commander Brady Hathaway—he supervised military operations run out of H.O.T. Watch while she was in charge of all civilian intelligence operations in the surveillance facility—exclaimed in surprise. "What the hell happened?"

"Rich Boy got away from his guards and all but tore the Ethiopian's head off with his bare hands. Who *is* this guy?"

A shocked pause was her only answer. Then Hathaway replied, "I have the same file on Winston that you do. Private prep schools. Harvard math undergrad. Master's in microbiology from MIT. Jet-set lifestyle since college—beaches in Monaco, skiing in St. Moritz, fast cars, yachts, beautiful women. Classic spoiled, rich kid."

"He violently murdered a man tonight. What the heck am I supposed to do with him now?"

"I wouldn't bring him back to the States. Our extradition treaty with Ethiopia will get him sent right back there to face murder charges, and I don't think that would make Leland Winston very happy. Go ahead and take him to Paradise Island for debriefing like we planned. Meanwhile the powers that be can sort this mess out."

Paradise Island also had the advantage of being close to the volcanic island in the Caribbean that housed the H.O.T. Watch facility. Normally, Paradise was a private getaway for H.O.T. Watch's staff when they needed a break from their high-stress jobs, but it occasionally doubled as a debriefing site.

Brady spoke again. "I'll do some more digging and see what I can find on your prisoner."

She caught a flutter of the American's eyelids. Awake, was he? Well, then. She murmured aloud in a theatrical whisper, "News flash. I think I may be the prisoner."

"What?" Brady squawked.

A quick movement made her look up sharply. It was the American. Holding out his hand expectantly, calloused palm up. The veins in his wrist were big and prominent. But then she already knew the guy was incredibly strong. It took tremendous strength to break a man's neck the way he had.

Without answering her colleague, she laid her cell phone in Winston's outstretched palm. She stared in shock as he crushed the thing in his fist, the plastic case shattering and the metal motherboard nearly folding in half.

No doubt about it. He thought she was the prisoner.

She forced herself to look him in the eye. She expected to see the same wildness from the road, the same murderous madness. But the blue eyes that stared back at her looked reasonably sane. At least for now. Was the guy schizophrenic or something?

"Why did you kill *El Mari?*" she ventured to ask.

"He was an animal. A butcher."

That was almost comical coming from him. She thought back frantically to her hostage training. Her best bet to stay alive was to get on this man's good side. Convince him she was a person with thoughts and feelings, and not some object to be crushed like her phone and cast aside.

"Would you like me to get that collar off of you?" she asked.

Surprise flickered momentarily in his cobalt gaze. Maybe even a hint of warmth shone there. The American was becoming more human by the second.

He slid out of his seat and knelt in the aisle beside her, offering her the back of his neck. Temptation surged to clobber him as hard as she could across the base of his skull. Except she wasn't at all sure she could hit him hard enough to knock him out. And if she failed, he'd do the same to her that he'd done to *El Mari*. Or worse. Memory of his ridiculously muscular body smashing hers flat flashed through her mind. She shuddered.

Nope, her best bet was to befriend this psychopath for now.

She laid her hands on the buckle, but jerked them back when the American groaned in what sounded like intense pain.

"Continue," he ground out.

What had the Ethiopians done to him? They must have tortured him brutally for even her lightest touch to hurt so badly. "I'll try to be gentle," she murmured, "but this buckle is really stiff."

The thick leather was almost too rigid for her to undo. But finally, the tail of the buckle gave way and slid free of the metal. The collar fell away from him. She kicked it toward the back of the plane in disgust. No matter how crazy this guy was, nobody deserved to be treated like an animal. His neck was raw and bloody where the collar had been.

"Let me get the first aid kit and clean up your neck. That must hurt."

One corner of his mouth turned up sardonically. She wouldn't exactly call it a smile. The distant relative of one, maybe. It was a start, though. As gently as she could manage, she swabbed the raw flesh ringing his neck. As the filth surrendered to her gauze pads and peroxide, his dirt blackened skin took on a pink and mostly human hue. She worked her way around to his heavy, dark growth of beard. She estimated he hadn't shaved in several months.

"How long were you in Ethiopia?" she asked.

He shrugged. Not the talkative type. Or maybe he'd just gotten out of the habit. If he'd been in solitary confinement for a while, he might not have had much opportunity for conversation with other humans. In her experience, once freed, such prisoners either wouldn't shut up at all, or they became intensely taciturn like this man.

Jefferson Randall Stanley Winston. The name didn't fit him at all. He ought to be called something like Gorilla Man. Or Jungle Giant. She snorted. *Or Sasquatch.*

Aloud, she asked, "Did the Ethiopians hurt you?"

He frowned as if he wasn't exactly sure how to answer that.

She rephrased, "Did they torture you?"

"In a manner of speaking."

What the heck did that mean? "Care to elaborate?"

"Nope."

She tried a different tack. "Your grandfather arranged for your release. He's been very worried about you."

That elicited a completely indecipherable grunt from him. Could be disgust, could be gratitude. No way to tell. Sheesh, talking to this guy was like conversing with a brick wall. Okay, Plan C. "Where did you tell the pilots to take us?"

He didn't even bother to acknowledge that one.

Ohh-kay. "Do you have any other injuries that need tending?" she tried.

He made a noise that might almost be a snort of humor.

She gave up. If he wanted to talk, he would clearly do it in his own time and on his own terms. Normally, she would get a man like this a good meal, let him take a shower and sleep a little, and then she'd sit him down and debrief him on what exactly had happened to him. But how she was going to get this guy to talk was a mystery to her.

She watched him through slitted eyes as he leaned back in his seat once more and seemed to all but pass out. Exhaustion, maybe? Except it looked more like he was bearing incredible pain in stoic silence. What was up with that?

What was up with everything about this man? What in the *hell* had happened to him?

Chapter 2

Just a little while longer. The plane would land in Bermuda where he'd told the pilots to go, and he would finally get the drugs his body was screaming for. And then, blessed relief. The pain would recede. It never went away entirely, but it would retreat into tolerable background noise. Until then, though, his entire skeleton ached as if every bone in his body was shattering into a million pieces. To call it excruciating didn't even begin to do it justice.

He was no doubt scaring the hell out of the woman across the aisle, but he was in too much pain to care. A need to do violence, to lash out against the agony eviscerating him from the inside out, nearly overcame him. He clenched his fists until he feared he might break the bones in his hands.

Finger by finger, he forcibly unfolded his hands until his palms pressed flat against his thighs. He could do this. He could survive this nightmare. Just a little while longer.

The woman's eyes popped open as the sound of the engines

changed pitch and the plane began its descent into Bermuda. Leland had a beachfront mansion there where Jeff could stay. More importantly, Doc Jones could fly there with his drugs relatively easily. He envisioned the hilly island in the middle of the Atlantic Ocean bristling with gracious, white stucco homes. He had good memories of summers there as a kid. It would be nice to be surrounded by familiar things again. It had been a long time. The past few years had been pretty crazy, culminating in the disaster in Ethiopia.

The plane bumped onto the runway and a groan escaped from between his tightly compressed lips, in spite of his best effort to restrain it. It was probably a perfectly fine landing, but even the lightest jarring sent daggers shooting throughout his body.

He glanced outside as the airplane came to a stop and frowned. Heavy tropical jungle? Since when did Bermuda have such vegetation? Alarmed, he surged out of his seat.

A pair of ominous, metallic clacks froze him halfway out of his seat. He looked toward the cockpit where both pilots, grim-faced, pointed heavy-gauge pistols at him. A glance to his right showed that the woman had joined them in aiming her sidearm at him.

Well, well, well. The lady had teeth, after all. Reluctant admiration coursed through him. Unfortunately, his soft tissue was as susceptible to lead as the next guy's. He subsided in his seat cautiously.

"Welcome to Uncle Sam Airlines, Mr. Winston," the woman bit out. "We do not necessarily fly the Friendly Skies. This is *my* plane and *my* crew. And you are *my* prisoner, not the other way around. Is that understood?"

She had guts to stand up to him like this. He'd be amused if he wasn't hurting so damned bad. But the prospect of having to wait even longer for his drugs threatened to swallow him in panic. He was out of strength to hold on. Out of endurance. Out of time.

With a roar, he surged up out of his seat. But the woman was surprisingly fast. She ducked down the aisle and out the door before he could lay a hand on her. One of the pilots passed her something as she raced by the cockpit, but he couldn't see what it was.

He followed her outside and came up short as she aimed a double-barreled shotgun at his chest. Her black gaze, leveled at him down the length of the weapon, was lethal. What little sanity he had left recognized death in her eyes. He pulled up short.

"Need us to restrain him, ma'am?" one of the pilots asked from the doorway of the plane.

Her gaze remained locked on him. She spoke slowly, as if she doubted his ability to understand her. He supposed he couldn't blame her for that. "Let's establish a few rules of engagement right up front, shall we, Mr. Winston? If you will give me your word of honor that you will not harm me in any way, I will swear not to sedate you or physically restrain you. But, if you break your word, I will not hesitate to do the same. Nor will I hesitate to kill you if it becomes necessary. Is that clear?"

"Crystal," he answered wryly.

"Do you give me your word?" she demanded.

He studied her curiously. She was a courageous woman to face him like this. But, then, she probably didn't realize exactly how courageous since she had no idea who he was—*what* he was. "I give you my word."

"Say it. What do you swear?"

Another wave of pain slammed into him and he ground out from between clenched teeth, "I give you my word I will not harm you."

She spoke to the pilot still hovering in the door. "If you'll off-load my bag for me, Captain, I'll let you be on your way."

"Are you sure you want us to leave, ma'am? We can stay here until more backup arrives to, uhh, help."

"No. The two of us will be fine. We have an understanding. I need you to go."

Jeff wasn't sure whether to be complimented that she trusted his word of honor or to despise her naïveté.

"All right." The pilot sounded deeply doubtful. *Smart man.*

The woman stood statuelike and continued to point the shotgun at him as her bag thudded to the ground, the jet behind them cranked up its engines and taxied off. He glanced away from the woman and her shotgun long enough to watch the white jet accelerate down the runway and lift off into the afternoon sky.

There went his best and fastest hope for relief from his private, living hell. He swore under his breath and looked back at the woman. How to convince her to get his drugs for him before he died from the agony of his withdrawal?

"Now what?" he asked her cautiously.

She lowered the weapon slowly. "Now we head up to the house. I imagine you'd like a shower, shave and a decent meal. Then we'll talk."

What he'd like was a nice fat injection of Doc Jones's magic serum. Although he had to admit, a shower didn't sound half bad. In the first days of his imprisonment, before his world collapsed down to a pinpoint of exquisite agony, he'd craved a hot shower almost more than he'd craved a good meal.

The foliage looked Caribbean... No way. They wouldn't have brought him to the one place he'd kill to go, would they? A low-level hum of eagerness to do violence vibrated in his gut. Patience. Someone would pay someday.

He fingered his thick beard. He must look like some sort of wild mountain man. Although maybe the look wasn't so far from the truth. Without comment, he followed as she slung the strap of her duffel bag over her shoulder then turned and walked toward a small, metal storage building.

She grasped the lock and dialed a combination. It didn't open. She tried again. No luck. She swore under her breath.

"Problem?" he asked.

"They must've changed the lock since the last time I was here. I'd call and ask for the new combination, but you destroyed my phone."

"What's inside?"

"A golf cart. Trust me, it's a long, steep hike up the mountain to the house without it. And it's really hot out here."

He shrugged. After the searing heat of Africa, this tropical climate felt almost gentle. Daytime highs in Ethiopia at this time of year routinely hit the high one-twenties. But the lady did look badly overheated. He eyed the lock and muttered, "Step aside."

"Excuse me?"

He brushed past her and she gasped as his arm came into brief contact with hers. Gritting his teeth, he ignored the light sound. He took the lock in his hand and gave it a sharp jerk. The hasp tore half off the building. He yanked again and a rectangular piece of galvanized metal sheeting gave way. The entire lock tore free in his hand.

"Door's open now," he announced.

She stared at him in shock. "How did you do that?"

He shrugged. There wasn't much to say. She'd seen exactly how he did it. He grabbed the lock and ripped it off.

"Do you have any idea how much strength it took to do that?"

He frowned down at the ragged hole in the building. "Aluminum of that gauge can typically hold something like twenty pounds per square inch. Given the size of the hole...maybe thirty square inches…that means it took about six hundred pounds of force."

Her jaw sagged.

"Of course, if there was metal fatigue, the required force might have been much less," he added lamely. What in the *hell* was he doing? He knew better than to show off for some woman he'd just met! Especially one who worked for the U.S. freaking government. It would be disastrous if she caught even a hint of his secrets, and here he was, laying them out before her like an open book for the reading!

He grabbed the handle and lifted the garage-style door hastily. Must distract the woman. Fast. His ploy seemed to work, for she ducked under the door as it was still rising and headed for the golf cart inside.

The vehicle groaned as he eased his weight down onto it. She threw him a strange look, which he pointedly ignored. After tossing her bag in the back, she drove the cart outside. He waited, arms folded, as she got out and closed the door behind them.

She guided the cart onto a dirt path that zigzagged back and forth up the steep side of a substantial mountain. It looked like a dormant volcano covered in heavy tropical undergrowth.

Near the summit, a small clearing opened up and a gracious one-story home came into view under a canopy of trees. It was long and low with a deep, covered front porch stretching its entire length. A ceiling fan cooled a pair of cane rocking chairs, and plantation shutters slatted the windows. Unquestionably Caribbean architecture.

The Caribbean, huh? So his guess had been correct. He eyed his companion speculatively. What were the odds she was attached to the secret government surveillance facility in that region of the world? The one that had gotten so many of his men killed and caused him no end of problems?

His more immediate problem asserted itself as a wave of molten agony engulfed him. He needed his drugs, and soon. At least he wasn't far from the United States. He should be able to get his drugs flown in here fast.

Assuming the prickly woman beside him allowed it.

He stared at his beard in the mirror. He would need clippers to trim it down enough to be properly shave-able. Not to mention, the idea of dragging a razor across his super-sensitized skin made him cringe in abject terror. There were not many things in this world that scared him, but the prospect of inflicting that kind of pain on himself was one of them. He was already stretched just about to the limit of his tolerance.

For now, he'd leave the beard be. He eyed the shower stall warily. Desire to finally be clean warred with his fear of the water hitting his skin. What if he couldn't take the pain? What kind of a wimp would he be if he couldn't even tolerate that small pressure? Fear won out over filth. Like his mother always said, a little dirt never killed anyone. But more pain could very possibly break him in his current state.

He backed out of the bathroom and headed down the hall toward the mouthwateringly delectable smell of meat charring.

"Steak okay for supper?" the woman asked from beside one of those indoor grill stoves that sucked down the smoke into a powerful fan.

He groaned as his mouth puddled with anticipatory saliva.

"That's the first time I've heard you make a sound of pleasure instead of pain. What did your guards do to you, anyway?"

Not much, truth be told. He'd ripped out of a pair of metal handcuffs trying to save his guard's life that first night in jail when the guy was murdered, and the rest of the jailers had stayed well out of arm's reach of him ever since. They thought he'd been the one to garrote the cop in the interrogation room with him. With *what,* he'd like to know, since he had no wire, rope, chain or other material on him or in the room strong enough or long enough to wrap around a man's neck and choke him to death. But that hadn't swayed the Ethiopians.

His big problem had been the other prisoners trying to kill him for the huge bounty *El Mari* had put on his head. As miserable as he'd been never coming out of his tiny, dark, sweltering cell, it had been better than getting killed. But three months living in a five-foot-by-eight-foot box had been hellish.

The woman was speaking again. "Look, you're far from the only guy I've debriefed. Nothing you can say to me will shock me. I've heard it all before."

He highly doubted she'd heard anything close to the story he could tell. He'd bet a million bucks his tale would shock her speechless. But that wasn't a theory he planned to test.

Wincing, he eased himself into a sturdy-looking kitchen chair. It held his weight, thankfully. If he were at anything remotely approaching full speed, he'd offer to help with the meal. Not that he could cook a lick. But he could've set the table or poured drinks or something. As it was, the room was starting to spin while invisible bad men poked him with cattle prods. His body jerked spasmodically as the pain assaulted him.

Clenching his teeth, he ground out, "What's your name?"

She slid a juicy slab of sizzling steak onto a plate and set it down before him. "Jennifer. Jennifer Blackfoot."

Desperate to distract himself, he concentrated on her name. Blackfoot? That sounded Native American. She looked Native American, too. Her face tended to roundness, her skin was a lovely walnut hue, and her exotic brown eyes were so dark they almost looked black. Her hair was true black with almost blue highlights glinting out of her long braid. He'd wager her hair reached past her slender hips when it was loose.

"What tribe?" he bit out.

"Despite my last name, I do not belong to the Blackfoot nation. My family is Chiricahua Apache. And yes, we were the violent ones who scalped white settlers and kidnapped white children. I am, in fact, a direct descendent of Geronimo, although in our tongue, his name was Goyakhla."

A warrior woman, was she? Not surprising based on what he'd seen so far.

"Do your friends call you Jefferson?" she asked as she sat bowls of cold Caesar salad and hot green beans dripping with butter on the table.

"No. Jeff," he muttered as he picked up a steak knife and fork. He swore as his palms cramped so violently he nearly cried out. The utensils clattered to his plate. His hands were too tightly clawed at the moment to master the fine motor skill required for steak carving.

The woman frowned but asked matter-of-factly, "Need some help with that?"

He scowled at her, too humiliated to admit that he couldn't control his hands.

She leaned down next to him and efficiently cut his steak into bite-size pieces. Through the haze of his despair, he noticed incongruously that she smelled good. It was a floral scent, but not overwhelmingly sweet. It was green and wild and entirely fitting for her. His instincts flared in response to the light musk.

She stepped back a bit too hastily. Scared of him, was she? Smart girl. She mumbled, "If the fork's too much to handle just now, go ahead and eat with your fingers. It won't bother me. It's how my people traditionally eat."

Too famished to stand on pride, he ended up doing just

that. God, he felt like a savage, shoveling food into his mouth with his bare hands. But to Jennifer's credit, he didn't catch even a single glimpse of disgust or revulsion in her eyes. He was stunned when she mimicked him and skipped utensils to eat with her fingers. She managed it quite a bit more daintily than him, of course. The compassion of the gesture startled him.

Near the end of the meal, which tasted better than anything he could ever remember eating in his life, she asked, "Any reason you didn't take a shower?"

Glaring, he muttered, "I need a *bath*."

She nodded evenly. "No problem. My bathroom has a soaker tub that even you should fit in. After supper, it's all yours."

He made eye contact with her just long enough to nod, but then he locked his gaze on his plate and refused to look back up. There was only so much embarrassment a man could stand.

Jennifer carried the empty plates to the sink as Jeff disappeared down the hall toward her bedroom. What a strange man he was. He'd fumbled with that knife and fork like he had no idea whatsoever how to use them. Which was absurd. The man was from one of the wealthiest families in the world and had the finest in education and lifestyle. Had he suffered some kind of weird memory loss where such basic skills were lost to him? More strange yet, she got the distinct impression that he was appalled at his own eating habits. Why, then, did he persist in eating like a savage?

Surely he wasn't trying to make some grand social statement, was he? The man didn't strike her as the type. He wasn't defiant enough for something like that.

He seemed about equal parts angry and desperate. But desperate for what?

The longer she was around Jefferson Winston, the more the mystery deepened.

Jeff eased into the tub of steaming hot water and was overcome by ecstasy that momentarily overwhelmed his pain. The bliss was so intense as to be almost sexual. He exhaled a long, slow breath of relief.

That same wild, sweet perfume he'd caught before swirled around him as he luxuriated in the water. His body shocked him by responding hard and fast to the scent of the woman. She was extremely attractive if a guy went for that whole earthy, natural thing. Which, he had to admit, he definitely did at the moment.

Just how much comfort was she authorized to give him, anyway? He pushed away the idea of bedding Jennifer Blackfoot. Not only was he in no shape to withstand the physical rigors of sex, the woman was so wary of him she looked about ready to jump out of her skin most of the time. And then there was that shotgun of hers to consider. Did sex constitute harming her? Would she kill him afterward for violating their deal?

That outcome was likely enough that he satisfied himself with merely imagining her slender, bronze limbs wrapped around him, her black eyes sparkling in pleasure, her body taking his into her and satisfying his long-denied lust.

When the additional pain of his aroused flesh became too much to bear, he forcibly turned his thoughts to his mission gone terribly wrong. That first night in jail, to his shock, instead of questioning him, his Ethiopian interrogator had whispered urgently of a conspiracy. Of classified military intelligence from the United States being sold to *El Mari* and used to ambush Jeff and his team. The interrogator's last words before the door burst open and a masked man jumped him and garroted him were that *El Mari* was determined to kill him. Even here in jail, Jeff would not be safe.

The guard had been right.

Thankfully, the other prisoners vastly underestimated his strength the first time they tried to kill him. They only jumped him with a half-dozen men armed with shivs. He beat them all to a pulp, retreated to his cell and never came out again to give them a second chance.

Jeff added more hot water to the cooling bath. When he found out who in *El Mari*'s organization had stepped into the bastard's shoes now that the guy was dead, he vowed to himself to take that guy out, too. The unholy work of *El Mari*'s mercenaries had to be stopped.

But more importantly, he would find and punish whoever in the United States government had sold him and his men out. Five good men dead on his watch. *God help Jennifer Blackfoot if she was part of the conspiracy that had killed his men.*

His grim thoughts grounded him back in the reality of his suffering. He supposed it was fitting that if he was the one man on his team to survive, he was also the one who would suffer the most for it.

The steaming bath gradually soaked loose the accumulated filth ground into his skin over a period of months. He picked up a surprisingly pink loofah—Jennifer didn't strike him as a peppermint pink kind of woman, but obviously he was wrong—and very, very carefully scrubbed the crusted dirt and caked sweat off his skin. It hurt like crazy, but being clean felt so good he was able to grit his teeth against the sensory stimulation long enough to finish washing.

As the tub drained, he stood up, naked, and let cold air

wash across him. His skin puckered with goose bumps, but it felt good. Even the most minor relief from his pain right now was a blessing. But it did not last. His skin dried and the fires of Hell resumed searing away his flesh layer by blackened layer.

Eyeing his disgusting clothes in a heap on the floor, he couldn't bring himself to don the filthy garments again. Gingerly, he wrapped a towel around his hips and headed for his hostess.

She was in the living room, reading a newspaper. Eagerness to find out what was going on in the world gripped him. Later, he'd read that thing front to back. But right now, he needed something to wear or access to a washing machine.

She glanced up and made a faintly choked sound. "Problem?" she croaked.

"Clothes. Mine are gross."

"Aah. If you'll look in the dresser in your room, you should find some men's clothing. Although I'm not sure any of it will fit you. But maybe you can find something that'll work until I can have larger clothing sent out."

He pounced on that like a lion on prey. "We can get things sent here? How fast?"

A delicate eyebrow arched over her right eye like a swallow's wing. "Is there something in particular you want?"

He eyed her warily. He didn't for a second underestimate the intelligence of this woman, his adversary. "I'll need to have some things couriered to me. Clothes for one. Medications. Business documents. I've been away from my company for too long. Things are probably a mess there by now."

She pursed her lips thoughtfully but made no immediate comment.

Rather than stick around to let her say no, he retreated to his bedroom in search of clothes.

Oh. My. God. Jeff Winston in a towel was one of the most incredible sights she'd ever seen. Sure, she worked around a lot of buff special forces operatives who were blatant exhibitionists when it came to showing off their muscles, but every last one of them would slink away in shame if they ever had to stand next to Jeff. Something primal and female stirred deep within her at the sight of this overpoweringly alpha male.

He looked a bit like a world-class body builder. Except where a body builder would sculpt his body for beauty, symmetry and an idealistic form, Jeff's body was built for sheer, raw power. The man looked like a rock. Or more accurately, a pile of bulging boulders and slabs of granite stacked into a humanoid shape.

No wonder he'd been so unbelievably heavy when he had landed on her and knocked her out of the way of the gun battle erupting over their heads. The guy hadn't ever heard of body fat, apparently.

As he retreated down the hallway, she noted that his back was no less defined than his front. He looked like he could lift a truck. Heck, he looked like he could pick up a truck and throw it.

Heat flared in her cheeks as she realized she was ogling her prisoner like some hot-to-trot college coed. She was a grown woman, thank you very much. Fully in control of her desires and not the slightest in need of a man in her life. But good heavens, what a man. She'd seriously never seen a specimen even remotely like him. He was a *beast*.

But as soon as the word crossed her mind, she frowned. His current appearance wasn't his fault. But with all that hair and that wild look in his eyes, it was hard to separate the man from the animal he'd had to become to survive whatever the Ethiopians did to him.

She cranked up her laptop and fired off a quick email to Brady Hathaway at H.O.T. Watch. She asked for additional steak to be sent to the island, along with a new cell phone for her. And then she ended the message with,

See if you can back channel an off-the-record conversation with the Ethiopian Army. What in the world did they do to this guy in prison to turn him into what he is now?

Chapter 3

Jeff stared at himself in the mirror. Both the T-shirt and cutoff sweatpant shorts he wore stretched too tightly across his massive physique. But they were the only garments that even came close to fitting him. If nothing else, they highlighted his power pretty blatantly. Hopefully, it would be enough to intimidate his hostess into sending for his drugs immediately.

He rejoined her in the living room, where she was most of the way through the newspaper now.

"Better?" she murmured as he sat down on the sofa opposite her.

"Indeed."

He waited until she glanced up at him questioningly, debating with himself while he waited. Indirect subtlety or direct and straightforward? How to get Jennifer to order his drugs brought in? His gut told him to go the direct route, but habit told him to approach all women circuitously.

"What's put that frown on your face?" she asked.

"I'm debating how to handle you," he replied frankly.

She smiled sardonically. "How about you let me do the handling for now?"

That sent his right eyebrow sailing upward. Did she mean the sexual innuendo? Surely, it had been intentional. She was too smart to make a sophomoric slip of the tongue like that. Thought she could use sex to manipulate him, did she? If he weren't in so much pain that he could hardly see straight, she would probably be right to think that. He'd played the field as hard as the next guy over the years. Maybe harder than most.

But since he'd met Dr. Gemma Jones, that had changed. The drugs had taken over his life. Now they were his one and only mistress.

"You didn't answer my question before," he announced. "How long does it take to get things shipped in here from wherever they get shipped in from?"

"Is there something specific you need in a certain time frame?" she retorted.

He glanced down at the shorts and T-shirt straining across his muscular body. "Some clothes that fit would be nice. Not that it would bother me to do without clothes altogether."

Her eyes widened and went an even smokier shade of coffee brown. *That's right, honey. Two can play that game of sexual innuendo.*

"I can have more clothes for you in the morning," she mumbled.

Overnight, huh? That meant this island was reasonably close to civilization. And fairly substantial civilization at that. Clothing in his size didn't come off the rack in just any old store. Back home, everything he wore was custom-tailored to fit his extreme physique.

He tried, "Is there a phone? I need to talk to my business partner. Not to mention my grandfather is no doubt waiting to hear from me."

Jennifer shrugged. "He'll have to wait a little longer. Until I finish debriefing you, no one speaks to you."

"Sorry," he replied lightly. "I'm not wearing any briefs."

Her gaze dropped involuntarily to his lap and spots of pink erupted on her cheeks.

"So what does this debrief entail?" he asked.

She blinked up at him as if she was struggling to organize her thoughts. "Uh, for a start, I need to know what happened that led up to your capture. And I'll need a full report of what happened to you while you were in the custody of the Ethiopians. And I need a satisfactory explanation of why you killed *El Mari*."

"And if I refuse to answer your questions?"

"Then you're not leaving this island any time soon."

He glanced out the picture window over her shoulder at a spectacular sunset over the distant ocean. If this place was close to the classified facility that had set up his men, he was happy to stay right here. "I can live with that. Can you?"

She leaned forward, forcing direct eye contact with him. "You will never be allowed to go home, Mr. Winston. Ever."

He shrugged. "I haven't been able to go home for a long time. That's nothing new."

She leaned back, frowning. "Why not?"

"Long story—"

"We've got all the time in the world, apparently," she replied dryly.

"—and I'm not sharing," he snapped.

"I'm going to keep at you until I get my answers," she warned him.

"Then you are doomed to intense frustration and the bitter taste of failure," he replied grimly.

She studied him intently like she was measuring the truth of his words. Finally she asked reasonably, "Why? I'm not the enemy."

He snorted. "From where I sit, that's debatable."

"Why do you say that?" she asked.

He studied her, as well. The temptation to confide in her, to tell someone the truth, to explain the real logic of his apparently inexplicable decisions, was strong. But he dared not. His secrets were far too explosive to share with anyone, particularly this woman who embodied the United States government.

"What did my grandfather say to you?" he asked.

She leaned back in her armchair. "I'll answer that question if you'll answer one of mine."

Aah. Clever. "Depends on what your question is."

"Why did you go to Ethiopia?"

Hmm. He could work with that. He nodded once, but immediately regretted the gesture. Daggers of pain shot down his spine and radiated out through his nervous system to every corner of his body. He groaned and fought down a wave of pain-induced nausea.

"Deal," he gritted out.

"You first," she retorted.

"Nope. You."

She stared at him curiously. *She wished.* He would never, ever explain the source of his pain to her. Finally she commented, "Your grandfather said you were in Africa on a humanitarian aid mission. That you and a team of your co-workers went out of radio contact about three months ago and that he was worried about you. He said he had hired private investigators, and they found sources in the Ethiopian government who said you had been thrown in prison."

She tapped a French-manicured nail on the wooden arm of her chair. "However, when we investigated through our sources, we found no evidence of a trial or even any charges being filed against you. For some reason, the Ethiopians ignored all of their own laws and simply locked you up and threw away the key. Why is that, Mr. Winston?"

"Jeff."

"Why is that, *Jeff?*"

"Not the question I agreed to answer." What sources was she referring to? Was it possible?

She huffed.

"I went to Ethiopia to solve world hunger."

She stared at him expectantly. "And?"

"And that's it."

She surged up out of her chair. "Look, Jeff. This isn't a joke. You murdered a man last night, and I have no compunction about returning you to the Ethiopian government to stand trial for your crime. You will be executed or worse. And believe me, in Africa, *worse* can be *much* worse than death."

She was magnificent in her fury. Anger sparked off her like fireworks and her body literally vibrated with her passion. She'd be a hellcat in the sack, for sure. The thought startled him. Since when did he sit around lusting after a woman like this? It had been years since he'd been that libertine playboy punk.

He leaned forward matching her intensity. "I'm telling you the truth. I went to Africa to solve world hunger."

She sank down into her chair. Watching her pull herself back in, containing her fiery energy was fascinating. In less time that he'd have imagined, she was able to ask him calmly, "And did you?"

"Did I what?"

"Solve world hunger."

He started to shrug but thought better of the unnecessary motion. "I have a good idea how to solve a substantial chunk of East Africa's food shortage."

"And how's that?"

"I didn't agree to answer that one."

She glared at him, but was otherwise outwardly composed. "Don't make this a war between us. I can make your life incredibly unpleasant." Her voice softened just a touch. "And I'd hate to have to do that."

He suspected he could make hers pretty unpleasant, too, but he refrained from mentioning it. He had no desire to antagonize her any more. After all, she really did seem to want to help him. Problem was, she had no idea how to do that. He'd asked for his drugs twice already, and she'd put him off both times. She didn't understand. And he *couldn't* explain it to her. But maybe he could talk around the edges of it.

He said in a conciliatory tone, "Look. I take certain medications, and I haven't had them for far too long. I need to get in touch with my physician and order up new prescriptions as soon as possible."

"Our doctors will have to review and approve anything you're prescribed. It may take several days."

Could Doc Jones disguise his meds so the government doctors wouldn't recognize them? Or would they be suspicious enough to run independent tests on the serum? No, he dared not even chance letting the government get its hands on any of his highly experimental medications.

He settled for, "In the meantime, could your people at least fly out some antibiotics and pain pills to help me get over the worst effects of my captivity?"

"Are you ill?" she asked sharply.

"I'm about to be," he replied soberly.

"Why?"

He shook his head. Nope. Not going there with her, either.

Thoughtfully, Jennifer watched Jeff retreat to his bedroom. He wasn't much less incredible in those tight clothes than he was in a towel. What would it be like to be with a man in such extraordinary physical condition? She made a policy of never dating any of the special forces operatives who worked out of H.O.T. Watch, so she didn't actually know.

The classified facility was home to a half-dozen Hunter Operations Teams. They did covert missions around the world with the help of the sophisticated satellite surveillance technology and intelligence analysts housed in the H.O.T. Watch headquarters. That facility was hidden on its own Caribbean island about twenty miles from here.

She added a few more details to what she knew about Jeff Winston. Beneath his rough exterior, he was highly intelligent. Cunning, even. And he was desperate to get his hands on some sort of prescription drugs that he was clearly in full-blown withdrawal from. That was the third time he'd mentioned getting medication sent to him.

She frowned. Was that why he'd been so wild and violent in Ethiopian custody? Had it been nothing more than the guy going through drug withdrawals? An odd sense of disappointment coursed through her. She'd hoped for better than that from him.

She opened her laptop computer and connected to the island's private wireless network to fire off a message to Brady Hathaway.

Please investigate possible drug addiction by Jeff Winston. And send out some giant clothes. Think NFL lineman…on steroids…and you'll have the dimensions about right.

Hathaway's response was swift.

Drug addiction?!!!

Correct. He appears to be experiencing some sort of drug withdrawal symptoms.

Do you need us to send out a team of doctors and relieve you from this debriefing?

She considered that one for a minute. In spite of her revulsion at Jeff's beastly appearance and behavior, there was something…fascinating…about him. He inspired a twisted compulsion in her to figure out what made this strange man tick. It had nothing at all to do with the unwilling attraction she bizarrely seemed to feel for him, of course.

Common sense told her this guy was a complete nut job. Definitely a candidate for a padded cell and a psychiatric team to pick his brains apart. Except, he'd been perfectly lucid through the meal and their recent conversation. He might be driven half-mad by the pain of his drug withdrawal, but that didn't make him crazy.

Was she seriously talking herself into turning down Hathaway's offer of a medical team to replace her? Apparently. Because the next words she typed were,

I'd like a few days to work on this guy. I've established the beginnings of trust with him. I think he'll talk to me given a little more time. I highly doubt he'd cooperate with a psych team.

Your call, Jenn. But be careful.

Right. Careful. There was nothing at all careful about being alone on this island with Jefferson Winston.

One thing he hadn't lacked for in prison was sleep. There'd been nothing else to do to while away the endless days, and sleep had been his only relief from the creeping advance of his pain.

Jeff dozed in his room for a few hours after he heard Jennifer's bedroom door close across the hall at about midnight. When he judged she'd had plenty of time to fall into a deep sleep, he eased out of bed and opened his door. He glided stealthily down the hall to the living room.

Triumph surged through him. Jennifer had left her laptop computer sitting on the coffee table. Now he could only pray it wasn't password protected. He turned it on and waited anxiously for it to boot up. Bingo. A welcome screen popped right up.

It took him a few missteps, but he figured out quickly enough how to connect to the island's wi-fi network. An internet connection opened automatically. He opened an anonymous public mail server and typed fast.

G., I'm somewhere in the Caribbean, and I'm a mess. Don't know how much longer I can hold on. You know that pain you predicted if I ever went off my health regimen? You have no idea how right you were. Have L. pull strings to find me and get me what I need ASAP. Hurry. J.

He hit the send button and leaned back, sighing in relief. He poked around her files for any hint of an association with the classified surveillance facility he sought, but found nothing. He'd be relieved if he didn't think she was too smart to leave that sort of evidence laying around. Quietly, he emptied the computer's cache and deleted all internet cookies and browsing history before shutting down the system. He crept back to bed and prayed for sleep to relieve him temporarily from his living hell.

Jennifer leaned back against her pillows thoughtfully, staring at the twin computer to the laptop she'd left out in the living room as bait. Who was G.? L. obviously referred to Jeff's grandfather, Leland. The regimen in the note no doubt was an oblique reference to whatever drugs the guy was addicted to, and his exhortation to hurry meant she was right. The guy was experiencing heavy withdrawal.

She forwarded the entire keystroke sequence from the time Jeff turned on the laptop until he turned it off to the computer guys at H.O.T. Watch. Her technicians should be able to track down this G. person with ease through his or her internet service provider. Her men's expertise, combined with the legal authority of the federal government, should unravel the mystery in a few hours. Probably by the time she woke up in the morning, they'd know who Jeff's drug supplier was and what drug he was hooked on.

She shook her head. No way was she letting Jeff get a fresh supply of his drugs. He'd been off them for a couple months already in jail in Ethiopia. He had to be pretty close to busting his addiction for good after so much time had passed. If he could just tough it out a few more days or weeks, he'd be clean. And then he could make a rational decision about his health. He didn't strike her as the kind of man who actually enjoyed being dependent on drugs.

Something about him suggested a sense of decency, honor even, under that uncivilized facade. And she was just the woman to help him rediscover that side of himself.

The State Department could probably spin the attack on *El Mari* as an unfortunate manifestation of his drug withdrawals. Temporary insanity.

But first, she had to get the real Jeff Winston back. For as sure as she was sitting here, the animal across the hall was not the man she'd read about in her dossier.

Chapter 4

"Wake up!" Something sharp slapped him across the face and Jeff howled in pain. He was being slow roasted in a giant oven and any second his entire body was going to burst into flames. Ye Gods, what a horrible way to die.

"Wake. *Up.*"

Was that insistent voice aimed at him? Surely not. He'd died and gone to Hell.

"I'm not kidding. I'll dump a bucket of ice water on you if you don't open your eyes and tell me what on God's green earth is going on, Jeff Winston."

The demon knew his name. And frankly, a bucket of ice water sounded like bliss. A fresh wave of agony ran over him like a ten-ton steamroller and he succumbed to white pain that blanked out everything else.

And then something else dawned on him. That was a female voice. "Gemma?" he mumbled. "Quit hitting me."

"Then wake up and tell me what's wrong with you!"

It was an enormous battle, but he managed to peel open one eyelid. His vision swam fuzzily as the vise crushing his skull tightened. God almighty, he was tough, but even he couldn't stand this. He whimpered, half in pain and half in terror. How much worse was it going to get before he lost his mind or his heart simply gave out and he kicked off?

The tone of the dark blob softened. "Where does it hurt?" *Everywhere.* Dark blob? Gemma was fair and blond. Everything about her was pale, even the light blue of her eyes. He squinted at this woman. Memory hovered close by. He was not in Ethiopia. And this woman wanted something from him....

The pain receded just enough to allow him a moment of lucidity. Jennifer, not Gemma. His captor. Although she was calling herself something nicer than that. Debriefer. Yeah, that was it. And she wouldn't let him have something—

She laid a hand on his shoulder, and the joint felt like it had literally exploded.

It was as if everything he'd suffered so far was a bare shadow of the pain that slammed into him now. As much as he hated himself for doing it, he screamed. And once he'd started, he couldn't seem to stop.

Jennifer reeled back from the man thrashing on the bed before her. A high-pitched keening tore from his throat, shocking her to her core. She didn't do anything! She just touched his shoulder. And he acted like she'd gouged out his eyes with hot pokers.

He barely looked human. He was hairy, huge and bathed in sweat. As if she'd landed in a really *bad* rendition of *Beauty and the Beast.* Where was the man from her dossier? Jefferson Winston was suave. Elegant. Sophisticated. He bore no resemblance whatsoever to this man.

Sheesh. If ever there'd been a better advertisement for

the evils of drug addiction, she'd never seen it. The man had become little better than a wild animal. It would be a tragedy if it weren't his own darned fault. She flinched as he let loose another bloodcurdling scream. And this time he didn't stop.

Freaked out, she retreated to the living room and turned on her laptop. She initiated a voice over internet protocol and called H.O.T. Watch headquarters on the Red line. It was reserved for life and death emergencies.

The duty controller answered with a terse, "Go." Most callers on this line had no time to fool around with the niceties.

"It's Jennifer Blackfoot. I need to speak with a physician who specializes in drug addiction recovery right now. I'll stay on the line."

"Roger." The controller's voice came back in a few seconds. "I'm patching you through to the substance abuse team at Wilford Hall Medical Center, ma'am," the controller announced.

A male voice came on the line. "This is Dr. Kinchon."

"Hi, sir. Jennifer Blackfoot. CIA. I'm debriefing a man who appears to be suffering from severe drug withdrawal symptoms. I need to know what to do to alleviate his reaction."

"What substance is he withdrawing from?"

"I have no idea."

"I need to know what he's coming down off of if I'm going to suggest a treatment. It could be dangerous in the extreme to respond incorrectly."

"Sorry, sir. He just came into my custody yesterday."

"What are his symptoms?"

She frowned. "Extreme pain. Delirium associated with his more extreme pain episodes."

"Is he scratching at himself? Hallucinating? Sweating profusely?"

"Yes, he is sweating!" she exclaimed, relieved.

"Do you have any idea how long it's been since his last fix?"

She had yet to hear back from Brady on what his off-the-record conversation with the Ethiopians had revealed. She pictured his thick growth of beard and guessed, "At least two months. Possibly several."

"Months?" the doctor exclaimed. "That's not possible. He would be long past any delirium tremens if that was the case. He must have taken something within the past few days."

At that moment, Jeff let out a scream that echoed through the house and sent an involuntary shiver down her spine. He sounded like he was dying.

"Please, Doctor. He's in terrible pain. Isn't there anything I can do?"

"You can try hot or cold compresses."

"He screams any time I touch him."

"Aah. Extreme tactile hypersensitivity. Don't touch him, then. Even the slightest contact may very well feel like a knife stabbing him. You might consider restraining him for his own safety."

Lovely. Just what she wanted to do. Torture the poor man. Not to mention she doubted any of the rope in the house would hold him down. "Please, Doctor. There has to be something more I can do to help. him."

"Find out as quickly as possible exactly what he's been taking and when the last time he had it was."

"Done." She wasn't sure how she was going to track down G. and bully the information out of the guy, but by golly, she'd make it happen if she had to show up on this G.'s front porch herself and beat it out of him.

Abruptly, silence fell over the house. Jennifer disconnected the call and raced for Jeff's room. Funny how the silence scared her even worse than his screams. At least when he was screaming she knew he was still alive.

He was alive when she got there, but he didn't look good. His skin was a ghastly shade of gray and his eyes were rolled back into his head. She risked touching him in his unconscious state and he was burning up. She'd never felt a fever burn so hot on a person's skin before.

A flash of her grandfather, who'd been a traditional medicine man, came to mind. What would he do with a patient like this? She recalled his whispery voice murmuring, "Heat a cold man, cool a hot man, child."

She sprinted for the linen closet and yanked out a bed sheet. She threw it in her bathtub, soaked it with cold water, and carried the sodden mass into Jeff's room. She spread it over him, settling the cloth against his body as gently as she possibly could.

His thrashing diminished slightly. But as soon as the sheet warmed to his body temperature, his whimpering increased in intensity. Damn. She fetched her laptop and called H.O.T. Watch again.

When the call went through, she demanded, "Who's G.?"

"Standby one."

She waited in an agony of impatience.

"No idea. G. has a dummy internet server. From it, your guy's message was routed all over the world. Assuming we can track it at all, it's going to take a while to follow the trail back to the target."

"Define *a while,*" she demanded tersely as Jeff moaned beside her.

"Two, maybe three, days, ma'am."

"I don't have that long." She thought fast. "Put me through to Leland Winston."

"Uhh, it's four o'clock in the morning in New York."

"Tell him his grandson is dying and I need his help. He'll take my call."

She wasn't wrong. The billionaire's gravelly voice came on the line in under a minute. "Who is this? And what's this about Jeff dying?" he demanded.

"Agent Jennifer Blackfoot. Your grandson's CIA debriefer. He's in horrendous pain. Appears to be withdrawing from some sort of drug. We need to find out what it is and when he last had it."

Strangely, Leland devolved into a bout of cursing fit to embarrass a sailor. Now why on earth would he react like that? Was this drug use an old problem of Jeff's that had resurfaced, maybe?

In an effort to break the old man's tirade, she interrupted. "Do you know someone with the initial G.? A friend or associate who might be supplying drugs to Jeff?"

Even more strangely, Leland abruptly went dead silent. So. He did know who G. was.

"Where's my grandson?"

"I'm sorry, sir. That information is classified—"

"Classified, my ass!" he bellowed. "Tell me where my boy is!"

"I can't, sir."

"Agent Blackfoot. That's your name, right? I'm about to roll a crap pile downhill onto your head like you've never seen before. Tell me where Jeff is, or I swear, I'll bury you."

She didn't doubt for a second he could make good on his threat. Men like him didn't have to bother with empty threats. She sighed. "I'm afraid you're going to have to pull your strings, sir. I have rules to follow and it's above my pay grade to deviate from them."

Leland's cursing grew so imaginative that, in spite of herself, she was a little impressed. She'd have to remember a few of his choicest phrases for the next time a Spec Ops guy stepped out of line and was due for a butt chewing from her.

He wound down soon enough, though. Into the heavy silence, she said merely, "And Mr. Winston?"

"What?" he snapped irritably.

"Hurry, sir."

Time ceased to have any meaning for Jeff. He was aware only of varying degrees of pain. Once his formidable self-control cracked, there was no putting that genie back in the bottle. The pain had gotten the best of him and no amount of self-discipline could give him the upper hand again. His bones felt as if they were being bent by degrees in vises. Which, in a more lucid moment, he wryly noted wasn't that far from the truth.

He'd known from the first that this outcome was a possibility. But he hadn't counted on the ambush in Ethiopia, nor upon being captured and thrown in prison for months before anyone found out he was even alive, let alone freed him.

The next time Gemma Jones said something might become a little uncomfortable, he was going to run away from the woman as fast and as far as he could and never look back.

With daylight came an apparent lessening of Jeff's pain. Jennifer offered him a glass of water with a straw to sip on. He'd been sweating like crazy for hours; he had to be badly dehydrated by now. She dozed in a chair beside his bed for a while, but woke immediately when he moaned. Her eyes popped open in alarm as she braced for the screaming to resume.

"What're you doing here?" he rasped.

"You had a rough night. I was trying to help. Although there's precious little I can do without knowing what you've been taking."

He frowned like he didn't know what she was talking about.

"Your drug addiction," she said impatiently. "I need to know what you were on so the doctors can tell me how to ease your symptoms."

"Need *my* doc," he muttered.

"Give me a full name and I'll get him for you right now."

Sharp intelligence abruptly shone from Jeff's blue-on-blue gaze. "Not nice to take advantage of the sick guy."

She frowned. "I'm not trying to trick you. I really need to know your supplier's name. You might die if we don't find out what you're hooked on and help you come down off of it safely."

He made a growling noise that might be a snort in a less torn-up throat. "Not. An addict." His teeth clenched as a wave of pain clearly assaulted him. "Call Leland."

"Stay with me, Jeff. I need more information."

His eyes started to fog over. "You stay. With me. Please…"

Her heart broke a little at the entreaty in his voice. He sounded so utterly lonely. She lashed out in sudden, irrational anger. "Look at you. You're a mess! You *are* an addict."

"Got that wrong…" he gasped before his voice broke and the screaming began again.

It was midmorning when a motorboat pulled up at the dock visible from the house. Jeff was unconscious for the moment, and she happened to be in the kitchen pouring herself a cup of coffee when she spotted the boat. Thank God. She'd asked for the strongest pain killers and sedatives in H.O.T. Watch's infirmary to be sent over here immediately.

She was startled to recognize the tall form jumping to the dock. What was Brady Hathaway doing here in person? She didn't have long to wait to find out. He strode through the front door, a backpack slung over one shoulder, a few minutes later. He'd made good time up the mountain. She was gratified to seeing him huffing.

"What's up, Jenn?" he demanded.

"I might ask the same of you."

"Where's the wild man?"

"Asleep right now. And for God's sake, keep your voice down. At all cost we don't want to wake him up."

"Gonna have to if Rich Boy wants the painkillers and sedatives I've got in my bag."

She leaped for the backpack eagerly.

"Whoa there, sister. You should use them as a bribe to get him to cooperate in your debriefing."

She laughed without humor. "Trust me. He's in no condition to answer questions."

"What are you talking—"

Jeff chose that moment to wake up, which meant he let out a banshee wail that sent Brady a foot straight up into the air. She was too exhausted to appreciate the humor of it. His face showing minor shock, Brady handed over the backpack. She rummaged in it frantically, as if she was the addict herself.

Meanwhile, he detailed, "My Ethiopian contact got back to me just before I left to come see you. Interesting report. He swears they did nothing to your boy. A guard tried to rough him up the night he arrived at the prison and Rich Boy supposedly killed him. But there are glaring discrepancies in that story. For example, the guard was garroted, but no murder weapon was anywhere in the room when the police arrived. And the prisoner was still handcuffed by one wrist to the table."

She demanded, "How do you strangle someone with a *table* dangling from your wrist?"

"Good question," Brady replied. "Apparently, the prison guards wouldn't get near him after that. His first day with the other prisoners, Winston beat the crap out of a bunch of them, then refused to come out of his cell again the whole time he was in jail. My guy is adamant that no one tortured him. Says your boy gradually went from crazy to really crazy. My contact sounded genuinely relieved to have gotten rid of him."

She poured out a handful of pills. Given his body mass, she figured she'd start with double the recommended dosage of both the sedatives and painkillers and see what those did for Jeff. She headed down the hall and Brady followed curiously.

Jeff had gone completely rigid in his bed, his body unnaturally arched off the mattress and statue-still. She rushed forward. "Jeff! Are you all right?" She knew it was a stupid question. But it was the first thing that popped out of her mouth in her panic.

He managed to open his eyes and seemed to struggle to focus on her voice. She spoke encouragingly as she picked up his water glass. "I've got painkillers for you, Jeff. I need you to swallow them. Can you do that for me?"

His entire body trembled with the effort, but he lifted his head off his pillow.

Brady jumped forward to support Jeff's shoulders while she fed the pills to her patient. He swallowed the last one convulsively and she caught herself sagging in relief.

Frowning, Brady eased Jeff back to the mattress. "Man. He's really dense."

"As in stupid to have done this to himself?"

"No. As in unnaturally heavy. The guy weighs a ton."

"Look at his arms and shoulders. His whole body's that muscular. Of course he's heavy."

Brady shook his head. "I've carried my fair share of injured Spec Ops guys across my back before. I know how much muscular, fit men weigh. And I'm telling you something's weird about this guy. He's really, *really* heavy."

She recalled Jeff landing on her during the gunfight. And the way the golf cart had groaned under his weight. Maybe there was something to what Brady was saying. "Well, I can tell you he's the strongest guy I've ever seen. He ripped the combination lock right off the side of the garage down by the airfield."

Brady glanced down at her patient. "Who *is* this guy?"

She threw up her hands. "That's what I've been *asking*. Now you know why I've been so hot and bothered for you guys to dig up everything on his past few years. How did he go from Ivy League, spoiled rich kid to *this?*"

She stared down at the man in the bed. Sympathy for his plight shuddered through her. No matter what transgressions lurked in his past, no human being deserved to suffer like this.

She and Brady spent the rest of the morning on their respective phones and computers, pushing their staffs mercilessly for any and every thing they could find on one Jefferson Winston.

A little new information was forthcoming. Jeff had apparently experienced some sort of political awakening after graduate school. He worked on the campaign staffs of several politicians who were generally social liberals and foreign policy conservatives.

He seemed to settle down after that and largely vanished from the jet-set partying scene for a few years. About a year ago he'd surfaced again, taking up his old lifestyle exactly where he'd left off. Except, of course, he'd obviously taken up body building in a big way during his prolonged absence.

A few of his acquaintances described him as less approachable after his return. Without exception, every close friend of Jeff's either was unavailable to talk to H.O.T. Watch's investigators or flatly refused to speak when asked even the simplest questions about him. Give the guy credit for having loyal friends.

Jeff was the CEO of one of the Winston Industries family of businesses. His firm, CompuWin, Inc. was a software applications development company. Which was a fancy way of saying they invented new stuff to do with computers. It was small, but prestigious, apparently.

An entire team of researchers at H.O.T. Watch worked on isolating what drug Jeff might have ingested. Jennifer was relieved to hear that no known steroid or combination of steroids was known to cause symptoms anything like the extreme pain Jeff was experiencing. Although it did raise the question of how he'd gotten all those massive muscles. Most of the experts thought he was having some sort of bizarre allergic reaction to the absence of his mystery drug.

Blessedly, the medications she'd given him seemed to take the edge off his pain and he slept quietly for a few hours. Jennifer experienced a profound relief that startled her. She knew better than to get personally involved with her prisoners. But darned if she didn't feel a connection to Jeff and his suffering. She couldn't help but admire his courage, even if the pain had ultimately gotten the better of him.

A boat arrived in the midafternoon to drop off a load of supplies that included clothes for her guest and a lot more food. Brady departed in that vessel, leaving her alone once more with Jeff. She was actually relieved when silence settled over the island. Whatever she was feeling for her prisoner was too private and personal to be shared.

Around supper time, Jeff moaned from his room.

She raced to his side. His eyes were open. She asked quickly, "How're you feeling?"

He blinked up at her, and she sagged in relief to see the man looking back at her. For the moment, the beast had retreated from his gaze.

"Are the painkillers helping?" she asked.

He nodded fractionally as if to move more would cause immeasurable pain.

"Need some more?"

Another tiny nod.

"Only problem with narcotics this powerful is you'll get addicted to them quickly. Particularly with us having to double up on the dosage to compensate for your body mass. Do you happen to know how much you weigh? The doctors want to know so they can dose you more accurately."

He shrugged. She'd take that as a no.

"Jeff, I really need you to tell me what you've been taking. I don't care in the least what it is. I just want to help you. I promise."

His gaze went opaque. Stubborn.

She swore aloud. "Help me out, so I can help you!" Her frustration threatened to spill tears onto her cheeks. She couldn't *stand* seeing him suffer like this.

"Lee. Land," he rasped.

She threw up her hands. "I've already been in contact with him. He assured me he's going to pull every string there is that goes over my head. For your sake, I hope your grandfather is even more influential than people think he is, and he gets here fast."

"Thank you," Jeff whispered. His eyes drifted closed.

"Give a shout out when you want more pain pills," she said with a tinge of sarcasm. And on that note, she pivoted smartly, dashed away the tears on her cheeks and marched out of the room. *Stubborn man. Wouldn't even help her help him.* For a moment she thought she felt his gaze on her back, but when she turned around in the doorway to check, he looked unconscious.

Which was just as well. She was very tempted to kill him.

Chapter 5

After the third dose of heavy-duty painkillers began to wear off, Jeff finally regained groggy consciousness. He remembered just enough about the past twenty-four hours to be glad he didn't remember the rest of it.

"Jenn?" he called out. His voice was weaker than he'd expected.

She careened around the corner immediately, her face haunted. She approached the bed carefully. Crap. What had he done to put that look on her face? "How are you feeling?" she asked cautiously.

"I've been better."

"You've been worse, too."

He didn't respond to that. No need to. They'd both lived through the past night and day. "I'm sorry," he rasped. His throat felt like rough, gritty sandpaper.

"Just tell me what you were on so I can make this go away."

"I can't. Really."

"Why not?"

"It's complicated."

"So complicated you're willing to die to protect it?"

"Yes," he answered without hesitation.

Her gaze snapped to his, the anger draining from her dark eyes and replaced by curiosity and rapid processing of new information. She blurted out, "If I had my guys hack into the classified government database of medical research, would I find you in it?"

He answered promptly and honestly. "No."

She must have heard the truth in his voice because her shoulders sagged.

"How's Leland doing?" he asked, praying desperately to distract her from her current line of reasoning which was uncomfortably close to the truth.

She laughed quietly. "Your grandfather's a piece of work. Took him under two hours to work his way all the way down from the White House to my direct superiors. But to answer your question, he's frantic. He really does care about you."

"I know." Jeff's father had died young in a car crash, and his mother had been more beautiful than reliable. Leland had been the stabilizing influence in his life that he would have otherwise lacked. Leland had taught him how to set goals and work to achieve them, how to be accountable for his actions, how to be a man, really.

"That's the first time I've seen you smile," Jennifer murmured.

He wasn't usually a grouch. In fact, he was known for his sense of humor and generally upbeat personality. He mumbled, "You haven't exactly caught me at my best."

"Hungry?" she asked.

"Famished." Maintaining his body mass required substantial infusions of calories every day. He'd been shocked that the Ethiopians had fed him as well as they had. They must have been afraid he'd kill another guard if they didn't. But the plentiful food they'd brought him had been gamy-tasting meat and bland gruels for the most part.

"Solid or liquid?" she inquired.

"Steak."

She laughed. "It'll take me a few minutes to heat up the grill, but one king-size T-bone coming up."

He noted wryly when she carried the plate into his room that she'd already cut the meat for him. He was startled when she sat down beside him and picked up a piece of the rare meat with her fingers. She shocked him outright when she leaned forward with a wicked smile and held it out to him, murmuring, "Open up."

He obeyed, and she popped the piece of steak into his mouth. His body reacted with intense pleasure to the protein it so craved.

They fell quickly into a rhythm of feeding and chewing.

And then on one bite, he closed his lips quickly as she withdrew her fingers, capturing her fingertip between them. She pulled her finger loose slowly, allowing him plentiful time to caress the captured digit with the tip of his tongue before it finally popped free.

Their gazes met over the next bite of tender steak, and fire blazed in her midnight eyes. He shouldn't tease her, but for the life of him, he couldn't seem to stop himself. Her breathing was light and fast, and a flush pinked her cheeks. It was probably all a ploy to get him to let down his defenses with her. But even so, it was impossible to resist falling under her spell. She was so exotic. Beautiful in a strong, wise, grounded way. Totally different than most of the women he'd dated before.

Not that he could ever contemplate dating her. Not with her job. Her employer.

But still. He savored her intimate attention almost as much

as he did the meal. He watched with interest as she sucked steak juice from her palm. Her mouth was lush and full, and her lips glistened as she licked off the juice. His body reacted powerfully to the sensual frankness of it. She would probably be as direct in bed as she was in everything else. He liked women who knew what they wanted and weren't afraid to tell him. More pleasure for everyone, that way.

"What do you like?" he muttered.

He was surprised when she actually answered, "In hobbies, I like to surf, hang glide and read. In food, I like a good steak and ice cream in any flavor. In life, I like to be outdoors and feel the sun on my skin. In men, I like honesty."

He winced. Okay, he probably deserved that. "I haven't lied to you," he avowed. "Everything I've told you is true."

"I believe you. However, you've also refused to answer even the most basic questions, including the ones that might save your life."

He sighed. "I'm sorry."

"Don't be sorry. Be straight with me," she snapped.

Maybe the last day of hell had stripped away some of his self-control. Or maybe he was just too exhausted to fight her any more. But he looked at her intently and appalled himself by admitting, "You're partially right. I am dependent on medication. But it's not a recreational drug. It's therapeutic. And I may very well die if I don't get more of it. Soon, probably."

He lifted a hand when she would have interrupted him. She subsided and his hand fell back to the mattress. He winced as a thousand needles pierced the length of his arm.

"I can't tell you what it is. It's experimental and it's a secret. I just need you to trust me."

"What's wrong with you?"

"Nothing, as long as I have my meds."

Despair gleamed in Jennifer's gaze. Or maybe that was tears. He couldn't tell for sure. "That's not an answer."

"It's all I can give you."

She studied him for a long time. It was clear in her eyes that she was absorbing the knowledge that he was, in fact, dying. She finally whispered, "I'd touch you if it wouldn't make you scream."

His heart leaped at the idea of her hands on him. He'd love nothing more than for her to touch him when he wasn't so hypersensitive that air wafting across his skin was nearly unbearable. "I think I can stand it if you're gentle."

She reached out with her right hand and laid her palm as lightly as a feather on his cheek. "Tell me if it hurts too much."

He nodded fractionally under her palm, which was warm and baby soft against his face. Funny to think that the exact same hand had pointed a shotgun at him not too long ago. Her fingertips trailed lightly across the edge of his beard. Traced his brows. Tracked down his temple to curl ever-so-lightly around the shell of his ear. He exhaled carefully. His entire body clenched, but with need, not pain.

The pain actually receded in the face of his driving desire. Had she discovered a remedy for his suffering? If only. Continuous sex with this woman sounded like a great alternative to screaming torture.

"That feels nice," he breathed.

"Yes, it does," she agreed with a hint of a smile. She ran her fingers lightly through his shoulder-length hair. "Do you usually wear it this long?"

"Hardly."

"I've seen pictures of you with it short. And without your beard. You're a handsome man."

He couldn't remember the last time he'd been so pleased that a woman found him attractive. Her simple words pierced his usual defenses against suck-ups and gold diggers as easily as a knife through air. Resolve to cut his hair and shave as soon as possible filled him.

"Please don't die," she whispered. "Fight to live."

Her entreaty sounded real. From the heart. And it broke him. He'd suffered the fiery tortures of Hell in stoic silence, but the idea of hurting this woman was too much for him. He opened his mouth with the intent to tell her everything. But then Jennifer glanced up, frowning, and he tensed. "What?" he bit out.

His usual adrenaline surge in response to a combat threat didn't come. He must've burned out all his available adrenaline fighting the pain. Now he only felt damnably weak. If something bad happened to her because he was too wiped out to protect her, he'd never forgive himself.

"Jet," she replied cryptically.

"Good guys or bad guys incoming?" he bit out.

"I highly doubt any bad guys know this place exists. Even most of the good guys don't know we're here."

"Do you need to go get your shotgun?" he prompted cautiously.

She pursed her lips. "Anyone who's been allowed to approach this island so closely has the approval of my superiors or they'd never have made it within visual range of this place."

Good to know.

"I'm going to go see who it is. You stay put, eh?" she told him.

He smiled, or at least tried to. Hopefully, it didn't look too much like the grimace it turned into as soon as she left the room. And hopefully, it meant help was on the way for him. He was hanging on by a very thin thread. And when it broke, he had a sinking feeling he was done for good.

Jennifer guided the golf cart down the path through the trees to the island's runway. She suspected she knew who was here. If she was right, it wouldn't do to keep her guest waiting.

Or two guests, as it turned out. She was right about one of them. Leland Winston stepped down onto the tarmac. But Jennifer hadn't been expecting the drop-dead-gorgeous blonde woman who followed him. *Please let that be Leland's personal assistant and not Jeff's significant other.*

Jennifer stumbled to a halt. Since when did she care if Jeff had a girlfriend who'd rushed to be at his side?

"Ms. Blackfoot?" Leland growled.

"Welcome, Mr. Winston."

"This is my son's colleague, Dr. Gemma Jones. She will be taking over my grandson's medical care henceforth."

Gemma Jones. G. His drug supplier. Although if Jeff was telling the truth, those drugs were keeping him alive. Did she dare believe him?

In the meantime, she wasn't about to let Leland Winston bulldoze over her like this. "I haven't released him into your custody, Mr. Winston. No one does anything to my prisoner until I say so."

"The President of the United States told me I could see my grandson."

"And so you may," she replied evenly. "But my statement still stands."

Leland shot her an assessing look. She stared back at him, refusing to be the one to break eye contact. She knew the type all too well. Show one millisecond of weakness, and a man like this would leap all over it and eat her alive.

Finally, Leland grinned. "I think I might just like you, girl."

She grinned back at him. "Shall we? Jeff is waiting for you." She gestured toward the golf cart, taking the lead. Winston's flunkies could carry his bags for him. She was not about to be his errand girl.

They arrived at the house and the gorgeous doctor spoke for the first time. "I'll need to be alone with my patient to examine him."

The physician's voice was sultry and smooth and as perfect as the rest of her. It positively set Jennifer's teeth on edge. She checked herself sharply. She was not in competition with this woman over Jeff. "In the first place, Dr. Jones, he's not your patient, yet. In the second place, I want a few answers before I allow you to pump more drugs into his system. The ones you've given him so far have made a complete wreck out of him."

"It's the absence of those medications that have caused the withdrawals," Gemma replied coolly.

That's what Jeff said, too. "What are these medications of yours?" Jennifer asked. She was intrigued when Gemma shot a quick glance at Leland, who gave back an infinitesimal negative shake of the head. What was that all about? Her field agent's finely honed antennae wiggled wildly. There were things these two weren't telling her and clearly didn't plan to.

Gemma answered lightly, "They're prototype medications. The scientific names are long and unpronounceable, I assure you."

"What, exactly, do they do? What's wrong with Jeff?" It was hard for Jennifer to keep her voice even and calm, but she was proud of the results of her efforts.

"At the moment, his skeleton is being physically distorted by the pull of his overdeveloped muscles. They're literally pulling his joints apart. That's what causing him the intense pain."

Horror flowed through Jennifer. That was…gross. And it sounded excruciating. "And these drugs? They stop his muscles from doing that?"

"Not directly. But it's close enough for your purposes."

The good doctor no doubt didn't intend any insult, but it was hard not to take offense at the faint condescension implicit in the woman's answer. Her lips pressed tightly shut, Jennifer led both Leland and Gemma through the house to Jeff's bedroom.

She stepped forward and spoke quietly. "Jeff? You have visitors."

His eyes fluttered open groggily, no doubt from the powerful narcotics he'd been sucking down like candy. He caught sight of her and smiled sleepily. "Hi, beauti—"

He broke off, staring over her shoulder. "Pops?"

Leland stepped forward. "Hey there, Boy. You look like crap. How're you feeling?"

"Worse," Jeff retorted dryly.

"Gemma's here. She'll fix you right up."

"Whoa, there," Jennifer interjected. "I haven't okayed these drugs of hers, yet."

"But you will," Gemma replied stonily. "Unless you want to watch this man die by agonizing degrees over the next few weeks. This isn't anywhere near as bad as it's going to get. When his muscles start breaking his bones, one by one, distorting his fingers into misshapen claws, his ribs slowly being crushed into his lungs and suffocating him by inches, just remember, it will be your fault."

Jennifer looked down at Jeff for confirmation. She saw it in the fear that flashed in his eyes before he carefully blanked it out. The bitch wasn't lying.

Jennifer nodded, her neck stiff. "Do it."

Gemma took charge with all the confident grace Jennifer expected of her. If only the woman were overtly nasty or obnoxious. Then Jennifer could genuinely hate her.

The doctor wasted no time digging into her medical bag. She pulled out a Styrofoam cube about eight inches square. It opened to reveal a vial of vaguely gold-tinted serum. The woman pulled out a hypodermic syringe and loaded it from the vial.

"Hold this." She thrust the syringe at Leland. Gemma pulled out a length of surgical tubing next. "Normally, Jeff's veins are of sufficient size that I don't have to use a tourniquet to bring one up. But he's so dehydrated at the moment that I don't see a good one."

The woman looked up at Jennifer. "Help me hold his arm down. In his current state, this is going to hurt him, and he might jerk."

"Touching him hurts him," Jennifer mumbled a little resentfully. "He *might* scream."

"Jeff," Gemma said sternly, "I need you to do your best to hold still. I'm going to give you your meds. Do you understand?"

He rolled his eyes. "Yes, Gemma. I'm not an idiot."

"I didn't know if you were lucid."

Jennifer laid her hands on Jeff's massive biceps as gently as she could. Wow. Her hands didn't even come close to spanning the bulge of it. She threw him an apologetic look and she thought a smile passed through his cobalt gaze. Jennifer had to give the doctor credit. Gemma was fast when it came time to put the tourniquet on Jeff's arm above the elbow. He sucked in a hard breath through his teeth and beads of sweat popped on his brow.

"Lean on me, Jenn," he gritted out.

She put more pressure on his arm.

"Harder, or I'll jerk. And I really need this shot."

Distressed, she made eye contact with him as she put her entire body weight on her hands. She saw the moment the needle pierced his skin because agony exploded in his gaze. "You're doing great," she encouraged him. "Almost done."

Gemma straightened away from the bed and pressed a

gauze pad over the site of the injection. "Hold this in place," she ordered Jennifer.

Jeff's entire body trembled visibly. And then, abruptly, he went still.

Leland blurted, "What's wrong?"

Gemma frowned as she reached for Jeff's neck and the carotid artery there. "I don't know…."

Jennifer answered the older man, "He's fainted. Again. The pain was too much for him."

Gemma's frown deepened. "Jeff has enormous pain tolerance. You have no idea how high."

Jennifer snorted. "Yeah, well, he reached the end of that tolerance yesterday. He screamed his head off for hours until I could get some painkillers sent over here."

"What's he on?" Gemma demanded.

Jennifer named the narcotic and the dosage it had taken to ease Jeff's suffering enough to beat back the delirium.

"I told him he shouldn't go to Africa," Gemma burst out. It sounded like the comment was directed at Leland. "Until his transformation is permanent, he has no business exposing himself to the possibility of being deprived of his meds. I *told* him this would happen!"

"You know how stubborn he is, Gem. It was his choice. His consequences. He won't blame you for this. And neither do I."

Jennifer's mind raced. *Transformation?* That was a fascinating word choice. Abnormal muscle strength? Experimental drugs? What was Jeff? Some kind of freak trying to turn himself into a superhero? Hoping to catch Dr. Jones off guard, Jennifer asked without warning, "What do those drugs do to Jeff's muscles?"

"Nothing," Gemma answered, her brows arched in surprise.

Hmm. The woman answered quickly, without hesitation,

and more importantly, without exhibiting any of the usual body language tells of a lie. In fact, all the tells pointed at honesty.

"How soon will he feel better?" Jennifer asked.

Gemma considered. "It could be several weeks before he's back to the normal status quo. He should feel significant relief of pain within a week, I should think, particularly if he stays very still and relaxed."

"A week?" Jennifer exclaimed. "He'll be dead from the strain of the pain long before then!"

The doctor looked sharply between her and Jeff. "Just how much pain was he in before the painkillers? Did he actually scream?"

Jennifer answered honestly, "I thought he might die. I was worried his heart would give out under the strain. And yes. He screamed himself hoarse."

Gemma looked genuinely appalled. Okay, so maybe she wasn't an entirely bad person, after all. "We'll continue the narcotic regimen, of course. I'm going to prescribe muscle relaxants, too. And I've got an experimental pain receptor blocker that might be helpful with his generalized hypersensitivity. Assuming, of course, that you will approve it, Agent Block-foot."

Jennifer didn't correct the blatant mispronunciation of her name. Teeth gritted, she responded tightly, "Anything so I don't have to listen to him scream for the next week."

"The medications are in my other bag." The doctor retreated, leaving Jennifer and Leland alone with Jeff, who was still out cold.

"Mr. Winston, do you have any idea how your grandson ended up in an Ethiopian jail?"

"I imagine it had something to do with the Ethiopian police arresting him."

"Don't play games with me," she snapped. "Your grandson

murdered a man during the prisoner exchange and is in a lot of trouble."

"The way I hear it, Jeff did the world a service by taking out that butcher. Plenty of people in the Ethiopian government—and our government, for that matter—are delighted that *El Mari* is dead."

"Nonetheless, the law stands against Jeff on this one."

"You'll figure it out," Leland said dismissively.

"*I* will? It's not *my* problem."

"But you like him, don't you? You'll do your best to help my boy because you can't help yourself."

Jennifer reeled back. *Excuse me?* She liked Jeff Winston? She felt sorry for his suffering. Admired him for his stoic tolerance in the face of overwhelming pain. Perhaps even had a crush on him. But *liked* him? Uhh, *no*.

Leland's blue eyes, so much like his grandson's, sparkled with humor. "I see Jeff's landed himself a wildcat this time. Should be fun to watch the show." But then his voice dropped in timbre. Changed tone. "A word of warning, young lady. Don't fall too hard for him. He always moves on. He'll never settle down in any kind of permanent relationship."

Chapter 6

When Jeff woke again, the sun slanted into his room from the east. Morning, then. He reached gingerly for his pain and was immeasurably relieved to discover that it had retreated to a dull roar. He still hurt like hell from head to foot, but it was as if the swords piercing him had been dulled just a bit. Enough that he could think past the pain if he concentrated.

His most immediate and pressing problem was a bursting bladder. Moving by slow degrees, he eased himself upright and swung his feet over the side of the bed. Man. He felt like he'd been worked over with baseball bats.

He went to the restroom and then eased on the pair khaki shorts and a soft, cotton polo shirt he found folded on his bathroom counter. He sighed at the simple pleasure of clean clothing that fit him. Now for the kitchen. He could eat a horse right about now.

Were Leland and Gemma still here? He couldn't tell from the closed bedroom doors ranging down the long hallway.

Thankfully, he wasn't completely incompetent in a kitchen. He managed to get coffee brewing and bacon sizzling on the stove. He scrambled a half-dozen eggs and was just sliding them onto his plate when Jennifer spoke from behind him.

"Did you make enough of those to share any?"

He looked up to smile a good morning at her, but his breath caught at the sight of her standing in a ray of sunshine streaming in through the kitchen window. She wore a sleeveless gauze dress that fell in a narrow column to her bare feet. Her long, unbound hair glistened iridescently around her like a raven's feathers, and her answering smile transformed her into an otherworldly beauty.

Belatedly, he replied, "I'll share anything of mine with you that you want. Just name it."

She helped him plate up their breakfast and slid into a seat across from him at the table. "How about you share some information with me?"

"Aah, yes. Your infamous debrief."

"Hey! You're back to using eating utensils!" she exclaimed as he commenced eating eggs with a fork.

He looked down at his hands. "Cramps are gone," he mumbled.

She reached across the table to lay her smaller hand on top of his. Her fingers were slender and graceful, shaped like an artist's. He was surprised to see an altogether feminine French manicure. The tough, all-business field agent was more of a girly-girl at heart than she liked to admit, huh?

"I'm so relieved you're feeling better, Jeff. I couldn't stand watching you suffer like that."

His entire body went on high alert as her fingers twined with his long enough to give a brief squeeze. Damn. He was hypersensitive again, but this time to her touch. He replied, "I'm sorry I put you through it."

Their gazes met in warm communication. Funny how

going to Hell and back with someone forged such closeness so fast. It was the foxhole effect, he supposed. Nearly die with a guy and you were buddies for life.

Jennifer was speaking again. "...hate to keep pestering you, but I figure you'd like to get on with your life. Dr. Jones is obviously eager to have you back home."

He looked up sharply at that. "Gemma and I aren't romantically involved if that's what you're implying."

"Does she know that?"

He laughed. "Oh, yes. She never gets involved with any of her patients."

"You mean there are more like you?"

Crap. He kept forgetting how good Jennifer was at inferring a great deal from just a scrap of information. "Honey, there's no one else quite like me."

Jennifer laughed and rolled her eyes. "I'd hate to meet the women that line works on."

He grinned back. "They'd drive you nearly as crazy as they drive me."

"I suppose having a lot of money gets in the way of normal relationships, doesn't it?"

"It does. But money allows a person to pursue his interests. And that makes up for a lot."

"What interests you?"

He pushed his eggs around on his plate. *Her.* She'd held up remarkably well to his screaming pain, and that couldn't have been easy. She was too smart for her own good, and she'd risen to his defense like a mother bear when she'd thought Gemma might harm him.

"Want some more eggs?" Jennifer asked.

He laughed. "When I'm not screaming, I'm always hungry."

She moved over to the stove and cracked a dozen more eggs into the skillet. As she added cheese, milk and pepper, she tossed over her shoulder, "Did the Ethiopians feed you enough?"

"Shockingly, yes."

"That doesn't sound like them," Jennifer commented lightly. Too lightly. As if she was suspicious of how he'd arranged that.

He sighed. "They were scared of me. I think they thought I'd hurt someone if they didn't keep me well fed."

"Would you have hurt someone?"

He frowned at the implication that he couldn't control himself. "Look. I don't run around randomly breaking people's necks."

"Could've fooled me."

"*El Mari* and I have…had…a history."

"Of what?"

Thankfully, he was saved from having to answer that by Gemma breezing into the kitchen. "Good morning! Jeff, that beard and long hair are awful. You need a haircut and a shave in the worst way."

"Good morning to you, Madame Fashion Police. I'm feeling much better, thank you for asking. And you?"

Gemma rolled her eyes at him and he grinned back at her unrepentantly.

"Of course, you're feeling better. I'm your physician."

He laughed. "Modesty, much, Doctor?"

"You wouldn't have hired me if I weren't the best, and you know it."

Jeff glanced over at Jennifer who, predictably, was taking in every nuance of the exchange. He might have been out of it yesterday, but not so out of it that he'd failed to register Jennifer's jealousy of Gemma. It was endearing, actually. Although he had no doubt Jenn would be mortified if he ever mentioned it to her.

"Earth to Jeff. Come in," Gemma announced sharply.

Startled out of his pleasant thoughts, he glanced over at his business partner. "What?"

"I'd like to run some tests on you. Her people wouldn't let me bring most of my equipment with me, but I did manage to convince them to let me fly in a portable X-ray machine."

He snorted. He'd bet she wanted to get a look at his bones. God knew what the past few months had done to his bone density. Gemma thought that if he continued the gene therapy long enough his extreme bone density would become permanent. But obviously, that hadn't happened, yet. He gathered from Gemma's rather elliptical answers to Jennifer's questions yesterday that his bones had been leaching calcium the past few months and had weakened his skeleton badly.

Jennifer sat a bowl of steaming scrambled eggs on the table and slid into her seat unobtrusively. Hiding in plain sight, was she?

Leland came into the kitchen just then, patting his ample belly. "Aah, this island air is good for the appetite."

Jeff grinned up at him. "Grab a plate and dig in." After everyone had served themselves, Jeff took all the remaining eggs and bacon.

"You need to eat fruits and vegetables, too," Gemma admonished as he polished off his plate. "I know you crave protein, but you need fiber and other nutrients."

He glanced over at Jennifer. "Now you know why we call her the Vegetable Nazi."

Jennifer smiled at him, and he asked her quietly, "Are you done eating?"

"Yes. Why?"

"Take a walk with me." As Gemma opened her mouth to protest, he sent her a quelling look and said with grim authority, "Not open to negotiation, Doc."

Jennifer followed Jeff outside cautiously. She wasn't any more thrilled than Gemma to see him up and about. She was still plenty creeped out at the idea of his muscles tearing apart his skeleton. "You've been very ill. You shouldn't overdo."

"And I won't. But you and I need to have a private conversation."

"So private you had to leave the house?"

"Are the trees bugged?"

She stared at him. "Excuse me?"

"I said a *private* conversation. That house is monitored."

"Actually, it's not. It's a vacation home for people like me. We can take a break from paranoia here."

Jeff pursed his lips. "In other words, you're not aware of it being bugged. But that doesn't guarantee that it's not."

Startled, she considered his statement. "I suppose your logic is sound. What's so private that you're not willing to take even the smallest risk of being overheard?"

He glanced over his shoulder briefly. It was an unconscious gesture, but the man really was worried about being observed. Why? What was the big secret?

"I have to ask you a question, Jennifer."

He sounded so serious he'd actually managed to scare her a little. And that was probably why she responded dryly, "I'm sorry, I can't marry a rich man. I'm allergic to money."

He stared, startled out of whatever he'd been about to say. A crack of laughter escaped him and she lurched. It was the first time she'd ever heard him laugh. He threw his head back and flashed even, white teeth as he laughed heartily. He threw an arm around her shoulders and dragged her close against his side in a casual hug. "Thank you. I needed that."

"Uhh, you're welcome."

Shockingly, he didn't turn her loose. He continued to walk with his arm looped casually over her shoulders. She saw what Brady Hathaway meant about this man being unnaturally heavy. His arm weighed a ton. Were she not in top physical condition, it would be uncomfortable across her shoulders.

The house disappeared out of sight behind them and he stopped. Turned to face her. "Seriously, there's something I need to ask you."

"Okay." She looked up into his eyes. The bright blue was flecked with silver. A ring of sapphire around the edges of his irises made his eyes seem darker than they actually were.

"Do you, by any chance, work at a facility called H.O.T. Watch?"

Whoa. H.O.T. Watch was *extremely* classified. Even its name was classified. Only the people who worked there and a *very* few people outside of that elite group had any idea it—or anything even remotely like it—existed. How did this civilian not only know it existed, but have an inkling she might work there? Did he know how close they were to the surveillance facility now? The idea blew her mind. This security breach was disastrous!

"What's that?" she managed to choke out.

"If you don't know what it is, I'm not about to tell you."

Thank God for that. At least he wasn't running around telling everyone he knew about the place. But how on earth did he know about it? "Why do you ask?" she threw out as casually as she could manage, which wasn't very casual at all.

"Because it's compromised."

Compromised? H.O.T. Watch? Her mind went completely blank. Only disjointed bits of thought came together. *No way. Compromised? For God's sake, how?* Eventually, she mumbled, "Why do you say that?"

His fingers trailed down her cheek with incredible tenderness from such a strong man. "Honey, you haven't denied working there. I need a yes or no answer from you. Do you work there?"

"I can neither confirm nor deny—"

He cut her off gently. "You have to tell me. Lives depend

on it. The lives of good men and women who are trying to do the right thing."

"I…" She trailed off. She had no idea what to say next.

He sighed. "I'm going to take your inability to come up with an answer as a yes. Which puts me in a bind."

"How so?"

He placed his hands on either side of her face and gently, but inexorably, forced her to look him in the eyes. "Have you ever sold information obtained from H.O.T. Watch's surveillance equipment to a non-U.S. government source?"

Dead shock poured through her. Rage exploded through the shock. She demanded in a terrible voice she barely recognized as her own, "Are you telling me someone's *selling* information from H.O.T. Watch?"

A relieved smile unfolded on his face. "Thank God. It's not you. I need you to leave this island with me. Now. Come with me somewhere where we can really talk. I need to show you something. But not here."

She was the CIA agent and he was her prisoner. She was the one doing the debriefing. The one who was supposed to put her subject off balance and get him to reveal his secrets to her. But she was the one reeling here. She was the one whose mind was blown with the things he knew about her. She was the one being deftly handled.

Jennifer shook her head. It wasn't possible. How he'd heard the name H.O.T. Watch was a mystery, and heads were going to roll when she found out who'd let it slip. Let alone what she was going to do to the traitor who was selling the place's secrets. That person was going to wish his head only rolled.

"Please, Jenn. Trust me."

It was the last straw. She blew up. "Trust you? You? The man who won't answer any of my questions, not even to save your own life? The man who breaks another man's neck in front of me and won't explain why? Who won't tell me even the most basic things about where he's been or how he ended up in an African jail? Or why he's addicted to drugs that will kill him by their absence? How am I supposed to trust you?"

Chapter 7

Jeff contemplated her soberly. He could see her point. He hadn't done a thing to earn her trust since they'd met. "Jennifer, I'm asking you to trust me because right now there is no one else you can trust."

Her eyes widened in dismay as that reality sunk in. He hated being the one to put that hurt and betrayal into her gaze. Nonetheless, he had to convince her. "H.O.T. Watch is compromised, and I can prove it. Come with me, and I'll show you. I swear on my word of honor."

She'd accepted his word before. Maybe she'd do it again. She looked…battered. Like his declaration had destroyed the foundation of her world. Surely she hadn't worked for the CIA for any length of time and managed to remain an idealist. But apparently, she had. The idea of her becoming cynical and jaded was painful to him. He had to make her see the truth, though. He owed it to her.

She spoke heavily. "No."

He supposed denial was a reasonable response from her. But he didn't have much time to overcome her objections. Her minders would get suspicious if the two of them were away from the house for too long. And no matter what she said, he had no doubt whatsoever that the place was under surveillance.

He pulled out his cell phone and dialed a number. The call would be monitored, but that couldn't be helped. He would just have to move faster than the response team eavesdropping on his conversation.

Leland answered the call. "What's up, Jeff?"

"I need you to collect Gemma and the pilots and meet me at the airstrip ASAP."

"What's going on?"

"Later. Quickly, Pops."

"Got it."

Jennifer stared in disbelief. "I haven't cleared you to leave this island! And I'm not about to now. Not after what you've just revealed. You need a full security briefing. There are legal documents I need you to sign…."

He waited her out with a patient look on his face. She knew she was babbling, but for the life of her, she couldn't stop. Things were moving too fast for her to process. It was too much to absorb. H.O.T. Watch compromised? This island under surveillance? What else didn't she know?

She was one of the two senior officials in charge of H.O.T. Watch. How could she not know about the surveillance here? Surely Brady Hathaway wasn't under orders to spy on her—or on the entire civilian side of the H.O.T. Watch house! Wouldn't she have been put under corresponding orders to spy on him, too? If only her staff was under surveillance, did that mean someone on her team was the leak? She couldn't believe any of her people were moles. She'd handpicked them all. Vetted

them out herself. They all had sterling records. Unquestion-
able patriotism. They'd all had plenty of opportunities to compromise missions, to make a little slip or omission here and
there that would have compromised operatives all over the
world, but she'd never seen even a hint of such a thing.

Jeff seemed so sure of himself, though. His body language
shouted that he was telling the truth. Unless he was trained
in how to lie with his body. It was possible, although it took
exquisite control to fool someone as experienced as her.

"Tell me you're not lying, Jeff."

Without hesitating, without any conscious thought, he
looked her square in the eye. "I'm not lying. Please trust me."

Dammit! Not even a *hint* of a twitch to indicate dishon-
esty!

"We need to go, honey. We're on a short timetable now."

"What are you talking about?" She really wished her brain
would quit feeling like caramel.

"That call I just made to Leland? If I'm telling the truth,
your boys at H.O.T. Watch heard me declare my intention to
flee the island. You know as well as I do that they'll send in
the cavalry to stop me."

He was right.

He took her by the elbow. Steered her farther down the
path. "Is there a shorter way to the airfield than following the
cart path?"

"Yes. There's a trail straight down the mountain. It's steep.
Bad footing. But passable."

"Show me."

She couldn't overpower him. It would be laughable to try.
So, she'd go along with his scheme for now. Head down to the
airfield with him. Show him that no cavalry was rushing in
to stop him. That he was being paranoid. That he was wrong
about H.O.T. Watch being compromised. Wrong about this
island being under covert surveillance.

A plan in place, her panic receded slightly. She led the way down the mountain. The narrow path was no picnic to navigate, and about halfway down she fell on a patch of loose scree that rolled out from under her feet, planting her on her behind in a scary downhill slide.

All of a sudden, a huge body was beside her. Jeff lifted her to her feet like she weighed nothing and lent her his bulk to balance on as they slid down the hill together in a rush. They pulled up sharply at the bottom of the scree field.

"Thank you," she gasped.

"My pleasure." He reached up to push a lock of her hair out of her face and tuck it behind her ear. The contact sent thrills racing through her.

The attraction in his voice was plain. No doubt about it, the two of them had something between them. Chemistry. And she *had* to ignore it. Had to keep her head. Whatever game Jeff Winston was playing, it was deep. And she would drown in it if she wasn't exceedingly cautious.

The rest of the hike went uneventfully until he put a restraining hand on her arm as they approached the airfield. The Winston Enterprises Gulfstream G650 stood at the near end of the runway, its door open and one of the pilots circling the jet doing a preflight inspection.

She glanced over at Jeff. "Why have we stopped in the trees?"

"H.O.T. Watch." He pointed at the sky and sick shock poured through her. He knew the facility used high-resolution satellites to watch the earth below? What else did he know?

She shrugged. "I can neither confirm nor deny—" she started.

He cut her off. "Spare me the party line. I'm looking out for your future career."

"My...huh?"

Without warning, he bent down and scooped her off her

feet. She squawked as he settled her in his arms like a child. He stepped out from under the canopy of foliage. "Feel free to kick and scream, but don't hurt me too badly, please."

Realization slammed into her. He was making it look like he was kidnapping her to whoever was watching this little exchange from above. Wait a minute. He *was* kidnapping her!

"Put me down!"

"Good. Do that again."

She pounded his chest with her fists. "I'm serious. Put. Me. Down."

"Sorry, honey. Can't. I really need you to come with me."

Chapter 8

"This is kidnapping!" Jennifer exclaimed indignantly.

"Kinda sexy, isn't it?"

Sexy? The word stopped her cold. Darned if it wasn't sexy being around a man who could pick her up and haul her off in his private jet like this. "Damn you," she gritted out from between clenched teeth.

He grinned down at her. "You are so hot when you're all worked up like this."

"Oooh!" she punched him in the jaw as hard as she could from her awkward position in his arms.

"Oww! Now that's carrying the act a little far." They'd reached the plane and he eased her body down the front of his in a delicious slide that stole her breath away. But his steely arm remained wrapped securely around her waist.

He called to the pilot, "Time to go. I know it's not procedure, but we'll be shot down if we dawdle."

The idea of being shot down sent the copilot hurrying toward the door.

"In we go," Jeff murmured to her.

She fought in earnest then. No way was she letting him force her into his jet. But she should've known better. He merely picked her up, this time in a muscular vise so tight she could hardly breathe, let alone move.

"No one's coming for us. And no one's going to shoot us down," she exclaimed.

Gemma and Leland were already aboard and humiliation swamped her to have them see Jeff carrying her like this. But the two merely made a production of gazing out the windows.

Jeff dropped her into an oversize leather seat and wrapped a seat belt around her. His hands fumbling in her lap were too much to stand. She grabbed the buckle from him and latched it herself while the first engine started.

"You may be expendable to your government, Jenn, but you're not to me. I don't plan to stick around here and find out if having you aboard is sufficient to stop them from shooting us down."

"Really, you're carrying this conspiracy theory too far."

"We'll see."

The second engine cranked up. The plane taxied a short distance, and raced down the runway. It lifted off, staying low as it banked over the ocean and picked up speed.

"Incoming!" the copilot called.

Jennifer looked out her window and spied a trio of wakes in the water below. Cold washed over her. The photo analyst in her recognized in an instant what she was seeing. Those were rigid-hulled inflatable boats, headed for the island. And RIBs had one mission, and one mission only. Carrying special forces operators into combat.

Holy Mother of God. Jeff was right. The island *was* under surveillance. The cavalry *had* come racing in to stop him

from leaving the island. Was he also right, then, that H.O.T.
Watch was compromised?

The jet turned away from the oncoming boats. It skimmed
over the ocean at barely a hundred feet off the deck if she
had to guess. She glanced over at Jeff, who was watching her
grimly.

She grumbled, "Please tell me your pilots are military
trained and know how to fly low-level at high speed like this."

He nodded and replied, "This plane is also equipped with
the latest in radar avoidance technology."

"You won't be able to avoid the satellites," she warned.

"We'll find a weather system and lose ourselves under or
in the clouds," he replied.

She fell silent. Jeff had avoided H.O.T. Watch coverage.
Meanwhile, her mind raced in circles. How had H.O.T. Watch
been infiltrated? Who was it? Why was the island being
watched? And how come no one had told her? But no matter
how many questions she asked herself, no answers were forthcoming.

Over the next several hours, the pilots took evasive action
that even she had to admit would confound the surveillance
capabilities of H.O.T. Watch. The plane landed in Mexico,
ostensibly to refuel, but she wasn't fooled. A plane like this
could cross an ocean on a single tank of gas. She'd bet the
crew was filing a flight plan under some dummy name to
allow them to slip into the United States.

The sun was setting over the Rocky Mountains when the
plane began its final descent. They landed and, under the
cover of an airplane hangar, transferred into an armored,
darked-out SUV. The drive, wherever they were going, took
about an hour.

The vehicle passed through a guarded gate and Jennifer noted that the security man and his booth looked neither

sloppy nor amateur. The Winstons took their privacy very seriously, apparently.

She gasped as a magnificent log-cabin mansion came into view against a backdrop of snowcapped mountains. It shouted of intense style. Limitless wealth. Its opulence was overwhelming. Rather like its owner.

Light shone through the windows, golden and inviting upon a landscape of spring wildflowers and grasses. Jeff smiled slightly beside her. "Glad to be home?" she asked him.

"You have no idea."

"Did you think you might not make it out of that prison alive?"

He glanced over at her wryly. "You can stop trying to debrief me now. You're off the reservation."

She didn't for a second think he was referring to her Native American heritage. He was using the phrase 'off the reservation' to refer to a spy who had gone rogue. Her. A rogue agent. It simply didn't compute. "I've been kidnapped. The government's going to come after you with both barrels."

"It'll take them a while to get through my lawyers and my security. And that will give me enough time to show you what I have to."

"Jeff!" Gemma exclaimed in alarm.

Jennifer looked over at the woman with interest. So. There were secrets here at the Winston estate that the good doctor didn't want her to see? Clearly, she had to see them, then.

Chagrin glinted in Jeff's blue eyes. "Stay out of this, Gem. It has nothing to do with you."

"And what is *this,* exactly?" Jennifer asked him under her breath.

"Patience. All will become clear soon. I promise."

Except she didn't feel particularly patient when she discovered she'd been locked in her luxurious suite of rooms, and the home's construction was fortlike. She'd never break out of here.

As night fell and stars began to twinkle outside, she stood by the floor-to-ceiling window and enjoyed the view. Although the granite Rockies were not her native red sandstone, the mountains still spoke to her soul.

Her door opened and she spun to face the threat. A tall, vaguely familiar man advanced cautiously into the room. She started to ask who he was, but then she caught sight of his eyes. Blue with flecks of silver and ringed by dark blue…

"Jeff?" she asked incredulously.

He flashed her an abashed smile. "Thought you might appreciate it if I got a shave and a haircut."

Wow. He cleaned up, umm, well. "You look like your pictures now," she mumbled, suddenly uncomfortable around his Ivy League good looks. Abruptly, he and his home felt foreign to her, far removed from any reality she could relate to.

"Had a dossier on me, did you? Did it say anything interesting?"

"What it didn't say was more interesting."

He strolled over beside her to gaze out at the stars. He smelled lightly of shampoo and expensive aftershave. It was intoxicating. Seriously? She didn't get light-headed over the smell of a man, thank you very much. It must be the altitude getting to her…at the exact moment when he walked into the room. Right. Altitude. She swore under her breath.

"What was so interesting by omission in my dossier?"

"How'd you go from spoiled rich kid to…this?"

He glanced sidelong at her. "'This' being what exactly?"

"You tell me. Who are you? *What* are you? What makes you tick?"

He turned to face her, and she was struck by just how large and powerful a man he was. She literally rocked back on her heels at his flesh impact. She wasn't so shallow that the mere fact of his godlike beauty made her suddenly hot for him. But the man *was* easy on the eye with all that Tarzan hair gone.

"Jennifer, I owe you my life several times over. And I'm eternally grateful for that. I also think you're one of the most attractive women I've met in a long time, and I'd love to do something about that if you're interested."

Her brain hitched like a broken wheel at the idea that her fantasies actually had a chance of becoming reality. And then it hit her. A) he hadn't answered her question, and b) the man could manipulate her thoughts like no one she'd ever met before. Belatedly, she realized he was speaking again.

"…some things about me and my life, however, that I cannot and will not share with you. Ever."

She knew the feeling. CIA field agents' lives weren't exactly open books, either. She considered him thoughtfully. "Do your secrets have to do with those injections the good doctor gives you?" She glanced down at a new bandage on his arm that announced he'd had another one of Dr. Jones's shots recently.

"If I asked you to quit asking questions and just accept me at face value, would you do it for me?"

"Why should I?"

He closed the gap between them and she sucked in a sharp breath. He reached out and, with a single finger crooked under her chin, tilted up her face.

"Because of this," he whispered.

His lips touched hers. Desire imploded within her, and she gasped as Jeff responded by sweeping her up against him, her feet dangling off the ground as he crushed her body effortlessly against his. It was as natural as breathing to wrap her legs around his hips and her arms around his neck as he supported her weight easily.

"I'm not hurting you, am I?" she asked breathlessly.

"Nope. Doc Jones's shots are doing their thing, and she gave me more of the pain receptor blocking stuff. Miracle drug. Winston Pharmaceuticals is going to make a fortune on it."

"You're not just saying that to be nice, are you?"

He laughed quietly. "I'm a lot of things, but nice is not one of them."

"Really?" she asked, surprised.

"Really. Gemma says I'm too blunt to be nice."

Jennifer hadn't worked in a male-dominated profession for a decade for nothing. She smiled up at him. "I truly do prefer honesty."

"Then I honestly want you to kiss me. Right now. And nothing you can do will hurt me."

"Promise?" she whispered.

"Promise."

She speared her hands into his silky hair and tugged his head close to kiss him deeply. And, oh, my, how he kissed her back. She'd never hungered for any man like this. If she could crawl inside his skin she would, so badly did she want to be with him. Her entire being strained toward him. And if the way he all but inhaled her was any indication, he felt the same way about her.

Her grandfather used to tell the legends of her ancestors, and she'd never understood the ones that talked about gods giving up their immortality for love. But this pull she felt toward Jeff, she could see giving up eternity for a little more of this. It felt *right*.

He groaned and turned to carry her somewhere. She didn't care where as long as he didn't let go of her. She felt small and fragile and safe in his arms and it was the most wonderful feeling in the world. He laid her on the bed and she clung to him as he followed her down. He propped himself up on one elbow, but she didn't want even that small distance between them.

"I want you, Jeff," she gasped against his mouth.

"I'll crush you," he muttered.

"I won't break."

"But you don't understand—"

"You *jumped* on me in Africa and I survived."

He grinned down at her. "Remember that, do you? It made quite an impression on me, too."

She stared back in surprise. "I thought you were going to kill me."

He kissed her lightly. "I thought you were going to kill me, too. But you didn't. You fired over my shoulder and got me out of there."

"The way I recall it, you pushed me out of the way of the bullets and then bodily dragged me out of that firefight."

He laughed quietly. "How about we call that one a mutual save, then?"

She smiled up at him. "Deal. If you'll shut up and get back to kissing me."

"As the lady wishes…."

To say she crawled all over him wouldn't be inaccurate. How could she not? He was so delicious and so very unbreakable. As he continued to be relaxed and not wince or gasp, she lost all fear that her strength and training would accidentally hurt him. For the first time in her life she felt free to do exactly what she wanted to without editing her desires at all.

Although when she reached for his belt buckle, he caught her hands and brought them to his mouth, kissing her knuckles regretfully. "As much as I'd love to see where that thought leads us, we have places to go and things to see this evening."

A whimper of distress actually came out of her throat. He groaned in response and kissed her deeply. Then he mumbled against her mouth, "Do you have any idea how tempting you are?"

"No, but I know how tempting you are."

He laughed in what sounded like pain. She took small satisfaction from the sound, though, because it mirrored her frustration.

He kissed her one last time, lightly, with regret at having to stop. "I like you enough to take this slow. And for what it's worth, I've never said that to a woman before."

She looked for the truth of it and found it in his open expression. Warmth filled her. She shoved back the loose tendrils of hair that had worked free from her braid during their passionate embrace. Lord, her cheeks were hot. What on earth had he done to her to cause such a violent flush? The wantonness of her behavior the past few minutes struck her forcefully. At the first opportunity that wouldn't cause him screaming pain, she'd thrown herself at him like a complete hussy. Thing was, she didn't *throw* herself at men. Ever.

He stood and offered a hand to her. She took it and floated to her feet like a feather. He pulled her into his arms and she went willingly, plastering herself against him, addicted to the feel of his body. So much for self-control. Apparently, she had none when it came to this man.

He groaned. "You're so damned delectable."

"Says the pot to the kettle," she grumbled as he resolutely stepped back from her and tucked her arm under his elbow.

"Come on. I promised to show you something. And so I shall."

The mansion was as impressive inside as out. It was outfitted with the latest in technology and lights went on in front of them and dimmed behind them automatically as they moved through the house. He led her through a great room à la hunting lodge decor that would rival any major hotel lobby in size and comfort. The rustic materials and touches of nature reminded her of home.

"Is this where you live most of the time?" she asked curiously.

"Yes. But don't get too comfortable. I'm betting the Feds will show up here momentarily looking for you. I'm frankly surprised they weren't waiting for us when we arrived."

"They'll move cautiously around you and your grandfather. You're powerful men and not good to tick off."

"Leland's the real mover and shaker."

"And you're the heir to the throne. You're still a force to be reckoned with," she retorted.

He smiled over his shoulder at her. "I can live with that, I suppose."

The house's technology was carefully disguised—dark touch pads blending in with the knotty pine paneling, a willow basket disguising a pile of remote controls. And a recessed, carved wood panel that turned out to hide a stainless steel elevator. Jeff stepped inside and held the door for her.

"Are we headed down to your secret sanctum?" she asked playfully.

"Actually, yes."

She blinked in surprise.

"Winston Enterprises is a global conglomerate with assets and interests that span the planet. We need to have our finger directly on the pulse of world events, and the facility I'm about to show you is designed to do that. The public is not aware of its existence, and I'd appreciate it if it stayed that way."

She pursed her lips, noting that the elevator was still going down. How deep underground was his secret sanctum? "You'll show me your hideout, but you'll have to shoot me if I tell anyone about it?"

His eyes glinted in dark humor. "Something like that."

The door opened and he stepped out, gesturing for her to join him. She took a single step forward and stopped in her tracks. It wasn't an exact duplicate of H.O.T. Watch headquarters, but it wasn't a far cry from it. The room was brightly lit, although the charcoal-colored walls, floor and ceiling prevented any glare. A jumbo video display—black at the moment—dominated one wall, and a half-dozen men and women sat in front of state-of-the-art computer displays with multiple wide-screen monitors at each station. Frankly, the surveillance and intelligence setup she was looking at was better equipped than H.O.T. Watch's.

A chorus of voices called out welcome-homes to Jeff. A good-looking red-haired woman wearing yellow-tinted glasses came over and gave Jeff a hard, brief hug. "It's great to see you in one piece, Jeff. You gave us a heck of a scare."

The mood in the room shifted in an instant to one of grief and loss. Jennifer watched on uncomfortably for the next several minutes as the staff offered Jeff their condolences on the death of his team. She knew all too well how it felt to lose men—the guilt and second guessing, the sleepless nights going over and over the mission and wondering what you missed that could have saved them.

With all Jeff had been going through personally, it was easy to forget he'd suffered a terrible loss just a few months ago. It hurt her to see the haunted look in his eyes as he accepted his people's offerings of sympathy and to know there was nothing she could do to fix it. Some hurts never quite healed.

As the staff finally wound down, Jeff introduced her to the woman with the funny glasses. "Sammie Jo, this is Jennifer Blackfoot. She's the CIA agent who pulled me out of Africa."

At the letters, *CIA,* everyone in the room froze. They all

stared at her like she was the enemy. She held out a hand and said pleasantly, "It's nice to meet you, Sammie Jo."

"You can call me Sam." The woman managed to be polite, but just barely.

Jeff announced, "Do we have a link to the CIA safe house in the Caribbean?"

"The one that they—" Sammie Jo glanced at Jennifer "—that she took you to?"

"Correct."

The redhead shrugged. "In fact, we do. When your grandfather found out where you were, he had us research ways to check up on you. I have to say, boss. You looked like hell, there, for a while."

Jeff muttered, "I felt like hell."

"What time frame on the safe house, sir?" one of the technicians called out.

"Within the past twenty-four hours," Jeff called back.

"It'll take a few minutes to contact the provider and download it," the technician answered.

Jennifer's jaw sagged as an interior shot of the living room of the house she'd spent last night in popped up on the large monitor. Her laptop computer was closed on the coffee table, her sunglasses sat on the credenza by the front door where she'd left them yesterday. A chill crawled over her skin.

"Looks like this was shot after Leland and Gemma left. This morning based on the angle of the sun," Jeff commented. "Fast forward it, will you? Let's see if the place had visitors after we bugged out."

Only the time/date counter in the corner of the picture changed in a blur for about ten seconds. Then, as she watched in horror, a dozen men in full combat gear burst through every door in an organized combat assault. Men she recognized from H.O.T. Watch. One of them touched his neck. Speaking into a throat microphone.

"Is there audio on this feed?" she asked hoarsely.

"No, ma'am," the tech answered.

"You okay?" Jeff murmured.

"No. I'm sick to my stomach."

He sighed. "It gets worse." He ordered his staff, "Pull up a military satellite feed from H.O.T. Watch. Something recent. I don't care what it is."

Jennifer actually staggered when a picture of H.O.T. Watch's satellite tracking map flashed up on the screen, reporting the position of every single satellite the facility used for intelligence collection. Jeff's arm slipped around her waist and she leaned against him, riveted as the shot shifted to a nighttime surveillance shot of...

"Oh, my God. Is that an American military team?" she gasped.

"Yes, ma'am. Looks like a Ranger patrol. Afghanistan if I had to guess from the terrain. I didn't request a specific location."

"Pull up another sample feed," Jeff ordered.

Her legs actually felt weak as pretty much the entire capability of H.O.T. Watch was demonstrated for her over the next few minutes.

"What about the super computer? Is its capability for sale, too?" she asked thickly. She really did feel like she might throw up.

"I don't know," Jeff answered gently. "Winston Enterprises has its own super array, so we've never been offered time on anyone else's."

She moved over to the console where the technician was typing commands into a computer to download more video feeds. She glanced up at Jeff in anguished entreaty.

"Let the lady have your seat," he directed the tech quietly.

She slipped into the guy's seat and donned his headset. Typing quickly, she called up the access port to H.O.T.

Watch's mainframe computer, fondly nicknamed Big Bertha. She typed in her access code. A beep denied her access. She tried a back door. Again, she was denied access. After a half-dozen tries to hack into the computer with which she was as familiar as anyone on the planet, she nodded and pushed back from the console. That was good news, at least. Big Bertha contained enough intelligence information to compromise at least half the special forces teams in the world.

"What's the verdict?" Jeff asked from behind her.

"The main frame seems safe. It's just the visual feeds that are compromised." She swiveled in the seat and demanded accusingly, "And how on God's green earth did you get access to those feeds?"

"Long story," he replied evasively.

"I'm all ears."

"Come with me. Let's chat in a more private place, shall we?"

He led her to the massive dining room and over to the window where a small table for two was set and lit by a cluster of candles. He pulled out one of the chairs and waited expectantly for her.

"I'm not going to be distracted by this wining and dining routine," she declared. "I want answers."

"I would expect no less of you. But there's no reason we can't get a bite to eat while we talk. The past few months have taken a toll on me, and I need to regain my strength."

She glared up at him as he pushed in her chair for her. "It's a dirty trick to invoke your recent suffering to gain my sympathy."

He sat down across from her and unfolded his napkin. "I never said I fight fair."

She rolled her eyes, as much at the thrill of feminine appreciation fluttering in her gut at his alpha male behavior as at his comment. "How is your pain? Rate it on a scale of one to ten."

He pondered for a moment. "What constitutes a ten in my world has reset in the past few days. I'd give this a three. It'll be a two once I've had something to eat."

Apparently he was none the worse for wear after having her throw herself at him earlier. Her cheeks heated at the memory of how she'd crawled all over him at the first opportunity that presented itself.

"Jeff, I don't like this."

"You don't like pork loin? I'll have the chef make you something else."

"That's not what I'm talking about. I don't like this." She waved her arm at the house in general. "I feel like I've stepped into a bad comic book. But this isn't a game. Real people's lives are at risk. You're tangling with real bad guys and real governments here."

"I got that memo, thank you," he bit out.

"What the heck are you doing then? This is madness!"

"What's any more mad about what I'm doing than the idea of a hollowed out volcano full of intelligence analysts and satellites looking down at any corner of the planet at a moment's notice?"

"H.O.T. Watch is funded by a government engaging in a global war on terror and with the intent to keep an eye on other world powers. You're a private citizen. A *cowboy.* I hesitate to imagine the events you're involving yourself in without any knowledge of what the government's policy or practices regarding those events are."

To his credit, Jeff took the rebuke calmly. "I have no interest in getting in the way of my—your—government. And as a rule I steer well clear of them."

"Then what is all this about?" She leaned forward to give her question added emphasis. "What are you up to?"

"I'm looking out for my family's interests. I rarely reach beyond the scope of Winston Industries."

She snorted. "Yes, but that's a major corporation with income greater than some countries."

"True."

She frowned when he said no more. "Why do you continue to stonewall me?"

It was his turn to stare at her intensely. "Are you sure you really want to know?"

She leaned back in her seat, studying him. So. He was up to something the government wouldn't approve of. She wasn't a CIA agent for nothing. She'd ferret out his secrets in spite of his head games and evasions. Oh, yes. She'd learn everything about him before she was through.

A man came into the dining room, wheeling a serving cart. He laid out the meal, and she was amused to see that Jeff's plate held at least twice as much food as hers, and there was no way she could eat everything heaped on her plate.

When she was done eating, she folded her napkin and said quietly, "Tell me about the men you lost."

He gathered his thoughts for a moment before speaking. "Winston Enterprises sends teams of people around the world for various reasons—to investigate new markets, to do humanitarian work, et cetera. We'd already lost one team in East Africa, and when we sent another one, I went with them personally."

She would love to hear more about that casually uttered *et cetera*. But she didn't interrupt.

"The attack on our group was well-coordinated, efficient and designed precisely to counteract our gear and skills. It was fast and deadly. They came late at night, drugged the hired guards with dart guns, then slit my men's throats in their sleep."

"Without any intent to be insensitive, how come they didn't kill you, too?"

"I was lucky. I heard the guy in the next tent gurgle and came partially awake as the guy assigned to my tent jumped me. He put a hand over my mouth and went for my throat with a knife in his other hand. But he didn't count on my being strong enough to sit up in spite of his grip on my face. I fought him off and bolted. By the time I got outside, the hit squad was finishing up." He added heavily, "And all my men were dead."

"How long was it before the Ethiopian Army showed up?"

"A few minutes. I had just finished checking to see if anyone was alive."

"Was the Ethiopian Army violent with you?"

His eyes were vague with relived memories. "No. I handed over the knife I had taken and they arrested me."

She frowned. If the Ethiopians had been in cahoots with his attackers, why hadn't they just finished him off? Why go through the charade of arresting him and acting civilized while they were at it? Clearly the Ethiopian Army had known of the attack and, furthermore, been close enough to intervene. Yet they hadn't. It could all mean only one thing. Their army had feared Jeff's attackers too much to interfere.

Was the same entity behind the attacks on Jeff's men and the theft of H.O.T. Watch's visual data stream?

Jeff was speaking again. "…a front operation, we bought access to the data. And then we started what I must say was an arduous process of tracking it back to its source."

"And your search led you to H.O.T. Watch."

"Correct. If it makes you feel any better, it took us nearly a year to get proof that the place even exists."

She gazed out the window at the black night. Her thoughts were nearly as dark at the moment. She was going to personally kill whoever had sold out the facility.

"What will you do now?" he asked quietly.

"Launch a full-scale investigation. Draw and quarter whoever's selling the data from the inside."

"It may not be that simple."

That made her gaze swing back to him sharply.

"In building our own facility, we learned a few things about places like H.O.T. Watch. The visual feeds available on the black market seem to come from every satellite feed you've got. Surely you designed a certain amount of compartmentalization into the place. Which means the leak's coming from above the level of the satellites. Or else there are multiple leaks."

The meal abruptly felt like lead in her stomach. She said slowly, "The military side of the house and the civilian side are completely separate. We duplicate systems in case of a breakdown, and we use them to double-check each other's findings."

"Then how is it I can buy feeds from both systems?"

"What are you saying?" She saw where he was headed, but her mind couldn't take it in, yet.

He took a deep breath and exhaled it slowly. "I'm saying I think the entire facility is compromised."

"But how?" she cried.

He shrugged. "When the American embassy in Moscow was built—by Russian contractors at the insistence of the Russian government—microphones and cameras were built into the walls and wired directly into the electrical system during construction. It's possible something similar happened when H.O.T. Watch was built."

The implications were staggering. Had the place been sending out pirated signals for *years?* The amount of damage to American military and intelligence operations was mind boggling. "You do know how to kill a girl's appetite."

They were silent for a few minutes. He looked regretful at being the bearer of such bad news, and she was simply numb.

Finally, Jeff asked, "Can I interest you in dessert? My chef is world-class."

"I don't doubt that, but no. No dessert for me."

"Maybe later. In the meantime, would you like to see more of the house?" He seemed to understand she needed a distraction to give her a little time to breathe. She didn't doubt he could prove everything he'd just told her. Her brain craved denial, and she let Jeff's mundane commentary about the mansion draw her out of her shock and dismay.

The home was a veritable museum of art, antiques and collectibles, and he was a charming host. This Jeff was about as unlike the savage on that road in Ethiopia as a man could get. But which one was real? How could the two coexist? Aloud, she asked, "How is it you're so different from the man I picked up at that prisoner trade?"

He frowned. "Same man. Less pain."

"Dr. Jones said the drugs treat your bones. What's wrong with them?"

"Density problem."

"You're telling me low bone density caused you the suffering I witnessed?" she asked skeptically.

"Something like that." He looped an arm over her shoulder and drew her near. "If I can't interest you in chocolate for dessert, can I interest you in me?"

He was blatantly trying to distract her. And darned if she didn't want to let him. Her body went liquid with desire at the mere thought of being with him. They could always talk later. After she'd softened him up…. Yeah, that was it. Sleeping with him was all part of getting him to talk. She could embrace that logic.

And then they were kissing and her body caught on fire and she wanted him worse than life. Maybe a little of her enthusiasm was her mind fleeing the horror of what she'd learned earlier. But most of it was lust, pure and simple.

"My bedroom's closer," he mumbled against her neck.

"How much closer?"

He laughed. "Just down the hall." And then his arm went behind her thighs and he swung her up into his arms and strode rapidly down the hall while she nibbled his ear.

His bedroom started to illuminate, but he barked a series of voice commands and the overhead lights went out. The drapes slid open with a quiet whoosh, revealing floor-to-ceiling glass panels and the splendor of the night. A gas fireplace lit across the room, throwing dancing shadows onto a massive bed. And then a huge panel in the ceiling slid back to reveal a skylight as large as the bed. He laid her down on a mattress the size of a small town.

This was, of course, insane. But darned if she wasn't feeling reckless after tonight's shocks. Even if she successfully plugged the leak in H.O.T. Watch, her career was over. She and Brady Hathaway would eat the blame for letting such an egregious security breach happen on their watch.

Even if bugs had been built into the place, Uncle Sam would need sacrificial lambs—her and Brady. Her dismay was too much to deal with at the moment. And Jeff was right here, right now, offering escape from the wreck of her life for a little while. What did it matter if she heaped fraternizing with a prisoner on top of all her other transgressions? And besides, the guy was smoking hot. She reached over her shoulder to pull the tie out of the bottom of her braid.

He took his time stripping her naked, kissing and tasting as he went. She writhed in an agony of need long before he was finished. "You do realize I'm going to get even with you," she threatened.

"I look forward to it."

Ha. He'd regret those words. She pushed his hands aside

as he reached for his clothes and did the task herself. She made sure he was groaning with impatience before she was done disrobing him down to his glorious, naked body. How much he worked out to achieve that physique, she didn't even want to contemplate. But the end result was worth whatever it took. He was, in a word, magnificent.

Impatient, she rolled onto her back and pulled him toward her.

"I don't want to hurt you," he explained as he resisted.

"You won't."

"You're right. Because we're doing this slow and easy."

"But I don't want that!"

He grinned down at her. "All in good time. For now, let's see if I can get you to make that sound in the back of your throat again."

"What sound?"

His mouth closed on parts of her that needed neither heat nor slick moisture to tremble with pleasure. She arched up hard off the mattress, her hands plunging into his thick hair to tug him away before she exploded.

"Oh, no. You don't get off that easy," he replied darkly. He ignored her ineffectual tugs and returned his attention to the volcano her body had become. In a matter of seconds, she was begging for more in between pleading with him to stop.

"Let go, Jenn. You're safe with me."

And that was all it took. An orgasm of such monumental dimensions as to be unbelievable slammed into her. It was like getting hit by an avalanche. It picked her up and tumbled her head over heels, flying her down a mountain and flinging her off a cliff, burying her in sensations so overwhelming she could hardly breathe. A keening cry of pleasure ripped from her throat. She collapsed back against the mattress, gasping for air.

"That sound," he said archly.

She laughed helplessly. The man played her like a violin and there didn't seem to be a thing she could do about it.

He kissed his way up her body, stealing away what little breath she had and establishing that he was going to be an exquisitely demanding lover. In moments, she was throbbing from head to foot with need, tugging him down to her and relishing the weight of him.

"I'll squash you," he muttered.

"I dare you."

"The lady likes to live dangerously," he chuckled.

"You have no idea."

"Show me," he demanded.

She pushed on his shoulders and he obliged by rolling onto his back. She followed, exploring him avidly with hands and mouth. When he let go of her to clutch the sheets in his fists and suck in air fast and hard between his clenched teeth, she raised her head. His head was thrown back, his eyes closed, and the muscles on his neck stood out in taut relief.

"Are you okay?" she asked in quick alarm. "Am I hurting you?"

He opened his eyes to glare at her. "Only if you stop."

"Well, then." She sat up, straddling his thighs. "Let's go for a ride, cowboy."

He laughed reluctantly. "Why do I feel like I've bedded a tiger?"

She laughed back, and finished pulling her hair free from its plaits. When her raven locks flowed around her body as wild and free as she felt, then, and only then, did she grasp his straining member in her fist. "Because you have," she murmured, guiding him into her.

She impaled herself upon him by millimeters, savoring the way his eyes went even blacker in the starlight. How his jaw rippled with the effort of his restraint. How his entire body shuddered with need by the time he was seated deep within her. She rocked forward slowly and her body shimmered with delight. Wanton, delicious impulses filled her. She ran her hands under her hair at the back of her neck and lifted her arms, letting the cool, silken strands flow like water down her arms and across her body.

And then Jeff's hands were there, his fingers combing through her hair, his fingertips stroking her body through the silken strands to new heights of bliss. Her hips liquid with desire, she rode him as slow and easy as he'd said she would, letting her pleasure build and build.

His jaw clenched, and before long, his entire body clenched beneath her. She cried out as another orgasm broke over her without warning, a tingling explosion that traveled through every inch of her body.

And then Jeff's hands were on her hips holding her so they remained joined as he rolled her over swiftly and rose up over her. He drove into her carefully. Again, deeper and with more power. She craved all of him and opened herself fully, whimpering for more.

He froze. "Are you okay?"

"Please, Jeff. More."

"Are you sure?"

"It's not polite to make a lady ask twice."

He laughed down at her. "My apologies, ma'am." And then he took her breath away as he did, indeed, let go of his formidable control. He drove into her until she shattered around him yet again.

She grabbed his arms, which were braced on either side of her head like steel columns, and wrapped her legs around his hips, desperately seeking the next explosion lurking just out of reach. His gaze locked with hers, and as they stared at each other with a naked intimacy that was shocking, found release together. He groaned his pleasure as she cried out hers.

And then his body was a delicious weight on hers, the relaxation of his muscles reflecting the limpid exhaustion claiming her. Still, he held himself propped up on his elbows as he kissed her leisurely and murmured, "You, my dear, are a miracle."

She was home. There was no other way to describe it. She'd never been a believer in soul mates, never held with silly, romantic notions like destiny. But she knew without a shadow of a doubt there would never be another man like this one in her life. Whether she was with him for a short time or forever, it wouldn't matter. He was the last man she would ever feel this way with.

He rolled to one side, his lovely body pressed against the length of hers, a hand propped under his ear. He used his free hand to push the tendrils of damp hair off her forehead while he smiled down at her.

"Nice view," she murmured.

He glanced up at the skylight.

"Not that," she corrected. "You."

He laughed quietly. "And here I was thinking the exact same thing. You're more beautiful than the night. Your hair is the sky and your eyes the stars. And you showed me Heaven."

"You look like you do, and make love like that, and you're a poet, too? Methinks you're pretty darn close to perfect, Mr. Winston."

They spent a long time just smiling at each other and murmuring about nothing in particular. But then the phone rang beside the bed, startling Jennifer.

Jeff reached over and picked up the receiver. "Yes?" He listened for a moment and then swore quietly. "Don't let them in, and don't tell them I'm here. Tell them to speak to my lawyers in the morning."

He put down the receiver.

"Who was that?" she asked soberly.

"The front gate. Uncle Sam's come looking for you."

Chapter 9

Jeff looked down at Jennifer grimly. Even when she was absorbed in unpleasant thoughts that put a frown on her face, he wanted her like crazy. She shifted restlessly, and he let her draw away from him. But he missed the warmth and softness of her body.

"What are you going to do?" he asked eventually.

"About H.O.T. Watch? I don't know. About the guys at the gate? Will they get past your guards?"

"Not a chance."

"Then I'm going to stay here a little while longer and hope you're as fit as you look."

"And why would that be?"

"Because I'm ready for dessert, now." She smiled wickedly at him.

He laughed aloud. "Leland always says never to stand between a woman and her treats."

"Smart man."

His bones felt like jelly when he and Jennifer finally collapsed side by side a long time later and stared up at the stars. He mumbled, "Wow. Just wow."

"Ditto," she murmured.

He was prepared to spend the rest of the night sleeping with her in his arms, but she had other ideas. She rose from his bed, bathed in starlight that turned her into a goddess. With her hair swirling around her like a dark cloud, she truly looked otherworldly.

"Where's the shower?" she asked.

He pointed at the bathroom door.

She disappeared, and he took a quick power nap while she played in his custom rain jets. The water turning off woke him and he swung out of bed. For the first time in several years, he actually felt unsteady. He grinned and just shook his head. That woman was a wonder.

By the time she'd combed out her hair and twisted it into a long braid, he'd finished a quick shower and dressed. As tempting as it was to interrupt her dressing, he left her alone. Her brow was furrowed in deep thought, and he'd never met a woman that liked to be bothered when something serious was on her mind. Finally, she looked up at him in decision.

"Yes?" he prompted.

"I need to make a phone call. One that can't be recorded or eavesdropped on."

"In the ops center."

They rode the elevator to the basement in silence. She retreated completely from him as the reality of their problems crashed back in on them. He felt strangely bereft. Quietly, he told the technician on the communications panel what she needed.

In a moment, the fellow passed her a wireless headset. "The line's secure, ma'am. I'll monitor the line throughout the call to make sure there's no surveillance, but I won't hear the conversation."

She nodded and donned the headset.

"Do you need me to clear the room?" Jeff murmured.

"Do you trust everyone in here?" she replied.

"With my life."

"All right, then."

He was shocked when she leaned down and commenced dialing a phone number. Just like that, she trusted him? Or maybe not just like that. He'd told her the truth about the island and about H.O.T. Watch and backed up both claims with hard evidence. But there were still a few truths he hadn't shared with her. And he didn't doubt the day would come when she demanded to know everything about him. Hell, after what they'd shared tonight, she deserved to know everything. Problem was, it wasn't just his neck on the line here. She wasn't the only person to whom he owed his loyalty.

Still, certain unspoken promises had passed between them. What they had was no casual hookup, no one-night stand. He didn't think for a minute that she was the kind of woman who jumped into bed with just any man. She was too self-contained, too mature, too professional, for that.

But they were headed for a wall beyond which he could not pass and behind which he could not allow her to go. When they hit it, she would walk away from him and never look back. The prospect of that caused him intense pain. And in his world, that was pretty bad pain.

Jeff made no effort to memorize the series of numbers she dialed, but he did note that it was longer than a regular phone number, even taking into account a country code and area code. A government number, then. Momentary panic clutched his gut. What if she was about to tell someone where she was and that he'd kidnapped her?

Trust was a two-way street, dammit. If he wanted hers, he had to give his to her, too.

"Brady, it's me."

Jeff heard a faint exclamation from a male voice at the other end of the line. His stomach muscles clenched until they cramped. *Trust, dammit.* No way would she do the things she had with him tonight if she was involved with some other guy.

Jennifer spoke quickly. "I'm fine. I can't tell you. And I can't tell you why. But I need you to trust me."

The man on the other end of the line said something fairly lengthy in response to that. Jennifer's gaze shifted to him and she smiled slightly at him. Jeff smiled back, but his mind raced. Whatever she was hearing was about him. He'd lay odds on it.

Finally, she said, "That's all very interesting. But it's not why I called."

A short pause.

"Look," she announced. "What I'm about to say has to stay just between you and me." Another brief pause, then, "Brady, H.O.T. Watch is compromised. Data from the satellites is being stolen and sold on the black market, and I can't tell you how I know that. But I do. And no, I'm not crazy."

Clearly, the man on the other end of the line thought she was, for she exclaimed, "Of course I'm serious! And no, I don't want you to investigate this. I've got it covered."

A short, sharp argument ensued. She ended it with, "I didn't tell you this to get you to do anything. I just need you to protect your teams. Make sure they don't get into any situations in the next few days where anything picked up on satellite telemetry could compromise their missions."

The technician spoke up, startling Jeff. "A trace has been initiated."

"I've got to go, Brady."

She disconnected the line. Looking disconsolate, she took off the headset and passed it back to the technician.

"Did he believe you?" Jeff asked.

"I don't know. But he won't take any chances with his men's safety. He'll operate as if I'm telling the truth until he knows otherwise."

"And what about you? Are you in trouble?"

"I didn't sound much like a woman being held against my will, did I? I probably should have pleaded for a rescue or something. But there wasn't time. I had to convince him to take precautions. That was more important."

"Sometimes it sucks being a good guy, doesn't it?" Jeff commented wryly.

"And how."

"Now what?"

"Now I think you need to tell me what happened in Africa."

He stared at her and hoped the chagrin churning in his chest wasn't visible. "I'm going to need coffee if we're going there."

She nodded and followed him silently from the ops center. He led her to the kitchen, and she sat on a stool while he did the one thing he knew how to do well in his kitchen and brewed a pot of strong coffee.

She sipped at the steaming mug for a moment, and then looked him square in the eye. "Quit stalling and spill it, Jeff."

"My people were in East Africa studying the problems with feeding the local populace."

She smiled wryly. "So you really were solving world hunger? What did you figure out?"

"We ran across a gang of thugs, led by *El Mari*. He and his men were stealing land from farmers—the good land with its own water supply that could feed a lot of people. They'd raid a farm, grab the women and children, and torture them until the farmer signed over the deed to his land. Then they'd murder the farmer and his family, of course."

Jennifer winced in commiseration like that sort of violence was not unknown to her.

He continued grimly. "We suspected that *El Mari* was, in turn, selling the land to big agro-businesses from China. The Chinese don't seem particularly interested in feeding the local populace. They're using the land to grow crops for making biofuel. My team was documenting all of it when we were ambushed."

She laid her hand on top of his sympathetically. "Any idea who jumped you?"

He shrugged. "Logic says *El Mari*'s people. But one has to wonder if it wasn't a Chinese hit squad, given how fast and efficient they were. I have a hard time believing a local thug could marshal that kind of discipline from his men."

Jennifer absorbed that for a moment. Then she surprised him by changing subjects. "My informants say you killed a prison guard, but I also hear there were irregularities with the murder scene that cast doubt on your guilt."

Her sources were very good, then. Better than he'd expected. He sighed. He hadn't planned to tell her this part, but he supposed it did no harm. "A local cop came into the room they were holding me in, ostensibly to interrogate me. Instead, he whispered a warning that I wasn't safe. That my enemies would finish the job they'd started and kill me in jail."

"Did people try to kill you there?"

He grinned. "Not after I scared them all into believing I was possessed by a demon and that bullets wouldn't scratch me. No one dared try a direct attack on me after I demonstrated my strength a few times. They knew I'd break them in half. I might have done a few things to intimate that I possess superhuman strength."

"Do you?" she murmured reflectively.

He looked her in the eye. "Any strength I have is one-hundred-percent homegrown. I earned it in the gym through sweat and hard work."

"Then what are all the injections and medications about then?"

He should have known she'd cut straight to the heart of the matter like a laser. "I really can't talk about those."

"I'm not going to reveal your medical discovery to some competitor of Winston Enterprises. I happen to have a bunch of security clearances that say I can keep a secret."

He shrugged, hoping against hope that she would follow him back to the subject of *El Mari* and Africa. "We didn't get our proof of the link between *El Mari* and the Chinese, but how else could some two-bit African strong man afford to buy surveillance footage from H.O.T. Watch to attack my teams with?" He added dryly, "For what it's worth, your images don't come cheap. Apparently, you guys are the best."

"Gee. That's good to know," she retorted.

She stared down at the quartz kitchen countertop. Apparently, his distraction tactic had worked. He hated manipulating her like that, but what choice did he have? It was that or destroy their relationship before it barely had a chance to get started. And he *really* wanted a chance with her. He sincerely hoped she wasn't allergic to money for real. While he had no great need for all this luxury, he did need substantial funds for his company's work. High quality medical research was *not* cheap.

Not to mention, he'd give his right arm to destroy her surveillance facility's capacity to kill his men. He owed payback for his men's' lives to whatever bastard inside H.O.T. Watch was selling the feeds. And Jennifer was his ticket inside the place. If he played his cards right, she would lead him right to the mole.

"I'm going back," Jennifer announced.

His gut leaped in vicious joy. "Back where?"

"To H.O.T. Watch."

Time for a little reverse psychology on the lady. After all, he dared not look too eager to break into the place. He rose up off his stool in what he hoped looked like genuine dismay. "Absolutely not. It's too dangerous."

"I wasn't asking your permission, Jeff."

Their gazes clashed. "Then I'm going with you," he declared.

"Too dangerous."

"Like it's not for you?" he demanded.

"I work there. Heck, I run the place. If I'm caught inside the facility all that will happen is my guys will ask me why I didn't come in the front door. You they'd lock up and throw away the key."

"Think about it, Jennifer. If I'm right, if the place is wired throughout with bugs and double feeds, then you're not going to be able to fix it. You're going to have to destroy the place."

She stared at him, her eyes huge. Shocked. Finally, she whispered, "Destroy H.O.T. Watch?"

It was a truly evil tactic to scare her like that. But if it turned out they only needed to kill off a single mole, it would be a relief to her by comparison to destroying the whole place. It was a classic Russian negotiating tactic. Make an outrageous demand and stick to it. Then, when you finally relent and offer something only mildly unreasonable, the competition leaps at the deal.

He sighed, disgusted by his own duplicity. She deserved better. "Let's take this one step at a time, Jenn. The first order of business is to find out exactly how much data is being stolen and how it's being done."

She snorted. "Based on what I saw in your basement tonight, I'd say we know what's being stolen—darned near all the visual data."

"Okay. How's it being done?" he asked reasonably.

"I have no idea, and I know that place like the back of my hand."

"Sounds like we need to take a look at the actual wiring. Check for duplicated and hidden feeds off the major data streams."

"Which means we'll need to go there in person."

He winced to hear her use the word "we." On the one hand it meant his tactic to use her to get inside the place was working. But on the other hand, it meant he was taking advantage of a woman he genuinely liked…and who would never forgive him for it if she figured it out. He asked, "Any idea how to approach the island unseen?"

She frowned. "Why not just walk in the front door and check it out in plain sight?"

"What if there's a mole in the place sorting the data streams and collecting the good ones for sale? Do you want to warn the mole you're after him? He'd either run, or worse, sabotage the place and then run."

She stared into her coffee cup for a long time. Finally, she looked up and said grimly, "It's possible you're right. I'm not sure about anything anymore."

"Would it help if I said you could be sure of me?"

"But I'm not!" she exclaimed. "You won't answer my questions about your health, you only told me about what happened in Africa after it didn't matter anymore, and for all I know, this is just an elaborate trick to get me to lead you into H.O.T. Watch so you can compromise the place even further!"

As he'd expected. She was no dummy, and the possibility of being used by him had occurred to her. It stung, though, that she would make love with him when she didn't trust him entirely. But she was a CIA agent, after all. Maybe she never fully trusted anybody. His gut twinged a warning at him. How was he supposed to have a long-term relationship with her if she wouldn't let down her guard entirely with him? But then, it wasn't like he had any plans to be entirely open and honest with her, either.

"Where do we go from here?" he asked in resignation.

She didn't hesitate. "Tell me exactly what those drugs you take do. How they work. Why you're on them."

He stared at her, frustrated. "Anything else. My life is an open book to you. Just not that."

"Why not?" she ground out.

"Other people's lives could be put at risk. If the government found out about our research at this juncture—" he broke off "—I'm sorry. I can't."

They stared at each other in frustration.

"All right, then," she said tightly. "How about this? Is there a way for you to wean yourself entirely off your medications? Permanently?"

The questions slammed into him like an invisible freight train that had managed to sneak up on him and flatten him entirely without warning. The truth was, he could get off the drugs. He would have to give his body ample time to lose muscle mass first, of course. But once he'd lost enough of muscle, he could come off the drugs safely enough just by stopping them. Gemma thought his bone density would return to normal and not be negatively affected by his having spent several years with it unnaturally boosted.

He stared at Jennifer in stubborn silence. If he admitted to her that he could stop the meds, she would never let it rest. Ever. He knew that with the certainty that he knew the sun would rise in a few hours.

"I see it in your eyes, Jeff. You can stop the drugs. Which leads to the next question. *Why haven't you?* You'd be insane not to. Who knows what damage you've already done to your body? You need to stop. Now," she urged.

He slashed through the air with his hand. "This is not open to discussion. It's my body. My life. My decision."

"Then that's it. I'm out of here."

Damn, they'd hit that wall fast. He should have known she'd see immediately that there was a way out from under the meds. She was too smart to miss the little clues. As it was, she knew far too much about the program already.

"It's unnatural, Jeff. You have no idea what it's doing to you. Stop now, before the damage gets too bad."

"I'm not damaged," he ground out.

"Don't even try to convince me that the agony I saw you suffer was okay. Can you seriously tell me you're willing to risk that again? It almost killed you!"

"As long as I don't go off the meds, I won't be in any danger of going to that place again."

"I'm not willing to risk it," she blurted.

"Nobody's forcing you to stick around and watch," he snapped.

As soon as the words left his mouth, he wished them back. She went silent and perfectly still. Pulled into herself emotionally.

"I'm sorry, Jennifer. I didn't mean that."

"Sure you did. And you're right. It's your choice to treat your body however you want to. And it's my choice whether or not I want to stay and watch you suffer like that the next time."

"There won't be a next time."

She snorted, and he added with no small amount of desperation, "You've only seen the downside of the project. You haven't seen the benefits of it, yet. Don't judge it, don't judge me, until you've seen what I can do."

"I have no doubt you can lift tall buildings and heave them

over your shoulder. I get that. I just don't happen to think it's worth the pain. I'd stop you if I could."

"Please. Don't interfere with this."

"I don't even know what 'this' is," she snapped. "You're asking me to expose a major classified facility to you with hundreds of lives at stake. But you won't extend the same trust to me and tell me exactly what you're doing to your body? That's not how it works."

He closed his eyes. Took several long, painful breaths. Was he really willing to lose her over his secrets?

Chapter 10

Jennifer watched in agony as Jeff waged an internal struggle with himself, her heart shattering by slow degrees. It could've been so good between them. But there was no way she could stand by and watch a man she cared about destroy himself.

Funny how much maintaining his enhanced strength resembled an addiction. How could he not see it? Whatever rush he got out of being abnormally strong was powerful enough that he wasn't about to give it up for her. He might be hooked on a classier poison than most people, but he wasn't so far from an alcoholic or heroin addict. She only wished his secrets weren't more important to him than she was. She slid off her stool.

"Should I walk to the front gate, or will somebody give me a ride?" she asked soberly. "I assume the Feds are still parked out there."

"Don't go," he ground out.

"Give me a reason to stay."

His entire body stiffened. And then, all of a sudden, the tension went out of him. "Fine. Is it possible for me to get off the meds? Yes. I would have to give my body maybe a year to lose muscle mass first. But eventually, once my muscles wouldn't tear apart my skeleton, I could stop the drug therapy."

She turned around slowly. "Would you go through those awful withdrawals again?"

"No. The only reason I was in pain was the torque on my bones. Take away the overpowering muscles and all that goes away."

"Then stop. Now! Become a normal man again."

"But I don't want to be normal. I like being strong."

"You're not strong. You're a freak."

His jaw rippled angrily. Didn't like hearing the truth, did he? That was too damn bad. The man was taking a completely unnecessary risk with their future—whoa. *Their* future? Since when had that happened? Were they a couple already? She didn't recall him giving her the right to make decisions for both of them.

"I'm sorry." She sighed. "I had no right to call you a freak."

He smiled without humor. "You are very good at that whole, spy doublespeak thing. You apologize and say you had no right, but you never actually admit you were wrong."

"I don't think I am wrong."

He pressed his lips together until a white line formed around them, and she suspected her mouth was the same. Clearly, the two of them would have to agree to disagree on this one. If he *could* stop, he would be crazy not to. Period. She simply didn't understand how he couldn't see that.

"Why did you start taking the meds in the first place?" she asked.

"The bad guys in the world are getting the best of us. The free world desperately needs to keep what little technological and scientific edge it has over them if we're to remain free. How many years do you think it would take our government to approve a program to fund and test something as controversial as Gemma's research?"

She winced. "Decades, maybe."

"Exactly. And we don't have that kind of time. The world moves too fast these days. New scientific discoveries come along all the time. Stem cell therapy is a hot field. Someone will duplicate Gemma's work before long, and then some other nation, maybe one not at all friendly to us, will start cranking out supersoldiers. And where will the good guys be then?"

She stared at him weighing his words. Finally she asked, "But did it have to be you?"

He shrugged. "I can't very well ask my employees to take a risk that I'm not willing to take myself."

Arrgghh. She hated that logic! But she also reluctantly understood it. As the civilian supervisor of H.O.T. Watch, she would never ask her people to do anything she wouldn't do herself.

"What other risks are there to this therapy?" she asked soberly.

Jeff frowned. "Gemma's still studying whether or not my DNA is actually being altered or not. It's possible my children would be born with bones like mine. If so, they would probably have to be delivered by C-section. Their bones might be too hard for a regular birth. Their growth would have to be monitored carefully."

"What about you?"

"So far, Gemma hasn't discovered any negative effects on my body. We watch my kidneys closely because of the amount of protein I consume to maintain this muscle mass. It turns out my cardiovascular system has kept up and grown stronger apace with my demands upon it. By building muscle through working out, my heart and veins had time to grow, as well."

Eeyew. But she supposed it was good to know he wasn't in danger of keeling over from a heart attack. "Anything else?"

"Ask me that in twenty years."

If only she was around in twenty years to do that. "You said there are other test subjects?" she asked.

"I never said that."

She rolled her eyes. "It's obvious there are. Like that girl in your ops center with the funny glasses. Is she one of them?"

Jeff scowled. "I'm not going to discuss anyone else who might or might not be part of the research and testing."

"Oh, please. No one outside this building would believe what you guys are up to if I told them, anyway. And in case you forgot, I keep secrets for a living."

"Let's say for argument's sake that there are other test subjects. You're asking me to put their lives in your hands."

"Like you're not doing the same thing to me when you insist on my taking you with me to infiltrate H.O.T. Watch?"

"Touché," he murmured. "I guess it all comes down to this, then. Do you trust me or not?"

Jeff watched Jennifer carefully. He realized belatedly that he was holding his breath as he waited for her answer.

Her mouth turned up in wry humor. "Some pair we make, circling each other like two dogs with a bone lying between them. Each one's afraid to break eye contact and look down at the bone, lest the other one attack while we're not looking."

He swept her up off the stool and hard against his body. "No more circling. No evasion. I trust you with my life. Do you trust me back or not?"

She stared up at him for a long moment, not as if she was hesitating, but rather as if she was considering the question. And then she nodded. "Yes. I do."

"With your life?"

She laughed with scant humor. "The answer to that seems obvious, since you can break my neck with your bare hands any time you want."

"Good lord, woman. We made love together. I could never hurt you!"

Her dark eyes went serious. "Fine. All jesting aside, I would trust you with my life if it came to that."

But he'd bet she wasn't willing to share all her secrets with him any more than he was willing to share his with her. Funny how trust and honesty were two entirely different beasts. "What about your employers?" he asked.

"What about them?"

"Are you willing to turn your back on them if it comes to a choice between me and them?"

She frowned, obviously not seeing where he was going with this. He elaborated. "My team and I occasionally work outside the law. Your government's law. I swear to you any laws we break are for the greater good. But as you've already seen, we use methods now and then that Uncle Sam might not approve of. If it comes to a choice, who would you choose?"

To her credit, she didn't evade the question. She looked him square in the eye and answered heavily, "I don't know."

It wasn't the answer he wanted, but it wasn't like he had any choice except to live with it for now.

He said gently, "One more question, and then no more tonight. I promise."

She looked up at him warily. She was coming to know him too well. "There's a bolt-hole out of this compound. You and I can leave right now. Long before Uncle Sam has any idea we were ever here. Do we make a run for it and go find out what's up with H.O.T. Watch, or do we stay here and hand you over to the Feds out front?"

Jennifer whirled out of his arms and threw up her hands.

"How am I supposed to answer that? You're asking me to determine my entire future this very second."

He refrained from reminding her that her future could include him. And that wouldn't be all bad, would it? He was asking her to give up her career, possibly become a fugitive from the law, maybe even give up her identity and assume a new one before this was all said and done. Yep, no doubt about it. Being a good guy sucked, sometimes.

She spun to face him, hair flying, eyes blazing. "The hell of it is I don't have any choice at all. I *have* to find out what's going on at H.O.T. Watch. No matter what it costs me personally. Too many lives ride on that place's security being intact."

As she stared at him, her chocolate gaze filled with tears. He instantly stepped forward and drew her into his arms. He couldn't make it better, but he could at least suffer with her. She sobbed against his chest until her grief and frustration drained away.

She said woodenly, "We probably ought to get going, shouldn't we? It'll be light outside before long."

He made another silent vow to himself to put the light back in her eyes, the smile back on her face, before this whole mess was over. He looped an arm over her shoulder. "C'mon. You're gonna love what I have to show you next."

Chapter 11

Jennifer stared as Jeff led her into what could only be likened to Batman's Bat Cave. A half-dozen cars were parked in the cavernous space, along with a pair of motorcycles and even a motor home.

She followed as Jeff strolled down the row of cars. "Something inconspicuous, I'd think." He stopped in front of a mid-size Chevrolet sedan.

"But what if we need to outrun someone?" she asked doubtfully.

He grinned at her. "Every vehicle in here is not as it seems. They've either been retrofitted with substantially larger engines than they usually come with, or in the case of the Chevy here, the body of a sedan has been mounted on the chassis and engine of a Corvette."

Of course he'd modified these cars. It was what a superhero did when he had all the money in the world. She shook her head.

"What?" Jeff asked.

"Boys and their toys," she grumbled.

He grinned. "Guilty as charged. Wait till you see the exit."

She climbed in the passenger side of the Chevy, and, indeed, when Jeff started the engine, she recognized the muscular growl of a Corvette. He punched a remote control and a metal door slid up in front of them. A long tunnel came into view. It was illuminated with halogen running lights low along both sides of it.

"Oh, good grief," she exclaimed, rolling her eyes.

He grinned unrepentantly. "If my team and I have to suffer for our abilities, we might as well have fun when we can."

She went silent at the reminder of the cost of his special powers. He accelerated down the arrow-straight tunnel until the lights were flashing past at an alarming speed. Finally, she blurted out, "I swear, if your tires leave the pavement, I'm going to make you stop and let me out."

Jeff grinned broadly without taking his eyes off the tunnel. "Chicken."

The passage ended as quickly as it began, with another metal garage door rising silently at its far end. She glanced behind them as they pulled onto a dirt road and wasn't surprised to see the door's exterior looked exactly like the rocks into which it nestled.

"Nice," she commented as he guided the car down the twisting road with his headlights off.

They drove slowly through the dark for maybe a half hour before he finally turned onto a paved road and flipped on his headlights. "Where to, Mata Hari?"

That one was a no-brainer. "New Mexico," she answered.

"What's in New Mexico?"

"Home."

* * *

Late-afternoon shadows softened the alpine forest around them as they wound up a mountain on a dirt road into a stand of spruce, fir and pinyon pines. A log cabin sat tucked among the trees, looking deserted. As she got out of the car, Jennifer took a long, deep breath of the sweet tang of pine sap on the air.

"Is this where you grew up?" Jeff asked as he stretched out the kinks of the long drive.

"No. This is my brother's hunting cabin. He won't mind if we use it. I'll give him a call to let him know we're here." She stopped on the porch to call her brother because cell phone coverage inside the cabin was notoriously bad. It was part of why Rex liked this place so much. His work—and his wife— couldn't bug him up here. "Hey, bro. It's Jenn."

"Sis! Long time no talkee. What's the occasion?"

"I'm at your cabin with a friend. Just got here. Mind if we shack up for a day or two?"

"Well, I dunno. I don't cotton to nobody messin' with my little sister," he answered in a fake drawl. "Is it serious between you two?"

Heck if she knew. The sex might have started out as casual, but she didn't think it had ended that way. She evaded a direct answer. "You'll like him." She added hastily in a blatant attempt to distract Rex. "Any chance you can run up with some food in the morning?"

"You're in luck. I'm just coming on duty, so how 'bout I swing up that way right now? I can be there in a couple hours. Is that soon enough?"

"That's perfect. And Rex, don't tell Dad that I'm here."

"You gonna tell me why?"

"Did you take that BIA job you were offered?"

"Nah, I'm still reservation police. Bureau of Indian Affairs cops take themselves too seriously."

"Then, yes. I'll tell you what's going on when you get here. And thanks."

"I may still shoot the boyfriend, so don't thank me yet."

She disconnected and headed inside. The cabin wasn't huge, but with Jeff inside, it felt hardly larger than a shoe box. And yet, the place fit him. He lounged in jeans and a T-shirt. She joined him on the sofa for a cuddle that quickly turned into a nap. It had been a long night and a longer drive. She woke up sharply, though, when Jeff went stiff beneath her and swore under his breath.

"I think I saw a police car through the trees," he muttered. "We've got to get out of here. Hide."

She put a restraining hand on his chest. "That's my brother. He's bringing us supplies."

"Your brother is a cop?"

"He's the other black sheep of the family. But he's cool. He won't turn us in."

"Are you willing to bet your life on that?" Jeff asked grimly.

"Absolutely."

"Will he have to turn us in when he finds out the Feds are after us?"

"Family history of fugitives, remember?"

"Yeah, but—"

"Blood's thicker than the law. And we take care of our own out here. This is Apache territory—not the United States of America."

Jeff didn't look entirely convinced as Rex's SUV pulled to a stop in front of the cabin. She stepped out onto the front porch while Jeff followed more reluctantly. Immediately, her uniformed brother swept her up in a rib-cracking hug, setting her down only when she squawked in protest.

"Great to see you, sis. You're looking good."

"You, too." He was going a little gray at the temples, with a few more laugh lines beside his eyes, but all in all, he looked happy and healthy.

"Rex, this is Jeff. Jeff, this is my brother, Rex."

Her brother was not a small man, but in the presence of Jeff Winston, he looked almost scrawny.

Rex took in Jeff's improbable physique with marked respect. "Wouldn't want to have to take you down in a bar fight," Rex muttered.

Jeff laughed. "Go for the taser. Drops me as fast as the next guy. And fortunately, I neither drink nor hang out in bars, so I won't cause any trouble in your jurisdiction."

Rex grinned. "I dunno. You know how kids can be. They'd see a guy like you and have to try you out."

Jeff nodded in commiseration. "Good news is punks mostly bounce off me and slink away to lick their wounds without me having to hurt them too bad."

"I've got a few punks on the rez I'd love to see get taken down a peg or two."

Jeff grinned. "Next time we pass through here, I'd be happy to oblige."

"That's a deal." Rex nodded over at her. "You were right. He's okay."

Relieved, she went over to the SUV to grab the bags of groceries in the back. She stepped inside just in time to hear Rex ask Jeff, "So what brings you out this way?"

Jeff answered smoothly, "I wanted to get to know Jennifer better. To see where she comes from. To understand her heritage."

Rex said nothing, but threw her a look that said he smelled a line of bull.

They all sat down at the kitchen table.

"So here's the thing," she started without preamble. "The place where I work has been infiltrated either by a spy or electronically, and Jeff gave me the evidence to prove it."

"You're protecting a witness?" Rex asked.

She winced. "Not exactly. Jeff and I both are on the lamb—"

"Jennifer," Jeff interrupted.

"I told you. He's my brother. He'll help us."

Jeff's scowl subsided but he looked decidedly tense as she continued, "We just need a place to stay for a day or two while we plan our next move."

"The Feds got a warrant out for you, sis?"

"I doubt it. Last they knew, Jeff had kidnapped me. The warrant's likely only for him. There's probably only an APB out on me."

Rex surged up out of his seat and Jeff mirrored the motion. Jennifer leaped up between the two abruptly bristling men. "Stand down, both of you!" she barked. To her brother, she said with desperate calm, "He didn't really kidnap me. I went with him voluntarily. He made it look like a kidnapping to protect my career. He's one of the good guys."

"God, I hope so," Rex mumbled, eyeing Jeff's massive arms, which were flexed in front of him at the moment.

The men sat back down and she perched in her seat again warily.

"What's next for you two, then?" Rex asked.

Jennifer glanced over at Jeff and took a deep breath. "Jeff and I have to figure out how to destroy the facility I work at."

Rex said hastily, "Okay, then. That's about all I need to hear about your plans." He made no bones about leaving quickly after that. Clearly, he wasn't interested in being put in any more compromising of a position than he already was. She couldn't blame him. But as she showed him out the door, he murmured as he hugged her, "If you need anything— anything at all—you call me. Family sticks together."

"I will." She punched him on the arm as he let her go. "Love you, bro."

"Right back atchya, kid."

His SUV pulled away into the night, leaving behind deep silence.

"Decent guy," Jeff commented. "Cares about you a lot."

She leaned against a porch post, staring out into the black trees. "Mmm-hmm."

"Penny for your thoughts."

She sighed. "It's going to be a big project to destroy H.O.T. Watch. I don't know if it can even be done. How am I supposed to blow up an entire mountain?"

He came up behind her and drew her back against the warm wall of his chest, his arms loosely around her waist. How was it his simplest touch could make her feel so safe? Of course, it also made her think about just walking away from it all, abandoning her duty and endangering the lives of countless operatives. Good men and women, many of whom she knew personally.

As long as they were going to be working together, she probably ought to keep her distance from Jeff. If she was being professional. *If she was concerned about doing the right thing.*

She mumbled, "Too bad the volcano can't just erupt. That would solve all my problems."

Jeff stiffened behind her. "You know. That's not a bad idea."

She turned to stare up at him. "Surely you don't know how to make an extinct volcano come back to life."

"No. But we could fake it. All we'd have to do is convince the people inside the mountain that it was about to blow. They'd evacuate, right? Rip out as much equipment as they could and take it with them?"

"That's brilliant!" Impulsively, she stood on tiptoe and kissed him soundly on the mouth. It was a mistake. She knew it the moment their lips touched.

She tried hard to argue herself out of it. Reminded herself to focus on work. That he might be using her for his own possibly violent ends. But then his arms caught her, holding her in place as she would have sunk back to her feet.

"Mmm. You taste good. I missed you today."

"We were together all day," she protested. She ought to put up a fight, but frankly, she had no will to.

"We weren't naked in bed together all day," he retorted.

She laughed in spite of herself. "We shouldn't."

"Why not?"

"We have work to do."

"Tomorrow."

"Jeff. Really..."

"Honey, if you want me to stop, I will. No questions asked. But I have to say, I'm not convinced you mean it."

"I should mean it," she responded in more than a little desperation.

He pushed a tendril of loose hair back from her face. Smiled at her a little. Trailed a finger down her neck and across her collarbone. Then murmured, "Have I told you today how beautiful and sexy you are?"

She tingled from head to foot, and her palms itched to slide over his glorious body, to take him into her and let him take her to the moon. She groaned under her breath. "Don't tempt me. I'm trying to be good here."

"How does that Mae West saying go? When I'm good, I'm very good, but when I'm bad, I'm better?"

She exhaled a breath of laughter as she leaned her cheek into his palm.

"Be a little bad with me," he whispered.

He backed toward the front door and she followed. It turned out Jeff took up most of the queen-size bed in the bedroom, which left her to drape herself either on top of him or beneath him. She blissfully spent the next several hours in both places.

Sometime after midnight, she dozed on Jeff's chest while his fingers combed lazily through her long hair. She murmured, "Regretting running away with me yet?"

His stomach muscles contracted as he lifted his head to glare down at her. "Never."

"You're a successful business man. You stand to lose a lot if you get any more mixed up in this."

"I'm already an accused murderer and in the United States illegally."

She frowned. "If you'd stayed on the island, the State Department could probably have made those charges against you go away. *El Mari* was a violent criminal in desperate need of killing according to many powerful people in the Nigerian government."

"There are plenty of places in the world that Uncle Sam doesn't have extradition treaties with."

"Jeff, I think you should leave me. You're a civilian. You shouldn't be mixed up in this."

"Not a chance," he replied forcefully.

"I'm serious."

"So am I, Jennifer. You need help with this thing. The kind I have the skills and resources to give you."

She pushed up to her elbows to frown at him. "You shouldn't be so cavalier about becoming a fugitive. People like me are very, very good at finding and bringing in people like you." His willingness to throw away his life worried her. If she'd lost a bunch of her men because someone had set them up, she'd be out for blood. Her suspicions notched up even higher that Jeff was using her to get inside H.O.T. Watch so he could find and take out the spy for himself.

Her goal was to fix the place. His might very well be able to destroy it. And yet, he was probably right that she couldn't do this mission alone. Did she dare take him with her and risk him turning on her at the worst possible moment?

"Why the frown?" he asked, lazily smoothing a finger across her brow.

"Just thinking about getting inside H.O.T. Watch."

"There's time enough for that tomorrow. Relax now. Enjoy the moment."

She smiled up at him. She had to admit the moment was pretty darned nice. Although an annoying sliver of guilt poked at her. It wasn't right to be suspicious of her lover like this. She really did trust him with her life if it came to a fight. The question was, did she trust all the rest of her people's lives to him?

Jeff was fully intelligent enough to run an elaborate scam on her. She'd wondered from day one if he wasn't outmanipulating her. Nothing had changed to make her stop wondering that, darn it. Sure, they made love together more sweetly and passionately than she'd ever experienced with any other man, but was she reading too much into it?

Was she at heart aware that she was getting older and time was running out on her to find a man and settle down? Was she grasping at emotional straws? She'd always told herself that her life was just fine without a long-term relationship in it. Was she lying to herself? Or was this just the dreaded biological clock ticking? Or maybe this was all a case of her being ridiculous and paranoid, and Jeff was exactly what he said he was—a concerned citizen trying to do the right thing. Ugh. It was so frustrating not knowing what was really going on with him!

Jeff murmured sleepily, "We won't know if the facility can be saved or is a total loss until we take a look at it. But given the quality and quantity of material that's been coming out of it, I think we should plan for the worst."

"Plan-for-the-worst is my middle name," she replied much more lightly than she felt. "It's why I'm good at my job." But she also knew she had never come up against a worst-case scenario anything like this before. This might just be the worst-case scenario that killed her. And Jeff, too, if she couldn't talk him into leaving. And soon.

Chapter 12

Jeff leaned over Jennifer's rough sketch of H.O.T. Watch and the island containing it. "How does the place get its electricity?"

"Nuclear power."

"Nuclear generator creates heat. Use heat to turn water to steam. Use steam to run turbines. Turbines put out electricity. Yes?"

"Yes."

He nodded, pleased.

"What?"

He grinned at her impatience. "There's steam. We can divert it to have it come out the top of the mountain. Make it look from the outside like the volcano is active."

She laughed in delight at the notion. "There'd need to be seismic activity, too," she added. "We'd have to set off some explosions in the deepest parts of the facility to shake the place a bit."

"Now you're getting the idea."

"Problem," she announced. "I don't know my way around the lower cave network. We didn't use those for the H.O.T. Watch facility, and I've only ever seen one map of them. The geologist who explored the caves in the first place showed it to me. That was years ago."

"Who's the geologist and how do we get in touch with him?" Jeff asked.

"Her. And she lives on the island with her husband. He's the one who recommended the island as the location for the H.O.T. Watch facility. The two of them supervised the building of the place, in fact."

"Sounds like we need to talk to them."

"They're totally loyal to the U.S. government. They won't help us."

Interesting how quickly she'd shifted to thinking of the government as the enemy. "Honey," he said gently, "you and I are totally loyal to the U.S. government, too."

She looked up, startled. "Right."

"How hard will it be to approach this couple?"

"About as hard as knocking on their front door. Although," she added, "they travel a lot at this time of year. I don't know if they'll be home."

He frowned. "But we'll have to get to the island undetected, right? How hard's that going to be?"

Jennifer grimaced. "No vessel, above or below the surface of the Caribbean can get within miles of that place undetected. Sensors and cameras ring the island."

"How close are civilian boats allowed to approach before someone challenges them?"

"Three miles."

He nodded. "We can work with that."

She shook her head. "The underwater buoys will pick up divers approaching the island. Their metal scuba gear or their metal self-propelled vehicles will trigger the alarms. And three miles is a long way to snorkel in the open ocean. The currents around the island are vicious. Particularly if we're hauling gear of any kind."

"Metal's the trigger for the sensors, then?" Jeff asked thoughtfully.

"Yep."

"Can you walk three miles?"

She snorted. "I ran the Marine Corps Marathon last year."

He laughed. "Well, then, I've got our approach to the island covered. We'll walk."

"On water?" she exclaimed.

"Exactly. One of the Winston companies makes a giant plastic bubble that holds a person inside. It's a novelty item. You can roll down a mountain in one, or you can walk on water. I'll have two sent to us. We can wear backpacks with whatever gear we'll need on the island."

A slow smile unfolded on Jennifer's face. "You *are* handy to have around in a pinch."

"That's what I keep telling you."

Her smile faded. "But I still don't like the idea of you participating in this mission—"

He stepped forward to stop the rest of that comment with a gentle kiss. When he had her thoroughly distracted he said, "We've already been over this. I'm going with you. End of discussion."

"But—"

"No buts. I'd worry too much about you if you went alone. I insist." That was his story and he was sticking to it. The first step was to convince her she needed him with her. The second step would come later—figuring out how to find the mole so he could kill the guy.

"Jeff. We've known each other barely a week. You don't

owe me anything. This could get really dangerous, and I don't want your blood on my hands."

Irritation chafed him. "I know we haven't known each other that long. But we've been through a shoot-out, saved each other's lives, been to Hell and back with my withdrawals, fled government surveillance and now we're fugitives together. We've crammed a whole lot of getting to know each other into that short time. Not to mention, you see a person's true stripes when they're under stress. I'd say I have a pretty good feel for who you are at this point. How about you? Don't you feel like you know me pretty well?"

She answered cautiously, "I know you can handle yourself under pressure and you won't hesitate to kill someone you believe is evil enough to deserve killing. I know the limit of your pain tolerance. Which," she added hastily as he opened his mouth to protest, "is extraordinary."

"And we've established that I'm loyal and smart and strong," he added.

"Well, yes."

"And that the two of us are reasonably compatible at sex."

A smile flickered across her mouth. "Reasonably," she allowed.

He rolled his eyes at that. They were amazing together and they both knew it. "What else is there to know?"

She huffed. "I don't know any of the normal stuff about you. Your favorite food. What kind of movies you like. If you want to have kids. Your dreams and ambitions."

"Steak. Thrillers. Yes—several. To make the world a better place. And most of all, to find a woman I can share everything about myself with and love forever."

She threw up her hands. "And that's another thing. You're too darned perfect."

"I was hoping not to have to confess how stubborn I can be.

Or how, once I make up my mind about something, I refuse to be swayed."

"Sorry. I already had those two figured out," she responded dryly.

"Flaws, huh? Ooh. Here's a good one. I don't pick up my dirty clothes. Comes from a lifetime of having a household staff to pick up after me. But as long as I can afford a butler, I figure that flaw won't make you too crazy."

"You don't have any idea how different our worlds are," she exploded in exasperation.

"Show me."

She scowled at him for a minute. In an abrupt decision, she snatched up the car keys off the counter. "Get in the car."

They drove down the mountain and headed into the heart of the Mescalero Indian Reservation. Truth be told, it was the first reservation he'd ever been on. They passed cattle ranches and neat homes that looked like they could be anywhere else in the southwestern United States. But then things began to deteriorate. The homes became smaller, older, dingier.

"This is what the entire rez looked like before the casino," she said grimly. She turned onto a street that took him aback. Something he'd expect to see in a destitute third-world country. "When I was a kid, this was all there was. My mom drank herself to death when I was about five. My dad shoveled manure on a ranch for a living and my grandfather made a few dollars here and there as a medicine man. If we were lucky, he got paid in food. I went to work in the fields when I was seven."

His heart ached for the child she must have been. He could picture her, long-limbed and scrawny with a braid flying behind her. He reached across the car to rest a hand on her shoulder. "Your father and grandfather did something very right for you and your brother to turn out like you did."

Tears glistened in her eyes, but she turned her head away

from him, likely to hide them. "They loved Rex and me fiercely. They taught us to be proud of our heritage and to love our country in spite of how it treated our people."

He nodded in understanding.

She spoke reflectively. "My grandfather was a medic in World War II. He was decorated four times for valor. And then he came home and nearly starved to death because he refused to take handouts from the government."

Given that she spoke of him in the past tense, he assumed her grandfather had passed away. He said soberly, "I would've liked to meet him."

"He would've told you what you've done to your body is unnatural. That you shouldn't play God."

Jeff smiled. "I've heard that one before. From my own grandfather."

Jennifer fell silent, contemplating the people whose lives were passing by outside. "I do what I can to help these kids. But my kind don't take charity easily."

"Thank you for showing me this," he said. "That you overcame such a difficult childhood makes the person you are now even more impressive."

"I'm who I am because of this, not in spite of this."

"While I, on the other hand," he replied lightly, "am who I am in spite of my upbringing and not because of it."

She stared at him. "You had everything you ever wanted!"

"Exactly. Which, in my experience, doesn't necessarily engender a deep sense of social responsibility, work ethic or meaningful life goals."

"What are your life goals?" she asked.

"I already told you two of them—to find a good woman to share my life with and to make the world a better place. Beyond that, I want to see this medical research through. Our country needs it, but the government can't do it. So I'm doing it for them."

"Do they know you're doing it?"

"Not yet. But we're getting close to having enough results to share."

"How many of you are there?"

He shook his head. "The less you know, the better."

"I can't believe you'd make mutants out of your own employees."

"We don't know if the modifications will become permanent or not. Gemma believes they will in time. That's one of the big questions we have yet to answer."

"My grandfather would have been right. It's unnatural."

"It's modern science. I admit it takes a little getting used to the idea. But the possibilities with this research are staggering."

Jennifer shook her head. "I've seen the downside of it. I don't think it's worth the pain."

"I'm not in pain as long as I stay on my meds."

"You're playing God," she muttered direly. "No good can come of it."

"Good already has come of it. I've captured bad guys, stopped a terrorist attack or two, and saved lives. All in all, I'd say the experiment has been a smashing success."

She turned the car onto a main road and accelerated toward the looming front range of the Sierra Blanca. "You and I will have to agree to disagree on that. I'll never forget the sound of your screams."

Guilt stabbed him. He'd never meant to put her through such worry. But by the same token, it was part of who he was. If they had any kind of a chance together, she would have to accept that part of him, too. He only hoped he got a chance to demonstrate the up side of his special gifts to her. It was part of why he was so determined to go on her search-and-destroy mission with her.

"So, nobody in your tribe lives in tepees and hunts buffalo anymore?" he asked, trying to lighten the mood.

"Each summer there's a festival here where some of that goes on. It's centered around the ceremonial coming-of-age rites for our youngsters. Sadly, it's as much for the tourists these days as for our own people. Times change."

They rode back to the cabin in silence, each lost in their own thoughts.

They made sandwiches for themselves and put their dishes in the sink before he couldn't take the silence any longer and said, "Okay, so we've established that you and I come from different worlds. I can accept yours if you can accept mine."

"What is there to accept about yours?" she asked, sounding surprised.

"You said a few days ago that you're allergic to money. Is that true?"

"I don't know. I've never been around someone as rich as you."

"I'll give it all away if you want me to. I'll have to keep some of it to fund Gemma's research, but I don't need the rest of it."

She snorted. "It's easy for you to say that because I'm not very likely to call your bluff."

He turned sharply to face her. "Go ahead," he said levelly. "Call me on it."

She stared at him hard, her expression gradually shifting to realization that he was serious and thence to disbelief. "But why? You barely know me. Why would you make an offer like that?"

Without breaking their stare he answered, "Because a good woman is worth more than all the money in the world."

"I'm planning to break into a government facility and sabotage it. That's the act of a terrorist, not a good woman."

"You protected me even after you saw me kill a man. You

stayed with me while I screamed my head off. You moved Heaven and Earth to get me help. You're willing to sacrifice your career—your *life*—to do the right thing. Trust me. You're one of the good guys."

A knife twisted in his chest when she merely frowned in response. It wasn't that he expected her to open herself up to him completely. At least not yet. She was too cautious a person for that. Not the type to wear her heart on her sleeve. But he'd hoped to see at least a bit of a thaw from her. Instead, she crossed her arms, moved across the room to sit on the sofa and commenced staring at the faded area rug.

He said lightly, "You look like I'm a terrible complication in your otherwise well-ordered life."

She made a sound somewhere between exasperation and humor. "You are."

He could live with that. For now. After all, it was a base to build on.

Jennifer didn't know whether to cry or scream, be thrilled or scared out of her mind, by Jeff's faith in her. In them. It was all happening so fast. She was a mature, reasonable person. She didn't leap into or out of relationships casually. She was thoughtful and logical about such things. But Jeff completely defied logic.

He was silent for a while, and she finally glanced up to see him sitting at the kitchen table, writing quickly on a pad of paper.

"What are you doing?" she asked warily. She half feared he was drafting up a prenuptial agreement for the two of them.

"Making a list of supplies we're going to need to make your volcano appear to blow."

"Why the big frown, then?"

"I'm worried about the amount of explosives we're going

to have to transport to the island. They're heavy, and we'll need a lot to shake the island."

"No problem. I've got all the access codes to H.O.T. Watch's armory. We'll just take whatever we need from there."

He smiled in relief. "Of course. Brilliant, Watson."

"How come you get to be Sherlock? It's my infiltration mission. You're the helper guy, not me."

"No problem. I'm Watson, then. Watson needs a kiss, Sherlock."

"Are you always this needy?" she asked as she strolled over to him. Lord, a girl could get used to the way his eyes lit up when he looked at her. Like the sun rose and set around her. But how was she supposed to know if he was for real or not? Would he stay like this for the next fifty years, or was this just the first flush of infatuation? Would it wear off in a few weeks or months?

"I'll always need you, babe," he murmured against her belly.

She wrapped her arms around his head and hugged him briefly. It was all she could muster past the panic he inspired in her. She felt like a trapped rabbit in the arms of a wolf. But then he kissed his way up her torso, feathering her face with kisses. He was such a lovely wolf, and he made the rabbit feel so very cherished.

Completely freaked out, she mumbled, "Show me your list."

He turned her loose with a sigh.

She touched his face apologetically with her fingertips. "This is moving a little fast. Be patient with me, okay?"

"Anything for you."

She was officially an idiot. Any woman in her right mind would be throwing herself at this man and not looking back. A new fear crept into her mind...that she would blow this thing between them. That she would be too afraid of getting hurt, too afraid of what could go wrong to let herself reach for happiness. Almost sick with terror, she doggedly turned her attention to his list, forcing her mind onto operational necessities. This was safe ground.

But then Jeff reached a hand across the table absently and twined his fingers with hers, and the ground beneath her feet heaved more wildly than ever. What on earth was she going to do with him?

Chapter 13

Jeff lurched awake as the disposable cell phone by his head rang on the night stand. Only Rex and Leland had its number and neither one of them could be calling at this hour with good news. "What's up?" he asked tersely.

Rex mumbled in his ear, "BIA informant spotted your car today. Feds are here. Gonna sweep the rez." It sounded like Jenn's brother was talking into a paper towel tube. Probably had his hand over his phone to hide it from said Feds. The guy was probably taking a terrible risk to warn them like this.

"We'll be out of here in five minutes."

"Head south. The Feds are starting at the north end of the rez. And stay off the main roads. Jenn will know the back ones."

"Got it. And thanks for everything. I owe you one."

The line went dead.

"Jenn—" Jeff began. But she was already awake, her dark eyes gleaming faintly in the dark.

"Who's coming our way?" she asked as she swung out of bed quickly and reached for her clothes.

"Feds. Rex said they'll come from the north and we should stay off the main roads."

She nodded. "You drive. I'll navigate."

Good thing Jennifer had insisted on keeping everything packed and ready to go, all the dishes washed and put away, and even the towels folded into the linen closet before bed. All they had to do now was toss the fresh food and their overnight bags in the car and wipe down the place for prints, and they were good to go.

He guided the car along the mountain carefully. It was slow going with the headlights off, but even in the trees, they dared not chance lights. They hit the lower elevations, and Jennifer guided him along dirt roads that were sometimes little more than twin tracks through the scrub country.

But finally she announced, "Okay. We're off the reservation. In about a half mile we'll come to a paved road. Turn left and that will take you to Hwy 82. We can take it west into Alamogordo, and then catch Hwy 54 South to El Paso. From there, I'm not sure what we'll do."

He smiled over at her. "If you'll pass me that last disposable phone, I'll take of what comes next."

Next arrived at the El Paso International Airport not long after they did—an unmarked corporate jet belonging to Winston Enterprises.

"The FBI will spot this flight and track it," Jennifer warned.

"That's why my pilots are filing a half-dozen flight plans. By the time the FAA tracks down which one we actually flew, we'll be long gone and the trail will be cold," he replied.

"And which one are we actually flying?" she replied.

"The one that takes us to Kingston, Jamaica. We need a

boat for our mission, and that's a major port not too far from H.O.T. Watch. We'll be able to rent something there."

She smiled reluctantly. "I admit it. You're definitely handy to have around."

"Just handy?"

"Okay, a godsend."

"That's more like it," he declared.

It took most of the day to get to Jamaica. Jennifer was intrigued when Jeff produced a fake passport at Jamaican customs. But then, so did she.

As they rode in the back of a cab toward the harbor, he put his arm around her shoulders. "Having fun yet, Mrs. Smith?"

"This is better than most of the business trips I take."

"Your honeymoon is supposed to be better than work, silly." Clearly, he was talking for the benefit of the cabbie. Newlyweds in this part of the world were a dime a dozen. But still, the idea of being married to Jeff was a shockingly seductive fantasy.

She had the driver let them out several blocks from the ocean. Funny how quickly all the paranoia of her days as a field agent returned to her. It had been years since she'd been an operator, but the trade craft came back as naturally as breathing.

The big question in her mind at the moment, though, was where did Jeff learn such things? He crossed streets and switched back on their route like a pro as they wound through alleys in a circuitous route toward the pier.

They'd ducked into a cheap souvenir store and were just about to step outside again when something triggered a mental alarm for Jennifer. She put a hand on Jeff's arm to stop him. "Just a sec," she murmured.

"What do you see?" He stepped behind a rack of T-shirts

and rifled through them while watching the street out of the corner of his eye.

"I don't know. I thought I saw a man come around the corner and then back out of sight."

"Want me to go check?" he muttered.

"Are you bulletproof?"

"Not the last time I checked, although I can probably take a small-caliber shot with less damage than most folks."

She rolled her eyes. "My question was rhetorical. We wait these guys out."

He shrugged and moved away from the store's front window. They browsed in the store long enough that the shopkeeper was starting to get suspicious, but nobody got sent into the place to check on them. Jennifer's tension gradually eased. It was probably nothing, just some guy remembering something and changing direction abruptly.

Still, she asked the clerk as the guy rang up the T-shirts she'd randomly selected, "Is there a back way out of here?"

The man frowned but pointed toward a storeroom. She paid quickly and headed for the back of the store. Jeff followed without comment. They slipped out into the alley, which was wreathed in shadows as the sun set on the city.

They'd taken maybe ten steps forward when four men stepped out of doorways and nooks around them. Chagrin washed over her. She hated being outmaneuvered like this. Worse, she'd apparently become predictable.

"Good evening, gentlemen," she said evenly. "Can we help you?"

The men shrugged and moved in closer to ring her and Jeff more tightly. But then one of them muttered something to his companions—in Amharic. These guys were from *Ethiopia?* How in the heck had they found her and Jeff? For his part, Jeff went very still. He'd recognized his captors' native tongue, too.

Jeff relaxed beside her and moved away slightly, no doubt to give them both room to fight. He'd been ambushed in an alley before, had he?

"This is going to end badly for you fellows," she warned calmly. "I'm going to give you a chance to turn around and walk away before we do this."

The four men traded looks—could they have been any more obvious that they were getting ready to jump her and Jeff?—and surged forward. When the first guy reached her, she lashed out with a vicious kick to the side of the guy's knee. He staggered and fell.

She didn't even bother to check on Jeff. He'd probably just picked up his attackers and knocked their heads together until they saw stars. The second man was more wary than the first and came in slowly, with his fists and defenses up. She blocked a flurry of punches and nearly went down as he leaped forward and hooked her ankle with his foot. But then a fist shot over her right shoulder from behind, crushing the man's nose in a single blow.

"That's my woman," a voice snarled from behind her.

The first attacker had regained his balance and straightened. He took one look at Jeff advancing on him, spun on his good leg and took off down the alley in a limping run. Scrambling noises behind her indicated that the assailants behind them were bugging out, as well.

"Are you okay?" Jeff bit out.

"Yes. You?"

"Fine. Want to go after them?"

She shook her head. "I doubt they're alone. They'll lead us to their reinforcements, who will likely be armed and more dangerous than those scouts. Best to get out of here before they come back."

Jeff grinned. "They'd have to bring a lot of reinforcements to take the two of us. You handled yourself like a pro."

"I *am* a pro."

His gaze roamed briefly down her body and back up. If her cheeks weren't already hot from exertion, they lit up like a torch now. "Am I correct that those were *El Mari*'s guys?" she mumbled.

"That was most certainly Amharic the guy gave his buddies instruction in. Although it's possible they're not *El Mari*'s goons, I don't see how it could plausibly be anyone else."

"How on earth did they find you?" she asked. "We've given the FBI, CIA and H.O.T. Watch the slip. So how did these guys pull it off? Could they have some sort of tracking device on you?"

Jeff frowned. "I'm not wearing any of the same clothes I did in prison. I had no jewelry, no personal possessions to put a tracker on."

"What about you?"

"Come again?" He looked confused.

"Were you ever knocked unconscious in jail? Drugged, maybe? Sleep an unusually long time after a meal?"

"What are you getting at?"

"Did you get any small cuts in prison? Maybe somewhere hard to see or feel, like between your shoulder blades or the back of an upper arm or thigh?"

"You think they put a tracker inside me?" he demanded incredulously.

"I think it's worth getting you naked and checking it out. But first, we have to leave this place. Get some distance from these jokers. My suggestion is we hustle down to the pier, get ourselves a boat and get out of here as fast as we can."

"Agreed. But first…" He stepped forward and wrapped his arms around her, drawing her close against him. He kissed her gently, but oddly enough, she didn't want gentle. She wanted wild and woolly. She wanted to know she was really alive and well. Or maybe it was just the adrenaline of the attack coursing through her. But either way, she backed him up against a brick wall and kissed him like she planned to inhale him right then and there.

Jeff tore away with a half laughing groan. "Boat. Leave. Check. And then we'll continue this…discussion." He grabbed her by the hand and all but ran out of the alley toward the docks. But who ended up dragging who was open to debate.

Thankfully, it didn't take long for them to find and rent a nicely outfitted, forty-two-foot cabin cruiser that would be perfect for their purposes. Jeff paid with a Swiss credit card that she expected would trace back to a nameless, numbered bank account, and he plunked down various sailing and radio licenses that seemed to make the boat's owner comfortable letting them take out the vessel by themselves. She was proficient with small sailboats, but this cruiser was beyond her experience.

As Jeff expertly backed the *Island Princess* out of her slip and into the channel headed toward open water, she asked, "Where'd you learn how to drive a boat like this?"

"My grandfather owns a yacht. I've spent some time on her."

"Let me guess. Leland's yacht makes this one look like a laundry tub?"

Jeff ducked his head a little. "You might say that. But a boat's a boat at the end of the day. You push the throttles, the boat goes forward. You pull them back, the boat slows down. You drop the anchor, the boat stops. It's not rocket science."

She eyed the sonar, depth finder and various radios askance. "Right. Let's just unanimously nominate you Captain and call it good."

"You do understand that the crew—that would be you—has to do exactly as the captain—that would be me—orders at all times."

"Or else what?" she replied playfully. "Will you make me walk the plank?"

"I'm sure I can come up with a more creative punishment than that," he threatened, grinning.

They sailed into the setting sun, and Jennifer had to admit that as escapes from bad guys went, this one was pretty darned pleasant.

Once they were well clear of Kingston and certain that no boats had followed them away from Jamaica, Jennifer turned to Jeff. "Off with your shirt, mister."

He grinned widely. "I like the way you think."

"I'm not getting frisky. I need to look for evidence that a tracking device was planted under your skin."

"Party pooper."

It took her about two seconds flat to spot the scar. It was less than a quarter inch long, high between his shoulder blades where he couldn't possibly reach it. When she rubbed the pad of her thumb hard across the spot, she thought she felt something small, flattish and hard under his skin.

"Ouch!" he yelped.

"You can withstand the fires of Hell, but a little poke like that makes you yell?" she asked wryly.

He grinned sheepishly.

She handed him his shirt thoughtfully. "Since when is a local warlord in the Horn of Africa equipped with subcutaneous tracking burrs?"

"You think *El Mari* got it from someone like the Chinese?" Jeff asked grimly.

"I think it's highly likely. But I also think it's a problem for another day. Right now we need to figure out how to deactivate the thing." She tapped a tooth with a fingernail. "Or at least disrupt the signal."

"Mind if I engage in a little outside-the-box thinking?" he queried.

"By all means."

"Why deactivate it? Let's lead these guys straight to H.O.T. Watch. In a best case scenario, they'll get mowed down by the special forces guys stationed there. Worst case, they compromise the facility and only add fuel to the fire of shutting the place down and relocating it."

She grimaced. His suggestion flew in the face of everything she was trained to do. But he did make a certain sense. It was a practical approach that solved two problems at once.

Jeff pulled out a navigation chart and spread it on the captain's worktable. "Okay. Where's H.O.T. Watch?" he asked.

She gulped. This was it. Once she told him where the facility was, there would be no turning back for her. She would have committed a felony by divulging classified information. She poked at a spot on the map where only an uninhabited island called Timbalo was charted. "It's here."

And just like that, it was done.

A look of satisfaction flitted through Jeff's gaze. Oh, God. Had she just told a killer where to find his next victim? Had this all been an elaborate ruse, after all, to trick her into revealing H.O.T. Watch's location? Had she just played right into his hands?

She watched in appalled silence as Jeff plotted a course and set the boat's autopilot to steer along it. She felt like a yo-yo bouncing up and down on a string. Wielded by one Jefferson Winston. Of course, she was using him, too. Using his wealth and resources to accomplish her mission. Using his physical strength as a shield.

He glanced up, did a double take in mild alarm. "You okay?"

"Yes. No."

He straightened up from the table to look at her searchingly. "What's up?"

"I'm worried about what we're going to find when we get to the island," she hedged.

"We won't get there until tomorrow depending on what the currents are like. No sense worrying about it before then."

Easy for him to say. He hadn't just ended his career. Being a CIA agent was all she knew. All she was. And she'd just given it all away. To him.

Anger flared in her gut before she reminded herself it had been her decision. She knew full well she was trading her career for the safety of the people whose lives depended on H.O.T. Watch. It was a noble sacrifice, darn it. Worth one lousy career. But still, it hurt.

"You might as well go below and get some rest," Jeff said quietly. "The next few days could get pretty busy. I'll take first watch. If you're not comfortable keeping an eye on the autopilot while I sleep, we can lay anchor while I catch a few hours' rest."

She was abjectly relieved to crawl into the big bed below by herself. It wasn't that she didn't enjoy making love with Jeff. In fact, she missed his big, warm body more than she cared to admit to herself. But her head was in such turmoil she could hardly stay in bed and not pace the tiny stateroom.

Jeff eased open the door sometime after midnight. He must have sensed her disquiet for he merely gathered her close in a silent hug. She clung to him until she worried she might not ever be able to let him go. But fear of depending on him like that made her turn him loose long before she wanted to.

She assured him that she and autopilot would get along together just fine and exhorted him to sleep. And, indeed, she dutifully wrote down their GPS position every hour and plotted it on the chart through the night. The autopilot was keeping them perfectly on course.

Between readings, she stared at the stars overhead and the fathomless blackness of the ocean below. She cast back in her memory to the very first moment she'd laid eyes on Jeff bursting out of that wooden crate in Africa. She analyzed and reanalyzed every minute with him, every conversation, every time they'd made love. In the most objective opinion she could muster, she concluded that she had not been brainwashed. She'd acted of her own free will and she was not unduly influenced by him.

Although she was also forced to conclude that it was entirely possible she and her logic were addled by her infatuation with the man. He was larger than life, figuratively and literally. How could she not fall for him?

As the sky grew rosy in the east, Jeff came up to the bridge, rubbing his eyes and his hair sticking up endearingly. Boy, she really did have it bad for the guy if his bedhead even turned her on.

"You were supposed to wake me up hours ago so I could relieve you," he complained.

"I wasn't tired. I decided to let you sleep."

"Why the insomnia? Worried about getting into H.O.T. Watch?"

"Actually, that's the least of my concerns."

He stepped close behind her and held her quietly as they watched the first sliver of the sun peek above the horizon. "It'll all work out, Jenn."

"If only I shared your optimism."

His optimism held when, in early afternoon, the island that housed H.O.T. Watch came into view as a low, dark hump on the horizon about five miles away.

"We should sail for the east side of Timbalo. All the people are clustered on the west side."

"Out of the direct path of hurricanes?"

"Exactly. But there's a house on the east slope. And that's where we're headed."

"The geologist and her husband's house?"

"Exactly."

He didn't ask for details. If only she had the same absolute assurance in herself that he did. Then maybe she would have a little more confidence in this mission to succeed and for the sacrifice of her entire life not to have been in vain.

Chapter 14

Jennifer watched in minor disbelief as Jeff used a small, motorized pump to inflate two gigantic beach balls. They were clear and nearly ten feet tall with small tunnels leading to hollow interiors a man could stand up in easily.

"Take your shoes off but leave your socks on," he instructed as she slid her backpack—its frame not aluminum but rather some high-tech polycarbonate, compliments of Winston Plastics—into the ball. He steadied the ball for her beside the boat while she crawled inside, and then he closed the flap over the tunnel, encasing her a clear, spherical chamber. They'd waited until night to do this both because it would be cooler inside the enclosed balls, and because the ocean would be at its calmest.

Wobbling on the squishy floor, she donned her backpack and stood up. She took a shaky step forward on the gently upsloping floor in front of her. The ball rolled forward a few feet on the surface of the water. She stepped again. Before

long, she found the balance of the thing and walked steadily
forward, propelling the ball across the ocean toward shore.
He wasn't kidding when he'd promised they would walk on
water. Jeff's ball rolled along easily beside hers.

It took nearly two hours to walk the four miles from their
boat to shore, but finally, she walked her ball up the sandy
beach. Gratefully, she crawled out of the stuffy space and
helped Jeff deflate and hide the balls in the bushes.

She took her bearings. She hadn't spent much time on this
half of the island, which was privately owned by Carson Gray.
He was the first person to scout this island as a possible location for the H.O.T. Watch facility. His wife, Lucy McFadden
Gray, was a geologist and had done the initial site surveys of
the underground cave complex that had ultimately become
H.O.T. Watch's home.

The couple had a home a mile or so down the beach, and
Jennifer hoped it was where they had stored the original geo-
logical maps of the island. "This way," she whispered.

They slogged down the beach, and it was slow going. Her
heavy pack weighed her down and the sand was deep and
soft. After walking in that squishy ball for two hours, and
now this, her legs felt like noodles. But she wasn't about to
complain in front of Jeff.

"Give me your pack," he ordered without warning.

"Excuse me?"

"We'll make better time if I carry both packs."

"But that would be well over a hundred pounds of gear!"

"Give me four or five hundred pounds to haul and you
might slow me down. Hand me your pack. You've proven that
you can pull your weight. But I've had enough of watching
you suffer."

"But Jeff—"

"Let me do this for you. What's the point of taking all those medications and risking my life if we don't use the advantage it gives me?"

"But—"

"It's for the good of the mission. There's no reason to wear yourself out before we even get to the hard part."

That argument won her over. She passed Jeff her backpack and was stunned to see him casually fling the thing over one shoulder like nothing more than a gym bag.

As she rolled her eyes, he commented, "Let me know if you get too tired to go on. I'll piggyback you for a while."

"Show off."

"Aww, c'mon. Let the guy impress the girl a little with his cool superabilities."

"Okay, fine. I'm impressed."

"Honey, you haven't even seen the good stuff yet."

"I don't know. When you ripped that lock off the door back at Paradise Island, I was pretty impressed."

He laughed. "I knew I shouldn't have done that the moment I did it. But you were so sexy pointing that shotgun at me I couldn't resist flirting with you."

"That's your idea of flirting?"

"You have a lot to learn about men, Agent Blackfoot."

She snorted. "I know men plenty well, thank you."

"Mmm. I'll say."

She swatted his arm, and they trudged on in companionable silence.

When they neared the perimeter of the Gray estate, she touched Jeff's arm and signaled him to let her take the lead. There was no sense trying to sneak through the jungle to the house. The external security system was either armed or it wasn't. Jungle or path made no difference if the thing was turned on.

She turned off the beach and followed the boardwalk snaking up the hillside toward a sprawling Georgian mansion sitting graciously under a canopy of trees. No lights were on in the house.

Her stomach jumping nervously, she walked around the fountain in the circular drive and boldly approached the front door to ring the bell.

"Seriously?" Jeff muttered. "This is your big plan to break in?"

"This is the 'in case they're home, it's the only way we'll get inside' approach," she replied.

They rang again and waited nearly two minutes before she was convinced no one was home. Now for the actual big plan to break in. She reviewed it quickly. "I'm going to pick the lock. Once I open the door, we'll need to find a landline telephone, not a regular phone but a direct line to H.O.T. Watch. I should be able to use it to access Big Bertha and disable the house's internal security system. But we'll have about sixty seconds to find the phone, get me logged on and get the correct access codes entered."

"And if we don't, the cavalry comes, right?"

She nodded grimly. The contingency plan in that case was to run like hell and hope the two of them could get off the island faster than the gang at H.O.T. Watch could find them using helicopters, tracking dogs, the latest in heat-seeking technology and dozens of special forces soldiers who knew this island like the back of their hands.

Jeff would search the library and office inside and to the left, and she would head for the kitchen and staff office in the back of the house. The door lock was original to the home and took her only seconds to click open with a pair of lock picks.

"Ready?" she asked Jeff.

He put a hand in the middle of her back by way of an answer. She took an instant's comfort in the warmth and strength flowing into her from him and then opened the door.

As she'd expected, no audible alarm gave away their intrusion. But without a shadow of a doubt, an alarm had been tripped.

The interior was elegant and airy, a masterful blend of antique and modern furnishings. She raced through the grand foyer and down a hallway toward the kitchen, where she turned on the lights and did a fast visual search. No sign of anything resembling a phone.

Vividly aware of the seconds ticking away, she headed for the office. A phone sat on the desk. She picked up the receiver and listened to the dial tone. Dang. A regular signal. The phone to H.O.T. Watch would have a slightly deeper tone. She looked at her watch. Twenty-nine seconds elapsed.

"Got it!" Jeff's voice was faint.

She tore out of the office and toward the front of the house. "Where are you?"

"Library."

Jeff stood behind a massive mahogany desk that looked more like a piece of art than actual furniture. He held out a phone receiver to her.

"Time?" she asked as she jammed it to her ear and heard the distinctive tone they were searching for.

"Thirty-seven."

Crud. It was going to be tight. Bertha might be a fast computer, but the thing still took a few seconds to process and execute commands. She typed in a rapid series of numbers on the phone's keypad and prayed this would work. *C'mon, Bertha. Answer, baby.*

Of course, this entire plan hinged on Brady Hathaway having not revoked her security codes in the past few days. She sincerely hoped that their seven years working together had earned her enough trust from him to cut her some slack, even if she did sound crazy at the moment.

The phone line made a series of rapid beeping noises and

then went silent. She typed in a numerical command code that ought to deactivate the alarm system in this house. It was a general override code that was programmed to work on all but the most sensitive systems in the H.O.T. Watch facility.

Three short beeps were all Bertha gave her back.

"Time?" she bit out.

"Fifty-six seconds."

She hung up the phone.

"Did it work?" Jeff asked tightly.

"I don't know. If I was sitting at my console in H.O.T. Watch, I could tell you. If the cavalry shows up in a few minutes, we'll know it didn't."

He didn't look too thrilled at that answer, but it was all she had. She said, "I'd suggest we start searching for the maps in here."

He nodded. "I expect they'll either be laid out flat in a map drawer, or rolled into tubes of some kind."

She looked around the room for the distinctive wide, flat drawers that would hold maps. She didn't see anything like them. A closet, maybe. The room, where floor-to-ceiling bookshelves weren't covering the walls, was lined with gorgeous oak paneling. She moved along the wood panels, pushing and tapping in search of a hidden closet.

Abruptly, the wall rang hollowly beneath her fist. "Here. There's something behind this panel."

Jeff moved over beside her, took one look at the wall, pushed on the panel, and a door popped open. An automatic light came on and illuminated a well-stocked wet bar.

"Nice setup," he commented. "I'd pour myself a snifter of that Louis XIII brandy if we weren't about to be arrested and thrown in jail for the rest of our lives."

"Keep looking," she responded.

Jeff took over searching the walls and in a few seconds opened another panel. This time a closet was revealed. And better, it was lined with shelves and filing cabinets. She stepped inside with Jeff and searched quickly. Bingo. A half-dozen cardboard tubes stood in the corner. She scooped them all up and carried them out into the library.

"Time?" she asked.

"Five minutes."

"I'd say we're clear. The cavalry would be here by now if I had failed to turn off the alarm."

Jeff nodded in relief and reached for a tube. The first tube yielded blueprints of the house they were standing in. But the second tube was a home run. An outline of the island unrolled on the desk, and an extensive network of tunnels and caves was drawn on it. There were five maps in all, each showing a different level of underground caverns.

Jeff gathered up the other tubes and returned them to the closet while she quickly photographed the cave maps for handy reference. He came back to join her. "Do we need to wipe down the room for fingerprints?" he asked.

"If they figure out someone has broken in by using Big Bertha to deactivate the alarms, they won't need to use fingerprints to identify the intruder. They'll know it's me."

"What's next?"

"We need to study these maps. Find an entrance to the caves that the gang at H.O.T. Watch either doesn't know about or doesn't monitor."

"And you're sure you'll recognize every entrance?"

"Jeff, I run the place. Believe me, I know every inch of the facility."

"You didn't know about the surveillance on the first island we were at."

She fell silent. He had a point, even if she didn't like the implications of it very much. Finally, she responded, "It's our only shot at getting into the place undetected. If you want to bail out now, you surely can. This is my problem, not yours. I'm truly grateful for all you've done to get me this far."

Jeff flared up. "Are you trying to get rid of me? Because I don't bail out on my people. Ever."

His people. She liked the sound of that. Although the violence of his reaction to the idea of his leaving should probably scare the hell out of her. "All right, then," she replied. "Help me look at these maps."

"Here?" he asked in surprise.

"We're safer inside this house than just about anywhere else on the island. And you have to admit, it's more comfortable in here than sleeping on the ground with all the bugs and critters."

Jeff chuckled. "I thought you were a big back-to-nature girl."

"Hey. Living in a tepee is great if that's all you've got. But a snazzy suite at a four-star resort is a whole lot more comfortable."

"I think you're getting over your allergy to money very nicely."

"As long as you never forget that I am actually capable of living in a tepee when necessary."

"Duly noted. I'll count on you to remind me if I ever forget."

She stared unseeing at the map. That sounded an awful lot like he was thinking about a long-term relationship with her. Shock and elation washed over her before she could tell herself to be realistic. Not to expect too much.

As a child, she'd learned that life was a great deal less disappointing if she didn't allow herself to hope for anything. That way any good things that did come her way were a pleasant surprise. Jeff Winston was a whole lot more than a pleasant surprise, though. He was more than she could ever dare dream of, let alone actually hope for.

* * *

Jeff frowned as he studied the complicated maps laid out before him. They looked like crude drawings of spaghetti and meatballs, but Jennifer seemed to be making sense of them. She traced various tunnels with her fingers and muttered to herself as she mentally walked herself through the facility and compared it to these maps.

"Here," she murmured. "This tunnel is walled off. We need to mark it."

He searched in the desk and found a mechanical pencil. He drew a line across the tunnel as Jennifer's finger backed up and headed another direction. It was frustrating being unable to help her with this. He hated feeling helpless in general, and he was already feeling far too much of that sensation around this woman.

There had to be something he could say or do to convince her that his taking the medications to enhance his body hadn't been a mistake. He understood her argument that what he'd done wasn't natural. But how natural was most of modern medicine these days? Nano cameras, robotic surgery and stem cell transplants? It was all pretty far-out in his book. He stood by his argument that someone had to learn about this body enhancement stuff before the other guys did. Better him than someone with no ethical compass at all.

"There's another wall here," she announced.

Over the next hour, he drew in the boundaries of the H.O.T. Watch facility at her direction. At least half the cave complex was undeveloped, although the parts that weren't developed were mostly small caves and narrow tunnels if the scale of the drawings was accurate.

Jennifer moved on to the deeper layers of the facility. She pointed out where the nuclear reactor was housed and where the tunnel was for small submarines to enter the facility. She even pointed out a cave where smugglers had hidden rum and treasure over the centuries.

When she'd finished mapping H.O.T. Watch, he stared at the drawings in deep concentration. "Do air vents lead to the surface of the island?" he asked.

"The air circulation system has intakes and vents all over the facility. There are three primary exits for stale air being vented from underground. They come out here, here and here."

Perfect. One of them ran right past the island's steam plant. And even better, the armory was just around the corner. He pointed at the map. "Here's the spot we should use for our break-in. We can steal explosives to create our mini-earthquakes here, and move over here to divert steam from the generators to this exterior vent."

She nodded in agreement. "Now. How to get to that spot from the non-H.O.T. Watch side of the island?"

"Do you know if the caves on this side of the island are blocked off from the outside?" he asked.

"Not to my knowledge. Although, I should probably check to see if the caves on this side of the island are on our security monitoring grid. I'd need to get into Big Bertha to do it, though."

"Can you access Big Bertha from the internet? I'll bet this house has wi-fi."

She nodded. "I'll need my laptop. Bertha will recognize its electronic signature."

"Will using your computer set off any alarms?"

"Not if Brady Hathaway trusts me."

"And if he doesn't?"

"Then we'll never make it inside H.O.T. Watch, anyway. He'll be waiting for us when we get there."

Great. She really was big on the whole trust thing in her relationships with people, wasn't she? If only she would extend that trust to him. He felt her holding back on him emotionally, and he was stumped as to how to break through her reserve.

Out of Jennifer's backpack, he retrieved a laptop computer and handed it to her. "Only way to find out if this Hathaway guy trusts you is to give it a try."

He watched over her shoulder as she booted up the laptop and, indeed, was able to connect to the internet. She logged onto Big Bertha rapidly.

"I'm going to run a low-level security scan. Nothing that should catch anyone's attention inside H.O.T. Watch."

"Don't do it if you think you'll get spotted," Jeff said in quick alarm.

"Nothing ventured, nothing gained."

"Nothing ventured, nothing lost," he retorted.

"How'd you get so rich with an attitude like that?" she demanded as she typed.

"I inherited everything I have. Never earned a dime on my own. Leland's the big risk taker, not me."

"That's such a load of bull. I ran your financials before I went to Africa to get you, and you've made millions with your computer business alone."

"Can you imagine how much money I'll make when I can offer people a chance to become a superhero?"

"You wouldn't sell the technology, would you?" she blurted out in horror.

"Never. I just wanted to get a rise from you."

She subsided in her seat, glaring at him. "Very funny."

"Just keeping you on your toes."

Kind of like she managed to keep him on his toes most of the time. He'd never met another woman who challenged him or fascinated him like she did. Life would never be dull with her around. Assuming he could convince her to stick around for a long, long time. He might joke about her getting used to money, but he didn't for a minute think she would stay with him because of it. If anything, she would choose to be with him in spite of his wealth.

"Nope. No motion sensors on the caves on this side of the island that are connected through to H.O.T. Watch," she announced.

"Great. We're in, then."

"Well, there's the whole business of busting through a solid rock wall and breaking into the armory without being discovered."

"Bah. Kid stuff. Leave the heavy work to me, honey."

As she backed out of H.O.T. Watch's computer system, he suggested, "How about we go find ourselves a guest bedroom and resume planning mayhem and destruction tomorrow?"

While she packed up her laptop, he carried their backpacks upstairs. She rounded the corner and put a foot on the first step of the sweeping curved staircase when he came into the hall above. "Stay there," he called down to her.

She frowned but waited. He joined her at the base of the stairs and she asked cautiously, "What's up?"

"This." He swept her up into his arms and cradled her against his chest as he climbed the stairs.

"What on earth are you doing?" she demanded.

"Don't tell me you've never fantasized about being carried up a staircase like this. Have you *never* seen *Gone with the Wind?*"

She laughed up at him. "I'd make the worst Scarlet O'Hara in history."

"I don't know about that. You're smart and tough and resourceful…and beautiful and sexy and passionate. And as for me, I'd make a smashing Rhett Butler."

"You certainly have the disreputable rake bit down pat."

"Darn tootin'." He carried her across the wide hall and into a sumptuous suite, kicking the door shut with his foot. Just enough moonlight filtered past the curtains to outline the dark shape of the bed. As he laid her down on it, he murmured, "Haven't you ever wondered what happened to Scarlet after Rhett carried her up the stairs that night?"

"Are you planning to show me?" she replied a little breathlessly.

"Frankly, my dear, I am."

Her laughter joined his as he quickly stripped her out of her clothes then strode over to the fireplace mantel where he lit the collection of candles that had made him choose this room. He returned to her doffing his shirt as he went. Jennifer reclined on the bed watching him, her long hair a swirling sable mist around her. The air conditioner blew quietly, setting the gauze bed curtains swaying lightly and raising tiny goose bumps on her beautiful copper skin. He shed the rest of his clothes and placed a knee on the mattress beside her. She crossed her arms over her chest shyly.

He said, "I'm fairly certain Rhett didn't allow Scarlet to hide behind any false modesty that night. Once and for all, he had to show her the depths of passion which she was capable of with him, to break down her walls and get her to admit how she really felt about him."

"Oh? And how was that?"

"Shall we find out?" he replied darkly.

Vague alarm crossed Jennifer's face. While he would never do anything to scare her, he also had no intention of letting her retreat behind her emotional walls tonight. He started out by kissing her. All of her. Wherever his explorations took him. She protested faintly, but eventually relaxed and gave him free access to anything he wanted.

"So tell me, Scarlet. Is it so hard to believe that we might develop strong feelings for each other?"

"I suppose it's possible."

"I think most people have trouble working up the courage to admit it." He kissed his way across her belly, which contracted tightly under his mouth. "I know I'm not a coward. How about you?"

"I'm usually not. But I'm a little afraid right now."

He raised himself up on his arms over her. "Afraid of me, or of yourself?" He gazed directly into her eyes, not allowing her to look away. Tonight he would give her no quarter. She was going to be completely honest with him and with herself.

"Myself." She sighed. "I see where you're headed, and it scares me."

"Where am I headed?"

"Toward a place where I have to face my feelings for you."

"And that scares you?" he asked quietly.

"To death."

He lowered himself toward her by slow degrees. His arm muscles bulged and her fingers strayed to his biceps. "I would never hurt you."

"I believe you."

He lowered his mouth to hers, stopping a mere breath away. "Then what is there to be afraid of?"

"Reaching a point where there's no going back."

"That's the entire point." His mouth completed the journey and claimed hers, lightly at first, and then matching her hunger as she kissed him back. And so it went for the next hour. Every time she balked at opening herself to him, he gently insisted until she let go of her resistance. But finally she came to the point he was waiting for.

She grabbed him by the back of the neck, looked him in the eye and demanded, "Make love to me right now, or I'm going to have to hurt you."

"Scarlet, Scarlet," he chided. "So impatient."

"I don't care how strong you are. I'll find a way to make you suffer."

As if he wasn't already suffering intense discomfort.

Grinning, he eased himself up her body, until they were face-to-face. "You admit, then, that you have nothing left to hide from me?" He had literally explored every single inch of her body with eyes and hands and mouth, had claimed it all for himself, branded her irrevocably as his.

"Fine. I admit it," she grumbled.

"And you also admit that I can play your body like a violin? That I can make you sing like an angel with pleasure and cry like a baby with need?"

"That's it. I'm finding some part of you that I can break right now." She reached for his fingers, and he yanked them out of her reach quickly.

"Aah, but if you broke my fingers, I couldn't do this with them. Or put them here. Or here." He plundered her body until she writhed upon his fingers, head flung back, eyes closed, keening in ecstasy.

Eventually, she rejoined him in the land of the living, panting, her eyes glazed.

"You were saying?" he murmured.

"What are you doing to me?"

"I'm treating you like the incredible woman you are. I'm showing you that you're my woman whether you choose to admit it yet or not. And I'm about to make love to you until you can't remember your own name."

Her body shuddered against his. "That sounds lovely. And my name is Jennifer."

Aah, so spirited, she was. A force of nature. He joined their bodies by slow millimeters, staring into her eyes and stopping whenever she would have closed her eyes, forcing her to open them once more. Gazes locked, they became one. He moved slowly within her, savoring the tight pull of her body against his.

Establishing a slow, steady rhythm, he refused to be hurried, even when she wrapped her legs around his hips and begged for more. This was not about one moment's pleasure. Tonight was about winning the lady's heart forever.

"Jeff! Please," she panted.

"Please what?"

"Please, more."

He pressed more deeply into her but did not change his pace.

"Faster. Harder. Don't be so gentle with me. You're driving me crazy."

"What's your name?"

"Jennifer."

He smiled and held his ground. Her breathing came faster and shorter, hitched, and then broke on a cry of pleasure. He paused just long enough for her to catch a breath, and then resumed his slow torture. She writhed beneath him as yet more pleasure built between them.

"Your name?"

"Uhh. Jenn."

"Mmm. Better." He picked up the pace just enough to push her over the edge again but did not stop. The flush on her cheeks spread to her breasts, and the pauses between climaxes became shorter and shorter as he drove her ever onward. His own body shouted for release, but he hung on with iron control. Not. Yet.

As she clawed at his back, out of her mind with need, he captured her wrists and pulled them up over her head, holding them with one hand. He drove into her harder now, deeper. He let loose more of his prodigious strength, and she absorbed it eagerly, her body clutching at him, demanding even more of him.

Gritting his teeth against the climax tearing at him, he ground out, "What's. Your. Name."

"Jeff!"

She wasn't so far wrong. He wasn't sure where he ended

and she began. Maybe they shared his name, too. She surged up against him, and what little control he had left snapped.

He drove powerfully into her, holding nothing back. He stared down at her, allowing her to see into the depths of his soul as he took her with his entire being and made her his. The end roared toward them like a freight train, deafening thunder rolling over them.

"Your. Name." He hardly remembered his own name as wave after wave of pleasure pounded through him.

She cried out incoherently, her eyes huge and black and unfocused as she stared up at him. She cried out again, the sound breaking off. And then, as he exploded from the top of his head to the bottoms of his feet, she let out a long, trembling cry and poured out every last drop of pleasure left within her for him.

He collapsed onto his elbows, his chest heaving, his forehead resting against hers. If that didn't make the point to her that they were made for one another, he gave up.

"What's your name?" he panted.

"Scarlet."

His lips curved and he kissed the smile off her mouth. Now was probably not the moment to remind her that Rhett and Scarlet were married. There would be time enough for that later. Assuming they lived through the next twenty-four hours.

Chapter 15

Jennifer blinked awake to bright sunlight streaming around the edges of the curtains. She wasn't quite sure what Jeff had done to her last night, but she knew one thing. Her life would never be the same. No way would Rhett have walked out on Scarlet if the two of them had shared a night like that together. And as for Scarlet? Would she have been able to deny her true feelings for Rhett after that? Somehow, Jennifer doubted it.

Reason argued that a long-term relationship wasn't all about the sex. But dang, last night had been epic. Sex like that could sustain a girl for a good long time. And it wasn't like Jeff was a bad guy. He was a pretty incredible guy. The only glitch was his little superhero problem. But it was a deal breaker. How was she supposed to watch the man she loved destroy himself by slow degrees? No way could she survive another episode like the one at the island with him.

A door opened and Jeff emerged, his hips casually wrapped

in a towel, his hair wet. Yep, the sight of all that macho muscle could keep a girl going for a *good* long time.

Spying her gaze on him, he smiled and moved to her side. "Good morning, Scarlet."

"Morning, Rhett."

He sat down on the edge of the bed beside her and pushed back her tangled hair from her face. "How are you feeling? I apologize in advance if you're sore."

She stretched luxuriously. "Nothing a hot bath won't soak away."

"I left you some hot water. Why don't you go have a nice, long soak while I take a look at those maps. I've been doing some calculations on how much dynamite we're going to need to rock this island. I want to double-check the numbers."

"There will mostly be military grade C-4 in the armory."

"All the better. A little bit of that stuff makes a big explosion."

"And you know so much about explosives, how?" she asked.

"Winston Mining."

Of course. "Is there anything you can't do?"

He considered her thoughtfully. "I don't know how to knit."

She laughed. "Neither do I." She climbed out of bed and headed for the shower. One thing she could say about this mission for sure. She'd never done a field assignment—heck she'd never heard of a field assignment—that had taken place in the sort of luxury that this one had. But that's what a girl got when she tangled with a Winston, she supposed.

Jeff had laid out a cold breakfast of food from their packs when she joined him in the library. Thankfully, he didn't insist on talking about their relationship like he had last night. Her cheeks heated up at recollection of just what form most of the "discussion" had taken.

"Hot bath?" Jeff asked as she joined him.

"Uh-huh." Yeah, that was why her cheeks were bright red.

They ate quickly and cleaned up after themselves. No need to trash the Gray's house just because they'd broken into the place. From her acquaintance with the couple, she doubted they'd mind in the least that she and Jeff had let themselves into the mansion, especially when they heard the reason why. Carson Gray was a patriot. And he understood that sometimes the end justified the means.

She frowned. That was one of the arguments Jeff used to explain his medical experimentation. Did his end justify his choice of means? She was grateful when Jeff distracted her by launching into a recap of his calculations to determine that they would need about a half-dozen blocks of C-4 per explosion to cause a noticeable shaking to the folks in H.O.T. Watch.

"The big problem," he elaborated, "is going to be choosing spots for the explosions that won't weaken the structure of the H.O.T. Watch facility itself. We don't want to collapse the place on anyone's heads."

"If we stick to the perimeters of the lower-level caves, I'd think we'll be okay," she replied, studying the maps.

"Agreed. So. How do we get into those caves?"

It was reasonable that the narrowest tunnels on the maps were also the smallest, but that was all they had to go on. Even armed with these maps, they were going to have to do some old-fashioned spelunking to find a back door into H.O.T. Watch.

Jeff shifted topics. "When do you want to hit the armory?"

"Late tonight. When only the night crew's on duty," she replied.

"I'm going to suggest we head out around sunset, then. And besides, that lets us spend the day in air-conditioning."

"For a man who can stand a lot of pain, you sure do like your creature comforts."

Jeff grinned. "Nowhere does it say we have to suffer unnecessarily to be heroes."

"I thought that's what being a hero is. Pushing beyond one's limits to do the impossible."

He rolled his eyes. "Been there, done that, got that T-shirt. It's overrated."

They spent the rest of the afternoon plotting out their best guess at a course through the tunnel network and estimating where on the island they would find a surface entrance to the underground complex of passages.

Finally, she announced, "We can swim out to these cliffs and look for this entrance, here. If we stay close to shore, the currents aren't bad."

Jeff frowned. "I'm not exactly nimble in water. I don't have enough body fat to counteract my muscle mass. Makes swimming hard work."

"Guess we'll have to get you some of those inflatable water wingies little kids wear on their upper arms. You'll be adorable."

"Gee. Thanks."

"We might be able to approach the cliffs from above and climb down to the cave entrance."

"It's worth a try," he replied in obvious relief. "But in case that's a bust, I think I'll go explore the garage and see if I can find something to help my buoyancy."

While he did that, she rolled up the maps and lashed their storage tube to her pack. To pass the time, she did one last inventory of their gear. Flashlights, climbing harnesses, hard hats—

Jeff burst into the library without warning. "Problem. Someone's out there."

"Someone who?" she asked in a reflexive whisper. "Where?"

"In the trees behind the house."

"Are you sure it wasn't just an animal you heard?"

"Yes, I'm sure. I saw a man out there. He was wearing jungle fatigues and carrying a big damned gun."

She frowned. "If the special forces guys from H.O.T. Watch are out there, no way would you have seen them. They're too good for that."

"Then someone else is skulking around getting ready to assault this house."

Jennifer stared at him in dismay. "Our Ethiopian friends? Have they found your tracking burr?"

"If you're certain it's not your guys, then it's probably mine."

"Any idea how many men are out there?"

"No. I just saw the one. But he didn't look like the kind of guy who'd be traveling alone."

She swore under her breath. "I guess we get to see just how good your stealth skills are now."

"Most of the field guys who work for Winston Industries are ex-military. I picked up a thing or two from them."

Yes, but he was a really big moving target. And the slightest mistake on his part could get them both killed. Trust, darn it. Trust. She could trust him. Hadn't she opened herself up to him completely last night?

They slipped outside in the gray of twilight, easing along the front of the house to where the jungle came closest to the drive. She debated crawling the expanse of grass and decided they'd be spotted regardless. They might as well just make a dash for it. She signaled Jeff and took off running across the lawn. They dived for the cover of the heavy brush and crouched there, panting. Nobody had shot at them. This was good.

They moved out cautiously. It wasn't dark enough for night vision goggles to be useful, which meant they had to rely on their own sight and hearing to detect any threats. It also meant any bad guys out here were in the same boat.

Jeff insisted on taking point, and she gave in rather than cause a serious argument. He'd have to pull his weight out here, anyway, if they were to succeed. She might as well find out right now if he could move quietly or not.

She followed as he glided off into the trees. Truth be told, he did a good job of blending into the shadows and varying his movement to avoid creating a rhythmic target that would be easy to spot. She mimicked his halting progress, her gaze roving constantly for possible threats.

She almost shot a wild parrot, and something small and furry that skittered off into the trees nearly gave her heart failure, but otherwise, all was quiet. Well, quiet being a relative thing as night fell in the jungle. It was a screaming madhouse of insects and night creatures. Jeff angled away from the house, roughly paralleling the coastline like they'd discussed, moving cautiously enough that they didn't disturb the night's symphony. She was actually impressed.

But then the volume of the critter chorus diminished sharply. Jeff froze without her having to touch his shoulder. He eased into the shadow of a massive palmetto and she joined him. Now, patience was the key.

They'd stood, statuelike, for maybe three interminable minutes when Jennifer spied a tiny movement in the distance. Something tall and two-legged was moving through the trees, angling away from them.

Jeff tensed beside her. He'd seen the guy, too. He indicated that she should follow him as he moved to tail the target. What was he doing? The idea was to avoid getting caught out here, not tracking down random patrols and engaging them!

But he was already a half-dozen feet ahead of her. Irritated and alarmed, she headed after him. They tracked the man for perhaps a quarter-mile. Their quarry was moving quickly. Not quite carelessly. But he definitely didn't think anyone else was out here with him.

Jennifer's pulse spiked as she spied movement ahead over Jeff's shoulder. It looked like three men waiting for the scout they'd been following. The cluster of men drew close together to murmur to one another. She tugged at the back of Jeff's shirt, but he ignored her warning to stop. What was he doing?

Shocked, she eased forward in a crouch just behind Jeff. He was going to get them caught! And whoever these guys were, they undoubtedly weren't playing games. They were carrying AK-47s, for crying out loud.

Jeff paused behind the trunk of a palm tree and she mimicked his stance. Tiny bits of conversation drifted their way. The hostiles couldn't be more than twenty feet from them. Her trigger finger itched and her whole body screamed of danger. But then the conversation began to register. That wasn't English. In fact, it sounded...Chinese? What the heck?

The island *was* under attack! Or at least being invaded. The Ethiopians must have called in the big guns after the encounter in Jamaica. Here was the proof they needed that *El Mari* was working for the Chinese.

Did that mean the *Chinese* were behind the suborning of the H.O.T. Watch facility? She *had* to shut down H.O.T. Watch now. Not to mention, she had to get in touch with Brady Hathaway somehow and let him know to deploy his men out here and catch these bastards.

She began to ease backward, away from the intruders. Jeff frowned, but she ignored him. It was imperative that she get in touch with Brady. Now. Jeff could sit there and watch bad guys for all she cared.

But he chose to accompany her as she glided away from the party of men. When she'd put a hundred yards or so between herself and the men, she picked up speed. She didn't lose her head and take off running, but she did move quickly through the trees until she had sufficient distance between herself and the intruders to use her cell phone. She pulled out the instrument and powered it up.

"What are you doing?" Jeff demanded in a whisper. "H.O.T. Watch can track the position of that!"

"We'll just have to take that chance. I'm betting they won't be looking for the signal, and by the time they pull up the tracking information, I'll be done talking and turn it off."

"You're warning them, aren't you?" he asked grimly.

She nodded and started to dial.

"You do realize that if they flood the island with soldiers we'll get caught, too."

"I guess we'll just have to be better and faster than the soldiers, then."

He shook his head in disgust as the phone began to ring in her ear.

"Jennifer?" Brady's voice asked in disbelief.

"Yes. Listen fast. There are armed intruders on the surface of the island. At least four, and they're speaking Chinese. Unless you're running a hell of a realistic exercise, the island's been breached."

"How do you know that?" Brady bit out, all business. She could picture him typing in a scramble order into his computer as he spoke. Of course, he could also be typing in the command prompt to bring up the GPS locator program and zero in on her current position.

"How do you think I know, Brady? I saw them. I swear, I'm not lying. Lock the place down and initiate the attack plan." She disconnected without saying any more. She'd warned him. It was all she could do. Of course, the question now was, how were she and Jeff going to get inside the facility with the place on high alert?

* * *

"I hear someone coming," Jeff breathed. He dropped flat and rolled partially under a bush of some kind.

Jennifer dropped beside him and laid perfectly still. He heard the quiet sounds of men passing by and listened tensely as they faded into the distance. The island wasn't that big. And if Brady believed Jenn, the place was about to get a whole lot more crowded.

He turned his head and placed his mouth on her ear. "We need to get into those caves before this place is crawling with special forces types."

She nodded and stood up, pointing off to their right. The ocean was that way. He concurred with her thinking. So much for approaching the cliffs by land. Looked like he got to go for a swim tonight, after all. He sighed. Thankfully, he'd found a boogie board in the garage and could use it to help float himself.

They emerged from the trees, and a narrow stretch of beach gleamed silver in the moonlight. They slithered awkwardly to the water's edge on their bellies. No time to stop and take off shoes. They went straight into the ocean.

The water was calm, with waves no more than a foot high rolling in quietly. He crawled through the shallow water on his hands and knees, then in a crouch, and finally, wading until he stood in chest-deep water. Jennifer was submerged nearly to her neck. She untied the second boogie board from her pack, and he helped her lash the two backpacks to it. She put the board's ankle lanyard around her arm and took off swimming in a modified breast stroke.

He hoisted himself onto his boogie board, which sank a foot or so under his weight. But it was enough for him to keep his head out of the water with reasonable ease. Feeling like a very clumsy sea turtle, he took off after her. It was slow going, but they gradually made their way around a headland and came to the east side of the island and its tall, black cliffs.

The waves were stronger here and buffeted them, pushing them toward the treacherous rocks. It was a tricky maneuver to find a spot where they wouldn't be torn to shreds on outcroppings of jagged volcanic rock. But finally, they washed against a cluster of smooth boulders.

Jeff grappled at the slimy rocks, seeking a handhold. Finally, he found one and dragged himself onto it. He reached a hand down for Jennifer and pulled her up beside him. They lay on the boulders panting for several minutes.

"Now what?" he asked when he'd caught his breath.

Jennifer rustled in her pack and came up with a pair of binoculars. "Now we find that cave."

Recalling the maps from earlier, he tried to picture the various openings in front of him depicted on paper. There was one cave that led directly into the underground tunnel complex about halfway along this stretch of rocks. It had been annotated as being twenty feet or so above the shoreline at high tide.

"What's this tide?" he asked.

"About halfway to low tide."

Drat. The lower the water line, the farther they would have to climb. "Do you see that cave we talked about this afternoon?" he asked her.

"I see about six caves that could be the one we're looking for," she muttered.

"Well, pick one and let's go for it. I don't like being exposed like this. Your boys are going to turn their satellites on themselves and spot us if we're not careful."

She sighed. "Good point. How about that far cave up high?"

He looked where she pointed and winced. She'd chosen the highest cave and likely the most difficult one to reach. "Done."

They had donned their climbing harnesses and safety checked them before they ever left the house, for which he was grateful now. He slung a coil of climbing rope over his shoulder, grabbed a hammer and a fistful of crampons and carabiners, and started to climb. With his strength, he was the obvious choice to be lead climber.

Hauling himself up by raw force, he made slow progress up the cliff face. The good news was the weathered stone had tons of cracks and crevices that made for great hand- and toe-holds. The bad news was the stone was brittle and he had to choose extremely carefully where to hammer in anchor points for the climbing rope.

Bit by bit, he created a trail for Jennifer to follow. She wasn't a half-bad free climber, but when she reached the last part of the climb—straight up a vertical face in a technical climb, she began to fatigue. He gained the ledge in front of their target cave and lying flat, reached down to haul her up by the rope. When she was an arm's length below him, he reached a hand down to her. She grabbed it and he pulled her up and over the edge in one massive heave of bunched muscles.

"Handy to have a guy as strong as you around," she panted.

He nodded as they caught their breath for a few seconds. "Ready to press on?"

She nodded and started to climb to her feet, but slammed back to the ledge as the *thwocking* of a helicopter abruptly overwhelmed the sounds of the ocean below. He rolled for cover fast and she followed.

"Thank God," she murmured when they were safely inside the pitch-black space. "Brady believed me."

"Even if he didn't believe you, he's got no choice but to act on the warning. Maybe it pulls a bunch of guys out of the facility and makes our mission easier."

"Not likely." Her voice floated out of the darkness. "They'll be on high alert and have wandering guards both inside and on the surface. It's going to be a nightmare to get past them."

"We'll figure something out," he replied encouragingly. The first order of business was to see if they could even get close to the developed portion of the complex via these unused tunnels.

He helped Jennifer stow the rope, crampons and carabiners she'd collected as she came up the cliff behind him. They dared not leave their climbing rope behind as evidence for Brady, nor as an easy aid to the Chinese intruders to finding this place.

"Here's hoping I chose the right cave," Jennifer mumbled. "I'd hate to have to do that cliff with helicopters out there."

No kidding. He followed as she turned on a flashlight and pointed it toward the rear of the cave. The total blackness was broken only by the thin beam of her flashlight. He pulled out his own light and flashed it at the uneven floor.

The cave elongated into a rough tube. Millions of years ago, hot magma would have flowed toward the sea, melting its way through the softest rock until it found the quenching waters of the primordial ocean. The two of them weren't the first humans ever to set foot in this tunnel, but it felt like they were. A sense of wonder overcame him.

Jennifer pulled up short. "Rock fall," she announced. "Blocks the tunnel."

"Lemme see." He moved past her in the tight tunnel to examine the pile of boulders. "I think I can move these. But you'll need to stand back so I don't roll one down on you."

"Are you kidding?" she exclaimed. "Those things are huge!"

"Hello. Man who lifts small trucks here."

She laughed reluctantly. "Even you can't move some of those."

"You'd be surprised. And I don't have to move them all. If

I can create a minor avalanche, the weight of the rocks and gravity will move some of the others."

"A good plan, in theory."

She stepped back as he put theory into action. It took him a few minutes, and even he had to shove and pull for all he was worth, but he did, indeed, dislodge enough of the medium stones to force a few of the biggest ones to roll down the pile and out of the way. An opening beckoned at the top of the pile.

"If I can squeeze through, we know you can make it," he told Jennifer.

"And if you get stuck? Will I be able to pull you out?"

"You can always go back to the house and get some butter to grease me up and slide me right out."

"Not encouraging," she grumbled as he wedged himself into the narrow opening. For a few seconds, there, he thought he might stick. But he pushed and pulled with his mighty strength and popped through on the other side of the blockage. Jennifer passed the packs through and then wiggled past the block to join him.

"Onward," he muttered.

"Hoorah."

Time became wildly distorted as they made their way farther and farther down the tunnel. Whether or not this was the tunnel depicted on Lucy Gray's map was anyone's guess. But the thing clearly did lead deep into the heart of the island. Only by checking his watch periodically, did he get any sense of the night passing outside.

It was a little after midnight when Jennifer exclaimed quietly from in front of him, "We did it!"

"What did we do?"

"This tunnel dead ends into a cinder block wall. We've found the edge of the H.O.T. Watch facility."

"Do we go ahead and break through the wall, or do you

want to change the plan, based on the new wrinkle topside?" he asked.

She stared at him, looking like a little girl beneath her yellow hard hat. "I don't know. What do you think?"

Wow. That was a first. Jennifer Blackfoot indecisive? He considered the wall before them. "What if we make a little hole and take a peek at what's on the other side before we make a final decision?"

"Can you do that? Make a peephole, I mean?"

"My dear, I'm an artist with a pickax. Of course I can." *He hoped.* Whether he could actually strike the wall lightly enough not to bring the whole thing down was another matter entirely. He stepped forward and tapped on the blocks gingerly near one corner of the wall. Nothing happened. He struck a little harder. Still no progress. Gritting his teeth, he gave the wall a mighty whack and a three-foot-long, zigzagging crack appeared along the mortar joints.

"Jeez. Don't knock the whole thing down," Jennifer exhorted.

He went back to tapping and chipped away a little piece of the cinder block. He kept at it, and eventually he waved her forward toward the hole he'd made. "You'll have a better idea of what you're looking at than I will."

She slid past him, her luscious body rubbing against his on the way. He would *never* get enough of that woman.

She peered through the hole for just a few seconds. "We did it. Armory's down the hall to the right. Utility room with access to the air vents is about fifty feet down on the left."

"Any sign of guards?"

She shook her head.

"Want to break through now?"

Another negative shake of her head. "Let's wait for a guard patrol to pass and then go. It'll give us the most time before someone comes back this way."

Logical. "Let me take a few more whacks at the wall while there's no one in sight and soften it up a little."

He swung the pickax at the wall being careful not to hit her as she peered through the hole.

"Stop!" she hissed.

Someone must be coming. He waited in tense silence until Jennifer let out a long breath and signaled him to continue. He winced at the booming sounds of his blows echoing through the tunnel. Might as well make all the noise short and sweet. He swung with all his strength, and in a matter of seconds, the wall crashed into the hall beyond. They'd done it. They were inside. So close to the bastard who'd killed his men he could taste it. He clambered through eagerly after Jennifer, who was already sprinting down the hall toward the armory.

She punched in a series of numbers on a pad beside the door and a green light illuminated. He followed her down a long aisle of tall shelves to where blocks of C-4 were neatly stacked like bricks. He threw as many as would fit into the bag he'd brought for the purpose.

"Time," Jennifer bit out. She'd estimated they would have thirty seconds in here before they had to get out and hide from the security patrol that would come to check on the late-night entry into the armory.

He turned and ran for the door. He dived left into the hall and ran for the utility closet with Jennifer on his heels. Again, they stopped while she punched in a security code and then jumped inside. Just in time, too. The door had been closed maybe five seconds when footsteps pounded past. Shouts outside indicated the broken wall had been spotted.

Jennifer pulled a key ring out of her pocket and manually locked the door. Funny how a good old-fashioned double-action dead bolt could trump all of today's fancy electronic gadgets.

"When they check the doors, the pad outside will detect the dead bolt and show itself to be locked down."

"God, you're good," he muttered.

"I told you. I know this place like the back of my hand."

He moved away from the door toward the big, galvanized aluminum duct running up the back wall of the tiny room. The vent was nearly three feet wide and just as deep. But then, it was ventilating an entire mountain.

"Any idea how we're going to get the lower levels to set up our explosions now that there are soldiers running all over the place looking for that Chinese team?" he asked after more footsteps pounded past.

She eyed the vent speculatively. "We've still got our climbing gear."

He eyed the vent dubiously. "I'd barely fit in that thing."

"Which is why no one will think to look for us inside it."

"I don't like it, Jenn."

Another set of shouts disturbed the silence outside. She shrugged. "Well, then I guess we'll have to take our chances with all those soldiers running around. Did I mention they have orders to shoot to kill intruders?"

And that was how he found himself dangling from a rope inside an air shaft, his shoulders brushing both side walls, and testing the limits of his tolerance for small, enclosed spaces.

Jennifer pulled the cut portion of the ductwork back into place behind her, plunging the shaft into blackness. Her voice drifted down to him, "Okay. Let's go."

He turned on the light mounted on his hard hat and eased downward slowly. His foot banged the wall and he winced at the booming echo. For the most part, they managed the descent in silence. They only had to drop down around twenty-five feet—two stories—but it seemed to take forever. Finally, a vent cover came into sight.

Jennifer peered through it cautiously. "This is it. The bottom level."

Awkwardly, he used his big knife to slice through the galvanized aluminum sheeting. But eventually, he tumbled through the hole in an undignified heap. He helped Jennifer climb off her rope a little more gracefully. They moved over to the door of a utility room much like the first one.

"Ready to do this?" he asked her grimly.

"As I'll ever be. Let's go blow ourselves a volcano."

Chapter 16

Jeff's patience was strained as they waited for a patrol to pass by outside. It took nearly fifteen minutes, which was good news. The less frequent patrols down here would give them more time to maneuver. Jennifer nodded and they slipped out into the hall. Unfortunately, they had to travel in the same direction as the patrol, and the two of them proceeded cautiously.

Jennifer peered around yet another corner and slammed herself backward into him without warning. She signaled for him to run and he did without question. She passed him by and dived into a side passage ahead of him. He did his best to pant quietly as the patrol passed back by, heading the other way.

Jennifer slipped out into the hall again and they retraced their steps. The number pad she stopped at this time also had a gel handprint reader. And when they slipped inside the unmarked door, Jennifer had to pass a voice recognition test and a retinal scanner.

But finally, a second door opened. And then he saw the reason for all the security. They were standing on a catwalk overlooking a pair of massive steam turbines. H.O.T. Watch's power plant.

It didn't take them long to locate the steam outflow vents. But it did take them a while to find a spot where one of the steam-filled ducts ran close to a cool-air outflow vent that sent stale air to the surface. Thankfully, the turbine attached to the steam duct was currently offline during this low-power-demand period of night. Which meant viciously hot steam was not flowing through the duct at the moment.

"I think this is as good as we're going to get," he murmured to her.

"Agreed."

These ducts were made of heavy gauge aluminum, and even his hands were aching by the time he sawed through the thick metal of each. He pulled out a tarp made of a special heat-resistant polymer that Winston Plastics had invented a few years back. Using duct tape, he joined the two holes together. The next time this particular steam turbine came online, a column of hot steam should shoot the air vent to the surface.

Jennifer had to go through much the same protocol as before when they backed out of the power facility.

"Won't someone upstairs see that you've come in here?" he asked, eyeing the various scanners doubtfully.

"If they're looking for it. Had we tried to get into the nuclear bunker, now *that* would have set off alarms like crazy."

They paused at the hallway door, listening for movement outside. Jennifer grinned over her shoulder at him. She was *enjoying* this? Oh, yeah. She was one woman in a million.

"Ready to make this place shake, rattle and roll?" she murmured.

"Let's do it."

They headed out, dodging yet another patrol, and made their way to the farthest reaches of the complex. They crouched at the end of a hall at another cinder-blocked wall marking the end of the H.O.T. facility.

"Let's set a charge here," she whispered. "If the maps are accurate, there's an old cave on the other side that smugglers used. It'll lead to several more good tunnels for explosions."

Jeff passed her a block of C-4, and she commenced slicing it efficiently into smaller chunks and daisy chaining them together with slow-burning igniter cord. The trick was not to create one massive explosion, but rather a long series of small explosions that would simulate the long, rumbling movement of an earthquake.

At the end of the chain, he attached a full brick of C-4. It would punch through the cinder block wall much more quickly than he ever could and would blend in with the rest of the explosion. It took them nearly a half hour to set the charges. But thankfully, this off-the-beaten-track little corner of the facility didn't garner any security sweeps.

Finally, he and Jennifer backed around the corner from their handiwork. They put in earplugs and pressed their hands over their ears, and she stepped on the small remote control with her foot.

Boom-boom-ba-boom-boom. *Boom*.

A choking, gray cloud of dust filled the air until he couldn't see his hand in front of his face. A hand grabbed his arm and he reached for Jennifer. They felt their way forward through the mess and he stumbled on chunks of rock and debris on the floor.

He used his free hand to feel his way along the wall. Suddenly, nothing but air met his seeking hand. A tug on his sleeve and he veered into the ragged opening. He nearly fell over the knee-high remains of the wall, but then the air cleared enough to see. They'd stumbled into a cave maybe a hundred feet long and twenty or so feet wide and tall.

"Hurry," Jennifer urged. "That explosion will definitely bring people to investigate."

They picked their way across the uneven floor of the cave toward a series of tunnels branching off at the far end. He watched, perplexed, as Jennifer pulled out a piece of chalk and made a mark just inside the opening of one of them. She backed out and headed for the next tunnel over.

"What's that for?"

"Misdirect. It's standard spelunking practice to mark your path with chalk so you can retrace your steps if you get lost."

"You're an evil woman. I like the way you think."

"And don't you forget it," she murmured half under her breath. "C'mon."

The tunnel turned out to be relatively large and smooth-floored, and they risked a jog down its length. Jennifer paused a few minutes later and pulled out her cell phone. She pulled up the maps she'd photographed earlier and the two of them conferred on their location. When they were certain this tunnel led to several other ones, they laid another set of charges like the ones before. But to this batch they added a timer set to go off in an hour.

They jogged on, stopped again, verified their position again, and laid another set of charges. It took them most of the remainder of the night to lay nearly two dozen sets of charges, all on timers to go off at various intervals over the next two days. The first timed charges were already detonating before they finished.

To the later charges they added extra C-4 to really shake things up inside H.O.T. Watch. Finally, they used up the last of their explosions. Now it was time to wait. Once the facility was evacuated, they'd go topside and take a hard look at the satellite surveillance system and its wiring.

They settled down on a smooth patch of sand and Jeff drew Jennifer into his arms.

"Mmm. You make a pretty good mattress, Mr. Winston."

"You make a pretty good blanket, Ms. Blackfoot."

"Get some rest. I imagine it'll take a while for folks to clear out of here."

He felt her lips moving across his chest through the material of his shirt. "Don't tempt me," he muttered.

She laughed softly in the darkness. "You're always tempted."

"With you around, you're damned right I am."

Jennifer closed her eyes. It was easy to sleep after the night's heavy exertion and with the total blackness of underground to lull them into believing it was still night, even though her watch said the sun had risen outside. And it didn't hurt, of course, that Jeff's arms were warm and secure around her.

How much later she jolted awake with the beam of a blindingly bright flashlight in her eyes, she didn't know. "Jeff, get that thing out of my eyes," she complained.

"That's not me, darling," he murmured from right beside her.

Crap.

"Hi, Jennifer. You're looking...comfortable."

She lurched into a sitting position. "Brady. What on earth are you doing here?"

"Funny. I was about to ask you the same thing."

"Need me to take him?" Jeff breathed.

"No." She sighed. "Brady, this is Jeff Winston when he's not screaming in pain. Jeff, meet my military counterpart, Commander Brady Hathaway."

The two men nodded cautiously at one another.

Then Brady burst out, "Would you care to tell me what in the hell is going on, Jennifer? Are you actually trying to blow the place up? Please tell me this guy brainwashed you or something."

"He hasn't brainwashed me. We're trying to convince everyone the volcano's going active again so they'll evacuate the facility."

"Why?"

She winced at the contained fury in that single syllable.

Jeff piped up evenly, but with a definite threat underlying his tone. "Give her a minute to explain before you jump to the wrong conclusions."

"You stay out of this," Brady snapped.

"That's enough, Brady," she snapped back. "Jeff's in the thick of this whether you like it or not. If it weren't for him, I'd never have learned that H.O.T. Watch is compromised. And when I say compromised, I mean totally. The place has to be shut down."

Brady opened his mouth to protest, but shut it again at a warning look from Jeff.

"Tell him what you discovered, Jeff," she pleaded.

Jeff described the loss of his team in Africa, his people's suspicions and the search for answers that led to purchasing satellite feeds from H.O.T. Watch.

"And before you tell him he's lying," Jennifer interjected, "I've seen the feeds with my own eyes. And I wasn't here. I was in Colorado. They were all for sale, Brady. Everything."

He stared at the two of them in stunned silence. "You swear you're telling the truth?" he rasped.

"The God's honest truth, Brady. I swear on my honor, on everything you and I have worked to accomplish in this place."

He staggered slightly before righting himself. "What's the plan?"

"Don't answer that, Jenn," Jeff bit out.

"We can trust him," she retorted. "I've worked with Brady for seven years. He's as honorable as they come."

"He also has a job to do. He thinks he needs to protect this place. We can't trust him."

She stared back and forth between the two men. She'd known Brady a lot longer, but she'd also known Jeff a heck of a lot more intimately. Who to trust? How was she supposed to choose? Her head said to trust Brady. But her heart told her to trust Jeff.

"Don't make me choose," she finally ground out. "Brady, will you withhold judgment until we get a look at the wiring of this place?"

"The wiring?" he exclaimed.

"Jeff thinks duplicate wiring was built into the facility at the time of its construction, and that's how whoever's stealing the video feeds is bleeding them off the system without being detected."

Brady swore in disbelief. "You mean…" He trailed off as the implications of the place having been spied on for years sank in.

"Explains a few things, doesn't it," she replied bitterly. The missions gone wrong for no good reason. Enemy responses that were too fast and too accurate to have been random luck.

Brady stared at her. "They'll blame you and me."

She nodded. "We make a great pair of sacrificial lambs, don't we?"

He sank down to his haunches in the tunnel and simply shook his head. She knew the feeling.

"Stay with us," she urged. "Help us check the facility out from top to bottom."

"I'll do you one better than that," he announced. He reached into his back pocket and pulled out a cell phone.

Jeff lunged forward and tackled the navy man. Brady fought, but he never stood a chance. Jeff got his arms around him and held him in a grip of steel until Hathaway gave up.

"Jeez, you're strong. Do you take steroids or something?" Brady grumbled.

"Or something," Jeff ground out.

"I was just going to call upstairs and order the evacuation now," Brady explained as Jeff cautiously turned him loose.

"Promise?" she demanded.

"Jenn. How long have we worked together? I didn't revoke any of your security clearances to this place, did I? I took you at your word and protected my teams without any explanations from you that I should. And I'm the one who came looking for you—alone—after your access codes were used to enter the steam plant."

She sighed and nodded. "Make the call."

It took about four hours to clear out the place. Most of that time was spent shutting down the nuclear generator and packing up the armory and critical computer components. Big Bertha would be moved in her entirety along with a portable generator to keep her internal cooling systems running during the transition.

But eventually, Brady's phone beeped with an incoming text. He glanced at the message. "That's it. The place is cleared. Let's go see what the hell's going on with your wiring."

This was it. Her entire future rode on the next few hours. If she was right, she'd go down as a hero. If she was wrong, she was about to go to jail for a very long time…if she was lucky.

Chapter 17

Jeff made a point of walking behind Brady Hathaway as they made their way back toward H.O.T. Watch. Were it not for the shiny new wedding band on the guy's left hand, he'd be more than just leery of the navy man. The guy obviously had a great working relationship with Jennifer. But, he reminded himself, when she glanced over her shoulder, it was to smile reassuringly at him, not Hathaway.

They'd passed through the smuggler's cave, taken another tunnel and stopped at a steel access door when an itching between his shoulder blades reminded Jeff. "By the way, did your guys catch that Chinese hit squad on the surface?"

"Chinese…what?" Brady squawked.

"The infiltration team I called you about," Jennifer clarified in alarm. "The four men toting AK-47s and skulking around in the woods."

Brady's jaw rippled. "I ran that down and the duty controller said it was an exercise. No live men were on the surface."

"He lied," Jeff bit out.

"Who was the duty controller?" Jennifer asked ominously.

"Sergeant Ordonez," Brady answered grimly. "One of my guys."

Jeff commented, "Sounds like you may have found your mole." He memorized the name carefully. Ordonez was a dead man. And meanwhile, a bunch of Chinese irregulars were still running around.

"Isn't Ordonez Venezuelan?" Jennifer asked.

Hathaway nodded grimly. "I'd bet my next paycheck he was clean when he came to H.O.T. Watch." But then he added, "He's been here since the beginning, though. I wonder if someone got to his family."

Jennifer replied gently, "It doesn't matter how they got their hooks into him at this point. Now it's all about damage control."

Huh. And revenge. Blood for blood.

With the complex emptied out, it was an easy matter for the three of them to head for the electrical wiring room that handled most of the facility's satellite feeds. They dropped the metal panels and stared at the jumble of colored wires.

Jeff suggested, "If you have access to this place's wiring diagrams, I'm an electrical engineer. I might make sense of this faster than the two of you."

Jennifer asked, "Big Bertha's down, right?"

Brady nodded. "We'll have to get the paper plans out of the safe in my office."

The three of them headed back out into the white, unmarked hallways. Jeff asked, "How do you guys find anything down here? Everything looks the same and nothing's labeled."

Jennifer laughed. "That's the point. When you live and work here you learn your way around. But outsiders are lost in a heartbeat."

"Count me lost."

"Stick with me, big guy," she retorted.

He did, however, carefully memorize the turns, and was fairly sure he could find his way to the massive control room they emerged into a few moments later. The place looked like a storm had blown through recently. Computer cables all over the place announced where laptops and monitors and satellite feeds had been hastily unplugged and carried out.

The three jumbo screens high on the wall were black now and the long rows of desks where analysts would sit were deserted. This place was as impressive as hell and it wasn't even up and running.

He waited on the main floor while Hathaway ran up a flight of metal stairs to an office overlooking the ops center. The floor rattled beneath Jeff's feet just then. Their explosive charges were doing a great job of simulating small earthquakes. Hathaway emerged in a few moments with a thick roll of blueprints under his arm, and they retraced their steps back toward the electrical room.

Jeff judged they were about halfway back to their destination when, without warning, a gunshot exploded behind them. Hathaway grunted like he'd been hit as the three of them took off running and dodged into the next hallway.

"Who the hell was that?" Jeff demanded.

Jennifer and Hathaway traded grim looks. She answered, "I'd guess it's Ordonez, or the Chinese, or both. Let me see your arm."

"The bullet just winged me. I'm fine," Hathaway ground out.

Jeff rolled his eyes. The guy didn't have to be a hero to impress *his* girl, thank you very much. "Just show her your arm. You know she won't let up until you do."

Hathaway grinned. "Getting to know her pretty well, aren't you?"

Jeff's comment was cut off by the hiss of pain Hathaway sucked in as Jenn poked at his arm.

"The bullet's lodged in there, you idiot," she announced.

"Yeah, I know. But we can't stop now to deal with it," Hathaway retorted.

She rolled her eyes and opened her mouth to lecture him, but Jeff cut her off gently. He knew that look in Hathaway's eyes. "Give it a rest, Jenn. The sooner we get out of here, the sooner he'll let you take care of his arm."

"God, I hate dealing with macho men," she groused.

"Say that to me the next time we're alone in the Grays' mansion," he retorted under his breath.

She blushed scarlet and turned to head for the electrical room without comment. Hathaway's eyebrows shot up, but the guy had the good sense to make no snide comments. Which was good. Jeff would hate to add a broken nose to the guy's injuries.

They barricaded themselves in the utility room, bandaged Hathaway's arm and let the navy man guard the door, holding a pistol in his off hand.

With the schematics, it was an easy matter to see that, indeed, H.O.T. Watch had been double-wired. Where the schematics showed a single connection, the box on the wall had two. Over and over, Jeff found instances of duplicate wiring.

While he took over guard duty, Jennifer and Hathaway commenced taking pictures with their phones of both the blueprints and the actual wiring. It was just the opportunity he'd been waiting for. His companions were engrossed in gathering evidence to prove that H.O.T. Watch was completely compromised.

With a last check to verify they weren't looking, he slipped out quietly into the hall. Somewhere out here was the guy who'd killed his men. If not directly, this Ordonez guy had certainly set up his team for the slaughter.

* * *

Jennifer felt sick. It was as if a doctor had told her that her beloved child was dying and there wasn't a thing she could do about it. No matter how long she stared at the electrical wiring system, no matter how desperately she might wish for it, she couldn't find any other diagnosis. H.O.T. Watch was finished.

Nearly a quarter of her life she'd poured into this place. She and Brady had turned it into one of the premier intelligence gathering and analysis facilities in the world. And it had all been stolen from them. She felt violated. Betrayed.

God, she needed a hug. She turned to Jeff to get one—Where was he?

Frowning, she looked in every corner of the utility room. No sign of him. "Brady, did you see Jeff leave?"

Her colleague glanced up in surprise. "No."

Crap. Crap, crap, crap. Surely he didn't slip out and go after Ordonez. But her gut told her otherwise. Had he totally used her, after all? Had this all been a gigantic setup to get him close to the guy who'd killed his men? Had all of it been a lie? Had *they* been a lie?

"I can't run, Jenn. Sorry."

"That's okay. I've got this one. Stay here. Keep documenting the evidence." She jammed her camera in her pocket and raced out into the hall. Empty. She took off running, but she didn't have any idea to where. For the first time in her life, she was lost inside her own home.

Jeff had spent a ton of time studying the maps of H.O.T. Watch yesterday, and he'd paid close attention when they'd been walking around the facility. He was confident he could navigate the unmarked hallways. He moved fast down the main hall in search of the shooter from before.

Where would he go if he were a saboteur trying to cover

his tracks? Jennifer had mentioned that the armory would be emptied as part of the evacuation. That left the obvious target, then. The nuclear generator. Jeff headed toward it.

He swore when he saw the shattered remains of the number pad hanging beside the door to the outer control room. The reinforced steel door hung half off its hinges, its surface singed black. Somebody else must have done a little extracurricular C-4 shopping in the armory recently.

Please, God, let the nuclear facility be shut down in its entirety. Surely, the staff wouldn't have left the island with any portion of the reactor running.

Of course, nuclear reactors stayed hot for years after they ceased operating. And by *hot,* he meant the rods stayed at thousands of degrees centigrade. He thought back to his lone nuclear engineering class in college. The saboteur probably wouldn't be able to breach the actual reactor. But the guy might be able to vent radioactive steam into the H.O.T. Watch facility and render it uninhabitable for a very long time to come.

Jeff lifted the door aside far enough to slip inside. He'd barely cleared the door when a terrific blow landed on the back of his head. It would have shattered a lesser man's skull. But as it was, it only knocked Jeff flat on his face and made stars dance in front of his eyes. Disoriented, he rolled to his back and was in time to catch the two-by-four as it arced down to finish him off.

He grabbed the board and yanked it with all his strength, sending the man wielding it flying over him and across the room. Jeff rolled and pushed to his hands and knees. Nausea overcame him and he retched, unable to stand.

He *had* to move. The guy would no doubt pull out a gun as soon as he realized a more quiet approach to killing Jeff wouldn't work. He forced his limbs to move. The fuzzy shape in the corner moved, as well. Groaned. Jeff crawled faster.

The guy pushed up onto an elbow. It was now or never. Jeff shoved to his feet and staggered across the room toward the saboteur. The guy looked Latin, not Chinese.

Savage satisfaction coursed through him. *The mole.* But satisfaction turned to dismay as Ordonez lifted a pistol and took aim at him. At this range, the guy wasn't going to miss.

Jennifer swore as two gunshots rang out somewhere nearby. They sounded close, but it was hard to tell with the stone tunnels distorting the sound. She looked around for a moment to locate herself and swore again. The nuclear reactor control room was just ahead.

Of course. Any saboteur would head there, and Jeff had figured that out. Small problem: Jeff didn't have a gun. Which meant those bullets had been fired at him.

She put on a burst of speed as panic rolled through her. She was going to kill him for using her and lying to her, but no one else had better beat her to it!

The burned and broken door came into sight and her heart skipped a beat. Pulling her pistol from its holster, she eased forward. Another shot rang out and she bolted through the doorway. She recognized both men immediately. Jeff was wrestling with Sergeant Ordonez, the two men grappling over a pistol between them.

She knew better than to shout out Jeff's name and distract him, so instead, she raised her weapon and yelled, "Freeze!"

Both men did exactly that.

And then the pistol discharged once more, flashing between their chests. Blood sprayed everywhere and she couldn't help it. She screamed.

Jeff groaned as the round hit the meaty part of his upper right chest. It felt like the bullet broke his collarbone. But he knew a thing or two about pain. Gritting his teeth, he literally fell on top of the shooter, using his weight to smash the man flat.

The man struggled, swearing, beneath him. "Who in the hell are you, and why won't you die?"

Jeff ground out as he grappled with the man, "I'm your worst nightmare. You got my guys killed. And now it's payback time."

"Jeff! No!"

He didn't bother to glance over at Jennifer.

"This isn't open to negotiation," he snapped. "This man dies. Now."

"Don't do it, Jeff! You'll have to live with it for the rest of your life."

"I can do that. I already live with the faces of my men who this bastard got killed."

"Huh?" Ordonez's muscles slackened slightly in his confusion. Jeff wrenched the guy's arm practically out of the socket and forced the man to roll onto his belly or lose his arm. Literally.

"Are you the bastard who's been selling the satellite feeds?"

"No!"

"Don't lie to me." Jeff jacked the guy's arm up against the resistance of ligaments and tendons until Ordonez screamed. To her credit, Jennifer didn't interfere in his rather extreme interrogation technique.

"Let's try that again, Sergeant. Did you sell those feeds?"

"Didn't sell them," the man panted. "Blackmail. They blackmailed me."

"Who?"

"Venezuelan death squad got my family. Mother of God, ease off my arm!"

"Keep talking."

"They're holding my family hostage. Seven years, man. Seven years!"

"The Venezuelans managed to get this place double-wired and put you inside?" Jeff asked in disbelief.

"Not them. The Chinese. They wired the place. They probably leaned on the Venezuelans to turn me."

"That's all I need to hear. And now I'm going to kill you very slowly. And while I rip your limbs off one by one, I'm going to tell you the names of my men who died. The names of their wives and children, damn you."

"Jeff—" Jennifer started warningly.

"Please!" Ordonez cried, cutting her off. "I did what I could. Diverted the most critical feeds. Protected the missions I could. I'll talk. I'll tell you everything I know. Names. Contacts. Money trail. Sweet Jesus, my arm! I'll give you the Chinese!"

Jeff was tempted. But the faces of his men haunted him, their families' grief at their funerals burned into his memory. But then another face intruded upon his rage. This one real and at a distance of about twelve inches.

"Take his offer, Jeff. This guy's just a pawn. Go for the real killers. I'll help you. Uncle Sam will help you. We'll nail them all. But you have to let this man live."

Jeff threw himself off the other man in disgust. Absently, he pressed a hand to his bleeding gunshot wound.

He jumped as Ordonez quickly lifted the forgotten pistol to his own mouth and pulled the trigger. But Jeff was too late. Dead, glassy eyes stared up at him from a pool of blood and gore. Jeff stared down in satisfaction. Finally. Justice was done.

And then the pain hit him. Damn, getting shot *hurt*.

Jennifer was swearing steadily and violently. She probably didn't even realize tears were streaking down her face. He started to reach for her, but daggers of agony stabbed through his right shoulder.

He moved to put his left arm around her to guide her to

the door, and that was when he noticed the panels of buttons and gauges going crazy.

"Uh, Jenn. We may have a problem. It looks like Ordonez breached the containment chamber."

Jeff's words shocked Jennifer out of her reaction to Ordonez's death. On the one hand, she was glad the man who'd betrayed her and H.O.T. Watch, who'd shot Jeff, was dead. But on the other hand, it was back to her and Brady taking the fall for everything.

"Breached…" she echoed. She glanced up at the control panels and gulped. She was no nuclear engineer, but she knew enough to know that Jeff was right. They had a major problem.

"See this smashed panel? It looks like he opened an emergency pressure relief valve and has disabled the controls that would close it again. We're about to have a major leak of radioactive steam. As soon as the ducting fails, if I had to guess."

She stared at Jeff in dismay. "Can we fix it?"

"Don't know," Jeff muttered, studying the other panels. "Good way to cover his tracks. Make it so no one can come down here to find the double-wiring for a few hundred years."

"We have to fetch Brady. Get out of here. Evacuate the island."

Jeff nodded, now studying the nuclear reactor below them through the glass windows. "You go get Brady and leave."

"You have to come, too!"

"How many people are still on the island?"

She frowned, thinking. "There's a small town topside. Maybe five hundred civilians. Family members of the H.O.T. Watch staff mostly. Some support people. They won't have cleared out, yet."

"Get them off the island as fast as you can."

"What are you going to do?" she asked suspiciously.

"Buy you some time. I think I can reach that valve and manually close it at least partially."

Horrified, she blurted, "You can't. You'll get irradiated."

"How did Spock put it in the *Star Trek* movie? The good of the many outweighs the good of the one?"

"No!"

"Go."

"Absolutely not, Jeff. This is madness."

"This is necessary." He grabbed her by the shoulders and kissed her hard and fast. "I'll join you on the surface as soon as I'm done. Leave the lights on and the doors unlocked until I come out, okay?"

He gave her a little push toward the doorway. When she resisted, he reminded her gently, "The locals are civilians. Women and children. Someone has to warn them. They deserve that much."

It was a cruel gambit. He knew she couldn't deny the validity of that particular argument. She talked fast. "There's an elevator in the ops center under the big screens. It's an emergency exit."

He nodded, then said grimly, "I love you, Jenn. Now get out of here."

He turned away and put his hands on the locked glass door leading down to the reactor core containment area. He gave a mighty heave and the door shattered as he ripped the handle off of it.

"I love you, too." The words came out as a sob, but hopefully he understood them. "Come back to me, Jeff."

"I promise."

He was lying. But she loved him for it.

She turned and ran.

Jeff made his way quickly to the valve. It was a simple job, really. Grab the circular metal plate and rotate it from its open position to a closed position. A ninety-degree pivot. No big deal. Except the valve was three feet across and weighed several hundred pounds. Worse, the servos holding it open were exerting hundreds of pounds of additional pressure on the plate to hold it open.

Heat poured off the cement sarcophagus housing the reactor core behind him. It was filled with water, and the steam heat in here was nearly unbreathable. He didn't even want to think about the radiation dosage he must be getting. This was suicide, and not in the figurative sense. But Spock was right. One life versus hundreds of innocent lives was no choice at all.

He placed his hands on the plate and yanked them back as the hot metal scorched his palms. He tore off his shirt, ignoring the stab of pain from his busted collarbone. Wrapping his hands in his shirt, he grabbed the valve again with his good arm and pulled. It didn't budge.

He braced his feet against the wall and tried again, straining with all his might. Something in his shoulder popped. A tendon giving way, maybe, but still he pulled, yelling against the agony tearing through him.

He thought he felt the valve move a bit. He took several deep breaths, gathered himself and threw everything he was into closing that valve. He pictured Jennifer. Her laughter. Her passion. The love in her eyes when she didn't remember to hide it from him. And he found the strength.

Slowly, slowly, the valve gave way. He trembled from head to foot, straining with the effort, blood and sweat and tears drenching him. But finally, it closed.

He staggered and fell to his knees, panting. He probably ought to get out of here. Even if he was a dead man, it would be nice to see Jenn once more before he kicked the bucket. He really had been looking forward to spending sixty or seventy years with her.

He pulled his broken body up the wall painfully and stumbled toward the stairs. One step at a time. Just one step.

Jennifer could hardly see through her tears as she and Brady ran for the ops center.

"This way, Jennifer." Brady guided her to the elevator that would dump them out at Pirate Pete's mail delivery service. It was a little-used emergency exit from the facility, but it earned its keep this day.

She stumbled out of the elevator and into the funky storefront. They stepped onto the beach. Chaos was the only word to describe the scene. In the flickering light of tiki torches, boats of every size and description were either pulling away from the pier or waiting to approach it and pick up passengers. Men, women and children milled around in consternation in the darkness while soldiers from H.O.T. Watch herded them into rough lines to board the boats.

"They've got to hurry," she mumbled to Brady. "The leak will happen as soon as the radioactive steam melts the ducting."

Brady nodded grimly and moved away to impress upon his men the urgency of getting everyone off the island *now*.

Jennifer sat down on the front steps of Pirate Pete's and just stared. So, this was what the end of a dream looked like. Everything she knew and loved was going up in smoke before her, and there wasn't a damned thing she could do about it.

It dawned on her that she was just sitting here, staring at her toes when there was work to be done. Her heart might be broken into a million pieces, but she'd never been the kind of woman who simply gave up. She'd keep fighting to the end. She owed that much to Jeff.

The thought of him made a sob tear at her chest. But she pushed to her feet, anyway, and dived into helping board refugees.

It took nearly an hour, but finally, the last of the civilians were off the island, and most of the soldiers, as well. Brady came over to her, looking nearly as haggard as she felt.

"Any sign of him?"

"Not yet."

"Last boat's getting ready to board."

"I'll stay," she declared.

"Jennifer. You can't. If he didn't get that valve closed, you'll die from the radiation."

"He said he'd come back to me."

Brady wrapped her in a hug, but she remained rigid against him, refusing to accept his comfort. "It's time, Jenn. You have to let him go."

"I can't. *I can't!*"

"I know it hurts. But you have to come away. It's what he would want."

She just couldn't do it. She tore out of Brady's arms and ran, stumbling through the heavy sand, back to Pistol Pete's. Behind her she heard one of Brady's men shout something about being ready to cast off. Brady yelled something back, but she didn't hear his words.

She tore inside Pirate Pete's and headed for the storeroom which hid the elevator. She jammed the button that would open the door. Odd. The door didn't slide open. Either it wasn't working…or the elevator was downstairs…which meant someone had called for it.

She heard Brady shouting for her outside but ignored him, frantically staring at the elevator door. "Don't you give up on me, Jeff Winston," she raged at the door. "You walk out of there right now!"

A whooshing sound startled her. With a slight pop, the elevator door slid open. At first she didn't see anyone. But then she spied Jeff lying in a heap on the floor. She bolted forward. He was alive, but barely. And he was unconscious.

There was no way she could pick him up by herself, adrenaline burst or no.

"Brady!" she shouted at the top of her lungs. "Help me!"

Not only did Brady careen into the storeroom, but a half dozen of his men came with him. They must have been coming to pick her up bodily and carry her down to the boat. Well, they could carry Jeff instead.

"Pick him up," Brady ordered.

"Carefully," she added frantically. The special forces soldiers grunted in surprise as they hoisted Jeff between them and hustled him outside. Jennifer hovered beside them as they jogged down to the pier with Jeff and boarded a rigid inflatable boat. The vessel pushed away from shore.

"Give me your phone," she demanded of Brady. He passed her his cell phone without comment and watched as she quickly dialed a number.

"Gemma, it's Jennifer. I need you to get to Kingston, Jamaica, as fast as you can with everything you've got to treat severe radiation poisoning. I'll be there with Jeff in two hours."

And they were the longest two hours of her life. Jeff never regained consciousness. The special forces medic on the boat cleaned and bandaged Jeff's gunshot wound and set his broken collarbone. The guy also fixed Jeff's dislocated shoulder and set up an IV drip to push fluids and painkillers into Jeff. But that was all they could do for him.

The hospital in Kingston added potassium iodide to the IV drip to protect his thyroid from the radiation. But the doctors were grim and uncommunicative after they finished testing Jeff with radiation dosimeters that went black when pressed against his skin.

Gemma and Leland arrived sometime after sunrise. Time had ceased to have any meaning for Jennifer as she waited for

Jeff to wake up. He'd said he would come back to her. And he wouldn't break his promise. He *would* wake up.

After a quick conference with his doctors, Gemma stepped into the room with her and stood quietly on the other side of Jeff's bed. "Jennifer, I have to ask you something."

She looked up in surprise. The doctor's voice was surprisingly gentle.

"The good news is Jeff's body mass allowed him to absorb more radiation than most people could survive. The bad news is the radiation has destroyed most of his bone marrow."

Jennifer pressed a hand over her mouth. That was not good. "Is he going to die?" she whispered.

Gemma frowned. "We can try a bone marrow transplant. Leland's a match and has volunteered to donate marrow for him."

Jennifer heard the "or" in the doctor's voice. "What's the other choice?"

"I can give Jeff megadoses of the stem cell medication he's already been using. It ought to grow new marrow for him."

"But?" she asked cautiously.

"But after such large doses of the medicine, the changes to Jeff's bones will likely be permanent. It has always been my premise that we would stop this experiment when we'd collected enough data on it, and that my test subjects' bodies would return to normal in time."

Jennifer frowned. "Why are you asking me this? Shouldn't you be talking to Leland as Jeff's next of kin?"

"Leland said I should leave the choice to you. It's what Jeff would want. He loves you, you know. Intends to marry you."

A sob threatened to escape Jennifer's chest, but she fought it back. "Which option gives Jeff the best chance of surviving?"

Gemma shrugged. "They're about a wash. Either way, Jeff's in for a fight."

Jennifer stared down at him. His smooth face offered her no clues as to which option she should choose. She glanced up at Gemma. The doctor was equally impassive.

Dammit, she made life and death choices all the time in her work. This was no different. Weigh the merits and drawbacks, calculate which option offered the best chance of mission success, make the call and don't look back.

Except this was Jeff. And she had to choose between giving him the normal life that she wanted for him or the enhanced life she knew he wanted…along with all the dangers and unknowns of that life.

It was no choice at all. She knew what she had to do.

Chapter 18

Jeff squinted against the glare of a painfully bright light.

"Jeff? Can you hear me? Can you open your eyes?"

He blinked his eyes open and smiled—or at least tried to smile—at the sight of Jennifer leaning down close to him. Her hand was warm and strong gripping his. Her hair fell down around him like a sable curtain and blocked out the worst of the glare.

"Hey." It came out a harsh whisper.

There was a flurry of activity as Jennifer shouted that he was awake and a raft of doctors and nurses swept in to poke and prod at him, foremost among them, Gemma Jones. That woman had a sadistic streak a mile wide.

He rasped up at her, "Am I gonna live?"

"In spite of your best efforts to nuke yourself until you glow, yes."

"People make it? Off the island?"

"Yes. And the nuclear reactor is fine. You contained most

of the steam and there was only a small release of radiation. Nothing dangerous to anyone but you."

He smiled as Jennifer elbowed the doctor aside. She looked anxious as she took his hand again. He tried to give it a reassuring squeeze but was stunned at how weak he was. "How long have I been out?"

"Almost two weeks."

Wow. "Did I scream again?"

Jennifer smiled in warm communication with him. "Nope. No pain this time. We just had to regrow you a whole bunch of bone marrow."

He frowned. "How?"

"Gemma's miracle drugs. She injected your stem cells into your bones, and sure enough, they're regenerating new bone marrow for you. Thing is…" Her voice trailed off.

"What?" he asked in alarm, looking back and forth between the two women. He was further alarmed when Gemma quickly herded the medical staff out of the room and left him and Jennifer alone.

"What the hell's going on, Jenn?"

She took a deep breath. "I had to choose. A bone marrow transplant from Leland or the drugs. They made me choose. Gemma had to use massive doses of the stem cells on you. She thinks the changes to your bones are permanent. I hope you don't mind being a superhero for the rest of your life."

She'd chosen the drugs for him? She had known what he would want, and she'd set aside her own desires for him? If he'd loved her before, he positively worshipped her now.

He must have come pretty close to dying to put those dark circles under her eyes. One thing was for sure. Life was too short and too uncertain to waste a single minute of it. "Jennifer, I can't exactly get down on one knee at the moment, and I don't have a diamond ring at hand—although I promise to buy you an enormous one—but will you marry me?"

She stared down at him and her hand clenched his convulsively.

When she didn't answer he added in desperation, "I love you with all my heart. I have no idea what the future will hold for me, particularly in light of my new physical status. But I'd give anything to spend it with you, come what may."

"Come what may," she repeated softly.

"Is that a yes?" he asked cautiously.

"For better or worse, in sickness and in health," she said reflectively.

"That *is* a yes, isn't it?" he demanded.

"Yes, Jeff. Oh, yes. Count me in. I wouldn't miss this ride for anything in the world."

She leaned down to kiss him, and he found the strength to raise his left arm and pull her even closer against him. For her, he'd always find the strength. She was his wellspring. His life. His one true love. With her at his side, they could accomplish anything. She was what made him a superhero.

He murmured against her lips, "If you're going to be my sidekick, you need a cool nickname."

"How about Mrs. Winston?"

"That's perfect."

Perfect, indeed.

* * * * *

Captain John Murdock, USMC, Retired, with the strong hands and gruff sarcasm, was all male, all muscle and a mystery to her.

Maggie's mind replayed every moment of that encounter with her new neighbor. She could still hear the deep voice demanding she do the right thing despite her fears—still feel the big hands that had accidentally warmed her and made her feel unexpectedly secure when he'd clasped her fingers. She could easily recall her gratitude that he'd spoken kindly to her chatty son even though she'd done nothing to encourage any type of conversation. John Murdock was bigger and stronger than her in every way.

She should be afraid of a man like that.

And yet she'd run to him for answers and assurances.

But blindly trusting a man like that was a mistake she couldn't afford to repeat. Was she a fool to believe the military cut of his golden-brown hair and proud carriage of his shoulders meant he was a man who'd defend her?

THE MARINE
NEXT DOOR

BY
JULIE MILLER

Julie Miller attributes her passion for writing romance to all those fairy tales she read growing up, and to shyness. Encouragement from her family to write down all those feelings she couldn't express became a love for the written word. She gets continued support from her fellow members of the Prairieland Romance Writers, where she serves as the resident "grammar goddess." This award-winning author and teacher has published several paranormal romances. Inspired by the likes of Agatha Christie and Encyclopedia Brown, Ms Miller believes the only thing better than a good mystery is a good romance.

Born and raised in Missouri, she now lives in Nebraska with her husband, son and smiling guard dog, Maxie.Write to Julie at PO Box 5162, Grand Island, NE 68802-5162, USA.

Prologue

"Maybe there won't be a wedding!"

"How can you say that?"

Hidden by the trash bins where he'd been working after regular customer hours, the man lingered in the shadows outside the Fairy Tale Bridal Shop near downtown Kansas City and watched as the back door swung open and the young couple stormed out into the parking lot.

An older woman, her hair gleaming like brass in the illumination of the trendy neighborhood's wrought-iron lights, hurried after them. "You ungrateful little girl."

"Please." The shopkeeper following behind her tried to intervene but wasn't assertive enough to be paid any heed. "You shouldn't be making big decisions right now—"

"No, Mother." The young woman whirled around and he caught his breath. She was so classically beautiful. So perfect. So like… *No, don't go there.* "It's young *woman. Grown* woman. Not *little girl.* You can't force this on me. It's too big. Too much. I don't want this."

"You still want *me,* right?" The tall man in the tailored suit reached for her.

She shrugged off his touch with an unladylike grunt and no answer.

"Sweetheart." The tall man smiled and clasped his hands around her shoulders, trying to soothe her temper.

"Let's go to our dinner reservation and use the time to cool off. It's been a long day."

"I'm not hungry." She shook him off.

The man in the shadows smiled beneath the mask he wore over his nose and mouth. That one had fire. An insidious awareness of her feminine strength licked through his veins and made him clench his fist around the bag he carried.

"Then let me drive you home. We'll talk."

"No!" The young beauty spun around and stamped her high heels toward the sidewalk that ran along the street. "I'll catch a cab."

"Sweetheart?"

"She really shouldn't—"

When the young man and mousy shopkeeper moved to follow, the mother stopped them both. "Don't bother. She's been like this for weeks now. I'll try to talk some sense into her when she gets home."

Seriously? They were letting her march off by herself? Not that this was as dangerous a neighborhood as it had once been now that buildings were being renovated and new shops and young professionals were moving in. And the Shamrock Bar just a couple of blocks over, where a good cross-section of KCPD cops liked to hang out after hours, offered some degree of crime deterrence. Still, a woman alone, brave enough to face the city at night—too upset to be truly aware of her surroundings…

The man glanced up. The last vestiges of graying twilight were giving way to stars and a dim crescent moon. Night was falling, and it would be a dark one. Traffic was light between the race of rush hour and the incoming surge of the city's nightlife.

She wouldn't find that cab anytime soon.

The forgettable woman went back into her shop. With

a silent nudge, the bossy mother and groom-to-be climbed into their car.

His pulse raced in anticipation at the opportunity at hand. The shop door locked. The car drove off. It would be so easy. It had been so long.

"Don't." A voice of reason inside his head tried to warn him off the impulse heating his blood. *"You don't need this anymore. You're better than this."*

But he wanted. Hungered.

And she was all alone.

He dropped his bag to unzip his jacket and reach inside his pocket. Everything he needed was in his vehicle. It would be so easy.

"I told you to get rid of those things. Don't think this way. Stop."

But he'd done without for so long, he'd been so good. Still, the rage burned inside him every time he thought of…her.

And the hurt. The humiliation.

It wasn't his fault. She couldn't do this to him. Not again. He wouldn't let her. He needed her to pay. He needed to take back all she'd stolen from him.

"It's not the same. You're confused."

"Shut up," he muttered, feeling his own hot breath moisten the fibers of the mask he wore.

He moved from the shadows to peek around the corner of the brick building. The street was practically empty. Storefronts were dark. The apartments above them were far removed from a world that was quickly shrinking to the quick, purposeful strides of the blonde woman and his own raging need.

Sliding his hand into his pocket, he turned off his phone, in case someone called and distracted him. In case someone thought they could track him down. This was just him and the woman now.

"Stop. She isn't worth it," the voice argued.

But the white-hot haze inside his brain wasn't listening. He ran to his vehicle and started the engine. He looked to the right, to the left, then pulled out of his parking space.

And even though the sun had set, he put on his dark glasses and followed her up the street.

Chapter One

I want to see you.

KCPD desk sergeant Maggie Wheeler had never seen an uglier flower. Not that there was a thing wrong with the cultivated shape and color of the pink spring tulip or the matching ribbon and tall bud vase.

But the florist's card burned her fingertips, and everything the flower that had once been her favorite represented stirred like a swarm of angry bees in her stomach. She breathed a measured sigh between tight lips. Why couldn't the past just stay buried in the past?

If the young man who'd delivered the gift hadn't already disappeared, she'd have sent it back to be delivered to a hospital or nursing home where the tulip and baby's breath could be appreciated. But because that option had left the building, she had no choice but to drop the whole thing into the trash at the end of the counter and empty out the shavings from the front desk pencil sharpener on top of it. She wadded up the card and tossed it in for good measure, too.

"Maggie." Fourth Precinct chief Mitch Taylor tapped the counter as he strode by, then flicked his finger toward the bank of meeting rooms on the far side of the maze of detectives' desks that filled the main floor. "You're with me. Bring your computer and sit in on this meeting."

Maggie shot up to attention, as startled by the order as
she was by the interruption. "Me, sir?"

The chief turned and winked, walking backward without slowing his pace. "If you want to see how a task force
works, get in here and take notes for me."

"Yes, sir."

She didn't wait to be asked twice.

The flower was forgotten as Maggie grabbed her laptop
off her counter, made sure Officer Allen could cover her
station at the front desk, and hurried down the hallway
after Chief Taylor. She followed him through the door into
Interview Room A and quickly slid into the closest empty
seat around the long conference table.

She was used to handling odd jobs around the precinct
office, but anticipation had her perched on the edge of her
chair. Her gun and badge were just as real as the other
hardware in the room. And even though her expertise was
paper pushing and patience, she was more than ready to
move up in both pay scale and prestige at the police department. At thirty-five, she might wind up being the oldest
rookie detective on the force, but she'd finally earned her
college degree. She was ready to take on investigative
work, ready to take the professional rank test and do the
interviews to earn her detective's shield. A little casework
experience, even vicariously tagging along at the inaugu-
ral meeting of KCPD's new major crime task force, would
look good on her résumé when she put in for the promotion.

Per the chief's specific request, she'd notified each of
the law enforcement professionals gathered here this morning. Detectives. A police psychologist. Uniformed officers
like herself. A representative from the crime lab.

You deserve to be here, she reminded herself. It had
taken her a long time to feel like she was worthy of any-

thing good or exciting in her life. Sometimes, a new situation like this one could still make her flash back to that awful time when she hadn't believed in herself—when she hadn't even thought she'd survive.

But she believed now. She was here for herself. Here for her ten-year-old son, Travis, and their future. She was in this room because Chief Taylor believed she should be.

Letting those positive thoughts drown out the unsettled worry over the message and flower she'd received, Maggie wiped the perspiration from her palms on the navy twill of her pant leg, steadied her nerves with a quiet breath and opened her laptop. All right, so maybe she was just here as a glorified stenographer to take notes, but her pulse still raced. This was the kind of work she wanted to do. Not just man a desk and be the smiling, efficient, nonthreatening face of KCPD that most citizens saw when they came into the building.

Maggie knew Chief Taylor had a soft spot for her. She'd served in his precinct back when he'd been the newly appointed captain of the first watch. Now he was running the show. She'd lost a little girl, given birth to a son, gotten divorced and worked her butt off to maintain a full-time job to support her child while she'd taken classes to earn the degree her ex had once denied her. The chief understood how badly she wanted that promotion and had no doubt invited her to sit in on this meeting to give her some real experience and a taste of where she wanted her career to go.

She was expecting formal introductions, maybe some kind of pep talk to get them fired up for a particular project. At the very least, she expected Chief Taylor to spell out the new team's purpose and why the commissioner had charged him with the job of selecting a task force for a special investigation.

She wasn't expecting the terse greeting from her barrel-chested boss when he reached the head of the table. "He's back."

He followed up the cryptic pronouncement by slapping a file folder on top of the table.

Even from the opposite end of the room, she could see the crime scene photos that spilled out. She could make out a woman's blond hair and a puffy, bruised face. She could see a lot of crimson on those photographs. Blood.

Nick Fensom, the stocky, dark-haired detective sitting closest to Chief Taylor pulled the folder in front of him and opened it. "The Rose Red Rapist?"

"That's right."

Maggie's stomach knotted beneath her thick leather belt and her gaze darted up to the chief's brown eyes, questioning him. Maybe his invitation to sit in on the meeting hadn't been an impromptu gesture of kindness after all. She'd once been in photos like that.

But Chief Taylor wasn't even looking at her. What if she had a unique understanding of that victim's emotions—shock, betrayal, pain, rage, fear, distrust? That didn't mean the chief had an ulterior motive for inviting her to the meeting. A decade had passed since that horrific time, and she'd put it behind her to focus on the present and future. She was simply overreacting to a gruesome coincidence. She was a cop. A future detective. A fast typist.

Not a sacrificial lamb lured into the room to be probed and profiled by the others at the table. *Get a grip, Sarge.*

Maggie's nostrils flared as she eased the prickly instinct to defend herself on a deep, quiet breath, and dropped her gaze to the screen in front of her. While that feverish impulse to guard against any sort of attack dissipated through the pores of her freckled skin, she concentrated on typing in the names and initial comments of everyone in the room.

Chief Taylor spelled out the details included in the file. "Same M.O. as that unsolved serial rapist case we worked a few years back. Blitz attack. Threat of a weapon once the victim is conscious. None of the victims have been found at the actual scene where the rape occurred, although how they're moved from one place to another isn't always clear. We've got nothing but the vaguest of descriptions of our perp. Male. Tall. There's not even a consensus on his race. He wears gloves and a mask. None of them have seen his face although this most recent victim has some other identifiers that might give us a lead."

"Other identifiers?" Detective Spencer Montgomery, whose short red hair had occasionally earned a question about whether he and Maggie were siblings—other than her son, Maggie had no relatives in the Kansas City area—sat across from his partner, Nick Fensom. Detective Montgomery adjusted his tie and leaned forward. Glancing around the room, she could see he was the senior detective, and his cool and confident demeanor reflected that status. "Such as?"

"His voice."

"Voices can be altered," Montgomery pointed out.

"Smells," the chief countered. "She thought she detected something chemical."

"That's pretty vague." Detective Montgomery wasn't easily convinced.

A dark-haired woman, wearing a CSI windbreaker and sipping something from a stainless-steel travel mug, introduced herself as Annie Hermann, the task force's liaison with the crime lab. "If we can identify the chemical or compound the vic smelled, then that could be a significant clue. It might give us the perp's profession or a medical condition. Or tell us something about his vehicle."

Detective Fensom shot CSI Hermann a look across the table and shook his head. "The perp leaves a red rose with each of his vics. It's probably fertilizer or preservative from the florist's shop."

The petite Annie Hermann straightened in her chair. "Then maybe he works with flowers. The back of a florist's van would be the perfect place to hide a body. The lab is running tests right now to isolate and eliminate any chemicals absorbed by the rose."

Maggie continued to type. Analyzing a rose? Would an analysis of the tulip she'd just trashed reveal the motive behind the anonymous gift? Not that she had any doubt as to the sender and the seeming innocence of his request.

"It's a viable clue," Annie Hermann insisted.

"We'll see." Detective Fensom rocked back in his chair, unconvinced.

The CSI poked the tabletop with her finger. "Science gives us facts. It eliminates false leads and solves cases."

"Not without any context to put those facts in. Cops solve cases. I'll bet my gut has led to more arrests than your science."

"Back to your corners, you two." Chief Taylor silenced the debate. "The perp's smell isn't much to go on, but it's a lead. Hermann, I want you to follow up on it." He turned to the dark-haired detective. "And, Nick, I want you to use that gut to lead you to anyone on the streets who can tell us about this guy or these abductions. Anything is more than we've got right now."

"Yes, sir, Chief."

"Yes, sir."

As the detective and the CSI settled back in their chairs, Maggie typed in the information, ignoring the crawl of memories over her skin beneath her uniform. Smell was indeed a vivid identifier because it left such an impression on the senses. Some of the most indelible memories she had from that hellish weekend her ex had gone off the deep end were of the smells—blood, booze, smoke, sweat—and the flowers he'd given her afterward. And to this day she would not use scented fabric softener or scented detergent in the laundry because of the memories that particular fresh smell evoked.

She nodded in silent approval of the victim's power of observation. If she could identify her attacker by whatever scent was uniquely his, then the task force had a good shot at nailing him.

Provided they could catch him first.

Detective Fensom grumbled as he gathered up the photos. "What's with the rose, anyway? It's as though he thinks that hint of romance makes it an act of passion instead of violence." He shoved the folder onto the blond woman in an elegant suit sitting beside him.

Dr. Kate Kilpatrick was more interested in skimming through the transcript of the report from the investigators who'd originally handled the case. Although Maggie had received counseling from the police psychologist years earlier, she'd never known Dr. Kilpatrick to work actively on an investigation before. "Maybe it's a sign of remorse?"

"More like a sick memorial for everything he's taken from her." Edison Taylor was the only other uniformed officer at the table. But the patch on the short sleeve encircling his biceps indicated he was a specially trained K-9 cop. "I thought he was off the streets, Uncle Mitch. What's it been? Eight—"

"Ten years, Pike," the chief answered, using a nickname that Maggie knew referred to the surname Edison had before he'd been adopted into the Taylor family as a young teen. "Either he went away to prison for some other crime and now he's back on the streets, or we've got us a nasty copycat."

"So why exactly am I here?" Pike asked. "I'm not an investigator, a profiler or a lab tech."

"I'm counting on you and your unit to provide extra security around the crime scenes. Run searches for us and so on."

Dr. Kilpatrick nodded. "Everything I've read so far on the case indicates our perp is someone who blends into the community well. His victims appear to be unfortunate targets of opportunity. Yet no one seems to notice anything suspicious, much less feel threatened, before the attacks. It would make sense that he'd also be around after the fact, perhaps reliving the assault by watching the neighborhood and police response to his crimes."

"Flying under the radar the entire time," Chief Taylor continued. "The commissioner and I agree that stepping up patrols all across the city might drive our perp underground and create an unnecessary panic. If this is the same guy from before, he'll stick to a part of Kansas City he knows. I want to narrow down the area where he hunts for his victims and use your unit and the dogs to keep a close watch in the neighborhood where he's most likely to strike again."

"And that would be?"

"Right now we're looking at Irish Town and the City Market district. There are a lot of new businesses, renovated offices and apartment buildings there. Plenty of women live or work there, or travel in and out to shop and socialize. That's where he abducted his latest victim." He circled the table to scan the file for the info he needed. "She was abducted just after an appointment at the Fairy Tale Bridal Shop."

"I know the area well enough." The blue-eyed officer reached down and scratched between the ears of the muscular German shepherd stretched out at his feet. "Hans and I will be ready."

Mitch Taylor returned to his chair at the head of the table. "Maggie?"

"Sir?" She snapped to when the chief called her name, forcing herself to interact instead of just recording information.

"I want you on the computer getting me the name of every violent offender whose prison term fits the time frame for when our perp was missing in action. The conviction doesn't have to be rape. Look for physical assaults, armed robberies."

"Specifically, crimes against women," Dr. Kilpatrick clarified. "This guy is all about power. Either he's punishing his victims for some perceived wrong done to him by a woman, or he's compensating for a real or self-perceived weakness—and women are easier for him to control. He feels stronger, more masculine, by putting someone else down."

"He could just be some sexual deviant nut job," Fensom groused.

"Possibly," the doctor conceded. "As I recall, there's no real pattern to his victim type. He's assaulted a Black woman, an Asian, blondes, brunettes. There has to be something that ties these women together—that makes them his type."

Okay, support. Tech support. Maggie wasn't the best-trained person when it came to researching through the KCPD database, but she was a fast learner. "I can do that. Look for men recently released from prison convicted of crimes against women."

She could already name at least one suspect who fit the

description without typing in a single keystroke. And she'd tossed his gift into the trash.

Annie Hermann had a different idea. "You know, some sickos can suppress their urges for a while. Or maybe the crimes just haven't been reported."

Despite the subtle tension between Annie and Detective Fensom, the chief thought her idea had merit. "It's possible he took his game to some other town and now he's back."

Maggie raised her gaze to the chief's and put forth an idea of her own. "I'll access the FBI's database and run a nationwide scan for any reports that match our perp's M.O."

"Better make that international," Spencer Montgomery suggested. "Our guy could have been way off the grid."

Maggie opened up a note pad on her screen and jotted down the task. She scooted the case file with the haunting photos around the table while she typed.

Chief Taylor pulled back the front of his suit jacket and propped his hands at his waist. "I know all the scenarios to explain why he's back in KC, doing this sick stuff to women. I want to know how we stop him."

"Is this…" Annie set down her drink and pulled an 8 x 10 of the latest victim from the file.

"Bailey Austin." Spencer Montgomery plucked the photo from her hand, perhaps looking at it a little longer than necessary for simple identification before picking up the folder and sliding it back inside. But he was a hard man to read, and maybe Maggie had only imagined the hesitation regarding the victim's picture. "It doesn't help that his first victim out of the block is the stepdaughter of one of the wealthiest men in Kansas City. Her stepdaddy, Jackson Mayweather, will do whatever it takes to protect his family. That could generate a lot of press we don't want."

"And makes us look bad that he's still on the street," his partner added. "That has to feed this perp's power trip."

Chief Taylor nodded. "I've already gotten a call this morning from Mr. Mayweather, after he talked to the commissioner. He's agreed to use discretion and defer to us, at least until we get our investigation under way."

"Is Miss Austin okay?" Montgomery asked.

"Look at the pictures," Annie said. "She was brutalized."

"I'm asking, did she survive? Is she alive? Coherent?" Maybe Maggie had only imagined an emotional reaction from Detective Montgomery because he cleared his throat and his tone became every bit as clipped and clinical as a scientist discussing his research. "I'd like to question her—as soon as Dr. Kilpatrick here thinks she can handle it. If we can't talk to a suspect, the next best thing is talking with the vic. If we could get a grasp on what she was thinking and doing that made her pop up as a target for this bastard, that might give us a lead to track him down."

Dr. Kilpatrick held the detective's gaze across the table. "I'd suggest sending an interrogator with a little more tact and compassion than you, Spencer."

"I get the job done," he argued.

The police psychologist was unfazed by the chill in his tone. "Whoever interviews the women who were attacked needs to understand their victimology. Rape victims require an intuition, an empathy, even, to get them to communicate. You may be dealing with anger, extreme distrust, fear of reprisals. They could be shut down and unreachable. Research indicates that some women even feel they deserved the attack, and won't cooperate with police to catch their rapist."

Nick Fensom swore beneath his breath. "Nobody deserves what happened to her."

Kate Kilpatrick nodded. "Unless you've been through that, though, it's difficult to understand the victimology."

The letter *k* repeated in row after row on the computer screen as Maggie's fingers stilled on her keyboard. Chief Taylor hadn't asked her into the meeting just to take notes after all. She was certain of it.

Detectives, a police psychologist, a crime lab liaison and a security expert. Their presence on the task force made sense. Now she understood that her presence here made sense, too.

Maggie knew what it was like to be a rape victim better than anyone else sitting at this table, as far as she was aware. She'd long ago locked down that part of her life and moved on the best she could to raise her son and provide a healthy, normal existence for them both. But if she could help Bailey Austin recover from her attack—if she could get the other victims to talk or offer some unique insight that could prevent the Rose Red Rapist from striking again…then maybe it was time to for her to unlock that terrible expertise.

Her attacker had been a free man for precisely forty-three days now. And even though a court order legally prevented Maggie from ever having to deal with her ex-husband again, she'd awakened every morning and fallen asleep each night for the past forty-three days, wondering if this was the day Danny Wheeler would return and finish what he'd started ten years earlier. The tulip this morning told her she'd been right to worry. She knew how frightened Bailey Austin was feeling right now—how wary and exposed and unable to trust she'd be until the bastard who'd raped her was put behind bars.

Maggie Wheeler understood victimology. Chief Taylor was a smarter man than he sometimes let on. He'd known

exactly what he was doing when he'd asked her to join this
meeting. Some favor.

"I'll let you all work out the details." He was wrapping
up the meeting. "Montgomery's running this show, but I
want a daily report. Anything you need, don't wait and go
through channels if there's any kind of delay. You need a
warrant, you need to talk to another division, you need
access to sealed records—whatever it might be—you come
to me and I'll expedite the request. As of now, this investigation is priority one." Maggie deleted all the extra letters
and saved her notes, working up the courage to raise her
hand and interrupt. "I have a wife and a daughter. I want
this bastard off the streets."

The answering chorus of "Yes, sirs" told her the meeting had ended. People were breaking into smaller dis-
cussions. Pike Taylor urged his dog to its feet. The chief
opened the door and was leaving the room.

Do it. Ten years of recovery and a hard-won independence urged Maggie to rise to her feet. One gift from her
ex wasn't going to intimidate her into sitting on her hands
and allowing another woman to be hurt. She had a unique
skill that no one else in this room could bring to the table.
She breathed in deeply and made her decision. Men like
her ex-husband and the Rose Red Rapist didn't get to ter-
rorize the women of Kansas City. Not when she could do
something to help stop them.

"Do it," she whispered to herself, closing her laptop and
hurrying after Chief Taylor. She caught up to him in the
hallway just outside his executive assistant's office. "Chief,
could I talk to you a minute?"

He pulled back his sleeve and checked his watch before
offering her half a smile. "I was hoping I'd pique your
interest." He nodded to the woman at the desk in his

outer office as he ushered Maggie through to his office. "Brooke, hold my calls."

"Right, Mitch." Brooke Kincaid, probably Maggie's best friend here at Fourth Precinct headquarters, mouthed a question to Maggie. *Are you okay?*

Maggie nodded, trading a thumbs-up sign with her friend, even though she was certain she looked pale as a ghost. She had to do this. She needed to be a part of this team.

Chief Taylor closed his office door and gestured to a seat on the near side of his massive walnut desk. "I know you don't have investigative experience yet, Maggie. But I also know how much you want to make detective. I hate to lose the efficiency you bring to running the front desk, but I think you could be an asset to the team. You'd be invaluable talking to the victims." His leather chair creaked as it took his weight. "I don't want to force you because I know it's a personal subject for you, but—"

"You don't have to give me a sales speech, sir," Maggie assured him. "You know my history with Danny. And I know that's why you asked me to join that meeting."

A much younger Mitch Taylor had been the arresting officer when her ex had finally answered for his violence against her. "I didn't want to give you too much time to think about it. I figured you might talk yourself out of helping."

"If you want someone who understands the victimology of the women the Rose Red Rapist preys on, I'm… qualified."

"You're sure? This could bring up some painful memories." He braced his elbows on the desk and leaned toward her. "And I won't lie to you—Danny has been out of prison a couple of months now, hasn't he? This has to be a particularly trying time for you. Nothing about this investigation will be easy."

She should have known a cop as experienced and on-the-ball as Mitch Taylor would be aware of her ex-husband's release from prison. Maybe he even considered her ex a person of interest because Danny Wheeler's time locked up in Jefferson City roughly matched the gap in the Rose Red Rapist attacks. She didn't know whether Danny would target any other woman except her, but then she hadn't known the extent of the violence he was capable of when she'd married him either.

"I want to do this, Mitch." This was her chance to prove to Chief Taylor that she was not only ready, but that she also deserved to make detective. It was also her chance to prove to herself that she truly had moved beyond the past that had once shadowed every aspect of her life. She was a fighter. A mother. A cop. A college graduate. She was nobody's victim anymore. "Some things, no matter how difficult they are, are worth doing. I want to fight for these women—be their advocate if I can. I want to join your task force."

Chapter Two

This was getting old.

John Murdock's thick arms and thighs flexed easily as he lifted two more boxes of books from the back of his pickup and shut the tailgate. But his right knee ached, and shards of phantom pain radiated down into his ankle and foot. He'd been at this all day—long enough for the sun to go down outside—packing, carrying, unpacking, hauling some more. Even though he'd made the trip several times already without incident, habit had him checking the cars on either side of him, and behind each crumbling brick-encased support pillar as he limped across the cracked concrete of the parking garage below his building.

He wondered how long the pain that wasn't really there would stay with him—possibly the rest of his life according to many of the doctors and therapists who'd worked on him. He wondered how long it would take before it stopped feeling like he was just going through the motions expected of him by *civilized* society, and he truly felt like he was home. He was getting used to the quizzical looks from strangers, setting him apart because they viewed him as some kind of hero or they felt sorry for him. Either option set his teeth on edge and made it hard to interact without second-guessing every word or gesture directed his way.

He wondered when he'd feel like celebrating surviving

his last tour of duty in Afghanistan, when he'd feel like un-packing his Purple Heart, Silver Star and other medals and deployment ribbons. He wondered when he'd be ready for a beer with old friends or facing the job—and the woman he loved but could never have—that he'd left behind. It didn't matter that he'd lived his whole life in Kansas City before reupping with the Corps. He felt like a stranger in his own town, with his own things, inside his own skin.

He'd left a part of himself behind on that roadside in Afghanistan. In more ways than one.

Returning to the Corps was supposed to have been a fresh start for him—coming home after his stint was up, the beginning of a brand-new chapter in his life. Yet he felt stuck, like nothing had changed. He'd loved the wrong woman, raised a sister who no longer needed him, given his spleen and a good part of his right leg, a couple of friends and half of his soul to the enemy he'd gone to fight.

Inside, he was still a long way from coming home.

Adding boxes of books and kitchen supplies, along with a few civilian clothes, to the boring beige of his furnished apartment didn't do much to make this feel like a home-coming. But it got him out of the spare bedroom at his sis-ter's place so she could sell it and get on with marrying her fiancé. And, it was mindless exercise that tired him out and didn't require much thought. Right now it was enough to feel less like a burden and to look forward to a decent night's sleep.

John slowed when he heard footsteps ahead of him. Two sets of footfalls on the far side of that last pillar. He was a big enough man that it'd take a pretty bold mugger to come after him. But size alone wasn't a deterrent if the perps were hyped up on some kind of drug or they took a closer look at his disability and mistook him for an easy mark—if there was a mugger at all.

Running into normal, everyday people who expected normal, everyday conversation out of him was almost more daunting than facing someone who wanted to hurt him. He'd been in survival mode for over a year now, and adjusting to *normal* was taking just as long as the psychologist who'd debriefed him when he'd mustered out had said it would.

The curve of a butt in navy blue slacks disappearing between the open doors of the garage's elevator almost made him stop in his tracks as he rounded the last pillar and passed the wall of junction boxes and access panels and fire emergency equipment. So the challenge would be normal, everyday civility if he got on that elevator. Would the woman who owned those curves notice the empty pant leg? Or the carbon-fiber composite rod sticking out of his boot? Would there be a slew of curious questions or politely stilted silence as she avoided eye contact with him? Maybe she'd just stare at the scars on his neck, arm and hand. A vein ticked along the column of his throat as the relative tranquility of being alone warred with his common sense.

Who knew how long he'd have to stand there holding the heavy boxes before his ride returned again? The Corsican might be rich in architectural history and renovation potential, but the building had just the one elevator that ran to all ten floors. He might as well start dealing with *normal, everyday* now rather than putting it off indefinitely.

"Hold the elevator," he called out, lengthening his stride.

The woman gasped. Maybe he'd just startled her. "Hurry up," she muttered—to her companion.

John bristled at the whispered slight. Were they trying to get away? Maybe she'd gotten a glimpse of him as well and wasn't thrilled about the idea of sharing the tiny space with him either. But if he could make the effort to be civil, then the woman attached to that backside could damn well do the same.

"Hold it," he ordered in a sharper tone. He heard a *"Mom,"* and then a slender, tanned arm shot out to catch the door as he slipped inside. He looked straight into a pair of emerald-green eyes, silently telling the woman that he knew she'd tried to leave him behind. "Thanks."

But when the doors closed and John retreated to the opposite corner to rest his boxes on the railing, he wondered if he'd made a tactical error. That verdant gaze, sparkling with defiance or warning or some other kind of intense emotion, followed him all the way to the back of the elevator before the woman blinked and turned away. Seeing her adjust her stance to position herself between him and the chestnut-haired boy with her made John wish he'd waited for the next ride up after all. *Nice to meet you, too.* He felt her wariness of him like a punch in the gut.

And he'd been worried about making small talk.

This woman meant business when it came to protecting her son from the big, bad strangers of the world. Despite the copper-colored hair twisted up in a bun at the nape of her neck, with a dozen fiery gold wisps popping loose to curl against her skin, she was no dainty female. She was tall, standing nearly six feet, judging by the mere five or six inches John topped her by when he normally towered over most women. She was in uniform and she was armed.

One hand rested on the butt of the GLOCK 9 mm holstered at her waist as she inched closer to the boy who was peeking at him from beneath the bill of his Royals baseball cap. John was pretty sure the protective-mama move was intentional when she turned so he could clearly see the

KCPD badge hanging from the chain beneath her starched collar.

"What floor?" she asked politely enough. But her green eyes darted as though they were assessing his height and width and the distance between them.

"Seventh."

"Travis." She squeezed the boy's shoulder beside the backpack he wore, drawing John's attention to the fact that her skin wasn't tanned so much as it was dotted with hundreds of freckles.

The boy, whom John put in the nine- to ten-year-old range, slipped his ball glove over the handle of the bat he carried before pushing the button and then twisting from his mother's grasp. "Do you live on the seventh floor?"

Well, at least someone in this elevator didn't think he was the spawn of the devil. "That's why I'm going there."

"We just came from baseball practice," the boy announced. "I play in the outfield, but I want to be the second baseman or shortstop. Do you like baseball?"

"Trav." The redhead chided her son in a soft tone that belied her tough-chick image. "What did I say about bothering people?"

"He's no bother, ma'am." Now where did that reassurance come from? He should have been happy she didn't want to talk to him.

The boy named Travis tilted his face up to John's, giving him a clear look at the inherited freckles sprinkled across his nose and cheeks. "I'm not supposed to talk to strangers, but Mom says I need to know all the neighbors on our floor in case she's not home and I need to go to a safe place. We're on the seventh, too. I'm Travis Wheeler."

Safe place? Although there were other eighty-year-old buildings on this block that were in the process of being reclaimed like this one, one of the reasons John had chosen this particular neighborhood was so that his sister could stop in for a visit whenever she wanted to. The fact that Miranda Murdock was a cop, like this woman, didn't matter. Big brothers looked out for their little sisters—even if she was engaged to a man who was just as protective of her as John.

This building was safe. The remodeled structure now surpassed fire codes and he'd been assured by the landlord that retired tenants and young professionals—not gnarly devil men who terrorized women and children—populated the place.

"I'm Captain—" *normal,* civilian *conversation, remember?* "—John Murdock. I work for the Kansas City Fire Department. Out of Station 23."

"You're a firefighter? Cool."

"Sorry." Mama clasped her hand over Travis's shoulder and pulled him back to her without sharing her name and completing the introductions. "You're new here?"

"Yes, ma'am. I've been deployed overseas or stationed in the DC area for a couple of years now. Moving in today." There he went, making a rusty effort to put her at ease.

"What apartment?"

"709."

"Mom, that's right next door to us."

"So it is." The smile for her son faded when she faced John again. "Don't worry, I'm not looking for babysitters. Travis won't be stopping by."

"I'm not a baby—"

"If he needs to—"

"He won't." John almost grinned at Travis's frustrated groan when his overprotective mama hugged her arm across his chest. "There are plenty of other tenants in the building we tru—"

Her gaze wavered and dropped to the middle of

John's dusty gray-green T-shirt where she could read the letters *USMC*.

Trust?

Yep, no need to worry about polite civility with this woman. He was free to be his moody, isolated self, as far as she was concerned.

So why did it bother him that she turned away to watch the buttons for each floor light up without making direct eye contact with him again?

"Can you play baseball with your leg like that?"

"Travis!"

Mama put her fingers over her son's mouth and John finally got the silence he'd thought he wanted until the elevator jerked, an alarm bell rang, and the whole car jolted to an unexpected stop. The redhead yelped as she tumbled into the back wall, but she caught her son and clung to the railing with a white-knuckled intensity, keeping both of them upright.

"What the hell?" John swayed on his feet, but the boxes anchored him into place. The light for the seventh floor was lit up above the door, but the doors didn't open. Beneath the blare of the alarm he listened for any sounds of cables and pulleys reengaging. He reached across the elevator and pounded the alarm button with his fist until it shut off. He tilted his face toward the trap door and machine works above them. Silence. Almost like the building's electricity had suddenly shut off. But why were the lights in the car still on if there was no power to the rest of the elevator? They were good and stuck. So much for life returning to normal. His gaze zeroed in on the ashen skin of the policewoman. "Does this happen often here?"

"Mom?" The kid tugged on the sleeve of his mother's uniform. A worried frown veed between the boy's eyes as he turned to John. "She's got a thing about elevators. She doesn't really like them."

"That's nonsense. I'm fine, sweetie." She cupped her son's face and flashed a smile for his benefit. But John wasn't buying it. Freckles there definitely had a phobia about something. Being trapped? Closed-in places? Fear of falling? "I've never gotten stuck in the elevator here before. But it's an old building. Stuff happens."

"It didn't happen on any of my other rides up and down from the garage."

Her glare told John that she didn't appreciate his pointing out that fact. "We just have to notify the super, Mr. Standage, that we're stuck, and he'll get things moving in no time." Assuming an air of nonchalance, probably to reassure the boy, she crossed to the rows of buttons and opened the emergency phone panel. Only, instead of pulling out the telephone, she dropped down in front of the opening. "There's no phone in here."

"What?"

"It's gone. There's nothing but wires."

"Let me see." John set the boxes of books on the floor and knelt in front of the panel beside her. He'd seen billiard balls ricochet across a pool table slower than the woman shot to the opposite corner of the car, pulling her son with her. So maybe *he* was what she was afraid of.

That didn't bode well for her staying calm in this crisis.

Drawing on years of training to keep victims or locals calm during a rescue attempt with KCFD or raid on insurgents overseas, John pushed aside any insult or guilt he might feel at her obvious aversion to him, and kept his voice as calm as he could make it. It was a little harder to control the jerky movements that might startle her as he pushed to his feet and locked his bum leg into place.

But the woman was wearing a KCPD uniform with ser-

geant's stripes on the sleeve. There had to be some training that she could draw on, too. "You have a cell phone on
you, Sarge?"

"Yes."

He remained by the door and simply spoke over the jut
of his shoulder to her. "If you've got Standage's number,
call him directly. If not, call 9-1-1 and ask for the fire department. They'll know how to deal with elevator emergencies."

She pulled her phone from the bag looped over her
shoulder and opened it to make the call. Good. "You said
you were with the fire department now. Do *you* know how
to get us out of here?"

"We'll find out what I can remember."

John wedged his big fingers into the slit between the
doors. He grunted with the strain on his forearms and
biceps until he created a gap wide enough to slide his
hands in all the way and get a better grip. "Let's see where
we are."

"Joe? This is Maggie Wheeler from 707. We're stuck on
the elevator. Are you working on the wiring? Or did the
power get cut somehow? Yes. There are three of us."

Once he could get his shoulders and body weight into
it, John pushed the doors all the way open and took a step
back to assess the concrete wall across from his feet. There
was a gap about a yard wide at the top that revealed a white
number 7 painted on a pair of outside elevator doors.

"Joe says he'll be right up," Maggie reported, stowing
her cell phone. "Of course, that means he'll be taking the
stairs, and with his arthritis, that could still be a while. Are
we between floors?"

"Yeah." John wasn't looking forward to spooking the
woman any further, but right now he was a little glad that
he'd gotten stuck in the elevator with the flame-haired

Amazon instead of someone more petite. He glanced back
to link up with those rich green eyes. "You got a name,
Sarge?"

She nodded. "Maggie."

"Maggie, can you reach those doors and help me open
them?"

After a moment's hesitation, she stepped up beside him.
Good. That was an old trick that still worked apparently.
Calling a person by his or her name got them to focus,
maybe even trust a little. Giving that person a specific job
to do was often the easiest way to distract her from her
fears.

Even though he felt her flinch when their hands brushed
against each other, she didn't hesitate to slide her fingers
between the doors and help pull them apart. Now they
were looking out onto the carpeted hallway of the seventh
floor. Weird. The only time he'd seen an elevator not align
with the exterior doors was when the power had been deliberately cut by firefighters battling a blaze.

John glanced up. But the damn light for the seventh
floor was still lit up. He wouldn't be able to see out into
the hallway if the lights were off there, too. What kind of
crazy wiring did they have in this place?

"What do we do now?" Sergeant Maggie asked.

John was all for getting off this carnival ride until he
could figure out just what the heck was going on. "Son?"
He turned back to Travis Wheeler. "Are you a climber?"

"Yes, sir."

"Careful," Maggie warned, understanding what John
was asking of her boy. "Shouldn't we wait?"

"Give me the bat and glove first," John instructed.
"Backpack, too." The boy handed over his prized possessions and John slid them through the opening onto the
eye-level floor above them. "Hold on a sec. So your mama

doesn't worry." He met the wary glare of deep green eyes as he picked up the two boxes of books and wedged one against either of the open doors. "That should buy us a few seconds in case anything happens."

"What could happen?" Maggie asked.

John nodded to her purse. "Call Standage back. Tell him not to touch or do anything until we give him the all clear. We don't want the power to suddenly reengage."

While she called the super, John laced his fingers together and bent down to give the boy the boost up he needed.

"Cool, Mom." Travis paused with his fingers and chin resting on the hallway floor. "This is just like that movie I watched at Juan's house. The one where the elevator crashed and almost cut that lady in two when she was climbing out."

"Oh, Lord," came the maternal gasp from behind.

John cringed at the boy's enthusiastic but ill-timed observation and pushed him on through the opening. "Not the time to be talking movies, kid."

As Travis crawled several feet beyond the opening and retrieved his things, John turned to the redhead clinging to the back railing. Without the freckles, there'd be no color to her skin at all. He reached out a hand to her. "Your turn, Sarge."

She clung to the railing. "Joe says he'll wait until I call him again."

"Good, but we're not going to wait. I don't think you want to be stuck in here with me any longer than you have to be."

"You know, it's not really you," she insisted.

"If you say so." But scared was scared, whatever the cause. John's hand never wavered. "Come on, Maggie."

With her eyes locked onto his, her shaky fingers revealing the same distrust, she finally reached out and slid her palm into his. She took a step toward him. "It's been a stressful day. Normally, I'm not a basket case like this. I just…really do have a thing about elevators."

"Fair enough." John pulled her up beside him, then stooped down to create the same step-up with his fingers. "I've decided I've got a thing about this particular elevator myself. There's something wrong with the wiring for parts of it to work and parts of it to stop cold like this. I think I'll be calling KCFD to make an inspection of the place. In the meantime, I say let's get out of here."

"Okay."

She braced one hand on John's shoulder and he lifted her. As she crawled out onto the carpeted floor, she started to slide back and John's hands automatically latched on to…those curves. The flare of her hips and rounded arc of her bottom were an easy grab. And a nice, firm fit.

John swallowed hard and shook his head. He had no grounds to fault the boy for bad timing.

"Sorry," he apologized, giving her a second boost. His hands and eyes had already lingered longer than an impersonal firefighter's should. But the lady cop broke the contact just about as soon as the nerve endings in the tips of his fingers sparked to life at the warmth and suppleness they detected beneath her crisp navy blue trousers.

The view was over and gone within another second, and Sergeant Maggie rolled to safety on the floor above him. John eased a tight breath out between his lips. Something dormant inside him had unexpectedly awakened. Was it just the fact that he hadn't touched a woman for two years? Hugs with his sister and handshakes with doctors and therapists hadn't zinged through him and thrown him off-kilter like this. And prickly redheads had never been his type.

He supposed he should be pleased to discover that life-threatening injuries and months of recovery hadn't destroyed the baser urges heating his blood right now. But he was just beginning to get comfortable with being closed-off and antisocial. Just a few minutes ago, working his way up to normal civility had been a stretch. And now he was wondering if that whole sexual lightning bolt had been a fluke or if he was going to have to curb his natural instincts to maintain a "just friends" relationship with his new neighbor.

Busy sorting through his observations and emotions, and putting them away in various mental compartments, he was startled to see the long, freckled arm poking back into the elevator. "Come on," Sergeant Maggie ordered. "Your turn."

Her tone was much more authoritative and coplike coming from the free air of the seventh floor than it had been in the tight confines of the elevator. Intriguing. Maybe he ought to latch onto that chilly timbre instead of remembering how she'd filled up his hands if he wanted to keep a polite distance from her.

He chinned himself up on the edge of the outside door track, then reached for her hand. With a surprisingly firm grip, she gave him the extra momentum he needed to hoist himself out onto the floor. Allowing himself a moment to catch his breath, John rolled onto his back. "Thanks, Sarge…"

But the prickly redhead was already slipping her son's backpack onto his slim shoulders and urging him to their front door. Nope, he didn't need to worry about hormones going on alert, being confused about social expectations of him or trying to be casual friends at all. Sergeant Maggie's quick retreat spoke volumes about how the two of them were going to get along.

Still lying on the rug, John realized that a nearby

door was propped open and someone with black hair and glasses was peeking out at him. He obliquely wondered if the short, shapeless person was a man or a woman, but there was no mistaking the unblinking curiosity. "Elevator isn't working," he explained. "Welcome to the neighborhood, right?"

The door snapped shut and John laughed at the irony of his worrying about being the antisocial one here on the seventh floor. He sat upright and pushed to his feet. He picked up his boxes from the stalled elevator opening and headed for his apartment. "Yeah, this is one hell of a homecoming, John."

"Excuse me?" the redhead asked.

John shrugged off the polite query. "Nothing, Sarge. Nice to meet you."

Her hesitation spoke volumes. "Nice to meet you, too."

"Hey, Mom. Look."

Great. They were right next door to each other. This could be awkward if the woman preferred him to keep his distance. John shifted his boxes and scooted around mother and son as the boy plucked down a folded piece of white paper that had been tacked to their door.

"Let me see that." Maggie snatched the note from the curious boy's fingers and unfolded it while John fished his keys out of the front pocket of his jeans. "That son of a... This isn't happening. Not now."

"Sarge?"

They both stopped with their keys turned in the locks of their respective doors. The instinctive urge to ask if something was wrong died on John's lips when he saw the color bleed from her cheeks. She stared at the words scribbled on that paper as though hypnotized. Whatever was in that note scared her just as much as the stalled elevator had. Something was definitely wrong.

Not your business, John. She wanted nothing to do with him, her kid asked too many questions and he wasn't looking to make new friends, right?

"Mom?" Travis's fingers touched his mother's arm. "Is it from—?"

"Go inside."

"But—"

"Go." She snapped out of her fixated shock and whisked his cap off his head to press a kiss there before reaching over him to open the door. "There's a snack in the fridge to hold you until dinner."

But Travis, his expression looking oddly mature for one so young, seemed reluctant to leave her. "I was just joking about that movie, Mom. I didn't think you were really going to get cut in half."

John nudged open his own door, giving them some privacy while his neighbor summoned a smile for her son. "I know, sweetie. I know. Wait for me to go through the mail and check the answering machine, though, okay? Now go."

John's muscles were weary with the exertion of the move and their great escape from the elevator as he set the boxes on the carpet. Yet when he turned to close the door, everything in him tensed with guarded apprehension. *She* was there, standing in the open door frame, the note wadded in her left hand while her right hovered near the gun on her hip again.

The warm smile she'd given her son had vanished. "Did you see anyone out here?" she asked. "A man who might have left this note?"

"No." He was vaguely irritated that she seemed to be sizing him up again. Yeah, those green eyes had noticed the fake leg. They swept over the scars. He bristled under her scrutiny. Did she suspect him of tacking the paper to her door? "What's it say?"

"Is this your first trip up from the garage?"

He took a step toward her. This was *his* apartment after all. *She* was the uninvited guest. "My sixth or seventh. What's in the note?"

She braced her feet in an overtly defensive stance and he stopped. What the hell?

John backed up a step and her words came spilling out. "Was there anyone on the elevator with you during any of those trips? Maybe you saw someone in the parking garage you didn't recognize? Was there anyone messing with the wires or controls on that elevator? Or flowers—did you see anyone trying to deliver flowers?" She glanced around at the closed doors behind her. "Sometimes the florist will deliver them to someone else if I'm not at home."

"I didn't see anyone tampering with anything, I don't know anybody here. And I sure as hell didn't get any flowers."

"Did you see a guy with a shaved head and tattoos?"

"I've only met the super, Joe Standage." And the older man wasn't the shaved-head type.

"His hair used to be black. Sometimes he dyes it."

"Joe does?"

"No, my…" Her freckled skin suddenly flooded with heat. Was she embarrassed by her ranting? Intimidated by his unapologetic scrutiny? Alarmed to suddenly realize *she* was the intruder here?

"Is this how you welcome all your new neighbors, Sergeant—" he dropped his gaze to the name badge on her chest pocket, pulled taut by the Kevlar she wore beneath her uniform "—Wheeler? Blow hot, blow cold? Make nice and then freak out? We haven't even been properly introduced."

Whatever this woman's secrets were, she wasn't telling. Instead of answering his accusation, she stuffed the note into her uniform slacks pocket. Then she huffed up in all her warrior Amazon glory, tipping her chin as her skin cooled to peachy dots over alabaster. "I'm Maggie Wheeler. Travis is my son."

"John Murdock."

"Are you military or KCFD?" She eyed the Corps logo on his T-shirt and the jarhead cut that he wore whether he was overseas with his Reserve unit or home in Kansas City, working for the fire department.

"Both. USMC, retired. For about a week now. Moving back to town after my last tour and some rehab. Firefighting is the job I'm coming back to after serving my stint in the Corps." He made another stab at moving closer. "Sarge, um, Maggie…are you okay?"

Her eyes widened as though the question had startled her. Or maybe it was his advance. Before she answered, she retreated into the hallway. "Of course I'm okay. Thank you for serving our country—*Captain* Murdock, was it?"

"Just John now."

She nodded. "I apologize for Travis being so nosy. He's going through a phase where he's completely nuts about baseball and firefighters and…everything. And he's never been shy about speaking his mind." She barely paused for a breath. "I'm sorry I freaked out on the elevator. And the note. It's just that I… Like I said, it was a rough day. Well, you don't need to know that. Welcome to The Corsican, John."

Yep, that sounded sincere.

By the time John reached the door, Maggie Wheeler's was closing. He heard not one, not two, but three separate locks sliding into place.

Something about that message, or the person who'd left it, had his neighbor spooked even more than getting stranded on the elevator had. Even though she wore a gun

and a vest and sergeant's stripes, indicating she was no
rookie when it came to law enforcement, the woman was
spooked.

John narrowed his gaze and looked up and down the
hallway. Beyond the super checking him in this morning,
and the curious person from the apartment down the hall
who hadn't spoken, he hadn't seen a single soul out here
all day long. A familiar niggle of unease crept along the
back of his neck like when he'd sensed a sniper's rifle focused on him up in the Afghan mountains.

He shook off the hyperawareness and retreated into his
apartment. Afghanistan was seven thousand miles away.
His years of service were done and he was reporting back
to KCFD Station 23 this week to start his new job as an
arson investigator assigned to the ladder company with
whom he'd once fought fires.

He had plenty on his plate right now to deal with. Leggy
redheads and curious kids and somebody else's bad news
weren't his concern tonight.

John locked the door behind him and leaned back
against it, sweeping his gaze across the beige apartment
decorated in wrapped furniture and sealed boxes.

So this was where he was going to live now.

It beat the cot and caves and blood he'd left in the
Middle East. It beat the VA hospital and physical therapy
units where he'd learned how to walk again.

But with nothing but bare walls and the paranoid lady
cop next door, the jury was out on whether he'd call this
new place home.

Chapter Three

"I know it's an imposition, but it would be a huge help. Thank you, Coach Hernandez. Yes, I know. Thank you, *Michael,*" Maggie corrected at his insistence. "I'll make it up to you, I promise."

Maggie locked her double-cab pickup and hurried after the other woman and two men striding through the sliding glass doors into St. Luke's Hospital. She'd been working the task force for nearly a week now, and this was the first time she'd been invited to leave the precinct office. If chauffeuring the members of the team was the only way she could get out and do some field work, then a chauffeur she'd be.

"I should be able to pick up Travis after practice this evening. With my new assignment at KCPD, my hours aren't as structured as they used to be, and I just can't get away today to pick him up after school and get him to Little League. But I'll be there by the time you're done."

With an apologetic frown, Maggie nodded to the reception desk volunteer who was pointing to the sign requesting cell phone usage be limited to the lobby and outdoor areas of the hospital. But Michael Hernandez was saying something about his son having Webelo Scouts after practice and that his late wife used to take care of all the transportation stuff anyway, and would Maggie and Travis want to go out to dinner with him and his son afterward? Maggie wasn't finding any polite way to break in to end the conversation with the man she'd asked the favor from.

Seeing Nick Fensom's beefy hand holding the elevator doors open, and withering under the glare from the volunteer, she opted to simply interrupt and wrap up the personal call she'd had to make. "I've got work to do, Coach," she apologized, carefully avoiding using his first name and encouraging anything that might be construed as a personal interest in him. "But I'll call the school to let them know Travis can leave with you. No, I'm quite sure about dinner. I appreciate your help, though. Thanks."

Worried that she'd kept the other task force members waiting, Maggie snapped her phone shut and darted through the open doors to an empty corner of the elevator. As the doors closed, she tried not to make too much of the feeling of déjà vu that skittered along her spine. Was it just last week that she'd gotten stuck on an elevator with her new neighbor, John Murdock? She'd been just as nervous about sharing the tight space with the imposing former marine as she was about joining other members on her first victim interview.

Joe Standage's assertion that he didn't know what the heck was going on in his building, and that he'd have to wait for an expert to help him repair the elevator before it went back into service, was hardly reassuring. Maggie and Travis had gotten into the habit of taking the stairs down to the parking garage anyway, so it wasn't that much of a hardship to use them coming back up, as well. And even though dinner conversations with her son, and her own dreams at night, had centered around the possibility of crashing elevators and being trapped on one with a monster far less interested in helping them escape than John

Murdock had been, Maggie refused to let her fears keep her from doing her job today.

For the trade-off of a free ride this morning, she'd get the chance to observe some of KCPD's best in action. Maggie figured she'd learn more about how to conduct an investigation in one morning by watching the real thing than she'd learned in an entire semester of her interrogation tactics class.

But as the elevator moved upward, it wasn't the anticipation of doing actual field work that had her heart pounding in her ears. Irrational as it might be, sharing an elevator with a man was always a challenge for her. Getting stuck on one was a real nightmare. Perhaps if she'd chosen to take the stairs ten years ago instead of allowing herself to get cornered in the elevator by her enraged husband, she might have gotten away. She might have been spared the attack that had forever changed her life.

She was justified in her aversion to sharing tight spaces with someone bigger and stronger than she was. Even compared to her, standing six feet tall with her work shoes on, John Murdock was an imposing man. Maggie's gaze flickered to the red-haired detective in the tailored suit and tie. Spencer Montgomery was tall, but John Murdock was taller. She looked to the shorter, stockier detective in the black leather jacket. Nick Fensom was broad across the shoulders and muscular, but John was bigger. Not even the artificial leg and obvious limp could lessen the intimidation factor of the unsmiling Goliath who'd moved in next door.

At least, not in her book. Captain John Murdock, USMC, retired, with the strong hands and gruff sarcasm, was all male, all muscle and as much a mystery to her as the handwritten note that still haunted her nights.

Mags—

*I miss you. I know I've done you wrong in the
past, but I'm a changed man. I've got me a job
and I'm not drinking.
I've paid my debt.
When can I see you?
Love,
Danny*

Maggie's nostrils flared as she breathed in deeply, willing the frissons of terror still sparking through her system to dissipate so that she could concentrate on the job at hand. The elevator snafu had to be a horrible coincidence that had made Danny Wheeler's note seem that much more threatening. Still, she'd put in a call to her attorney the next morning to discuss getting a new restraining order against her ex-husband. Having the flower delivered to a public building like Fourth Precinct headquarters was easy enough. But how had he found her unlisted address? How had he gotten into the building, past the security gate at the garage and Joe Standage? And why had not one of her neighbors on the seventh floor—whose doors she'd knocked on before some of them were even awake that next morning—seen Danny come and go? Not even those piercing green-gold eyes of John Murdock had seen anyone lurking around her apartment.

Was she living with a bunch of hermits?

Were the tenants in her building too elderly, too foreign, too nearsighted, too hard-of-hearing, too afraid to step up and get involved with their neighbors? If they ever got to know Danny Wheeler the way she did, they'd be smart not to come out of their doors.

But one man had stepped up. Although circumstances

hadn't given him any choice, Captain John Murdock had gotten involved.

As Dr. Kilpatrick and the two detectives discussed their strategy for approaching Bailey Austin, Maggie's mind replayed every moment of that encounter with her new neighbor. She could still hear the deep voice demanding she do the right thing despite her fears—still feel the big hands that had accidentally warmed her backside and made her feel unexpectedly secure when he'd clasped her fingers. She could easily recall her gratitude that he'd spoken kindly to her chatty son even though she'd done nothing to encourage any type of conversation. John Murdock was bigger and stronger than she in every way except for the fact she was armed and had two good legs. She should be supercautious about developing any kind of a relationship with him. She should be afraid of a man like that.

And yet she'd run to him for answers and assurances.

Why had she expected him to be alert to the comings and goings around her apartment, and concerned about her troubles? Yes, he'd stayed calm and gotten her off that elevator when her own fears had kept her from thinking straight. But blindly trusting a man like that was a mistake she couldn't afford to repeat. Did she think his handicap, and the burn scars on his arms and neck from an obviously terrible injury, meant he couldn't harm her? Was she a fool to believe the military cut of his golden-brown hair and proud carriage of his shoulders meant he was a man who'd defend *her?*

Danny had done a stint in the Navy right out of high school. She knew better than to think that just because a man wore a uniform, he was a good guy. She was smarter than that—smart enough to know that outward appearances and little flickerings of awareness in her pulse were no way to judge the true character of a man. She'd fought too hard for her independence to let one panic attack and a lingering curiosity about her mysterious, attractive neighbor keep her from standing on her own two feet.

She would figure out what had gone wrong with the elevator. *She* would find out how Danny had gotten that note to her. *She* would make it clear that he could never be a part of her life, or their son's, ever again. It was what a strong woman would do, what a well-trained KCPD detective would do. This morning she needed to set aside her fascination with John Murdock, and her fears about her ex, to become that detective she wanted to be.

Still, *"Sarge, um, Maggie...are you okay?"*

When was the last time a grown man who wasn't an E.R. doctor or a fellow cop asked her that question?

She knew better than to make anything out of his concern. Heck, they'd barely spoken two words since that night. But it was nice to be asked. Nice that someone was polite enough to notice her distress. Nice to know that wigging out on a man didn't automatically mean he couldn't care. In a neighborly, we-just-survived-a-small-crisis-together kind of caring, of course.

Tamping down the smile that softened her lips, Maggie waited for the other task force members to exit the elevator and get a few steps ahead of her before falling into step behind them.

Bailey Austin's hospital room was easy to spot. It was the one with the John Murdock-sized SWAT cop pacing back and forth in front of the door. She recognized Trip Jones as a coworker who checked in at her desk every morning before the precinct's daily roll-call meeting. His wife was Charlotte Mayweather-Jones, stepsister to the rape victim they'd come to interview. Normally Trip greeted Maggie with a friendly smile.

But there were no smiles for any of them as they approached. "Detective Montgomery. Nick. Dr. Kilpatrick. Sarge." Trip shook hands with each of them. "So this is the new task force?"

"Officer Jones," Spencer acknowledged for all of them. He pulled back the front of his suit jacket to splay his hands at his waist. "How is she?"

Trip shook his head and shrugged. "It's not good. I'm afraid to go in there. I could tell I made her nervous."

"Did she say you remind her of her attacker?" Spencer asked.

"She didn't say anything to me. I guess I can be kind of scary when I'm in the mood to wrap my hands around the neck of the bastard who did this."

Dr. Kilpatrick squeezed his arm in reassurance. "That's an understandable reaction, on both your parts. I'm sure that somewhere inside she appreciates you being here for her."

"Maybe. This family has been through enough with Charlotte's kidnapping, the murder of that worthless stepbrother of hers, and now this. I don't know how much more she can handle."

The blonde psychologist reached for the door handle. "We'll be gentle with her, I promise."

Spencer Montgomery caught the door and followed her in, with his partner right behind them. But when Maggie reached the open door, she stopped. "Wait a minute. We're *all* going in there?"

"We need to question the victim while the incident is still fresh in her mind." Detective Montgomery looked faintly annoyed at having to stop and explain his actions when he faced her.

Maggie shivered with the memory of when *she'd* been the woman lying in that hospital bed. "Her mind's probably still in shock right now. And to see a crowd of armed police officers storm into her room—"

"We're hardly storming," Spencer argued in a hushed tone.

"We're not the bad guys here," Nick Fensom echoed.

Maggie looked over her shoulder to share a rueful glance that included Trip, as well. "Right now, in her mind, pretty much everybody's a bad guy."

A tremulous voice from the other side of the privacy curtain silenced the standoff. "Don't touch me."

Maggie had never met Kansas City socialite Bailey Austin, but she recognized the tenor of a woman fighting to hold on to normalcy and civility, and failing miserably.

A man's voice shushed her. "Sweetie, I'm just so worried—"

"I know."

"This doesn't change how much I love you, how much I want to still marry you. Tell me what you need." Frustration colored his voice. "Anything."

"Bailey, dear, Harper loves you."

"I'm sorry. I just can't… I don't want to talk about the wedding right now, okay?"

"Loretta, dear." That was an older gentleman's voice. Probably Bailey's stepfather.

"No." Loretta Austin-Mayweather's shrill voice took care of any need to be secretive about KCPD's arrival. "I'm going to make everything okay for my daughter. She's going to get married. She's going to have her happily ever after."

"Dear—"

"I just want everything to be the way it was before this happened."

"They're ganging up on her." Maggie whispered the thought out loud.

Nick Fensom's blue eyes narrowed at the observation. "They're family."

"Doesn't matter. They're not listening to what she needs right now."

Spencer was shaking his head as the conversation on the other side of the curtain escalated toward an argument. "We need to talk to her alone if we can. I don't want anybody else's well-intentioned comfort or defense of her to shut her down and keep her from talking, or taint whatever details she can recall."

Nick nodded his agreement. "She may not feel comfortable sharing some of the grittier details in front of her family, anyway."

"Divide and conquer, then." Kate Kilpatrick adjusted her fingers around the strap of her bag and headed for the curtain. She pulled the curtain aside to announce their presence and reveal a tableau of startled friends and family gathered around the bed. "Mrs. Mayweather?" Kate extended her hand to the beautiful blonde woman with the red-rimmed eyes. "I'm Dr. Kilpatrick from KCPD. I'm so sorry this happened to Bailey. As a mother I understand the grief and rage and helplessness you feel at seeing your child harmed." Dr. Kilpatrick had children? She'd never mentioned them. Maggie had never even seen a picture of any family in the psychologist's office. But the moment of surprise passed as the psychologist smoothly manipulated the startled family members. "I have some experience counseling the families of victims. Why don't you and I go out to the lobby and talk for a bit."

Loretta Austin-Mayweather latched on to the sleeve of her husband's suit coat. "I want to be with my baby."

Jackson Mayweather turned his shrewd eyes to Dr. Kilpatrick. "You can calm her down?" The police psychologist nodded, then he patted his wife's hand. "Loretta, I promise we won't go that far. But I think we should talk to the doctor."

Wrapping his arm around his wife's shoulders, the Mayweather patriarch guided her out the door behind the psychologist.

Maggie stepped aside, marveling at the smooth teamwork of the task force members. Nick Fensom said something to Trip's wife, Charlotte, about the red jacket of the certified therapy dog sitting at her feet, and soon the detective was escorting them out the door to join Trip.

But a tall, golden-haired man in a suit maintained his position at Bailey Austin's side. Her fiancé, Harper Pierce, according to an article she'd read in the Kansas City society pages, glared at Detective Montgomery. "You again? Didn't you torment this family enough when you kept harassing us with questions about the Rich Girl Killer?"

"I got the job done, didn't I? We got our man." Spencer's gaze settled for a moment on the bruised face of the young woman in the bed. "We'll get this guy, too."

The one blue eye that wasn't swollen shut blinked open to meet the detective's curiously blank expression. But just as quickly, Bailey closed her eye and turned onto her side, hiding her face toward the blinds at the window.

"You see?" Harper Pierce taunted. "She doesn't want to talk to you."

With his focus squarely back on the hostile fiancé, Detective Montgomery pulled back the front of his jacket, subtly displaying his badge, his gun and his authority to the other man. "You're with me, Pierce. If you truly want to help Miss Austin, that is. Because you were one of the last people to see her that night, I'd like to ask you some questions about the time and events leading up to your fiancée's abduction."

"Bailey needs me here."

"Go." Snatching her shoulder away from Harper's outstretched fingers, Bailey curled into a ball, making it clear that his touch might be the last thing she needed right now. "Please, Harper."

Several moments of silence passed before it fully registered that Maggie was alone in the room with the victim. She shifted on her feet in the shadows beside the door, wondering if she should excuse herself to go observe the interviews or just slip quietly out of the room.

But Bailey Austin's soft voice called to her before Maggie could decide. "You can sit if you want."

Maggie glanced back at the door, then over to the chair and rolling stool beside Bailey's bed. Maybe the young woman was one of those high-society trophy wives-to-be who'd been raised to have impeccable manners—under any circumstance.

But no woman in Bailey Austin's condition needed to be worrying about Maggie Wheeler's feelings right now.

"You need your rest." Maggie thanked her and backed toward the door.

"You don't have to go."

The other woman's voice sounded small, almost devoid of inflection, stopping Maggie's retreat.

She recognized the bleak sound of isolation, the belief that no one could ever truly understand what she'd been through. Maggie's eyes burned with tears of empathy. But she blinked them away, refusing to let another victim feel the utter loneliness and drifting sense of loss she'd endured. Opening up her well-guarded heart, Maggie crossed the room and took a seat on the creaking vinyl stool.

"Your family will be back soon. Or, if you don't want them here, I'm sure your brother-in-law Trip could make that happen." She talked to the gap in the gown between Bailey's shoulder blades. "I'm sorry this happened to you.

You're probably not ready to hear this right now, but I can recommend a victims' group and a therapist who specializes in counseling sexual assault victims."

The younger woman rolled onto her back, turning her puffy face to Maggie. "Were you attacked, too?"

Maggie nodded, going to that matter-of-fact place in her head where she could discuss such things. "January sixteenth—ten years ago."

"I guess it's a date you never forget."

"Haven't yet."

Bailey's bruised blue eye sharpened its focus. "Trip said more detectives who were experts in this kind of crime would be in to question me today. Is that who you guys are?"

Maggie spoke in gentle tones but didn't sugarcoat the truth. "KCPD believes the man who attacked you has raped several women. He disappeared off the radar for a few years, but it seems he's back in Kansas City."

"What he did to me, he did to other women?"

"The M.O.'s match. So our chief has put together a task force." She nodded toward the door. "Detective Montgomery, he's the task force leader. He'll want to ask you some questions when he's done talking to your fiancé."

"I know Spencer." Bailey hugged the blanket covering her up to her chest. "I don't want to talk to him."

She was on a first-name basis with the task force leader? Detective Montgomery had never mentioned a personal connection with the victim. But then, she'd yet to see the man reveal much of anything he didn't want to. "He's one of the best investigators we have."

"I know he is. He helped capture the Rich Girl Killer." But Bailey was sinking beneath the covers, pulling up the blanket like a sheet of armor.

"If there's some kind of problem between you, his partner, Nick Fensom—"

"No."

Maggie released a silent breath and tried again. "Maybe you'd feel more comfortable talking to a woman. Dr. Kilpatrick is a police psychologist, more of an adviser than a cop. She doesn't even carry a gun."

"Why don't you ask me the questions?" Oh, no. Was she serious?

"I'm just support staff. I'm not trained yet—"

"Is it crazy to just want to be left alone?" Bailey's gaze drifted off to a distant corner of the room. "Yet I'm so afraid of being alone now."

"Whatever you're feeling right now is normal." Maggie spoke from practical experience and the stories she'd heard in her support group. "Strangers may make you uncomfortable. For some rape victims, any man can make them nervous. For others, just leaving a familiar place can trigger a panic attack."

Bailey's gaze came back to her. "My sister—well, Charlotte's my stepsister—she was like that. She was kidnapped when she was in high school. For as long as I knew her, she would never leave the house. Until Trip came along. She still doesn't like crowds. And she has a therapy dog to help with the panic attacks." She shifted in the bed to face Maggie. "It took her years to be able to function normally. Is that what I have to look forward to?"

"Surviving a sexual assault is a lot like coping with the death of a loved one. It can affect each victim differently. The length of time it takes to learn how to cope and then move on with your life, and how you get to that point, is different with each person. There's no right or wrong way to recover. And you can't compare your path to anyone else's."

There was a long pause as Bailey processed the answer. Then she surprised Maggie by reaching for her hand. "I never even saw him coming. I was so mad at Harper and my mom, so overwhelmed by all the wedding plans, that I didn't even realize the screeching of brakes I heard in the street was for me."

All of a sudden, Bailey started talking about the attack. Maggie glanced toward the door for help, almost calling out for one of the experts to come back in. But the young woman's grip convulsed around hers with every memory she described. Tears glistened on her bruised cheek and Maggie didn't have the heart to leave her alone or risk her shutting down again.

Maggie thought of her classes, and formulated questions she should ask. But Bailey kept talking. Her eyes were closed, as if replaying events in her mind. "When I woke up, I was in this empty building. On the floor. I mean, on a mattress that was directly on the floor. It was covered in plastic. Everything was."

With one last glance at the door, Maggie gave up on willing reinforcements to arrive. *Do it.* She adjusted her position on the stool, clutched Bailey's hand a little more tightly. If she wanted to be a detective, she might as well start acting like one. "Do you remember anything else about the building? Were you in a small room? A large one?"

"It was sterile."

"You mean it was clean?" The report had mentioned odors she remembered. "Like the hospital?"

Bailey shook her head. "It smelled awful. There was no furniture except for the mattress. No decorations. There were partial walls—framing where walls and windows should go—like a big office or apartment building under construction. Or one being gutted and torn apart, I don't know. Mostly I saw the floor."

"What was the awful smell, do you know?"

"Pickles."

"Pickles?"

"I don't know. I was in and out of consciousness. And he swore he'd cut me or hit me again or put the hood back on me if I so much as spoke." She inhaled a deep breath. "But yeah, now that you say that, it *was* clean—what I could see before he blindfolded me and took me back to that intersection near Fairy Tale Bridal. The plastic underneath me was crystal clear. I remember looking through it and studying the design on the mattress, counting the stitches while he…" Bailey pulled her hand away and rolled onto her opposite side, curling into a ball.

Maggie knew the interview was done and didn't try to push her. "Thank you for talking to me, Miss Austin. I know it's not easy, but knowledge gives us power against this guy. It's the only weapon we have right now to keep anyone else from getting hurt. Thank you for your courage in talking to me."

Curling her fingers into her palm, Maggie fought off the urge to reach out and offer some kind of comfort. But sharing her compassion wasn't why Maggie was here. She'd come to St. Luke's to do her job—or rather, to learn more about how to do her job. Knowing she needed to report this new information about the assault to Detective Montgomery and the others, she adjusted the holster on her belt and stood.

Her fingers were on the door handle when Bailey's soft voice reached her. "Does it get better? Will I ever not hurt? Will I ever feel safe? Will I ever be able to trust again?"

Maggie knew honesty was the only way to answer. "The pain will fade over time." As for the rest? "Like

I said, every survivor's path to healing is different. It'll be tough, but try to remember the important thing, Miss Austin—we survived."

Chapter Four

Just another day at the office, John tried to tell himself as he pulled his pickup into the parking lot next to KCFD Station 23. Although he'd just spent most of his shift down at headquarters, sitting through orientation meetings and filling out paperwork, he knew it wasn't true. The last of his training at HQ was done.

Today was his D-day.

Storm the beach head of normalcy and find a way to fit back in to his old life again.

He breathed in deeply through his nose and let the doubt creep out between his lips.

Fire Station 23 had been his destination every workday for almost a decade, before he'd had enough of the wanting and not having—before not even having the right to think about Meghan Taylor had dulled his senses so much that he'd been close to becoming a hazard to himself and his team.

And he'd loved being a firefighter. At six-five and a good 250 pounds, he'd always been a physical being. He'd played sports in school, had relished the discipline of the ROTC program that had paid for his degree at KU. He'd opted to join the Corps after graduation, had served in both infantry and artillery support units. When his stint was up and he'd transferred to the Reserves, firefighting had offered the perfect schedule to give him the time off he needed to attend weekend trainings and summer deployments. His engineering degree had taught him how buildings were put together, and how fire and heat, chemicals and explosions could bring them down.

Being a firefighter wasn't all that different from serving his country. He liked using his hands to maintain, deploy and neutralize powerful equipment and dangerous explosives. He thrived on the teamwork involved in attacking the flames, developing close relationships with the men and women he worked with. He loved cooking for his buddies at the firehouse, keeping physically and mentally fit, wearing his uniform proudly, and protecting his city.

Each time the alarm had gone off, he'd eagerly answered the call.

When his country had asked him to go overseas for a year, he'd answered that call, too.

Getting the investigative assignment at Station 23 should feel like a well-earned reward, like he was finally coming home.

John turned off the engine and braced his forearms on the steering wheel to stare through the windshield. In the two years he'd been gone, the city had repainted the firehouse facade a cool steel-gray. He missed the warm, earthy brown of the old bricks. He missed knowing what was going on in the lives of his coworkers, several of whom were now moving in and out of the open bays, washing down one of the engines and trimming up the landscaping in front of the building. He missed knowing exactly what job he was doing and feeling confident that he was the best man for that job. He missed his damn leg and the friends he'd lost in that roadside bombing.

Muttering a curse, John leaned back, dropping his hand to rub his thigh and run his fingers across the elastic band

and molded polymers that added the illusion of a real limb beneath the material of his KCFD-issue cargo pants. He wouldn't be fighting fires anymore with the hardware he was wearing. He'd been *promoted* to arson investigator, a dubious honor that meant KCFD would honor his service to them and to his country, but that there really was no place for him on the front lines of a ladder truck unit anymore.

"You'd best get to it," he chided the hazel eyes squinting back at him in the rearview mirror.

He pulled the brim of his KCFD ball cap low over his forehead and opened the truck door. Despite the handicapped tag stuffed in his glove compartment, John had parked several spaces away from the entrance, giving him time to adjust his stance over his false leg and minimize his limp before approaching the station's open garage doors. The early-evening sky swirled with clouds that hinted at spring showers by nightfall. If he'd been a superstitious man, he'd have seen the coming storm as a bad omen. But John believed in what he could see and touch and trust. He knew this day wasn't going to get any better. The sooner he got this bittersweet reunion with his old job and friends started, the sooner it would end.

"John." As soon as he rounded the corner in front of the fire station, Meghan Wright Taylor set aside the flowers she'd been transferring to a decorative planter and pushed to her feet. Her smile was as sunny as her wavy blond hair as she shucked her gardening gloves and hurried across the driveway to greet him. "I thought my shift was going to end before you got here today." She stretched up on tiptoe to wind her arms around his neck. "It's good to see you."

Although he leaned over to complete the hug, John braced himself to absorb the contact with her shorter frame. Meghan had proved to be a good friend since they'd first been assigned to Ladder Truck 23 together more than fifteen years ago. But her heart had always belonged to one guy, and Gideon Taylor was a smart man to love her just as hard and deep in return.

Even in her black duty uniform, Meghan smelled like the outdoors and sunshine. John released her and stepped away before too many memories and what-ifs got stuck in his head and his first day back at the station turned maudlin. "I like what you've done with the place," he joked.

Meghan laughed and he noted lines of humor beside her warm brown eyes that hadn't been there before. Marriage and motherhood and—cripes, were those captain's bars pinned to her collar?—suited her well.

John flicked his finger beneath her collar, indicating the brass pin she wore. "Somebody got promoted while I was gone."

"This is my station now." She was a smart firefighter, and had earned the respect of her male colleagues long ago. "I'm running the show."

"Congratulations."

"Big John Murdock, I heard you were coming back." John turned at the voice of another familiar friend. Dean Murphy strode out of the garage with a big grin set on his face. "So how are you?"

"Still don't like to be called Big John." Images of tall tales and television commercials had never fit, even when he'd been 100 percent. He clasped hands with the younger man and exchanged a firm handshake. "You still causing trouble around here, Dean?"

Dean had been little more than a rookie before John was deployed. There was a new cloak of maturity around his trim, wiry frame now. "Not much."

"Not much?"

Meghan linked her arm through John's elbow and

pulled him into the station house. "Dean is as much of a player as ever. Claims he wants to settle down and get married before he turns thirty, but I've yet to meet any Mrs. Murphy-to-be."

"You cut me deep, boss." He clasped his hands over his heart in a mock show of pain. "I could settle down if I had to."

"If you had to?" Meghan teased.

Dean winked. "Can I help it if the ladies find me irresistible? I'm just doing my duty to keep 'em all happy."

"As long as you keep doing your job the way you do when you show up at my station house, I don't care how you charm the ladies on your own time." A drumroll of thunder rumbled in the distance and Meghan glanced skyward. "Dean, let's get these trucks back in the house before the rain hits." Her order, gentle yet succinct, got Murphy and some other men moving. But she tugged at John's arm, pulling him away from the sudden bustle of activity around the shiny yellow engines. "Come on, I'll show you your office."

John nodded hellos to old friends and introduced himself to the new hires before following Meghan into the hallway that led to the station offices. A lot had changed on the inside of Station 23 since he'd gone overseas, too. New paint, new staff. Going into an office where he'd work banker's hours and then go home instead of heading for the bunk rooms and lounge areas where the firefighters on seventy-two-hour shift work would sleep and hang out like a family until a call came in.

"We'll get your name and title painted on the door," Meghan promised. He didn't mask his sigh of regret as well as he'd thought. "Does it meet with your approval?"

He must have a thing for freckles on women. The little specks dotting the skin on Meghan's cheeks had been one of the first things he'd noticed about Maggie Wheeler, too. For a brief moment, his head filled with the memory of green eyes, deep and pure in color, wide and frightened and looking to him for answers he couldn't give. But the similarities between his next-door neighbor and the fire-fighter whose happiness with another man had prompted John to re-up with the Corps ended there. Meghan was sleek and compact while Maggie was tall and rounded. One was a sunny blonde, the other a fiery redhead. One was going out of her way to make him feel welcome while the other...

Hell, he'd never had another woman intrude on his thoughts before when he was with Meghan. The war must have changed him in more ways than he'd realized. Even his ability to concentrate was missing in action. Taken aback by the observation, John covered his surprise by pulling off his KCFD cap and making a joke. "I've been sleeping on cots, the ground or a hospital bed for the past year. Don't know if I can handle a plush leather chair and air-conditioning."

"You've earned the promotion, John."

But it would be a different job. He'd go in and analyze a fire scene after the fact, when his leg wouldn't matter. His days of being on the front line, of being the first man into the action were behind him.

Swallowing the bile of that admission, John tossed his cap onto the desk, claiming the functional office space as his own. "Bare bones but sufficient. Most of my job will be about analysis and writing up reports, so this will do just fine."

If Meghan sensed his melancholy over the irony of returning to work without really getting to do the work he'd been trained for, she hid it behind a smile and invited him next door into her office. In a marked contrast to the bare metal shelves and computer in his office, her space was decorated with awards, family pictures and abundant warmth.

He picked up the framed photo of Meghan surrounded by her husband and four adopted sons. "Good grief, all the boys are taller than you now."

She gently caressed the picture when she returned it to her desk. "They're not boys anymore." She pointed to a wedding photograph on the shelf behind her desk. "Our oldest, Alex, is married now—to a lovely young attorney named Audrey."

John knew the older boys had been teenagers when she and Gideon Taylor had adopted them. Still... "You're not old enough to be a mother-in-law."

Meghan laughed. "Audrey makes it easy. I'm only ten years older than she is so we're more friends than in-laws. And Alex is a SWAT cop now. Hard to believe he was in so much trouble when I worked with him as a foster child. And this one—" she picked up another photo of a tall, muscular police officer with an imposing German shepherd seated beside him "—is Pike. He's K-9 patrol with KCPD." She pointed to another photo, with two teenagers dressed in blue-and-gold letter jackets. "Matthew and Mark were little more than toddlers when Gideon and I adopted them. Now they're in high school."

The love for her family was evident in her voice. John breathed in deeply, wishing that could have been him in those pictures, but knowing he never could have made her happy the way Gideon Taylor did. He'd been relegated to big brother status on the day they'd met, and nothing would ever change that. The pain he used to feel might not grip as tightly as it once had, but it was still there. John covered the inevitable awkwardness with a teasing laugh. "And yet, you don't look a day over twenty-nine."

Meghan joined in. "Thanks, but flattery will get you nowhere. I run a tight ship, Murdock. I'll expect you to fall in line, too, now that you'll be based here. I requested you for my station house, you know."

"I suspected as much."

"We always made a great team fighting fires," Meghan explained. "You were solid, dependable. You grounded everybody here, especially me." She leaned over the desk and dropped her voice to a whisper. "Besides, there's not a one of those goons out there who can cook a meal the way you can. Not even me. And I've had such a hankering for your pork roast with that cheesy polenta and glazed carrots."

Okay, he could do this. He could make nice and be friends and pretend his world hadn't changed. "I'll be sure to check the pantry before the end of the day, boss."

"My taste buds are happier already." She headed out the door. "Come on, I'll show you the new upgrades in the kitchen—"

Forced or friendly conversation of any kind ended abruptly when the station alarm went off. Meghan checked in with the dispatcher and told him to make the call for the full team to suit up and respond to a warehouse fire near the Missouri River. The instinct to run out to the gear lockers in the garage with everyone else jolted through John's legs.

He was following Dean to the first truck when the adrenaline haze cleared and John reminded himself that he was only feeling that jolt in one of his legs. Any *instinct* he felt was all in his imagination. He wasn't cleared for front-line duty. Ever again. The call wasn't his to respond to.

He drifted back out of the way as the men and women climbed into the trucks and paramedic van. The flashing orange lights blurred, and the strident repetition of the alarm muffled his hearing as he faded back into the space vacated by the ambulance.

He startled when Meghan dashed up and touched his arm. "I'll call you myself once the blaze is contained so you can investigate the cause. Depending on the size of the fire, the structural damage and this weather—" she nodded toward the drizzle of rain outside the open garage doors that was coming faster and heavier by the second "—it may be morning before I can safely get you in there."

John nodded and she stepped up onto the running board of the engine and opened the passenger-side door. He limped over to catch the door while she climbed inside. So maybe he had been relegated to chief cook and side-line watcher—he wasn't going to let his punky mood hold anyone up and endanger the lives and property of the people who'd called in the fire.

"Are you all right?" she asked, pulling her hair up into a ponytail inside her white scene commander's helmet.

John closed the door and tapped it twice, giving the driver the all-clear to go. "Go do your job," he urged, then stepped aside. "Watch the roads. They'll be slick with this new rain."

With a nod, she picked up the radio and gave the order, "Let's move out."

The station lights stopped flashing and the alarm went silent as the last of the trucks pulled out, leaving him standing alone in the middle of the empty garage. The sudden silence and frustrated yearning for the life he'd once led filled him up and spilled out into the emptiness surrounding him.

Yeah, this reintegration into civilian life was going real damn well. He was making friends and doing important, useful things with his time.

Sarcasm was eating a hole in his stomach when John heard a telephone ring. He knew there had to be a skeleton crew on hand at the station 24/7. The dispatcher, at least, should still be in his office.

But the phone rang and rang, and no one was answering. Some of that same urgency he'd felt when the alarm had gone off sparked through him again, and he hurried back to the offices to discover that it was the phone on his new desk that was ringing.

No way had Meghan and Company 23 reached the fire, much less put it out. And he didn't know another soul who'd be calling.

The only way to stop the speculation was to pick it up. "Hello?"

"Captain Murdock?"

He'd have written off the young voice as a wrong number or a prank if they hadn't called him by name. "This is John Murdock. Who's asking?"

"Travis Wheeler." Son of a gun. Sergeant Green Eyes' kid was calling him? Why? "I'm your new neighbor, remember?"

"I know who you are, Travis. How did you get this number?"

"You said you worked at Station 23."

Resourceful kid. Admirable stick-to-it-tiveness. Although he wasn't sure if tracking him down through the KCFD help desk or through some online information system irked him or concerned him. John checked his watch. It was after six o'clock. "Are you reporting a fire?"

There was a long pause and a rustling of movement over the phone, as though the kid was moving around. "No, I'm at the ballpark. Abbott Field."

What the heck was going on? "Trav, I'm at work. I can't talk baseball right now."

"It's raining." Probably all across the city by now. "I tried calling my mom, but she didn't answer. Sometimes she has to turn off her cell phone at work, like when she's in a meeting. She didn't answer at home either. It said something was out of service. It didn't even ring."

So he'd managed to get a call through to John at the fire station, but couldn't get a line to his own mother? A vague sense of unease raised the fine hairs at the back of John's neck. First the elevator in their building was out of commission, and now the landline phone wasn't working? Travis had mentioned something on the elevator last week about needing to know a *safe place* where he could go. Those fine hairs jumped to full attention. What the hell was going on next door with Maggie Wheeler? "Why are you looking for your mom? Are you okay? Is *she* okay?"

"I don't know. Practice got done early because of the rain and there's no one here. Well, nobody I know. There are some people who were watching practice still here, but... She was supposed to pick me up, but she's late." Suspecting Travis was standing out in the rain was worrisome enough, but there was something ominous about the pause in the boy's voice. "Mom's never late."

John plucked his hat from the desk and pulled out his keys. "I'm on my way."

Chapter Five

"Are you kidding me? Two cops called my work this afternoon."

Maggie deleted the vile message on her phone and hurried up the steps of the Fourth Precinct parking garage. The clock on her cell phone flipped over to 6:30 as another message from Danny Wheeler began to play. Her uniform and skin were damp from the rain outside, and she could feel the loose hairs sticking to her face kinking into curls. But she hadn't bothered with a jacket or umbrella because she was running so far behind.

"They talked to my parole officer." Danny's voice was full of accusation. "They came to my job. What did you tell them about me, Mags?"

Nothing that wasn't already in his arrest or prison record. But, like usual, if things had gone wrong with Danny's day, it was somehow her fault. And if she hadn't caused the problem, then he expected her to save him from it.

Reaching the third level, she jogged across the concrete toward her truck. She hit Delete again, praying the next message would be another from Travis, telling her that the parents of one of his teammates had agreed to wait with him after all, or had given him a ride home.

If she hadn't been so busy pulling files and going

over them with the detectives, absorbing every nugget of wisdom about what made one convicted rapist a viable suspect and another one not, she would have gotten Travis's call. She would have excused herself from the debriefing with Montgomery and Fensom, even appealed to Chief Taylor if necessary, in order to leave early to pick up her son.

With no update from Travis after his first call, and his cell phone now going straight to voice mail, Maggie quickened her pace. It had always been her and Travis. As his only legal parent, he relied on her entirely for his transportation, food, love and safety. Letting him down, even when the weather and a chain of events beyond her control messed up her schedule, wasn't an option she could live with.

She pulled her keys from her leather shoulder bag and punched the remote to unlock her truck.

Oh, hell. Danny had left yet another message. Whether he was upset about KCPD approaching him over making contact with her or if this was about his being a person of interest in the Rose Red Rapist case didn't matter right now. "…asking me about *my* wife? *My* whereabouts? I remembered your favorite flower, didn't I? You're supposed to have my back, Mags. I am not going back to prison. Understand that? You will not send me back there."

"Officer Wheeler?" Startled by the real voice behind her, Maggie silenced her phone and whirled around. "Maggie Wheeler?"

"Yes?" Settling back into her skin, she made a quick assessment of the man approaching her. His dark hair and easy stride were familiar, although she couldn't place him. Civilian clothes. Unarmed. He looked friendly enough, but something about the piercing blue eyes put her guard up.

"Gabriel Knight. *Kansas City Journal.*" He flashed the

press card hanging alongside a camera around his neck "I've managed to get a few words from the other members of Chief Taylor's task force this week, but you about got away from me."

"I'm off duty now, Mr. Knight." She opened her truck door and dismissed him. "And I need to get going."

"Is everything all right?" He nodded toward the cell phone squeezed in her fist. "You seem upset."

She tucked the phone into her bag and tossed it onto the passenger seat. "I'm fine."

"Just two minutes of your time, Mrs.? Miss—"

"It's *Sergeant* Wheeler." She climbed in behind the wheel. Travis needed her. "And I'm sorry, but I don't have two minutes right now."

When she turned to start the engine, he caught her door and held it open. "Do you think KCPD will have any better luck this time catching the Rose Red Rapist?"

"I hope so. Excuse me." She tugged at the door handle, but the reporter didn't budge.

"You hope so? That doesn't inspire me with confidence, Sergeant Wheeler."

"Well, of course, we're doing everything we can. KCPD's best are on this case, I promise you." She tamped down on the red-haired temper sparking in her blood. No meant no in any situation. What didn't Danny and this guy understand about that? But the first thing she'd learned when she went to work as a KCPD desk sergeant was that she was the face of KCPD most people saw. And that meant she had to be a friendly, helpful, patient face. So she drummed up a smile for the reporter. "Do you mind?"

"If this is an example of the department's best work, then what is someone with virtually no investigative experience like you doing on the task force?" Maggie's fingers tightened around the steering wheel at the low blow to the department and to her. "Is it because your ex-husband served time for rape? Is he a suspect?"

There went *friendly*. "Mr. Knight—"

"I hear you have a real knack for getting the victims of these crimes, like Bailey Austin, to open up and answer questions. Can you tell me why that is? Why did you get results when a dozen other cops before you couldn't?"

"How do you know about—?"

"So you did interview Bailey Austin."

Helpful was off the table now, too. "There are confidentiality expectations in place with assault victims, Mr. Knight. Now remove your hand from my door before I arrest you."

He let go of the door but didn't move to give her enough room to close it. "Threatening the press? That ought to make a good headline."

And now *patience* was done. "Headline this—Single Mom Needs to Pick Up Son from Ball Practice. I have to go. You should speak to Dr. Kate Kilpatrick." She pointed toward the precinct headquarters building across the street. "She's the task force's liaison with the press. She can answer your questions better than I can."

He finally retreated. "You've given me more than enough to work with, Sergeant Wheeler. Have a pleasant evening."

Maggie's response wasn't nearly so civil. She slammed the door and peeled out of the parking garage, leaving Gabriel Knight and whatever he was texting on his phone behind her.

She hadn't expected to be interviewed by a reporter and hadn't handled it well at all. He'd gotten her while she was distracted with Travis and Danny, and had ferreted out answers she wasn't sure she was supposed to give. All her thoughts were exploding in a swirling mass of temper, frustration, self-doubts and second-guessing. She hated feeling out of control like this. She was a good mother. A good cop. She'd make a good detective, too.

But knowing the truth and feeling the truth were two different things. And right now, it was impossible to silence the taunts from the corners of her mind. Taunts that echoed in Danny's derisive voice.

Your child is stranded in the rain.

You just botched that press interview.

You will never get anything right on your own.

"Shut up, Danny." Voice in her head or face-to-face terror, he wasn't going to undermine her confidence anymore.

Maggie turned on her headlights and cranked the windshield wipers to give her a clearer view through the rainy streets that led to the ballpark near Travis's school. As the snail's pace of rush-hour traffic stopped her at yet another light, she toyed with the idea of sticking the magnetized flashers on her roof and turning on the siren. Instead of abusing her badge and busting through the line of cars, she picked up her purse.

Concentrating on evening out her breathing and keeping her panic in check, she pulled out her phone and continued checking her messages. There were three more from Danny, probably as sweetly apologetic as the first three had been rife with anger and accusation. She deleted all the messages once she saw that there were no more from her son.

Easing along with the flow of traffic, she called Travis's number again, forcing herself to keep thinking positive thoughts when it went straight to voice mail. Had he let the battery run down? Forgotten to turn it on? Had he set it down someplace and lost it, leaving him not only abandoned but also unable to contact her? She left a message just in case. "I'm so sorry I'm running behind, sweetie, but I'm on my way. Make sure you stay where the lights are and hang out with your friends if they're still there. I love you."

She called the apartment again to see if he'd found a way home but got a recorded message about the line being out of order. A follow-up call to Joe Standage gave her an answering machine message. She left a request asking him to check why her home phone wasn't working, and if he saw Travis at the apartment, to please call her. She was praying for a cut utility line or an incompetent building super, and not something more sinister.

But she'd once had a daughter, too. And even though Danny hadn't killed little Angel himself, he hadn't been above using his own daughter as leverage to ensure Maggie's cooperation. Danny said he wanted to meet, and she'd said no. If he'd taken Travis to punish or persuade her...

Maggie cursed rush hour and pressed a little harder on the accelerator.

Once she crossed over the I-70 overpass and veered off toward the east side of the city, traffic thinned. A glimpse of white in her rearview mirror made her vaguely aware of a square van a few vehicles back making the same turns she was. But there was still some going-home traffic in the area, and several cars were heading northeast like she was, so she dismissed it.

She was on her third unanswered call to her son when she turned into the parking lot at Abbott Field and saw that the ball field lights were off. The concrete concession stand and batting cages were dark and locked up tight, and the bleachers and dugouts were all deserted. With the clouds blocking off the last dregs of daylight, the only illumination came from the distant streetlamps and her truck's headlights. "Where are you, Travis?" she muttered in hushed fear before finally thinking clearly enough to dial a different number. "Coach Hernandez?"

Laughter in the background nearly drowned out his reply. "Mrs. Wheeler. Did you rethink dinner?"

Right. He'd taken his son to a Scout meeting. "Is Travis with you?"

"What? We're going to that pizza place over on Independence Avenue."

"I'm not interested in dinner, Coach." She tried not to scream her own frustration. "Is Travis there?"

"No."

"Then where is he? I came as soon as I got his message about practice ending early. I can't believe you'd let a little boy stay at the ballpark alone."

"I thought you'd already picked him up." His tone bristled at her criticism, and he was quick to defend himself. "Everyone was gone when I left."

"Gone?" Oh, Lord. She willed herself X-ray vision as she peered through the windshield and the rain. "*I'm* at the park right now and no one's here. Do you know who he got a ride home with?"

"No." Travis's coach must have walked out of the meeting because the background suddenly quieted. "I saw him making a phone call. I just assumed it was to you."

How could the man *just assume* her child was safe? But the priority was finding Travis right now, not arguing Michael Hernandez's fitness to be a coach responsible for her child's well-being. "All right. Thank you."

"Mrs. Wheeler?"

"I have to go."

"Let me know when you find—"

She disconnected the call and tried to think like a cop instead of a terrified mother. With her heart pounding in time to the quick rhythm of the windshield wipers, she pulled her KCPD windbreaker from behind the seat and grabbed a flashlight from the glove compartment. She left the headlights on but locked the doors when she climbed out to begin her search of the grounds.

The rain cooled her skin but did nothing to ease her anxiety. With her emotions so out of focus, she relied on her training to do a quick, methodical search of the park. The doors to the main facility were locked, the stands empty. She checked behind trees and trash cans and walked through both the men's and women's public restrooms. The ladder up to the scoreboard was empty. There was no glove, no bat, no balls, no backpack—no sign of a ten-year-old boy anywhere.

"Travis, where are you?"

With the rain washing away the traces of anyone having been at the ball field at all, Maggie headed back to the parking lot and her truck. Maybe she should call in for police assistance. Or go straight to the dispatch office and issue an Amber Alert. Maybe she should get on the phone and call every friend of Travis, every teacher, every human being her son knew to find out if anyone had seen him.

Or maybe, possibly…she should call Danny. He'd never been interested in having children. Angel had been an unfortunate accident in his book. And Travis wasn't even legally his. But Travis knew the name of the man who'd fathered him and knew he was now out on parole. Tension bubbled in her stomach at the idea of the two of them even meeting, much less calling on an absent, worthless father for help.

That's when she saw the white van. Again. *Boyle's Extermination Company,* with the logo of a bug and a rat painted on the side. It was parked out on the street, not half a block away from her truck. Too close to be a coincidence. Someone *had* been following her.

Going on alert when the van's front door slid open, Maggie lifted the hem of her jacket and unsnapped the cover on her holster. She made sure she had access to the radio clipped to her shoulder and shined the beam of her flashlight straight into the face of the stocky man who climbed out.

The light reflected off big, round eyes, vaguely reminiscent of one of the critters on the side of the van. Dressed in tan coveralls, the man hunched his shoulders against the rain and called to her across the parking lot. "Mrs. Wheeler?"

Conquering the urge to retreat at hearing her name on the stranger's lips, she braced her legs and straightened to her full height. The exterminator, according to the matching vermin logo on his coveralls, wasn't any taller than she was, but he was built like an ox. The bug eyes and the tattoos on the side of his neck warred with his friendly smile and the bouquet of roses in his left hand.

Van? Roses? Woman alone?

Maggie put up her hand to stop him from coming any closer. "Do I know you?"

"Lawrence Boyle. I'm a friend of your husband."

"I don't have a husband."

He laughed. "Danny said you'd say that. Here." He held out the drooping red blooms.

"I hate flowers."

When she made no move to take the gift, he laid them across the corner of her truck and tailgate, then shoved his hands into his pockets and backed up a couple of steps.

She wrapped her fingers around the butt of her gun and unsheathed it a few inches. "Keep your hands where I can see them, please."

The bug eyes darted to her weapon. "I'm trying to do you a favor, Mrs. Wheeler. I know we've never met, but I feel like I know you. I know things weren't always great between you and Danny."

"Hands, Mr. Boyle."

"He talks about you all the time." The exterminator with the bleached-white hair pulled his hands from his pockets, then leisurely laced his fingers together and rested them on top of his head.

He'd done that for a police officer before, Maggie noted, keeping him in her sights and inching to the back of the truck. The rain shredded the tissue paper as she pulled it aside to retrieve the note. The *Sorry. Love you* wasn't as troubling as recognizing the card from a florist shop in her neighborhood and knowing Danny had been within a block of her apartment. Had Danny made contact with Travis? Had he done something to keep her from reaching her son?

"He says he's sorry if he said or did anything that upset you today." Lawrence Boyle's hands went right back to the top of his head when she swung the flashlight back to his face. "I guess cops and lawyers make him nervous. He hopes the two of you could have a conversation sometime."

"Not likely." It wasn't the first time Danny had sent flowers as an apology for his unspeakable behavior, but she intended it to be the last. She eyed the van behind Boyle and wondered if her ex was in there, watching her right now. "Where is he?"

"At work by now, I imagine. I gave him a job a few weeks ago. Danny and I go way back."

Judging by the twining blue-and-green tats on his neck, including a trio of teardrops that indicated years of incarceration, she could imagine where they'd met. Just how much did he and Danny have in common? Did they share a penchant for hurting women? "I need you to step back inside your van, Mr. Boyle."

Although he wiped the moisture from his face and retreated a step, the conversation wasn't over. "Your kid has a strong arm. Can't hit worth crap, though."

Don't ask. The answer will only upset you. "How do you know that?"

"We watched practice for a while. Before the rain started."

We? As in Boyle *and* Danny?

The rain soaking through her uniform was suddenly cold against her skin. "Did Danny take Travis?"

"No, ma'am. I sent him back to the shop to clean up for the day, and cool off."

"Why were you following me?"

"To give you the flowers." He made a face as if that had been a stupid question. "I was taking them to the police station to deliver 'em when I saw you leave. Please, ma'am, they're getting ruined."

Think, Maggie. Think. She had to push through the haze of fear, anger and suspicion to find her son. Did she take his word about Danny's whereabouts or insist on checking the inside of his van?

When he moved toward the flowers again, she pulled her gun and he stopped. His hands went up in the air. "Easy there, Mrs. Wheeler. I don't mean you no harm. You're just worried about your boy, I bet. Danny said you were doing a good job with the kid."

Ultimately, a dubious witness was better than no witness at all. She had to ask, "Did you see my son leave the ballpark?"

"Yeah." Lawrence Boyle lowered his hands and slipped them into the pockets of his coveralls, despite her warning. "Some cripple in a black truck picked him up. Big guy— looked pissed off. Walking on a stick for a leg would put me in a mood, too."

Relief warred with anger inside her. *Cripple?* Lawrence Boyle could only be talking about one man. John Murdock. "That big guy is a war hero. And here's what Danny can do with his flowers."

She knocked the bouquet into a puddle beside her truck, climbed inside and drove away

"TRAVIS RYNE WHEELER, you couldn't have called me half an hour ago to let me know you were safe?" Maggie snapped into her phone. She was immediately contrite over raising her voice, but her emotions were still bubbling too close to the surface. Knowing that Danny had been at the park watching her son, and could have easily been the one offering him a ride home, had terrified her. She should be grateful Travis had had the sense to call someone more reliable. "Sweetie, do you know how crazy I've been with worry?"

"That's why John made me call you." His man-sized sigh made her wonder if there was a big, unsmiling marine standing over him as he spoke. "I left my phone out in the rain and I couldn't see the screen, and did you know none of the phones on the seventh floor are working? John asked Miss Applebaum and the Wongs, too."

"Nice try, pal. But you and I are going to have a re-fresher course in where and how you can reach me, no matter what you do to your cell phone or what happens in this old building." She reached the sixth-floor landing and paused to control her breathing after her evening sprint. "And we're going to talk about who's a stranger and who you can trust."

"Mom, I know that stuff. That's why I called John. Fire-fighter? Captain? Duh."

"Then you need a reminder about who you shouldn't be imposing on. Honey, we barely know him." Despite the burn in her thigh muscles, she stretched her legs to take the last flight of stairs two at a time. Time to end the call. "I'm here. You stay put."

Maggie shoved open the door and plowed into the super, Joe Standage. Her cell phone flew across the carpeted floor, a tray of tools spilled in a noisy avalanche and a stepladder crashed into the opposite wall.

"Sorry. Are you all right?"

"Where's the fire?" he asked, pushing himself upright.

Maggie was quicker to get back to her feet. She scooped up pliers and a screwdriver and dropped them into the tray, then slid her hand beneath Mr. Standage's wiry arm to help him up. The peppering of gray in his ruffled hair was a closer match to the arthritic knees that made him slow to stand. But the surprising fitness of his arm muscles made her think his turtle-paced, aw-shucks demeanor was more about personality than age. "Long day. I wasn't looking," she apologized. "Are you okay?"

"I'm fine. Been doing some work for Miss Applebaum in 716. She fried up another batch of those apple fritters." He straightened his clothes and picked up his tool tray. "I put in a call to the phone company to have those phones up and running again by morning. I must have accidentally severed a line when I was cutting through a wall to move the cable for her. Got the elevator fixed, though. Found a disconnected wire. No need for you to be taking the stairs anymore, Mrs. Wheeler. Say, have you had any trouble with ants? Miss Applebaum pulled out the sugar when she was baking and found a whole trail—"

While Joe chatted away, Maggie handed him the folded stepladder. The retired gentleman might have time for a friendly confab, but she didn't. Besides, after that weird encounter with Lawrence Boyle, bugs were the last thing she wanted to think about right now.

"My apologies again." Maggie scooped up her cell phone and hurried past her own apartment door.

"Don't you want to know about the ants?"

Ignoring the older man, Maggie knocked on the door of Apartment 709. "Travis?" She pushed her damp hair off her face and knocked again. "Travis, are you in there?"

Miss Applebaum opened the door behind Maggie and poked her wrinkled nose beneath the security chain. "Is everything all right, dear? I heard a crash. It's not that elevator again, is it?"

"No, ma'am. Joe says it's working now. Travis?" Maggie knocked again. If her son had added a lie about his whereabouts on top of everything else that had happened this evening…

"Now what?" a new voice asked. "Are the phones working yet?"

Miss Applebaum raised her tinny voice. "No, Bernard. Joe had to call the phone company for assistance."

Heat crept into Maggie's cheeks as two more doors in the hallway opened. "Come on, sweetie. Travis?"

The door of 709 suddenly opened in front of her raised fist and she punched John Murdock in the middle of the chest. The big man filled the doorway. He wore a barbecue apron beneath the belt of his jeans and was drying his hands on a towel.

Maggie pulled her hand back. "I'm sorry. Is Trav—"

"He's here. He's safe."

The concise words had no time to register before his hazel eyes darted to the left and the right. Instinctively, Maggie turned her gaze to follow his lead. Miss Applebaum was still checking on the commotion in the hallway. Bernard Cutlass stood in his pajamas and groused about rude people and needing to call his daughter in Belton. Joe Standage was holding the elevator doors open; his face was wreathed with concern. One by one she became aware of eyes at each of the occupied apartments on the seventh floor.

"It's just a miscommunication, folks." John's big hand closed around Maggie's wrist, the warmth and sureness of his touch jolting her again. "Everything's all right."

He pulled her inside and shut the door behind her before letting go. He angled his head down to hers, filling up her vision with a square jaw and narrowed eyes. "Did I just lie to those people? Or does every evening here have this much drama?"

"I'm sorry I hit you. Where's my son?"

The square jaw backed away. "Kitchen."

Maggie darted through the apartment, its layout mirroring hers next door, and found Travis at the table, doing his homework. "Hi, Mom."

"*Hi, Mom?* That's all you have to say?" Clothes were dry, face was smiling. He looked normal and safe and content, and she wrapped her arms around him and hugged him.

"Told you she'd be worried." John moved past them to check something on the stove. Maggie pulled Travis to his feet, nestled her cheek against his thick, damp hair and hugged him even tighter. "As soon as I realized you didn't know he'd called me, I had him use my cell phone."

"Do you have any idea how scared I was?"

Sooner than she wanted, Travis wriggled free. "Mom, jeez."

Maggie captured his chin in the palm of her hand and looked down into his sweet green eyes. "Don't you ever do anything like that again. I went to the ballpark. I couldn't find you. You wouldn't answer your phone."

"I couldn't." He squinched his face up in apology and sat back at the table.

"Coach Hernandez should never have left you…" *Cool it, Maggie.* The coach was someone Travis looked up to. She shoved aside the tendrils of hair sticking to her damp skin. "It was getting dark and it was raining and there was a man there—"

"What man?" Casual though an apron and soup ladle might make him appear, there was a probing intensity in John's eyes that reached her clear across the room. "The last couple of vehicles were leaving when I picked him up. No one was in the stands."

Maggie shivered at the assessing gaze that pierced through the armor she wore, inside and out. But she shook her head, dismissing his concern. Danny Wheeler and Lawrence Boyle and lousy timing were her problems, not his. She wound her arms around her own waist, trying to alleviate a chill that couldn't be entirely blamed on the wet clothes she wore.

"You're all I have, sweetie. And with work and that reporter and…" She fisted her hands beneath her crossed arms so she wouldn't embarrass Travis with another hug. "I couldn't find you. I didn't know you were safe."

"I borrowed Juan's phone to call the fire station and John came and got me. I took care of the situation myself. You don't have to worry about me." He did a very good imitation of mature, but his next sentence reassured her that Travis was still her little boy. "And please don't call me sweetie." His eyes flicked to the man at the stove and he dropped his voice to a whisper. "Not in front of other people."

A relieved laugh sneaked out. She just couldn't resist reaching out and mussing his hair with her fingers. She felt the dampness of it and remembered she must look like a waterlogged mess herself. "You're ten years old, not thirty. *I'm* supposed to take care of *you.*"

John set down the ladle and joined them at the table. "Come on, slugger. Finish that last problem so I can clear things off and set the table." He looked over the top of Travis's head to Maggie. "You two want to stay for dinner?"

Another dinner invitation from a man? When had she ever been this popular? And when had it ever been a good idea for her to think about saying yes?

"Please, Mom?"

The tug at her sleeve wasn't nearly as persuasive as the warmth that spread through her beneath John Murdock's focused attention. As her fear for her son's safety dissipated, other sensations were sneaking in—like the way John hadn't budged when she'd knocked on his chest. Like the distinctly masculine hills and hollows filling out his khaki-green T-shirt, and the way the color of the cotton intensified the pale green of his acutely observant gaze. And she couldn't help but notice that he was tall enough that even she had to tip her chin to see the color and expression of those intriguing eyes.

That surprising appreciation about a man made her self-conscious about how she must look. The rain had probably washed away what little makeup she did wear. Damp strands of hair had escaped from her bun and kinked around her face and collar. And even though it hadn't mattered for a long time, she knew her mannish uniform, thick belt and Kevlar transformed her figure into something about as feminine as the long plank table between them.

No, she needed to get out of here before she did something silly like accept his invitation. Travis was the only guy she needed in her life.

"We wouldn't want to impose."

"Aw, Mom." Travis moaned on three different pitches.

"I wouldn't have invited you if it was an imposition.

Food's made. There's plenty. Stay and eat. Or don't." John's matter-of-fact offer was an embarrassing reminder that he hadn't asked her on a date. This was about food, practicality and being kind. And they'd have a ten-year-old chaperon, for Pete's sake.

She must be in a pretty vulnerable state to be worrying about such things around a man who was more stranger than friend. Yet he'd rescued her son. He'd answered the call to protect the most precious thing in her life when she hadn't been there to rescue him herself. He'd touched her, and she hadn't minded. He didn't remind her of Danny Wheeler in any way.

Moody as he seemed to be, John Murdock was a good, decent man. Maggie had known far too few of those in her life. Maybe that's all this sudden attraction was. He was a good guy, the kind of man she wanted her son to know. The kind of man who should be their friend.

And whatever he was cooking, it really did smell wonderful. That was some kind of spicy stew, and corn bread if she wasn't mistaken. Her empty stomach grumbled in noisy appreciation. Oh, yeah, she was a real catch right now. Like she should worry about becoming anything more than friends.

"Do you have honey to go with that corn bread?" she asked.

"I bet I could find some packed in a box somewhere."

"Does that mean we can stay?" Travis really did seem to like the guy, and John didn't seem to mind the adulation.

"Can you give me five minutes to change into some dry clothes?"

John nodded.

"All right, then. We'll stay."

"Yes!"

Maggie rested a hand on Travis's shoulder to calm him down. "Just for dinner. We don't want to take up any more of John's time. And you and I will clean up the kitchen afterward."

Travis's groan was as loud as his cheer had been.

John grinned, transforming his chiseled features into something quite handsome and making her pulse trip over itself when he turned that smile on her. "Sounds like a deal to me."

"Finish your homework." She sat Travis back in his chair and returned to the living room. John followed her out to escort her to the door.

She'd been in such a rush on the way in that she hadn't paid any attention to the decor. While she had to admire a man who could move in one day and have most of his stuff unpacked and put away so quickly, she wondered at the lack of personal touches. The only shots of color in the room were the spines on a collection of books that filled an entire shelf from floor to ceiling—and the rich navy blue of his Marine Corps uniform in a plastic cleaner's bag draped over the back of the couch.

"That's impressive." Drawn to the subtle display of pride and patriotism, she detoured to the sofa to get a closer look at the brass buttons and royal blue slacks with the red stripe down the side.

"Just got them out of storage yesterday."

"My dad was a marine, too. But his uniform was a little different—he was enlisted."

"Ooh-rah." John stopped at the front door and turned. "Where did he serve?"

"Quartermaster Corps out in Barstow." She blinked away the grim memories of her teen years in Southern California. "He was killed in a motorcycle accident off base."

"I'm sorry."

Soon after, she'd met a young Navy seaman named Danny Wheeler, who'd seemed like the answer to her heartbreak. Her late mother had approved of Danny, had told her it would be good to have a man in the family again. Thank God her mother hadn't lived to see how her marriage to Danny had turned out.

Maggie blinked again and forced herself to concentrate on the computer-generated pattern of grays and tans on John's utility work uniform. She gently shifted the carefully pressed dress blues aside to get a better look. "Even the camouflage looks different from what Dad wore. That was a different generation, I guess."

Beneath the camo uniform she found an open box. She immediately recognized the Purple Heart container and reached inside to retrieve it. Danny had burned her father's service mementos one drunken night in an effort to keep her from putting any other man before him. She blinked away that raw memory, too. "Dad had one of these from his tour of duty in Vietnam. Before I was born."

She couldn't help but let her gaze slide over to the denim pant leg that folded in around John's artificial limb. "Can I ask what happened? Does it still hurt?"

John crossed the living room and plucked the felt box from her fingers. "That's a conversation for another night."

She noticed the felt covers of several other medals when he placed the Purple Heart back inside the moving box.

"Are you pinning these on your uniform?"

"No. Just haven't got them put away yet."

Another medal case caught her eye and she reached inside to pick it up. Her neighbor was even more of a hero than she'd defended against Lawrence Boyle that evening. "But you should, Captain. At least put them in a display cabinet. A Silver Star is something to be proud—"

He grabbed the medal and dumped it back with the others. Then he quickly scooped up the box and uniforms, shoved them in the front closet and shut the door—taking away any trace that he was a military man…beyond the buzz cut of pecan-brown hair and the proud carriage of those broad shoulders. "It's just John, remember? You'd better get out of those wet things before dinner gets cold."

"I'm sorry if I said something wrong. I was just admiring—"

"You didn't say anything wrong." He drilled her with a look that told her his words weren't entirely true.

She'd touched a nerve. But as someone who'd completely fried her own nerves for the day, she understood his need to avoid touchy subjects right now. She headed for the door he held open for her. "Okay, Just John. Thank you—for everything this evening. I'm not used to depending on anyone else." She wanted to say or do more, but the steely cast to those suddenly cold eyes told her that no apology would be welcome. So she opted for a simple smile and a quick exit. "I'll be back in a few minutes."

Chapter Six

11:47 p.m. John read the time on the table beside his bed and tried to remember the last time he'd gone this long without checking a clock or watch and wondering when something would end—like lying in a burning vehicle and listening to his comrades dying, pushing himself to the limits during a painful physical-therapy session, or working side by side with Meghan Taylor and pretending he didn't care.

But tonight he hadn't thought about time. He hadn't thought about Meghan. He hadn't really thought much about the war he'd left behind. There'd been no past to grieve or regret, no future to worry about. For a few hours tonight, he'd simply lived in the moment.

Dinner with the Wheelers had been surprisingly relaxing and fun and...distracting. Maggie was true to her word, taking only a few minutes to change and come back. She'd washed away the smudges of mascara that had shadowed the freckles beneath her eyes. And even though she hadn't released her hair from that practical bun she liked to wear, it was nice to see her in civvies and discover that the curvy hips and butt down below were balanced with equally sweet curves on top.

Not that he'd complimented her or flirted. He'd just noticed. A lot. He'd noticed the way she'd loaded up her corn bread with honey, and then licked the sweet golden mess off her fingers. She was genuinely pretty and unpretentious and crazy about her son.

And yeah, maybe his ego had taken a few strokes when he'd caught a soft smile or curious glance directed his way. But he wasn't looking for a relationship or date, or even the chance to exercise some of the other parts of his body that hadn't seen any action since the roadside bomb outside that Afghan village. He didn't need to be with anyone until he was sure his body could keep up with his brain, and he was certain he could keep the demons that sometimes still haunted him back in the past where they belonged.

Besides, Travis Wheeler had demanded the bulk of his attention at the dinner table. The boy had thoroughly tested John's knowledge of all things baseball, and only the promise of spending some time in the batting cage with him before his game on Thursday night had finally been enough to let John turn the dinner conversation to something other than sports.

Not that Maggie let the discussion stray to anything deeper than the jovial incompetence of their building super. Joe Standage was as friendly and helpful as they came, but it had already been a comedy of errors when it came to fixing things around here. The elderly lady whose apartment sat kitty-corner from John's had complained about a leaky toilet and wound up having to replace her entire bathroom floor after a visit from Joe. Then there was the stuck elevator, and the phones that were still out of order. He'd gone down to the basement himself to inspect the leads running through the building. Judging by the sloppy work he'd seen, the super was lucky that his power saw had cut through a telephone line instead of one carrying electricity to the seventh floor. Could the guy in charge of building maintenance really make so many mistakes? Or was someone deliberately sabotaging things on the seventh floor, leaving Joe to clean up afterward?

John had learned several other things about the tenants on the seventh floor. Maggie had warned him to expect gifts of baked good from Miss Applebaum. And that the Wongs would probably not come out of their apartment to interact with him, but that they would somehow know everything that was going on in the building anyway. Bernie Cutlass talked like a grouch, but he'd been a heck of a lot friendlier before his wife of fifty-some years had passed away last year.

John had learned that Travis loved science and math but thought reading was for girls. After the meal, he'd introduced Travis to his library in the living room, earning a hidden thumbs-up from Maggie. Then she'd insisted on putting away the food and loading the dishwasher by herself, urging John to keep her son interested in the books on his shelves. He'd been happy to lend Travis a couple of YA books—one about a dog who was adopted by an Army unit, and a classic fantasy by Madeleine L'Engle.

Inevitably Travis's curiosity about his injuries came up. And while *transtibial amputation* had tongue-tied the boy, pulling up his pant leg to let him inspect the knee joint and composite rod, as well as letting him inspect the specialized blade prosthetic John used when he was running or working out had kept him talking right up until the moment Maggie had to literally pull him out the door with reminders of brushing teeth and bedtime.

John slipped his bookmark between the pages of the novel he was reading and set it aside to ponder what it was about the family next door that could divert his attention even now that all was quiet on the other side of the bedroom wall that separated his apartment from theirs.

Maggie had been relaxed and friendly at dinner, curious

to hear about his sister's upcoming wedding; sympathetic to learn that he'd lost his parents as a teenager, too. She'd liked his cooking and was surprised to learn that he was the self-taught chef of the family who'd honed his gourmet skills by watching television and preparing dinners for his coworkers at the fire station.

John inhaled a deep, settling breath as he recalled the lines of strain beside those striking green eyes and pale rose lips. Most of Maggie Wheeler's relaxed charm had been an act.

He speculated about the weird convergence of events surrounding the lady cop. If there were enough strange things going on to make him suspicious, then she must be downright paranoid.

Something about night patrols and trusting his gut and experience more than he trusted his eyes and ears told him there was trouble lurking at the fringes of Maggie's life. The woman was hiding a secret or two. She'd been terrified that her son had been alone at the ballpark and out of contact with her. She'd mentioned a mysterious man. The woman wore a gun, a badge and body armor, yet she'd just about had a nervous breakdown when that elevator had gotten stuck.

John eyed the stump of his leg beneath the hem of the running shorts he wore to bed. He was hardly the warrior he'd once been, but he had a feeling that woman's troubles were going to nag at him until he had answers. In every cell of his body he'd been trained to rescue and protect. And while life had altered how he could respond, the instincts were still there.

Maybe that's all this bout of insomnia was—his instincts warring with his abilities. He was aware that Maggie had stirred something in him—a fact that was playing hell with his long-held assumption that Meghan

Taylor was the only female who would ever turn his head. And he knew Maggie was in trouble. But even though her son had invited him into their lives, she hadn't asked for his help. Hell, he wasn't even sure what he could do for her beyond volunteering for a little after-school transportation and some male role modeling for Travis.

Would that be enough to satisfy those protective instincts? That need to take action that drummed through his blood? Shouldn't the offer of neighborly friendship be enough to appease those rusty urges before he embarrassed himself by attempting to do things he was no longer capable of?

A telephone rang in the bedroom behind the thin wall, breaking the silence of the night and giving John his answers.

His hands stiffened into fists at his sides as he glanced at the clock. Midnight. They'd been hours without a line to the outside world, and now, at precisely 12:00 a.m. the phone was ringing in Maggie Wheeler's bedroom?

He swung a leg and a half off the side of the bed and reached for a shoe and the prosthetic propped against the bedside table. For months he'd attuned his ears to the subtlest nuances of sound, warning him of enemy movement in the middle of the night. For years before that, he'd learned to pick up on the sounds of human distress amidst the popping and crashing sounds of a burning building and roaring fire hose.

John concentrated on the methodical process of twisting the prosthetic into place until the suction of the tailored fit engaged, locking the false leg to his own.

Don't listen. Don't eavesdrop. Don't notice.

But the ringing phone wasn't half as alarming as the panicked words he couldn't quite make out, followed by a slamming sound and a scramble through drawers and a closet next door.

He couldn't wait and wonder. It wasn't in him to sit and do nothing. Something was wrong. Something was very wrong.

John pulled the elastic band into place over his knee joint, grabbed his T-shirt from the foot of the bed and hurried out the door. A quick glance up and down the hallway revealed no signs of movement, only shadows and the security light by the elevator doors. Was that…

His eyes zeroed in on the door to the stairwell next to the elevator. Had he imagined that gap between the door and frame? A sliver of light from the landing blinking out as the door closed?

"Hey!" His hopping, hobbling gait got him to the end of the hall in a matter of seconds and he pushed open the swinging steel door. The staccato of running feet echoed up from several stories below. What the hell? John jumped down to the third step in pursuit of whoever had been lurking on their floor. He nearly pitched forward on the fourth step, caught himself on the sixth and slowed his pace to keep his balance as he circled the middle landing.

Frustration poured through his system, telling his body to go faster. Maybe if he'd had on his running leg, he might have a chance of catching the guy. But the perp was speeding up and he was slowing down. John was halfway to the fifth floor when he heard a door slam open down below. The distant door closed again and he knew he'd never be able to catch the guy.

Swallowing his pride and changing strategy, John switched course and jogged back up the stairs. There was still no other sign of activity on the seventh floor when he stopped in front of Maggie's door. He knocked softly. Knocked again. "Maggie?"

He heard a shuffle of noise from inside the apartment, including one unmistakable rasp and click of metal on metal. John had been in the military long enough to recognize the sound of a bullet sliding into the chamber of a semiautomatic. He stepped to one side of the door, out of the potential line of fire, and knocked again. "Maggie, it's John. You can lower your weapon. Open up."

A shadow passed over the peephole, then the chain and dead bolt disengaged and the door opened. Wavy copper hair hung loose and danced over the dotted skin of Maggie's shoulder. She wore long pajama pants, a pair of tank tops and carried her GLOCK 9 down at her side. She'd opened the door just wide enough to flash him a smile he didn't buy. "It's late."

He wedged his shoulder against the door to keep her from closing it. "Tell me about it. You went to bed an hour ago."

"How do you know?"

"Old construction and thin walls. Your bedroom butts up to mine."

Her cheeks flooded with heat, and then he felt her shoving against the door. "Well…stop listening in, you Peeping Tom. Or whatever you call a spy like you."

What John lacked in speed and grace he made up for in brute strength. He planted his foot, braced his hand against the doorjamb and refused to retreat. "Look, I'm not the only one spying on—"

Her telephone rang again. She was wound up tight enough for him to see the leap of muscles beneath her skin. Then her shoulders sagged with some sort of surrender and she swung open the door. "Come on in. I don't want to wake Travis."

John closed the door behind him and threw the dead bolt while Maggie dashed into the kitchen to pick up the phone. "Hello?" He reached the archway into the kitchen in time to see her steady her posture and repeat the greeting. "Hello?"

The color draining from her cheeks told him as much as the gun in her hand that these late-night calls weren't a wrong number. Without breaking stride or asking permission, John plucked the phone from her hand and demanded an answer. "Who is this?"

A startled huff followed by the sounds of labored breathing were punctuated by a man's voice. "You can't have her. She's mine or nobody's."

Adrenaline burned through John's veins at the stark threat. "Listen, you son of a—"

The line abruptly disconnected.

John replaced the cordless phone in its charger, making a quick note that the woman needed caller ID before facing her. "Maggie?"

"What did he say?" She was staring at the phone, rubbing her free hand up and down her right arm. She shook as though a cruel prankster had just dropped a bucket of ice down her back.

"Doesn't matter." John reached out to touch her shoulder and she turned and walked right into his chest. Automatically, his arms wound around her. The thin layers of material between them gave him a clear impression of her healthy curves, shower-fresh scent and trembling fear. It was choice, not instinct, that made him shift his stance to draw her more fully against him and rest his chin at the crown of her soft, fragrant hair.

He didn't know what kind of danger this woman was facing, but he'd be damned if she'd face it alone. He felt a sob of heat against his neck, but there were no tears falling. She was rattled, stunned, too cold for his liking.

"Who was that? Same guy who called before?" He

gently pried the gun from her grasp and she curled all ten fingers into the front of his T-shirt, burrowing against his neck and chest. Her breath stuttered across his skin like a whispered caress. Her hips and thighs lined up squarely against his as if she'd been built to fit his big, brawny frame, yet there was no doubt that she was feminine and soft in every way he was not. He set the gun on the counter and flattened his palm near the small of her back, along the cool strip of skin exposed beneath the hem of her shirts and the low waist of her cotton pants. And even though his body awakened and warmed at the needy, full-body contact, John wanted answers. "Easy, Sarge. You're okay now. You tell me who was on the phone, what he said to you and what the hell is going on around here that has you so spooked."

"THERE WAS SOMEONE OUTSIDE? Why didn't you say something?"

Maggie picked up her gun from the counter, reloaded the magazine John had pulled out for safety's sake, and dashed out of the kitchen. Parts of her were still a little numb, a little in shock from the midnight phone calls and how easily she'd turned to John for comfort. And parts of her were firing with a panicked need to find where these threats were coming from and squash them into dust.

"You were a little preoccupied." John followed her into the living room. "He was there a few minutes ago, before I knocked. That guy is long gone."

She wouldn't believe it unless she saw it with her own eyes. If Danny had gotten this close to her home, this close to Travis...

"Why didn't you tell me there was an intruder in the building? Did you call 9-1-1?" She stopped at the front closet and slipped into her running shoes and windbreaker.

She grabbed her keys and badge, stuffed them into a pocket and opened the front door.

John's big hand reached around her and caught the door before she could get out. "You're chasing down a perp in your PJs?"

The square jaw and hazel eyes and look that said she was behaving irrationally were right there when she spun around. Sarcasm bubbled up as she looped the chain of her badge around her neck and pushed him back a step. "I'm a cop. We go after people who break into buildings."

"Especially when they're lurking outside your door at the same time you're getting crank calls?"

Not so irrational, after all, eh, big guy?

Breathing out a muffled curse, John opened the door and nudged her into the hallway. "Lock it."

Maggie shoved her key into the dead-bolt lock. "You should go back to your apartment. You've already run the stairs once tonight and you're not armed."

"Lock the damn door. I'm coming with you."

By the time she twisted the key, John was already at the stairs, holding the door for her. Maggie scooted past him to peek over the railing. There was nothing to see or hear as far as she could tell, but she wasn't taking any chances. "Keep to the wall. I'll take lead."

Despite the uneven rhythm of his gait behind her, Maggie was surprised to feel John at her heels every step of the way down the stairs. The dim wattage of security lights in the stairwell limited her vision to only a few steps at a time, frustrating her need to find the man who was turning the hard-won serenity of her settled world into a nightmare.

Every time she checked a hallway and passed an empty landing, she mentally noted a *clear* report. John was right. Whoever had been outside her door was long gone or so well-hidden that she'd never find him. But she couldn't stop. She couldn't give up on the desperate idea that catching Danny in the act of stalking her would be a simple seehim, catch-him, send-him-back-to-prison operation, and she'd be able to live a normal life again.

By the time they reached the last flight of stairs without seeing so much as a pet cat moving about the building, Maggie's adrenaline was waning and she was about to give up hope of putting an end to all the weirdness happening around her. Still, her training had taught her a thorough search meant inspecting every floor so that there were no surprises once a building had been cleared.

She slowed her pace as they reached the garage level and put up a hand to warn John to stay behind her. "Let me go out first. There are plenty of places to hide down here. What are you... Let go!"

John clamped his hands around her shoulders and forced her to an abrupt stop. She shrugged free of his grasp, but her protest stopped up in her mouth when he moved past her to feel the steel door and sniff the air.

"I smell smoke."

"Where's it coming from?" She took a deeper breath and the acrid smell stung her nostrils, shifting her concern from a man she couldn't catch to the more immediate danger. She craned her neck back, looking up into the murky shadows of seven flights of stairs. "Travis."

"Don't panic yet. Door's cold." John pushed open the door to the parking garage beneath the building. "The fire can't be that big or that close."

Maggie followed him out and turned 360 degrees. Concrete, brick, cars, trucks, laundry room, storage area, elevator. She lowered her gun to her side and darted out toward the rows of vehicles. "Could it be an engine fire? I don't see any flames."

She didn't see any signs of movement either. The laundry room was empty, and a padlock on the outside of the tenants' storage lockers told her their intruder must have run up to the street, ducked under the security gate and disappeared into the night.

Maggie came back to the stairs and elevator. "Do you think the fire's outside?"

"No." John didn't look any more like a firefighter in his red running shorts than she looked like a cop in her pajamas. But there was something so methodical and focused in his movements along the wall that he inspired both confidence and an uneasy sense of pending danger. He was trusting his nose, not his eyes. He ran his hands along the bricks, traced his fingers along the seams of metal access panels and smelled the air. Maggie jumped when he snatched his fingers back as though one of the bricks had bitten him. "It's in the wall. Localized from the feel of it." He glanced from the stairwell door to the elevator, then up into the support beams over their heads. "That won't last long if it gets into the infrastructure. There are all kinds of conduits behind this wall it can travel up. Phones, power, cable, heating and AC."

"The fire will spread to the seventh floor?"

"To the whole building. I'm guessing your friend rigged it as a diversion. Crossed some wires, maybe jammed a match into the insulation."

Travis.

Maggie spotted the fire alarm beside the elevator and ran to it. But John blocked her path. "We have to wake everyone up and evacuate the building," she argued. "Travis is asleep."

"There's no hammer." He grasped both sides of the emergency fire box mounted on the wall. "One more thing Standage is responsible for that doesn't work."

"Why do you need a hammer? Hit the alarm."

Instead, he wrapped his left hand around his right fist, flexed his forearm and shouted, "Don't look!"

Maggie jerked her face away as he smashed his elbow into the glass front of the fire extinguisher box. The glass splintered and bowed. A second blow showered glass down on the concrete at his feet. She spotted drops of blood in the shattered mess. "John?"

He set the fire extinguisher on the floor and pulled out the ax behind it. "Stand back!"

"John!"

With a mighty, home-run swing, he attacked a small hollow in the wall beside one of the electrical boxes. Chunks of brick and mortar flew out and Maggie dodged out of the way of the stinging projectiles. A second blow, a third, caved in the bricks. Wisps of smoke feathered through the expanding crevice.

With a fourth blow, John hooked the ax head behind the brick facade and pulled down several chunks, revealing black char marks and smoldering insulation. "Maggie, get the extinguisher," he ordered, swinging the ax against the wall with one last blow. The whole section of bricks tumbled out, forcing John back from the avalanche.

If he was hurt or his prosthetic was damaged, he never let on. He dropped the ax and reached for the fire extinguisher, but Maggie pulled the pin and rushed past him, squeezing the trigger and spraying CO_2 foam all over the insulation, wood slats, junction box and bricks.

"You got it." John squeezed his hand around hers, urging her to release her grip. "You got it, Sarge."

Maggie's hand popped open and she let John pull the extinguisher from her shaking hands.

"Are we out of danger?" she asked. "The fire won't spread?"

He set the empty red can on the floor and brushed the dusting of mortar and grit off his hands. He turned his forearm and, for the first time, noticed the gash above his elbow. "I don't think we're catching your intruder tonight. If he didn't have us beat before, he's had plenty of time to get out of the building while we were distracted with this." He bent down and reached into the white goop she'd sprayed all over the opening. "Here's our culprit."

He wiped off the squishy remains of a cigarette butt, then sniffed it, frowned and held it up by the light next to the stairwell door.

"It's fresh." He flicked the butt back into the abyss. "Nobody's that much of an idiot to drop a lit cigarette inside a wall."

She blinked against the gases from the chemicals and pungent smoke lingering in the air. "It was deliberate?"

"Oh, yeah." Blood seeped through the fingers John clasped over his elbow. "I don't suppose you managed to tuck your phone inside your bra?"

"You're a pro at only answering the questions you want to, aren't you?" She pulled her cell from the pocket of her windbreaker. "Now what?"

"You're calling the cops and I'm calling KCFD. There are too many things going wrong around here. And I'm guessing this isn't the only one that wasn't an accident."

Chapter Seven

Maggie cut another piece of adhesive tape. "I can't believe Travis went back to sleep so fast. I figured he'd wait until the last firefighter left."

Oops, the last firefighter in the building was still sitting at her kitchen table, letting her doctor up the glass cuts on his arm. She looked up from where she knelt beside him. "Sorry."

"Pretty exciting night for a ten-year-old, huh?"

"A little too exciting if you ask me. That was nice of your friends to let him climb inside the fire engine for a few minutes, though. I just hope he'll wake up in a few hours when I get him up for school."

Maggie carefully placed the tape over the gauze bandage and gathered up the first-aid supplies. She noted a couple of tiny scratches in the rod sticking out of his black shoe. Who knew what injury the collapsing wall might have caused had that leg been skin and bone. A sudden attack of weary, guilty tears made her eyes feel gritty, but she blinked them away and pushed to her feet. John Murdock had already risked so much keeping her and the rest of his country safe. And now she'd put his life in danger again because of her stupid choices and sorry past.

The kitchen tile was cold beneath Maggie's bare feet

as she crossed to the sink to throw away the soiled cotton she'd cleaned his cuts with and wash her hands.

"The cops cleared the building and the men on the first-response truck confirmed that the fire hadn't spread beyond that part of the parking garage." Maggie shivered at the deep, even sound of John's voice coming up behind her. He appeared beside her at the counter to pick up her GLOCK off the counter and dump the magazine. She watched the practiced efficiency of his long fingers opening up the firing chamber to remove the bullet there. He reloaded the bullet into the magazine and set both it and the GLOCK on top of the refrigerator. "So, are you going to tell me why you answer the door with a loaded gun?"

A chill traveled down Maggie's spine at the ominous question. She folded her arms in front of her and rubbed at the goose bumps pricking her arms. She couldn't blame him for asking. She'd been ready to shoot to kill when she'd heard the knock on the door and had come flying through the living room. He'd probably feel a heck of a lot safer if the crazy lady next door wasn't armed. But Danny and her past had never been easy to talk about, even to a qualified therapist.

She turned her head in his direction without making eye contact. "It's really late, and I think we could both use a little sleep."

But the wide chest wasn't budging. "That bastard said, 'You can't have her. She's mine or nobody's.' Now that makes it sound like this guy thinks you and I mean something to each other. And the only type of man I know who would care about something like that is an old boyfriend. Or an ex-husband."

The flinch in Maggie's shoulders apparently told John all he needed to know.

He leaned a hip against the counter to face her. And

even though he ducked his head to try to read what she was sure was an unnatural pallor to her chilled skin, she never raised her gaze above the earth, eagle and anchor logo on his T-shirt. "If that was your ex, making calls and setting fires and who knows what else, you need to call your attorney now."

How could the man who'd chased away a bone-deep chill just hours earlier make her feel so cold now? She hugged her arms tighter and nodded toward the clock on the stove. "Before three in the morning?"

"I don't mind waking him."

"Fortunately it's not your decision to make." Tipping her head to finally meet that probing gaze, she flashed him a look that she hoped would put an end to the conversation.

She spun around to retrieve her windbreaker from the back of a chair and slide her arms into the sleeves. What had she been thinking—allowing John Murdock into her home? Standing here in her pajamas? Turning to him for solace and support because a nightmare from her past resurrected itself and caught her off guard?

She needed to back off the whole idea of having a hero come to her rescue. She needed to be self-sufficient. She needed to think this through. "We can't even prove that that was Danny who called."

"Twice. In the middle of the night." He straightened from the counter, making the distance she'd tried to put between them seem insignificant.

"All he said was my name, too softly for me to identify a voice. Then some heavy breathing. And I didn't hear him speak to you. It could have been anyone." The arch of John's eyebrow told her he knew she didn't believe that. But she couldn't back down; she didn't want to admit that Danny had become a part of her life again. "And I never knew my ex-husband to smoke. He was always about being fit and working out."

"You don't have to smoke to have access to cigarettes and a lighter."

"You can't be sure it was him on the stairs either."

"He put a lot of people at risk tonight."

When the green-gold glare never wavered, she felt compelled to add, "Fine. I promise to call first thing in the morning and let my attorney know it's a possibility, okay? So just drop it."

John shrugged, his big shoulders creating a ripple effect in the kitchen's quiet atmosphere. "Like you said, it's not my decision. I can see I've overstayed my welcome."

With just a few steps, he strode through the archway and left her alone. *Alone.* With Danny out there in the world somewhere, watching, waiting for his next chance to get to her.

Maggie ran to the archway to stop him before he reached the front door. "Would you like some tea?"

So much for standing on her own two feet.

She held her breath as John halted in the shadows of the unlit room. She knew they both worked in the morning, and the hour was already late. She knew the former marine had better things to do than deal with her problems.

Maggie also knew she really didn't want to be alone right now. She'd never had an ally against Danny before, and had worked ten long years to get to the point where she didn't need one. But please, please, please, don't let John Murdock think she was such a crazy woman that she didn't appreciate his help and concern. Please let him turn around and stay until she could get these nerves worked out of her system and become a competent cop and confident woman and think on her own two feet again.

She was still holding her breath like some kind of

dumbstruck teenage girl who'd just asked the high school quarterback to the Sadie Hawkins dance when John turned around. "Tea sounds good."

It was too dark to tell if the glare had disappeared, but the quiet depth of his voice skittered like a caress against her ears. Her breath rushed out on a noisy sigh and she tiptoed back across the cool tiles to turn on the light over the stove and pick up the kettle.

Nervous energy thrummed through her veins as she filled the teakettle with fresh water. Was this relief crashing through her system? Trepidation at entertaining a grown man in the middle of the night? Anticipation of forming an alliance that could, at the very least, give her an outlet for expressing the fears she'd guarded close to her heart for so long, and, at the very most, give her an extra pair of eyes and ears to help her avoid Danny and keep her son safe? Maybe her inability to be still had to do with something else altogether—something she hadn't even allowed herself to feel for a very long time.

Awareness. Attraction. Desire.

She was so out of practice at relating to a man who wasn't a coworker or a perp, and whose age landed in the eligible range between father figure and ten-year-old that she couldn't be sure what she was feeling.

John Murdock was a fascinating mix of Jekyll and Hyde. Even if he refused to pin the ribbons and hardware to his uniform, he wore the medals he'd earned serving his country in every proud step he took. He walked on an artificial leg and had visible burn scars, but there was nothing weak or wounded about those broad shoulders and strong arms. He could be gruff and standoffish one minute, and almost possessively concerned the next. She should be afraid of a man who was bigger and stronger than she was. Yet every newly awakened cell of her body had been imprinted with the memory of what it felt like to be held by him—to be surrounded by his heat and strength, to feel secure in a way she never had before. And foolish as it might be, she longed to be held that way again.

History had taught her a bitter lesson about her inability to judge men. But tonight she was trusting another lesson she'd learned the hard way—that a man's merit shouldn't be judged by his outward appearance or his personality. Handsome charmers could be deadly. And maybe a damaged marine who showed up unannounced and uninvited on her doorstep in the middle of the night was someone she could trust.

"I figured you for a coffee drinker." She pulled out the tea tin and sorted through the bags inside. "I'm assuming you want an herbal blend at this hour. No caffeine?"

The oak chair creaked beneath his weight. "Surprise me."

Maggie opened the dishwasher and pulled out mugs and saucers. Trusting though she was willing to be, there was an unfamiliar intimacy about having a grown man in her quiet kitchen at this time of night that raised goose bumps along her skin. She set out the sugar bowl and asked if he wanted milk. Then she was back at the tea tin again, digging through it to find the precise flavor that appealed to her right now. Something to calm her ping-ponging thoughts? Or something to boost her courage? Maybe she was the one with the Jekyll and Hyde personality. She should double-check that Travis was still asleep with his ball glove. Maybe she should get dressed. Or at least brush out the sleep-rumpled hair that kept falling into her face.

"Maggie, sit."

The mug she held clattered in its saucer before she righted it with both hands. Her heart thundered in her chest. "I don't take orders like that very well. Especially from a guest in my own home."

"Fair enough. Sarge, will you sit with me, please?" The deep timbre of his voice could be downright mesmerizing when he softened it like that. "I know I'm barging into your life, and maybe I'm not welcome, but I think you need to talk."

She tucked her hair behind her ears, rubbed her damp palms over her hips and turned. A reassuring smile never quite took hold. "You're welcome here. Always."

"Sit."

John's quiet patience seemed to soothe her own rapid pulse. With a nod of acquiescence, she came to the table and pulled out a chair on the opposite side. "Where should I start?"

"Wherever you need to."

His hazel eyes glimmered gold in the dim light of the kitchen, encouraging her to open up. But she couldn't just jump into Danny Wheeler and the memories of pain and terror. So she pulled her feet up onto the seat and hugged her knees to her chest. She nodded toward the bedroom outside the archway. "I wish I had Travis's ability to fall asleep fast and stay oblivious to the world until the alarm goes off in the morning."

"That must make it easy for the tooth fairy to pay him a visit."

She nodded at the silly comment, appreciating the effort at humor, but knowing she needed to steer the conversation toward more serious matters. "I checked his cell phone. It's working just fine now. Maybe the moisture from the rain did mess with it, but I'm thinking he saw it as a way to spend some time with you. You've been a popular topic lately."

"Yeah, he asked a lot of questions before you got home

tonight—everything from timing his batting swing to wanting to know what it was like to drive a fire engine."

"He probably loved that."

"Well, I don't drive one anymore." His chest expanded with a controlled sigh. "But back in the day…"

"But you're a firefighter."

"Arson investigator. I go into a fire after the fact now." She could hear him tapping his false leg under the table. "I'm not on the front lines anymore."

"You were tonight." The regret she heard in his voice saddened her. Although she didn't see how having the brains, training and experience to do that kind of analysis and help put away criminals or prevent similar tragic accidents could be a bad thing. "Sounds a lot like detective work. I love the challenge of solving a puzzle like that. I'm hoping to make detective one day soon myself."

"Yeah?"

"Yeah. I just graduated with my degree in criminal justice in December." She shrugged her shoulders around her clasped knees. Maybe she shouldn't have revealed just how delayed she'd been about taking control of her life after the devastation of her marriage. But she suspected John had agreed to a cup of tea so he could get some facts to explain the harassing phone calls and arsonist in the building, not to trade stories. She needed to say something to alleviate his concern. She brushed a wayward strand of hair off her face and held it behind her ear. "Travis knows he could have called me at the precinct. Whether or not I'm in the middle of an investigation, they'd have gotten a message to me. I'm sorry he bothered you."

"It wasn't a bother. Compared to the way I used to live my life, it's nice to know that I can still be useful."

"Useful?" Surprised by the admission, Maggie dropped her feet to the floor and turned toward him, crossing her arms on top of the table. How could a man whose touch had blotted out her fears and whose quick action had prevented a small fire from becoming a big tragedy think he had nothing to offer? "You've taken on not one but two heroic careers. How do you figure you're not useful?"

"Is it possible the calls came from someone besides your ex-husband? I don't want to leave you exposed to more trouble because we didn't look at other possibilities. Is there something about a case you're working on now that makes you feel like you have to arm yourself at home?"

Ouch. She'd run into walls before. So it was fine for the man to come over here and question her, but if she showed any concern about him, the subject was closed. More Jekyll and Hyde. "I don't know who you used to be, John Murdock. All I know is the man you are now. And if I didn't think I could trust you, you wouldn't be here right now."

"So you let me in." She could learn a thing or two from his interrogation tactics. The man didn't mince words or waver from his goal. "But are you going to answer my question?"

Maggie exhaled a surrendering breath. If he was going to be rescuing her son and holding her in his arms and insinuating himself into their lives, she supposed she owed him some explanation. "I've been a desk officer for most of my career. Not a position where you make a lot of enemies. My chief assigned me to the Rose Red Rapist task force—sort of an internship for detective work. But I've been a part of that for only a few days."

"I imagine you could make enemies on a case as big as that." John leaned forward, seeming to assess every response she gave. Maggie drew back a few inches. "That bastard was in the papers back before I went overseas. The cops never caught him?"

She shook her head. "The crimes stopped for a while and any leads the department had went nowhere. Now he's back. There was a victim attacked with the same M.O. a week ago." Maggie fiddled with the corner of the place mat in front of her. The unsettling events these past few days struck too personal a note to be attributed to someone who didn't know her, right? Could there be another enemy out there? Was she so worried about Danny coming back into her life that she was overlooking a different threat? "I'm more support staff and investigator-in-training than a real detective yet. I blew off a reporter last night who thought I knew something insightful about the case. I don't."

"Would this Rose Red Rapist know that? Has anyone else on the task force been targeted?"

"Targeted?" The place mat crumpled between her fingers.

"Maybe your ex did send you flowers and a love letter. But an elevator mishap? Communication lines out just on our floor?" He pointed out just how personal the odd events had become. "Lines that were out until *your* phone rang at midnight?"

Her fingers fisted around the corner of the placemat. "Those things could happen anywhere, to anybody."

"If you make an excuse for one more thing—" Maggie snapped her gaze back to John and that focused intensity wouldn't let her look away again. He reached across the table and laid his fingers over her fisted hand. "Don't tell me it's nothin'. I know what scared looks like, and what a person does to cover it up. And, Sarge, you've got that look. If it's not the rape investigation, then I'm guessing it's your ex—and that it wasn't a friendly divorce."

A bubble of familiar terror stuck in her throat. Danny Wheeler wasn't something she'd talked about with anyone except her therapist and Chief Taylor. But the bubble burst with an exhale of relief that he'd guessed her secret, and her fingers relaxed and slid beneath the warmth of John's hand. "Pretty easy to figure out, huh?"

"He's the one who called tonight, isn't he?"

"I can't be sure, but I wouldn't put it past him to say something like that."

What was it about those beautiful eyes blocking out everything else but their focus on her that made her think she could trust this guy? "Can you talk about it?"

She was surprised to discover that she could.

"I married too young and I married wrong. Danny Wheeler was abusive. Very." Her fingers flinched as she spoke, but John's grip around her hand was rock-steady—the same way his arms had been when he'd held her so close. Just like before, his touch steadied her nerves and allowed her to choose her words very carefully. "That's why Chief Taylor thought I'd be a good fit for the task force. I'm a rape victim, too."

Those eyes finally blinked and looked away. She could only imagine what kind of curse or emotion that steely jaw was crushing into silence. With another blink, John looked at her again. His grip on her hand shifted. Tightened. The intimacy of the night shrank down to the graze of a callused thumb over the tender skin on the inside of his wrist. "Can you tell me about it?"

"I tried to leave him once. We had a daughter."

"Did he ever…?"

"Hurt her?" Danny had never laid a hand on their daughter. And yet… "Angel wasn't even in school yet when Danny took her. You know, to make me come back. He got drunk and passed out. By the time I got there, she'd wandered out of the motel room where he was hiding and got hit by a car."

John was observant enough to know how that accident

had turned out. "Please tell me there's something positive coming out of this story."

Maggie's fingers danced inside John's grip. The only silver lining to this story was asleep with his ball glove in the next room. "That's when I knew there was no chance at reconciliation, that even if Danny stopped drinking, I couldn't be with him again. I filed for divorce. I was moving my things out of our apartment when he…trapped me on the elevator."

John's hand squeezed painfully tight. Just as quickly, his fingers eased their grip. "I'm sorry. I'm so sorry. So you beat this bastard, right?"

In a way, she supposed she'd defeated her ex the morning she'd awoken in the hospital and decided that weekend of terror would never happen again. "I got my divorce, sent Danny to prison and had Travis all in the same year."

The stroke of John's thumb stopped. This time the curse was audible. "Travis is the product of your husband raping you?"

Maggie nodded. She reached out to hold on to John's hand with both of hers, easing his temper and rediscovering some of her own strength. "I haven't told Trav. I may never tell him. It's not like Danny wants to be a part of his life. Why tell my son he was born out of anything besides my love for him?"

"How long has Danny been out of prison?" John's fingers danced across the palm of her hand, sending a riot of goose bumps up her arm and kindling a slower, more languid heat inside.

Maggie wondered if John was finding comfort in these simple touches across the table, too. "Long enough for him to show up as a person of interest on the task force's suspect list. His term in Jefferson City ran about the same time that the Rose Red Rapist stopped his attacks here in K.C."

"Do you think he's the serial rapist?"

She'd been wondering that ever since the day of the first task force meeting when her ex's name had come up. "I never thought he'd hurt anybody but me. But I know that officers from KCPD have talked to him since he was released from prison."

"So even if he's not this Rose Red guy, he probably associates you with the police investigating him. That could explain the calls and the late-night visit."

"Isolation is a classic tactic of abusive men." She shivered at the idea Danny would have deliberately sabotaged her phone so that she couldn't have contact with anyone until he was ready to talk to her himself. She knew what she had to do. "I'll report the calls, the fire—everything—to the task force when we meet tomorrow." She glanced over at the clock on the stove. "Or rather, later this morning."

John read the clock, too, and pulled his hand away. "In the meantime, we're looking out for a man with a shaved head and tattoos."

Missing the warmth of his touch, Maggie tucked her legs up to her chest again. It was a little unnerving to realize that he'd paid such close attention to the comments she'd made during that first panic attack when he'd been moving in. Still, John was a civilian now. And as much as she appreciated his concern tonight, and how talking things through was starting to calm her fears, she knew she shouldn't ask for more from him. "*I'm* looking out for a man like that."

"Without any backup? What are they teaching at the police academy these days?" He leaned back in his chair, scrubbing his hand over the beard growth dusting his jaw. "You got a picture of this guy?"

With a wry laugh, she turned toward the bubbling sounds of the hot kettle on the stove. "Strangely enough, I didn't want to keep any."

"Do you have an address on the exterminator company he works for?"

Needing to take charge of something and move, Maggie got up to turn off the kettle before the whistle shrieked and woke Travis. "I'm sure it'll be easy to find. It's on my to-do list. I'll have a chat with Travis to remind him about staying safe, too."

"I'll have a look around the building tomorrow. Make sure I'm familiar with all the access points and exits here." She heard the chair scooting across the tile behind her and knew he was getting up. "I think I'll follow up on some of Joe's repair work, too."

"And what, check for signs of sabotage?" She poured the hot water over the tea bags in each mug before turning. "John, I'm not asking you to do anything like that."

"You worried I can't do the job?" he asked.

Why would he think... Oh. Her gaze lighted on his leg at just the wrong time, and his posture instantly changed. In the space of a heartbeat, the warmth and concern and soothing comfort he'd brought with him vanished. "I didn't mean—"

"Fine." He'd already backed through the archway and was heading through the living room. "But you get a co-worker to walk you to your car and get Standage to make sure the outside doors stay locked. Have him put up a security camera—"

"John."

Don't stand there, Maggie. Don't let him leave like this. Do it.

Maggie hurried after him. "John Murdock." The muscles in his forearm bunched beneath her hand when she stopped him at the door. With a gentle tug, she asked him to face her and read the sincerity in her eyes. "I don't doubt your abilities or your good intentions for one moment. You're a marine. Wounded or not, you're not afraid to go into battle. But this isn't your fight. I'm a cop. I'm trying to protect you." She wasn't sure if it was his arm or her fingers quivering where they still touched, but she knew she didn't want to pull away. "You don't know my ex. Danny claims he's changed. But the man I knew was violent and unpredictable. Smart, too. Sometimes, he'd just blow up and lose his temper. Those episodes were shocking and painful, but at least I knew they would end. I could recover from them and move on."

"What about the other times?"

Damn, the man was tall. And broad. And when he faced her like this, Maggie felt exposed and feminine and vulnerable. But he didn't need to know the details about Danny's traps and cruel, calculating games. He only had to be warned. "I don't want to form a neighborhood watch against Danny. He'll strike out at anyone who gets in his way. I don't want anyone else to get hurt because of me."

"Don't worry, Sarge. I'm all heroed-out. I just want to do a little poking around. Find out if anyone else around here needs to be worried about what your ex might try to pull. I'd like to know if the things happening around here are deliberate or spur-of-the-moment, and if Danny has any friends in the building."

She braced her hand at the center of his chest, petting him, gentling him, begging him to understand. "John, I'm not asking you to do anything like that."

"I'm volunteering."

"Why?"

He covered her hand with his. "Because some things are worth fighting for. Like the daughter of a fellow marine. The safety of the people where I live. The idea that a woman shouldn't have to take crap like that from any man. It doesn't matter whether it's my battle. It needs to be fought."

Some things are worth fighting for. She'd uttered the same words to Chief Taylor when he'd asked her to join the task force. The echo of that sentiment resonated deep inside her, telling her she had more in common with John Murdock than sharing the same address. "I thought you were all *heroed-out.*"

"Maybe I'd just like to be able to sleep at night."

Her gaze dropped to the clasp of their hands. "I'm sorry. I'm trying to be strong and independent. I never wanted my problems to become anyone else's."

A callused finger slipped beneath her chin and tilted her face back to his. "Would he use Travis to get to you? Like he used your daughter?"

Her silence was answer enough. John brushed a rebellious strand of copper hair off her cheek and tucked it behind her ear. And then, after a moment's hesitation and a catch of breath between them, he dipped his head and covered her mouth with his.

John's kiss was no-nonsense. There was no tentative exploration, no forceful claim. His lips moved over hers gently but surely. He smelled of smoke and dust and man, and Maggie couldn't imagine anything more empowering than answering his sensuous request. Maggie's lips parted, clung, explored with surprising welcome. Her hand drifted up to the strong line of his jaw and she tickled her sensitive palm against the soft rasp of beard stubble there. She hadn't kissed a man since Danny. Hadn't wanted to.

But she wanted this. She needed this. She'd had no idea how much she craved this intimate, human contact.

John's kiss was about trading warmth and support. It was about the surprise of the unexpected tension sizzling between them. It was about talking and listening and understanding each other in a way that only two people so wounded by life could fully comprehend.

It was a kiss that ended so abruptly that Maggie swayed on her feet.

But two strong hands were there to catch her. The room was still spinning when John leaned in to rest his forehead against hers. Her eyes popped open to look up into a sea of deep green flecked with shards of gold.

"I don't know how you're doing this to me, Sarge. I'm not ready to feel anything."

She wasn't ready to be having feelings for someone either. But ill-timed or unexpected as the tenuous emotions might be, there they were, taking root inside her. So she had no answer for him. The Marines had landed in her life, and she wasn't strong enough to keep pushing this one away.

"I'm keeping an eye on the place," he promised. "And on the two of you. Until you tell me otherwise, we're in this fight together."

Chapter Eight

"So KCPD's finest haven't been able to figure out squat yet."

He turned the black newsprint to the single lamp that illuminated the dark office and smiled at the news story in the early edition of the *Kansas City Journal*. Hot off the presses. The ink was fresh enough to smell, and if he used his imagination, the paper was still warm to the touch. He trailed his finger along each line of the story.

It started with a historical account of what had been labeled a "troubling chain" of sex crimes attributed to a single, unknown attacker. Then it went on to make mention of his latest conquest, calling her "the stepdaughter of one of Kansas City's wealthiest businessmen." Wealthy? Beautiful? Entitled? Then the woman deserved to be taken down a peg. He'd done the city a great service.

The woman's injuries got less comment than the discussion of her stepfather's assets and a lame quote about how a "substantial reward will be offered" for any solid leads on the attack. The story mentioned Fairy Tale Bridal Shop and a street name, but there wasn't even a description of a vehicle or alleged attacker mentioned.

For all the fine writing, there really wasn't a lot of meat to the story. There was more talk about the commissioner announcing a new task force than there was about anything else. It was a weak story. Far too weak. He read few facts beyond the names of the police officers, advisers and support staff assigned to the investigation.

One. Two. Three women's names were listed. He stroked his finger across each one. These women had no power over him. They couldn't touch him, couldn't hurt him. And this one woman, Maggie Wheeler—make that *Sergeant* Maggie Wheeler—had the nerve to brag that she'd been the first one to break any kind of lead on the case when she'd gotten the witness to open up to her.

A familiar, predatory urge stirred in his loins.

Maggie Wheeler. Worthless bitch. She only thought she'd gotten something useful from her interview with the blonde woman.

There was something extraordinarily satisfying about outsmarting the entire police department, about putting these women in their place. His nostrils flared as he breathed in deeply and savored the triumph coursing through his veins.

"Not a clue," he gloated. "Not one, single clue."

Yet a niggling bit of annoyance whispered in his ear. He hadn't done enough to assuage the hurt yet. The story wasn't important enough to make the front page. *He* wasn't important enough to be taken seriously. The Gabriel Knight article was buried on the second page between a political cartoon and an advertisement for a local theater.

"That's a good thing." The voice in his head tried to reason with the rage brewing inside him. *"You can't hide in the shadows any longer if you're plastered all over the front page. You made a mistake, had a moment of weakness. But you're better than that. You can control this."*

That's right. He was in control. No beautiful damn woman would ever make a fool of him again.

He reached the end of the column and saw that the article was continued on the last page of the section. The last page? He hadn't even merited a proper headline and now he was just a to-be-continued in the local paper? His breath constricted in his lungs and he rubbed at his chest.

"Ah, hell." He'd smeared a black mark across his clean T-shirt.

Angrily, he shot to his feet and tossed the newspaper onto the chair. He peeled off the shirt en route to the nearest bathroom and folded it into a neat rectangle before dropping it into the bag beside the sink.

"Easy," the voice warned. *"You don't want anyone to know the truth."*

"Shut up." He railed against the face staring back from the mirror over the sink. He was a handsome enough man, wasn't he? He had a job. He'd made a whole damn career for himself. People should respect him. But it wasn't good enough. *He* wasn't good enough.

"That's not true," the voice was quick to argue. *"You've taken a few hits, but you're a good man. Take a deep breath. Get a grip before you get yourself into trouble again."*

Get a grip?

He slowly opened his fisted hands and grimaced at the black ink staining every finger. He was dirty. An abhorrent sourness churned in his gut and he nearly retched.

His own thoughts, as well as the voice, went silent as he turned on the hot water and pumped palmfuls of soap into his hands. He scrubbed and scrubbed at the ink until his fingers were clean and the skin was pink. He splashed more soap and water on his face, then reached into his bag for a bottle of hand sanitizer and a clean shirt.

He wasn't sure how many minutes passed before the fog of his obsession cleared from his brain and he heard a knock at the bathroom door. He froze at the sound. How long had that person been listening in? How long had he been in here, washing away the filth and the rage?

"It's time."

His voice sounded surprisingly normal as he answered the summons to the morning meeting. "I'll be right there."

"I SEE WE MADE THE PAPER." Spencer Montgomery walked through the conference room door and circled the table, placing a copy of the *Kansas City Journal* in front of each task force member. Maggie opened her copy to the page he indicated. "So, in addition to having our plates full with this investigation, we all need to watch what we say to Gabriel Knight."

A quick skim through the article did little to alleviate Maggie's guilt. "I never said Miss Austin's name, I swear. He guessed the victim's name. His question about the interview at the hospital caught me off guard, and whatever I said or did was enough to confirm the guess."

"Relax, Wheeler." The red-haired detective sat at the far end of the table. "Knight talked to all of us. I just hope this doesn't have anything to do with those incidents at your building you reported. I'm not thrilled to see our names listed there."

Annie Hermann stuffed the last of the muffin she was eating into her mouth and grabbed her newspaper. "We are?"

"The information was in KCPD's official press release." Although Spencer Montgomery's words were meant to be reassuring, Maggie could tell by the pinch of a frown between his brows that he wasn't pleased. "I'd pay good money to keep our investigation out of the papers. Anonymity would make our job a little easier. Witnesses and informants will be more reluctant to come forward if they think they'll see their name in the paper. And if our perp gets any sign that we're onto him, it could drive him underground again."

"Or make him even smarter about how to cover up his crimes," his partner, Nick Fensom, suggested before taking a long drink of his coffee.

Kate Kilpatrick, looking enviously fresh and stylish so early in the morning, offered another warning. "The publicity could play in to his power trip as well, making him even more dangerous. The *Journal*'s readers aren't just here in Kansas City. Its circulation is statewide. And if the story gets picked up on the wire and internet, we'll be giving this guy national attention. A lot of people are going to be following every move we make."

Just like a white exterminator's van and unseen eyes had followed *her*?

Maggie stopped typing her notes as her thoughts drifted back to her late-night conversation with John Murdock. He suspected her work on the Rose Red Rapist investigation might be the cause of the unwanted calls and weird events that had rattled any sense of security she'd fought so hard for. Was it possible that a woman who'd purposely flown under society's radar for so long now had more than a vicious ex-husband for an enemy?

She hoped he'd be home when she got there tonight. She wanted to be there when he went poking around the building to find some sign of last night's intruder, or evidence of any of the building's breakdowns being deliberate. Not just because she needed those answers to plan out the best strategy for keeping Travis safe, but because having a friend like John in her corner made *her* feel safe. He made her feel a few other things, too, but she wasn't any more ready to acknowledge and explore those feelings than John claimed he was.

When her attention came back to the task force meeting, Spencer was still voicing his concerns. "We're under a microscope now. If we make mistakes, it'll hurt our credibility."

Nick Fensom chimed in. "And if our leads are publicized, that allows the perp to stay a step ahead of us."

Dr. Kilpatrick jotted a note in her planner. "I'll call Mr. Knight with an official statement, and explain the risks of giving the case too much coverage."

"He'll plead the First Amendment, say the public has a right to know." Nick scowled.

"And I'll argue victims' rights," Kate countered. "There's a fine line we have to walk with the press. We want Kansas City to be aware of Rose Red, but we don't want the city paralyzed by fear of more attacks. Nor do we want to hinder any victim's recovery or jeopardize any future prosecution."

"You're on Gabe Knight, then," Spencer agreed. He sorted through the printouts in the notebook in front of him. Something among the meticulous records diverted his attention.

Maggie typed in Dr. Kilpatrick's assignment to talk to Gabriel Knight at the *Journal.* She was sitting with her fingers poised over the keyboard to input the team's next directive when she realized Detective Montgomery was waiting for her to look up and make eye contact. Had she missed something? "What?"

Was that Spencer Montgomery's version of a smile? "I read your report of your interview with Bailey Austin. Impressive for a first-timer to get her to open up like that."

"Thank you," she answered hesitantly. The lead detective would clean up in a poker game. She couldn't tell if that was amusement or if she was in some kind of trouble for overstepping the bounds of a relative intern. "I think she just wanted somebody to listen to her."

"Possibly." So no pat on the back after all. "But when Chief Taylor said our prime witness could identify her rapist by smell, I was hoping for something more useful than pickles."

Maggie set her laptop on the table. "That's what she said the smell reminded her of—pickles."

Annie Hermann snapped her fingers and reached down to pick up the oversize bag she carried. She pulled out a bent file marked with the crime lab stamp. "Pickles would make sense with the preliminary results from the lab."

"How's that?" Nick wadded up the paper cup from the coffee he'd been drinking and shot it into the trash can beside the door. "That our perp likes to snack on gherkins and dills?"

"No, smart-ass." Annie handed the wrinkled report off to Detective Montgomery. "Vinegar. The lab found traces of vinegar in the victim's panties."

Dr. Kilpatrick sat forward in her chair. "That's not good."

"Pickles have vinegar in them, don't they?" Nick asked.

"Yes." Maggie already knew that Dr. Kilpatrick's concern wasn't about food. Maybe it was a good thing that Bailey Austin hadn't remembered every detail of her attack. "Women used to use vinegar as a cleansing agent after sex. There was an old wives' tale that it worked as a contraceptive."

"You think our perp is some old fart?" Nick asked. "How do you explain the physicality of the attacks, then?"

The CSI across from him groaned. "Listen, Mr. Neanderthal, our guy doesn't have to be old-school to use vinegar. Wives' tale or not, it's an effective way to clean up traces of DNA off the vic. That's why we haven't been able to find any kind of scientific ID on this guy. We can't even tell you what kind of condom he uses because any trace we manage to pull has been compromised."

"He disinfected her? After..." Nick swore under his breath. "If that bastard comes after either one of my sisters—"

"Relax, Nick." Spencer cooled his partner's outburst. "I think we're all in agreement that we can't get this guy off the streets soon enough."

"But we're back to square one," Nick argued.

Maggie piped up shyly, even though she hadn't been asked her opinion directly. "Miss Austin said she came to in an abandoned office building—either under construction, or being renovated or torn down. Could we start a search for properties like that in the area where she was abducted?"

Pike Taylor nodded toward the dog at his feet. "Hans and I are game."

"There's no evidence the assault took place in that area," Spencer pointed out, "only the abduction."

Nick looked at his partner. "You got any other leads, Spence? We need to try something."

"Wheeler's plan it is." After a moment to consider their limited options, Spencer agreed, closing his notebook. "Let's go pull construction and demolition orders for a six-block radius around the abduction site near that bridal shop. Pike, you'll get a search team together? Remember, nothing too big—we don't want to raise this guy's suspicions."

"Will do."

Wheeler's plan? Maggie dipped her head to hide her smile as a fledgling sense of pride and accomplishment swelled inside her. She could be a detective. She could help these victims.

But there was little opportunity to savor the success

of her idea. Without any official dismissal, the meeting seemed to be ending. Everyone at the table was getting up, gathering their things, moving with a purpose. It was business as usual at the Fourth Precinct, and Maggie was starting to feel less like the gatekeeper between KCPD and the public, and more like an integral part of the task force.

Detective Montgomery opened the door. "Annie, see if your lab can at least identify what brand of vinegar it is and find out where our perp could have bought the stuff."

"Could be a long list."

"It'd be more than we've got now."

Kate Kilpatrick filed past the red-haired detective. "I'll pull the files from ten years ago and start reading through them. See if there's any mention of vinegar or empty buildings in the victim statements."

Maggie was the last one to reach the door. "What should I do?" she asked. "Besides copy details of the meeting to everyone."

Detective Montgomery thought for a moment, then closed the door behind them. "Get with the doc on those old files and line up some interviews with the previous victims. You got Bailey Austin to open up, maybe you can get one of them to remember something more, as well."

"Yes, sir." Feeling more like the detective she aspired to be than she'd ever felt before, Maggie quickly crossed the floor back to her front desk station across from the third-floor elevators.

She spent some time at her desk, copying the meeting notes into an email and sending them out to Chief Taylor and the task force members. She verified the duty log for the day, then agreed to cover the desk for Officer Allen's fifteen-minute break so that he could manage the front on his own while she went upstairs to Dr. Kilpatrick's office to work on the victim interviews with her.

Maggie was giving a visitor directions when the elevator doors opened. Her training to be the precinct's first line of defense as well as its first opportunity to welcome guests had her automatically turning to identify the elevator's occupants.

She never heard the woman's thank-you or saw her walk away. Maggie's pulse was thundering in her ears, and her vision had narrowed down to the shiny bald pate and deceptively handsome face of Daniel Gable Wheeler.

He was coming this way, sauntering across the marble floor in his tan work coveralls. His laser-blue eyes locked onto hers, and he was smiling. He grinned that charming smile that had once knocked the teenage Maggie off her feet as though the abuse, the threats, the rape and that fire last night had never happened.

Run. Scream. Fight. Do something.

Danny rested his elbows on the counter and laced his tattooed fingers together. "Hey, baby. The guy downstairs said I needed to sign in here and get a visitor's pass."

Any civilized greeting escaped her. "You can't be here."

"Sure I can, Mags. Where do I sign?" The words carved into his knuckles—*LOVE, HATE*—were a mocking testament to their relationship, and gave graphic emphasis to the damage those powerful hands had done. "I volunteered to come in for questioning on the Rose Red Rapist case. I'm meeting with a Detective Fensom. I'm all about proving my innocence."

Fat chance. The sooner she got him away from her and out of the building, the better.

"Fine. When's your appointment?" She lay the clipboard and a visitor's pass on top of the counter and reached for the phone. While Danny signed the registry, she checked the duty log for Nick Fensom's extension. "I'll get you set up in an interview room and let him know you're here."

The hand that said *LOVE* shot over the counter and grabbed her wrist. Maggie instantly tensed and tried to pull away. Her struggle was subtle and brief. What if someone else on the floor saw her unable to properly defend herself? What if she went ballistic and created an incident that shouldn't have to happen? And why couldn't she decide what to do? It wasn't the offense of his unwanted touch that stunned her, but that the bruising strength still felt so familiar. Had she come such a short way in ten years that Danny's touch could still make her brain and backbone shut down like this?

"I'm being friendly here, Mags. And I don't even get a hello? I thought I'd at least earn a little credit for helping KCPD with the biggest case they've had in years." He leaned in for a more intimate whisper. "Actually, I could care less about anyone else here. I saw your name in the paper—read that this was your investigation. Now I understand why you sicced those uniformed officers on me at work to get an alibi for the last attack. You're moving up in the world. I'm proud of you, baby. I'm here to help you."

If he'd showed her anything but that sincerity in his eyes, she might have cowered. But some out-of-practice instinct that warned her never to believe what those blue eyes said finally kicked in. She could do the hushed intensity thing, too. "Danny, let go of me now or I'll throw you in a jail cell instead of an interview room. There are thirty cops working on this floor at any given time. If you try anything, all I have to do is say the word and they'll be here to back me up. So let go."

With an arch of one dark eyebrow, he eased his grip and she pulled away. While Danny put his hands up and retreated a step, Maggie put the call in to Nick.

A few minutes later, Maggie led Danny into an interview room and closed the door. "Detective Fensom is taking an important call right now. He'll be here as soon as he can." She knew standard procedure was to offer an uncuffed, voluntary interviewee a cup of coffee or glass of water, but she had no such niceties to offer her ex. It was all she could do to point to a chair. "Have a seat."

She waited until his butt was firmly planted in the chair before heading for the door. But escaping from Danny had never been easy.

"I saw your new boyfriend at the ballpark."

Maggie halted with her hand on the doorknob. "So you *were* there watching my son."

"I was waiting for you." He made his appearance sound like a romantic gesture. "I figured you'd come pick up the kid. Didn't know you'd have a boy toy to come do it for you instead."

No argument about Travis being *their* son. No remorse about driving away and leaving a child all alone after dark. No indication that he even remembered the daughter he'd taken to keep Maggie from divorcing him, and then allowed to wander into traffic and be hit by that car.

Angel's death had been the incentive to plot her escape from their marriage. Danny had punished her within an inch of her life the night he'd caught her on the elevator leaving him. Keeping Travis safe gave her the incentive to turn the doorknob. Years of training and therapy and healing gave Maggie the strength to believe Danny could never punish her again unless she let him.

"I'll guard the door from the outside until Detective Fensom gets here."

"I can see how ol' Peg Leg would make a good babysitter."

Maggie froze at the offhand comment. The logical decision to get away warred with the emotional need to put

Danny in his place, to teach him a lesson, to best him somehow for saying something so crude about the man she was falling in love with.

Before that revelation could fully register, Maggie pulled the door shut to hear Danny's next snide comment.

"But he ain't all there, baby. He can't give it to you the way I can."

She wasn't the one who was going to be forced out of a room at her own workplace. Task force or not, Danny Wheeler had to go. Maggie stepped away from the door and faced him. "Get out. Unless you plan to confess to stalking me at my apartment and setting a fire in the basement, you need to leave."

"I've got no idea what you're talking about, baby." His blue eyes hooded with an expression she supposed was his version of longing and regret. "We were once so good together, Mags. That's all I want. Like I said, I'm sober now. I'm holdin' down a job." He leaned across the table and reached out to her. "On our wedding day you promised you'd love me forever. I haven't forgotten those vows. I want to get back to the way things were when everything was right between us."

Maggie ignored the outstretched hand. "Nothing was ever right, Danny. I was just too afraid to realize I could have something better."

His fingers curled into a fist and he pushed to his feet. "And you think screwing old Sergeant Hopalong is better than being with me?"

How had she ever thought Danny Wheeler was hero material? Shaking her head, she turned for the door. "Leave, Danny. Now. Or I'll call your P.O. and tell him you violated your restraining order. I'll tell Detective Fensom that you had to reschedule your meeting."

She never reached the doorknob. Danny grabbed her by

the collar and swung her around to slam her up against the wall. "You uppity bitch. *I* tell you when we're done talkin'." His hand curled around her throat, and his hips butted up against hers, anchoring her in place with her toes barely touching the floor. But her hands were free. She clawed at his wrist but was rewarded with a tighter choke hold and his hot breath in her face. "I'm trying to be reasonable here. You won't meet with me when I ask nicely, so we have to have this conversation any way I can."

Rage spiraled up and twisted with the instinctive need to free herself. *Think. Take him down. Do it!*

Danny was the same person he'd been ten years ago. Maggie was not.

Twisting her legs free and fighting for breath, Maggie thrust her palm up under his nose, hard enough to feel the pop inside. Danny instantly loosened his grip and grabbed his bloody nose. "You stupid, stupid—"

Maggie sucked in a reviving gulp of air, pulled her gun and put it to his throat, backing him up until he hit the table and the steel legs screeched across the floor. "Keep. Your. Hands. Off. Me."

Just as quickly as the attack had come, Danny's outburst subsided. His warm blood dripped on her fingers and he started to laugh. Holding one hand up in surrender, he ignored the threat of the gun pressing into his neck and pulled a bunch of tissues out of the box on the table to dab at his nose. "Man, how I love that Irish temper of yours. So much passion there. Nobody ever could control that fire but me."

Control her? "Oh, my God."

Stunned by how thoroughly she'd just lost it, horrified to think she'd sunk to the same gut-level violence that Danny thrived on, Maggie pulled her gun away from the imprint she'd left on his throat. She'd just earned a college degree that had trained her to outthink rather than just react to a suspect like this. And outthink him was exactly what she intended to do.

He was still laughing when she grabbed him by the front of his coveralls and put him facedown on the table. "Turn around, Danny. Hands behind your back. You have any weapons on you? Anything sharp or dangerous?" After patting down his pockets, she handcuffed his wrist to the table and pushed him back down into the chair. "You're looking at assault on a police officer and violating a restraining order."

He grinned up at her. "You need my help to solve this case, Mags. I have friends on the street. I hear things."

"I don't need anything from you." She opened the door again, swung it wide so that any and everybody who walked down this hallway could see the man she'd handcuffed there. Not that she had any intention of staying. She met Danny's smile with the sternest, strongest look she could manage. "Don't you ever talk about John Murdock like that again. A woman would be lucky to have him love her. He's more of a man than you'll ever think about being."

"John, is it? And you're defending him? So it *is* personal."

She shook her head, remembering how impossible it was to reason with him, and stepped out into the cleaner air of the hallway. "Goodbye, Danny."

Lawrence Boyle was strolling down the hallway, peeking into each open doorway he walked past. Maggie sidestepped him when he approached, but he moved with her, blocking her path. "Ma'am?" He greeted her with a smile, with his hands held up in front of him to show he meant her no harm. "I was looking for Danny? The guy at the front desk said he was back here."

"In there."

"Whoa, dude, your nose." Deciding her personal desire to leave Danny as far behind as possible was secondary to leaving two former felons together and unguarded, Maggie reluctantly waited against the wall opposite the open door. Danny's boss turned his thick neck to ask her about the handcuffs. "Is he under arrest?"

Maggie hooked her thumbs into her utility belt and looked him straight in the eye. "You should go back to the waiting area, Mr. Boyle." She eyed the front of his jumpsuit for a visitor's tag. "You need to sign in."

"But he said he was only going to be half an hour." Boyle faced her fully to plead his case. "I've got my van parked downstairs. We've got a job to get to."

Danny pulled out another tissue to wipe the blood from his face. "It's okay. I may be a little longer, Lawrence. I have business to attend to."

"Yeah, I know what kind of business you're interested in." Maggie put a hand on Boyle's shoulder to keep him from entering the room. Although she felt him stiffen inside his coveralls at her silent command, thankfully, he was more willing to cooperate than Danny had been. With a nod, he promised to stay put and she released him. "Seriously, Danny? Breaking the law right here at the police station? What's the good of me giving an ex-con a break and hiring you when you go and get yourself into trouble again? And over a woman?"

"She's hot when she's all fired up and in charge, isn't she?" Danny seemed oblivious to his friend's frustration and her revulsion at the worthless compliment. "Nobody else will ever love you the way I do, Mags."

Lord, she hoped not.

"Everything okay here?" Maggie masked her sigh of relief at Nick Fensom's arrival, and channeled the raw energy coursing through her into the white-knuckled grip she had on her belt. Danny and Lawrence Boyle might top Fensom in height, but there was a cagey, badgerlike intensity about the stocky detective that made both men sit up straight and retreat a step. "I thought I asked only one of you to come in for questioning. I don't like a party."

Maggie was glad for the backup, but prayed her relief wasn't flooding her cheeks with heat. "Your appointment is in Interview Room D. Just so you know, Danny Wheeler is my ex-husband and coming within fifty yards of me is a violation of his restraining order."

Nick eyed the duo in matching coveralls before dismissing her. "I'll have a personal conversation with his parole officer, Sergeant. You get back to work."

"You interested in her, too?" Danny taunted from inside the room. "Come on, Mags, you're *my* wife, remember?"

Nick grabbed the door and flicked a thumb over his shoulder, warning Boyle out of his way. "You, out. You, shut up." Turning his attention to Danny, Nick closed the door.

The squeaky soles of Lawrence Boyle's shoes told Maggie he was hurrying to catch up with her. But she hadn't expected him to latch on to her arm or for her swerving release to be so obvious. She clamped her mouth shut and waited for the bleach-haired exterminator to speak.

"Sorry, Mrs. Wheeler. When Danny said he was in a position to do the cops a favor, I thought it was a good thing. I didn't know he was coming here to hit on you." *Hit on her?* Oh, the irony of that cliché. But those bug eyes were round and dark and smiling with good intentions. So she clamped her mouth shut and let him finish. "But Danny's a good worker. My business is expanding and I could really use his help. If Danny gets released again, I promise I'll keep him in line."

Impossible.

No one could keep Danny Wheeler in line.

No one could keep him out of her life.

Maggie saw the blood staining the sleeve of Boyle's coveralls and knew it had come from her hand. She hid her palm against her thigh and changed course to head for the bathroom. "Excuse me, I need to clean up."

Any extra confidence that the task force meeting had built inside her was gone. By the time she got inside the john, away from ex-felons and fellow cops, her knees were shaking so badly she had to grip the edge of the sink to keep them from collapsing.

After ten years Danny could still take her back to that place of insecurity and terror in an instant. She wasn't ready to be a detective. She wasn't ready to take a chance on a new relationship. She wasn't in any shape to be much good to anyone else as long as Danny could get to her like this.

Because until she could get a handle on the fear, the anger and the paranoia and second-guessing they inspired, she wasn't even any good to herself.

JOHN'S BOOTS CRUNCHED over the melted plastic and metal bits of the Wilson Irrigation Supply Company's collapsed roof. He'd replaced his ball cap with a hard hat, and his ax and fire hose with a flashlight and a computerized clipboard.

He saw the sweep of Meghan Taylor's flashlight coming up behind him before he heard her voice. "What does it look like to you, John?" She'd shed the heavy weight of her coat and breathing gear, but still wore her helmet, boots and overalls. The pale hair sticking to the sweat at her temples indicated she hadn't been home to get any sleep since yesterday's alarm. "Hazmat cleared the place of any toxic chemicals, but the rest of this place looks like a total wipe to me."

He followed her glance up to the skeletal walls and twisted metal shelves of what had once been a storage facility for miles of irrigation pipe. He agreed with her danger assessment of the surviving structure. "What's left is going to have to come down before they can do any rebuilding."

"I know they've lost a ton of inventory with this fire, but if they're going to claim it for insurance, I want to make sure it wasn't deliberate."

He nudged aside the mucky layer of water and ash with the toe of his boot and aimed his flashlight at the charred remains of an exposed wiring box. "I haven't seen any pour patterns that indicate the fire was intentionally set. But we might have a case for old age and negligence. It's a good thing your team turned off the gas feed or we'd be looking at an explosion instead of a slow burn. That junction box had probably been sparking and smoldering for days before it ignited."

John took a couple more measurements and entered his notes while Meghan climbed through the warehouse's wreckage with him. This warehouse was probably about the same 1930s vintage as The Corsican, the building where he and the Wheelers and an odd assortment of retirees and recluses lived. He wondered how many upgrades there had been as superficial and cosmetic as this place. While the fire department's visit last night had given him a plausible excuse to check on his neighbors and put together a list of all the building's recent mishaps and repairs that could be attributed to the decaying structure and quick, less-than-stellar fixes by Joe Standage, he was having less and less doubt that Maggie's problems hadn't been caused by age or accident.

"You okay?" Meghan asked, pulling him from his thoughts.

John dismissed her concern. "This just reminds me of another antique that needs to be fixed."

"I heard you had a small fire in your building last night."

"Yeah, a cigarette butt caught some old insulation wrapping on fire. We put it out with an extinguisher before the crew from Station 15 ever got there."

"We?" Meghan asked.

Two years ago—hell, even two days ago—John would have been more concerned about helping Meghan over a pile of rubble that had been knocked down to prevent it from collapsing on the firefighters who'd been fighting the blaze through the night. At the last second, he held out his hand to balance her on the climb down toward the exit. "A neighbor lady and I discovered it."

"But you don't think the fire was an accident?" He released her hand as soon as they hit solid ground.

"I'm beginning to think The Corsican is a death trap."

Meghan scoffed at his doomsday pronouncement. "Come on, I know you. I know you checked the inspections and building codes before you ever moved into the place."

She was right, he *had* made sure The Corsican met city safety codes before signing the lease. "Let me rephrase that. It's not the building that has issues—it's some freak who's trying to bring the place down around us."

"Why? What else has happened?"

It felt like a violation of trust to share any of the sick details about Maggie's disastrous marriage, even with a longtime friend like Meghan Taylor. "It's personal," was the only explanation he offered. "I need to do a little more poking around before I figure out exactly what's going on there."

He was surprised at how readily Meghan accepted his answer, and at how vehement she was about supporting his concern. "If you need anything, you put my number on speed dial. Or call the station. I haven't forgotten how you were there for me when that arsonist was setting fires in Kansas City, and I seemed to be in the middle of all of them."

"Gideon Taylor was there for you," John corrected her.

"The man I love, my boys and my best friend—" she squeezed his arm to emphasize his importance on that list "—were there for me. That's how I got through it, John. I owe you." She patted his arm and moved on ahead of him. "You call, whether it's another fire or anything else. We'll do whatever we can to help."

"Thanks, boss. I'll keep that in mind."

By mutual consent, they changed direction and headed outside to where Dean Murphy and the rest of the Station 23 crew were rolling up hoses and stowing gear. Before they hit asphalt and the jokes and shouts of the crew, Meghan stopped in front of him and turned. "I've been worried about you, John. You seem different. A heck of a lot more introspective. And here I thought it was me, that I made coming back to work uncomfortable for you. But if you've got something you're dealing with, maybe some issue with this neighbor lady you mentioned, then I won't worry so much. Unless you need me to. I don't make you uncomfortable anymore, do I?"

John looked down into the eyes of a friend. And even though there were certainly hints of regret and might-have-beens lingering inside him, the sharp pangs of unrequited love had truly dulled. His thoughts were centered on another woman now. One who just might need him the way he was beginning to need her and her son.

"No." The answer felt more honest than he'd expected.

"Yo, Big John!" John groaned at the taunt from Dean. "You know you miss this. Why don't you get your old bones on over here and show us you can still haul all this equipment."

"You're just trying to get out of work, Dean. I *am* old enough to be smarter than you and have your games figured out."

The younger man laughed and took a few more good-natured gibes from the rest of the crew before they all went back to finishing up the job at hand.

"You *do* miss it, don't you," Meghan observed. "Being in the middle of the action?"

"I get paid more than he does, and my muscles won't ache at the end of the day." Not from lifting the heavy hoses and gear at any rate. "Besides, I've seen more *action* than any man needs to."

"John, are you happy to be home?"

That was the million-dollar question, wasn't it?

Leaving it unanswered, he opened the door of his truck and tossed his hard hat and clipboard inside. "I'd better get back to the station and get my report written up. My boss is a real stickler for gettin' the job done fast and right."

Meghan smiled at the friendly jab but didn't back away from her concern. "If you need more time—to recover from your injuries or adjust to the new job or get better acquainted with the neighbor lady—"

"Are you matchmaking?"

"Do I need to?"

He climbed inside behind the wheel. "I'll see you back at the station."

Chapter Nine

A couple hours later, John was sitting in his office, pulling up the layout of the Wilson warehouse on his computer to add to his KCFD report. Although he'd bagged up some of the toasted wiring to be analyzed at the state fire lab, his preliminary findings were that the fire was accidental.

He brushed his fingertip over the top of the mouse and eyed the public building links on the screen in front of him. How hard would it be to pull up the blueprints on The Corsican—to double-check what should be in that building compared to what was actually there, and find out who had access to the building to perform inspections or maintenance on phone lines and elevator wires? Just how far should he go, following his instincts about there being something very wrong about the old building? Did one kiss, battling a fire together and a late-night heart-to-heart make him Maggie Wheeler's protector? How much of the lurking sense of pending danger surrounding Maggie was him trusting his gut? And how much was just a lost man without a purpose seeing enemies where none existed?

And was there something to Meghan's teasing about the *neighbor lady?* Was his brain still so fogged up with war and loss and recovery that he was missing something his station captain could see that he couldn't?

A soft knock at his door diverted his attention. "John?" Meghan pushed open the door. "You have a visitor."

"I do?"

Meghan stepped aside to usher in Maggie Wheeler. In that moment, John knew that his feelings for his boss were a thing of the past. He stood as the red-haired cop stepped into his office. Meghan's sunny blond hair faded into a pleasant memory as his pulse kicked into overdrive at the impact of Maggie's copper-haired beauty.

But the pale cast to the skin beneath her freckles tempered the rush of hormones. She stood tall and strong, a poster image for serving and protecting with her navy blue uniform, Kevlar and badge. But there was a searching request in those deep green eyes and a nervous fluttering of fingers through the wisps of escaping curls at her temple and nape.

"Sarge?" Meghan disappeared from the room and closed the door as he circled the desk. "What is it? Did something happen to Travis?"

She shook her head, alleviating that fear at least. "I saw Danny today. He came to the police station."

John guided her to a chair and shut the blinds on the office door. He brushed his hand across her shoulder as he perched on the edge of his desk facing her. Maybe he was offering comfort, or maybe he needed the feel of her strength and warmth for himself—a tangible reassurance that she was okay. "I thought you had a restraining order."

Maggie shot to her feet, avoiding both his touch and making eye contact. She dusted her fingers over the empty shelves behind his desk. "He had a legal way around it. He's a person of interest in the task force's investigation case. Detective Fensom wanted him to come in."

John stayed put, letting her pent-up energy carry her around the room. He couldn't imagine what kind of courage it required, and what kind of terror it caused, to come face-to-face with the man who'd raped and beaten her and stolen her child from her—a man she should have been able to trust. Protective anger fired through his blood, making it difficult to keep his own voice calm. "I'm guessing the investigation wasn't the real reason he agreed to help."

"Who knows? He could use some good karma with the police department, but...who knows?"

Beginning to understand her need to pace, John followed her to the bookshelf. Again he tried to touch her, but she crossed her arms and moved away. It was then that he saw the bruises on her wrist, the five purpling dots of violence that indicated Danny had put his hands on her.

Ah, hell. The marks were there beneath her collar, too. Double hell.

John pushed his fist against his mouth, bottling up his curse. Although he thought he could understand why Maggie might not want him touching her right now, he seethed at the idea that this wasn't the first time Danny Wheeler had hurt her.

Maybe sensing his growing rage—hell, maybe avoiding it—she abruptly changed the topic. "You don't have a single decoration in here. What about a picture of your sister? Do you have one with the two of you together? I know, you could put your medals and ribbons in a shadow box and hang them on the wall right next to your investigator certification. Or maybe frame your honorable discharge. You'd be doing this big, empty wall a favor. Showing off your accomplishments isn't bragging, John. It's just a statement of fact."

"Sarge... Maggie." He was stupefied by the sudden lightness of her tone but wasn't buying the "everything's hunky-dory now" attitude one bit. He moved in closer but didn't touch. "You didn't come here to decorate my office. When you ramble on like that, I know something's wrong. Why are you here?"

She turned to face him, eyeing his chest like she wanted to be there. He breathed deeply to conquer the urge to pull her into his arms. He squeezed his hands into tight fists down at his sides when she reached up to fiddle with the collar of his shirt—adjusting it, smoothing it, touching that one little corner of cotton knit like she was afraid to act on the need in her eyes…like she just might be afraid of him.

"Talk to me, Sarge. How do I make this right for you?"

She looked up at him then—and he was certain that green would forever be his favorite color.

Maggie pulled her hand from his shirt, denying him even that little bit of contact. But her brave, beautiful eyes never once looked away. "I want to go with you to check out our building. Now. As soon as you can get off work. If there's any way we can do it before I have to pick up Travis, that'd be great." He was ready to answer yes, but she had more to say. "I need to get ahead of this mess, John. I'm tired of just reacting. I'm at a disadvantage. I need to take control. I want to know for sure whether Danny has been in the building, and if he's responsible for any of the weird stuff that's been going on. I need to find out if there's any more crazy in store for me and the people who live there."

Her fingertips brushed against his fists and something like relief, acceptance—need—sparked between them at the shy request. John opened his hands and laced his fingers together with hers, holding on tight. It was a welcome, a promise. The trust in that simple gesture cracked open something cold and doubting that had encircled his heart.

And then he felt the grip of her fingers squeeze around his knuckles, holding on just as tightly to him.

"THAT AIN'T GOOD."

Maggie swung her flashlight around to peer into the storage unit where John had stopped. *Her* storage unit.

She curled her fingers through the chicken wire that lined the open frame of the door. Her heart plummeted to a place as dank and dark as the brick walls and wooden framework around her.

Those were her things inside the modest 6 x 6 cubby, recessed like so many others into the basement walls of The Corsican. There was Travis's tricycle she hadn't been able to part with, the collection of baseball bats that got bigger and heavier with every year and the high chair she might never need again but had been too sentimental over to part with.

That was her card table and folding chairs, set up as though someone was expecting company down here. There were her winter clothes, out of their boxes and draped over the chairs as though someone had been trying them on or sorting through them.

And then there were the pictures. Not *her* pictures. Pictures of her in shades of gray from a dozen newspapers. Taped all over the back wall. There was the task force article from the morning *Journal* that mentioned her name. There was a photo of her taken when she'd earned her sergeant's stripes. Every other officer who'd earned a rank that year had been cut out of the group picture. And there were others. A yellowed, faded image of her and Danny's engagement announcement from a naval base newsletter—she hadn't kept a copy. The lone color photograph was one of her crossing the street in front of the Fourth Precinct office. It looked as though it had been taken from above by someone standing on the top floor of the Fourth Precinct parking garage. With the greenery and sunshine of a clear spring day in the background, she knew it had been taken within the past few weeks, maybe even the past few days.

They'd been looking for signs of tampering with breakers, fuses and wiring. They'd checked windows and doors throughout the ground and basement levels, looking for any building access that was broken or had *accidentally* been left unlocked. Except for the main door and the security gate to the parking garage—both of which required a passkey or typed-in code—everything at the Corsican seemed to be locked up just fine. So how had he gotten in here? Any sense of normalcy she might have felt, any sense of privacy or security, rotated on its axis. "I think I'm going to be sick."

"No, you're not. You're in control, remember?" John went to the window at the end of the passageway and reached up to inspect it. "It's sealed tight." He swung his beam into the rafters above them. "In fact, they could use a little ventilation down here. Looks like the main door is the only access. When was the last time you were here?"

She thought back to when she and Travis had brought down the boxes of winter coats and extra blankets. "When the weather started warming up. I brought those clothes down."

"So that's been a couple of months."

"About the same length of time Danny's been out of prison."

"And no one else noticed it?"

"Maybe it just happened."

He returned to her side to shine his light over the creepy homage. "Let's get out of here."

Maggie was stunned by the violation of it all. Not only

had Danny gone off the deep end with his obsession, but he'd also broken in and done it in her own personal space. "It's like a shrine." Her breath stalled in her chest. "Or a setup for a wake."

"It's a sick mind is what it is." John's fingers wrapped around hers to pry them off the chicken wire. "We need to report this. And I want to talk to Joe and the landlord about the security here. As far as I'm concerned, it sucks."

"Wait. Not yet." She liked the feel of her hand inside John's sure grip, so she held on. But she planted her feet and only let him pull her away from the front of the unit. She wasn't ready to leave this part of the basement just yet. "I don't know what Danny's game is, but I'm going to figure it out. Why did he do this? How did he do it?"

John relented on his efforts to get her out the door, but he pulled her around the corner into the main passageway that cut through the two rows of lockers, probably so she wouldn't have to see Danny's handiwork. "Okay, then, let's think about this. All the tenants have a key to the main door dead bolt, right?" Maggie nodded. "So who has a key to the locks in here?"

"Just me." She suddenly thought to pull the ring of keys out of her pocket and went back to her locker. "I mean, every tenant puts his or her own lock on their individual storage unit. But everyone in the building has a master key to get into the catacombs here."

Maggie tried her key in the padlock on her door. When she couldn't get the key to slide in, John took it from her hand and tried it himself. "It doesn't fit."

"This isn't my lock."

He dropped the keys into her palm, then snugged her hand inside his and pulled her back. "That thug probably cut yours off to get inside, then replaced it with his own lock."

Now she was ready to leave and call it in. "I think breaking and entering is enough to put Danny back in jail for a long time and keep him there. Especially because he committed the crime against his former victim."

Something long and skinny crunched beneath Maggie's shoe. She tilted her flashlight down to the floor and backed up. "Eeuw." A line of large black ants were streaming from beneath the storage locker across from hers and disappearing under the door frame of her locker. Although the ants had now changed their path to curve around the squished carnage of her shoe, they just kept coming. Hundreds of them. Thousands, even. "Look at all of them."

"Carpenter ants."

"Joe said Miss Applebaum found some in her apartment. He went in and sprayed them for her, I guess. They must have relocated down here."

"Which means they're probably throughout the building by now." John didn't sound any more pleased to see the tiny invasion than she was.

Swarms of anything had always been a bit of an ick factor for her, but as Maggie and John stepped over what had looked like another crack in the floor until their lights showed it to be a moving, living thing, she had another disturbing idea and stopped. "What would draw them all the way down here? You don't think there's something else in my locker, something…rotting? Dead?"

"Don't worry. They eat wood. Besides, we'd smell it if something was dead." He wrapped his fingers around her elbow and kept her from going back to see Danny's artwork again. Together they headed toward the garage. "These ants aren't as destructive as termites, but they're not good. Just one more reason to add to the list of why I never should have moved into this place."

Maggie tugged against his hand and glanced up at him. Was he already thinking about leaving?

With only the hint of a smile to warn her, he leaned in and planted a quick, firm kiss on her lips. "Don't worry, Sarge, you're on the list of reasons why I'm glad I did."

Maggie was smiling, too, by the time they left the storage space and reentered the parking garage. She liked seeing John smile. He was usually so serious and guarded. The flash of boyish teasing warmed her heart.

She'd liked the faintly possessive stamp of that kiss, too. Although she'd never imagined she would enjoy any man showing possessive tendencies around her again, there was something healthy and respectful, and completely new about the way John liked to hold her hands or take her arm, to subtly touch her—or kiss her. It was like falling in love for the first time all over again.

He made her feel important. He listened. He got angry... on her behalf. John made her feel like a woman worth caring about, not a punching bag or vessel for sex or thing a man owned the way Danny had. He made her believe that with the right man—with John himself, perhaps—that it was okay for her to love again.

She walked to her truck to pull out a spool of yellow crime-scene tape and marked off the entrance to The Corsican's storage locker, giving herself time to sort through those new feelings. She tried to decide if trusting John also meant she could trust herself enough to act on those feelings. But final decisions about her heart and trust and awakening desire would have to wait.

As soon as she was done securing the scene, she put in a call to dispatch. John was still poking around in walls and crevices while Maggie paced in front of the storage entrance's yellow tape and finished her call.

"I'd write up the report myself, but because it's my

stuff…I want everything to be by the book. Thanks. Hey, can you patch me through to Nick Fensom?" She covered the phone while she was being transferred to speak to John. "He's the detective who interviewed Danny. Nick booked him into a cell overnight, but if he's looking at Danny as the Rose Red suspect, then he'll want to see this."

"That's not the only crime in town, Sarge." John joined her next to the open doorway. "Even if he's not the rapist KCPD is looking for, he still needs to be put away for stalking you like this."

The dispatcher was on the line again. So much for an immediate response. "He's out? Could you just copy him on this report? And give him my number. Yeah, a unit to watch the place in the meantime would be great. Thanks."

Before she ended the call, John's cell phone rang. He pulled the phone from his belt and flipped it open to answer. "Hello?" He turned to face Maggie. "This is John."

His eyes locked onto hers, warning her that the call was important.

"Trav, where are you?"

Maggie darted to John's side. Fear made her blood run cold. This couldn't be happening again. "What's wrong?" She tugged on the sleeve of John's polo and stretched up on tiptoe to put her ear closer to the phone. "Why did he call you?" she whispered.

John put up a hand, asking her not to panic. "Yes, I know where your mom is." Then he twisted his wrist to check his watch. "Then you've got half an hour before practice is over. I'd be happy to come and get you, but I know she's planning on it."

Was her son in trouble again? Abandoned at the ball-park? Maggie grabbed John's phone and rocked back on her heels. "Travis, are you okay? Is somebody there with you?"

"Mom?" She knew that tone. She'd heard it before when she'd caught him bringing a garter snake into the apartment. When he'd painted his own set of roads on the carpet of his bedroom to run his cars and trucks. He was up to something he shouldn't be.

"Where are you?"

"At Abbott Field. I'm on the bench, waiting for my turn to bat."

"Coach Hernandez is with you?"

She hated the slight pause but appreciated the honest answer. "He's on the mound pitching. Hey, did you know I caught a fly ball today? Off Jimmy Stecher? He's our best hitter, but I got him out."

Great news, but missing the point. "Why would you think I wasn't picking you up today? Yesterday was just a fluke. I told you I talked to Chief Taylor and he said I could work my new schedule around yours."

"Well, I just thought…could we eat dinner with John again tonight?"

Huh? Maggie glanced up at John, who bent his head toward hers to catch more of the conversation. "Sweetie, we can't invite ourselves—"

"And maybe…you could wear a dress."

"A dress?" John's curious eyes narrowed on her.

"And some lipstick like the lady on TV."

"Why would I wear a dress for dinner? Did you tell John you couldn't reach me again? My phone is turned on—you didn't even try."

John's green-gold eyes swept down her dusty uniform and lingered on her legs. "*Do* you have a dress?"

Oh. Maggie's mouth dropped open. Heat crept up her neck and flooded her cheeks—partly from the hungry appreciation darkening John's eyes, and partly from learning that her ten-year-old was already wise enough in the ways of men and women to understand that showing a little skin—well, showing something a little more feminine than starched pants and a flak vest—could get a man's attention. And, apparently, he desperately wanted her to get John Murdock's attention. She snapped her mouth shut and turned away to focus on the call. "We don't even know if John has plans tonight."

"Ask him."

John's warm breath danced across the back of her neck. "If that's an invitation to dinner, I accept."

"Mom?"

Say it, Maggie. You know you want to. Do it. She glanced over her shoulder to the man standing behind her. "Would you like to come to dinner at our place tonight?"

Travis probably jumped off the dugout bench. "Yes!"

She turned her attention back to her son. "It's just a dinner invitation, young man. You have to go to bed early anyway. You were up too late last night."

"Mom, a guy has to eat."

"A guy has to eat."

The same phrase echoed in both ears at two different pitches. She might be in trouble. Not a bad kind of trouble, for a change, but a very unfamiliar kind.

She covered the phone and pulled it from her ear. "My son really likes you."

"That works out well because I really like him."

"He may not understand exactly what he's doing, but I think he's playing matchmaker with us."

An unexpectedly devilish grin teased the corners of John's mouth as he leaned in. "Good." His lips brushed across her nape, discovering a bundle of sensitive nerves and short-circuiting all thought and concern. "As slow as you and I are moving, somebody needs to."

"But—"

John circled his hands around the front of Maggie's waist and pulled her back against his chest so he could nuzzle his way along the side of her neck. Although she couldn't feel his body through her vest, she could definitely feel what his lips were doing above her collar. Her mouth opened in a noiseless gasp as a zillion little pinpricks of pleasure danced along her skin, chasing along the path where John's moist breath and patient, thorough lips heated her skin.

Who knew she had an erogenous zone right there? Who knew she even had an erogenous zone? Her pleasure had certainly never been the goal of Danny's sexual encounters.

"You like that?" John whispered against her ear.

She was barely aware of the "Mom? Mom?" in her ear.

But she wasn't so starved for male attention that she'd forget she had a young eavesdropper on the line. She tilted her head away from the sensual assault and tugged at John's arms, trying to work some space between them so she could talk to her son in a fairly normal tone. "Travis, I'm on my way to pick you up in just a couple of minutes. That's great about catching the fly ball. Be thinking about what you want to have for dinner. Love you."

"Bye, Mom."

When she handed the phone back to John, he used her outstretched hand to turn her. And then his mouth was back, sliding over hers. He slipped his palm beneath the collar of her uniform to cup and soothe the sensitized skin at her nape. But his fingertips were teasing wisps of hair free from the bun there. His tongue was in her mouth, exploring the soft skin inside.

Her tongue darted out to shyly play with his. Her hands were at his face, stroking the square line of his jaw, testing the rugged angles of his cheekbones, discovering the tantalizing contrasts of his warm scalp and short, spiky hair.

Heat blossomed inside Maggie, making her vision hazy, her hearing muffled. Her lips and tongue and fingertips seemed supernaturally aware of every taste—coffee and something tangy and sweet from lunch—and every touch—warm, sun-leathered skin, supple muscles moving underneath.

She felt her own body straining against the stiffness of her uniform, responding to John's embrace. She felt the greedy hand squeezing her bottom, the fingers loosening her hair.

She felt her holster butting against her hip, and the Kevlar solid as a wall between them. *Reality check.* She was a thirty-five-year-old woman of the world. She wore a gun and a badge. She had a son waiting for her at baseball practice. She had a job to do.

She wasn't the kind of woman who made out with a man in a parking garage. At least, she never had been.

"John, I'm on duty." Maggie leaned back, struggling to get some of the cool, dank air around them into her lungs to calm her senses. Yet she couldn't help wanting a taste of the salty skin along his jaw. Her brain cells were fighting to remember sanity and decorum, yet she ached at the subtle difference in textures on his skin as she pulled her fingers along the column of his neck, tracing healthy skin and scars down to the strong pulse beating at the base of his throat. "You're on duty, too, aren't you? We have responsibilities. You can't just kiss me like this."

"Then you need to stop kissing me back." His deep voice was a husky caress, a dare, a promise.

Maggie pressed her feverish lips against his. She kissed him again, more gently each time, lifting her hands to cradle his jaw and look up into his eyes. "What's going on with you? You seem…different."

John pulled back with a heavy sigh that stirred the tiny tendrils curling around her face. "You know, you're the second woman to say that to me today." He moved his wayward hands to a more neutral location at either side of her waist, and rested his forehead against hers, giving her some of the space she asked for without releasing her entirely. "Maybe I am a different man. It's like something finally woke up inside me today. Here I was, in a perpetual mood over never being able to go back to my old life. When I think, all along, I was meant to move on to something new."

"Me?"

"I don't know. But doesn't it feel right? I'm way out of practice, though—maybe I'm misreading the signs."

"You're not." Thank goodness he wore his hair like a marine, or her hands would have left it a rumpled mess. Still, she smoothed her fingers across his forehead as if there was a need to straighten the short spikes there. "Look, you can't be more out of practice at starting a relationship than I am. I really like you, John. I feel safe with you. But—"

"If you tell me you just want to be friends—"

"But I need to take it really slow. I've got a ten-year-old son. He idolizes you now, but I want you to get to know him. Some days he's an old man, trying to take care of me, and some days, he's still such a child. Plus, I've got a lot of emotional baggage that comes with me." She turned her head toward the disturbing shrine in her locker. "And I've got that kind of crap to deal with."

John slipped his finger beneath her chin and tipped her

face to his again. "I can do slow. If I can learn to walk again, I can learn to do relationships, too."

That probing gaze told her he could be interested in making something work with her. But too many years of guarding her body and her heart against another mistake was a difficult defense to get past. "I'm not easy to care about."

"I'll argue that one. I've got a need to take care of you in a way I haven't felt for any woman for a long time. I'm guessing it's harder for you to believe it than anyone else."

"Scary ex, remember?"

"One leg?" He tapped his thigh.

Maggie shook her head. "That doesn't matter to me."

"Well, I guess that one's hard for me to believe."

She curled her fingers beneath the collar of his shirt. "If I try not to do the crazy lady too often or too severely, will you try not to talk or think about yourself as though you're anything less than a good, wonderful man?"

With a reluctant nod that made her think he was as skeptical about making a relationship between them work as she was, he let go of her waist and pulled her right hand into his to seal the bargain. "Slow it is."

The sound of a man clearing his throat interrupted the intimate handshake.

Maggie quickly pulled away to see Joe Standage and his toolbox standing there with a wink-wink smile on his face. "Well, look at the two of you. Looks like romance is in the air."

Joe's teasing didn't bother her as much as seeing the man with the dark, round eyes and tan coveralls standing behind him. Lawrence Boyle simply nodded. "Mrs. Wheeler."

John's movements were as purposeful and methodical as Maggie's quick escape and throwing up of her invisible armor had been. He angled himself slightly between her and the other two men and slowly extended his hand to the man in the exterminator's uniform. "I don't believe we've had the pleasure. I'm John Murdock."

Boyle stared at John for a few uncomfortable seconds before shifting the canister he carried into one hand and shaking hands with the other. "Lawrence Boyle."

Although he seemed more at ease speaking to her than to John, the bleach-haired man didn't exactly look happy to see her. "Your friends at the police department are keeping him for a while. Left me shorthanded today. Now I'm working a double shift."

Was he expecting an apology?

John thumbed over his shoulder toward the storage lockers. "I'm guessing you're here for the ants."

"Yes, sir. Came back to have a look."

"Lawrence is my brother-in-law," Joe explained.

For some reason, Maggie had assumed Joe Standage was a perennial bachelor. "I didn't know you were married."

"My late wife—Lawrence's older sister—passed away several years ago. Long before I retired and took this job." Joe reached over and smacked Boyle's immovable shoulder. "I like to shoot some work his way whenever I can."

The first time Maggie had met Lawrence Boyle and his white van, a suspicion had planted itself in her mind, but she'd been too frantic about Travis's safety for it to fully register. It did now. She moved up beside John. "You said you were *back* to look at the ant problem. Have you been in the building before?"

"Have you been in the building in the past week?" John clarified.

Bug-eyed Boyle shook his head. "This was one of Danny's jobs."

"Danny was here?" She looked from Lawrence to Joe and back. She didn't care who talked, she just needed to know. "When?"

John stood right behind her. "Answer her."

"He sprayed some old lady's apartment upstairs—"

"That would be Miss Applebaum," Joe interjected.

"And laid down some foam around the foundation down here. About a week ago."

"The day I got that note and the elevator stopped."

Boyle's shoulders puffed up as if she'd accused him of something. "Once he told me you lived here, I made sure he came during the day while you were gone. I know your fifty-yard rule. He used to talk about you every day."

"In prison?"

"Yeah. We shared a cell for a few years. I know what you said he did to you."

"What he *did* do," Maggie emphasized. She'd lived it, and the court had proved that there'd been nothing consensual about the weekend Danny had captured her, brutalized her, dragged her back to their old apartment and kept her prisoner until he'd finally drunk enough to pass out and she could escape. "That's why he can never come near me or my son again."

Boyle shifted on his feet, looking either embarrassed by his past or uncomfortable about sharing too much about a man he considered a friend. "Ma'am, I need to get to work. Like I said, a double shift means it's a long day."

"Was Danny in the storage unit, too?" she asked.

"I don't know. That's why I'm here to check his work. See if he missed something, or sometimes it just takes a second application to kill the buggers." Boyle held up the flat-nosed nozzle and hose, and translucent plastic canister that contained a thick clear liquid and was marked *Poison*.

"They can chew a lot of holes in the wood and lay a lot of eggs if we don't catch 'em."

When he moved around her to enter the storage area, Maggie grabbed his arm to stop him. "I'm sorry, but you can't go in there right now. It's a crime scene. You'll have to do your work another time, or work in a different area."

"What happened?" He looked down at the hand on his canvas sleeve as if he wasn't any happier about her touching him than he'd been to take John's.

Maggie quickly snatched it away. "Someone broke into my storage locker."

"You think Danny messed with your stuff?"

"Someone did." John grasped her shoulders and pulled her a step back from both men. He made no effort to mask his suspicions that Joe and anyone he hired would have complete access to the building. "Someone who has a key."

Chapter Ten

Thirty-six hours without hearing from a violent ex might sound like a reprieve to some women, maybe even an end to their troubles. But Maggie knew that going a full day and night without hearing from Danny was more likely to mean he was plotting something even more cruel than anything he'd done to her yet.

Still, it was heartening to have made it through almost two normal days. She thought if she had enough practice at it, she could learn to do normal without second-guessing every move or comment she made.

Her dinner with John had been by turns fun and awkward. Even with Travis between them to keep the conversation going, it had felt like a first date. The sundress she'd worn had been a hit, judging by the appreciative peeks beneath the table from John. But then she'd spilled her iced tea down the front of it and been forced to change into jeans and a T-shirt—and it seemed the glances were just as heated. She'd been nervous each time one of them asked a question that was a little too personal and the other paused before answering. And then, after putting Travis to bed, she and John had curled up on the couch together to share some more adult conversation. But the two hours of sleep she'd gotten the night before caught up with her and she'd promptly fallen asleep.

She'd warned John that she'd be a slow mover in the relationship department. But it was embarrassing to think just how much patience it would require of a man who wanted to be with her. She had to question if a man like John—so wounded by life the way she had been, and still searching for his own emotional healing—would have the patience and endurance to put up with her bad days as well as her good ones.

Work had gone a little better. She'd been invited to sit in on two victim interviews, one with Dr. Kilpatrick and one with Detective Montgomery. In the first interview, Maggie's sharing of some of the emotions she'd carried with her since her own attack had encouraged one of the Rose Red Rapist's earliest victims to share about her abduction. She'd been a young woman in graduate school back then, and had gone on to become a pediatric nurse, wife and mother of three children. Although she had no description of her attacker, she remembered being forced to bathe afterward—an early effort by the rapist to create a sterile crime scene that would leave no trace.

She'd met with the second victim this morning, an attorney who was more than willing to talk, but whose memory of the event had been blocked out by either emotion or time. Along with Detective Montgomery, Maggie had asked a few pointed questions that had helped the woman recall some specific details that matched Bailey Austin's account—the scent of chemicals—cleansers, perhaps?—and the clear plastic beneath her as the rape occurred.

Maybe she wasn't as successful about nailing Danny for stalking her, but she was beginning to feel that she was worthy of Chief Taylor's belief in her—that she might just make a good detective, and that she was making a meaningful contribution to the task force's investigation.

This afternoon, she'd joined Detectives Montgomery

and Fensom at the Fairy Tale Bridal Shop to conduct a different sort of interview—this time with the closest thing they had to an eyewitness of the attack, shop owner Hope Lockhart.

Maggie hovered in the background while she observed the two seasoned detectives in action. Hope was about as keen on being grilled by the two detectives as an actual victim would be. A plump young woman with glasses and curly blond-brown hair, Hope Lockhart fit the stereotype of a plain Jane. But because redheaded Maggie was the last person to relegate anyone to stereotype status, she focused on the woman's beautiful fashion sense and on the amazing diversity and apparent success of her business.

The entire time that the detectives were questioning her about the night of Bailey Austin's attack, Hope dressed a mannequin in a silver-colored satin wedding suit and added it to a black-and-white storefront display touting sophisticated second weddings. Even with her business partner, and the building's owner, Brian Elliott, on hand to offer his support, Hope stayed busy. Either she was worried about impressing her partner, or she needed to stay busy to keep her nerves from overtaking her.

"I really don't see what I can tell you," she said, swapping out a jeweled barrette with a netted hat to place in the mannequin's hair. "Of course I want to help. I've worked with Bailey and her mother for several months, planning her wedding. I'd like to think of her as a friend." She glanced at Detective Montgomery before switching back to the barrette. "But I didn't see anything."

Brian Elliott stood up from his chair in one of the seating areas near the shop's dressing rooms. "Exactly. Montgomery, is it?"

"Yes, sir."

Mr. Elliott handed off a file he'd been reading to his

executive assistant, a dark-haired woman named Regina Hollister. He buttoned the jacket of his expensive suit and invited himself into the conversation. "Hope is the most honest woman I know. If she says she saw nothing that can help you, then she saw nothing. Now we were having a business meeting when you showed up that I'd like to finish so I can get back to my office."

Spencer Montgomery slipped his hands into the slacks pockets beneath his own suit jacket, completely unruffled by the other man's defense of Hope and superior attitude. "You're free to leave anytime you want, Mr. Elliott. Miss Lockhart was one of the last people to see Miss Austin before the attack. She may have noticed someone lurking in the area who shouldn't have been there—"

"I didn't."

"Or seen an unfamiliar vehicle." Maggie noticed the wheels turning behind Hope Lockhart's glasses, as though she was trying to place something she had seen that night. "And she would certainly be able to tell us Miss Austin's state of mind when she left the bridal shop."

"She was upset." Hope worked the small hat between her fingers as she faced Spencer. "Bailey and her mother were arguing about the wedding. She wanted this classic outdoor ceremony in the backyard of her father's estate. Small, with family and a few friends—something to do with wanting her sister to be her matron of honor. But her sister doesn't deal well with crowds of people."

Spencer's attention was focused solely on the shop-keeper now. "I've met her sister. That would fit."

Apparently giving up on moving the interview along, Brian Elliott returned to his seat. Nick Fensom, who'd been wandering through the salon, casually looking at the displays of clothes, invitations and gifts, ended his exploration near the same seating area. Maggie guessed he was positioning himself to run interference for his partner if Elliott decided to intercede again, so that Spencer could concentrate on Hope Lockhart's story.

Maggie was beginning to rethink the shy appellation she'd given Hope earlier. Although her nerves were about to crush the small hat, she seemed equally determined to offer useful information. "To be honest, I felt like Bailey's mother and her fiancé were ganging up on her. Mrs. Austin-Mayweather said she'd reserved a date at a cathedral and wanted Bailey to look at big ball gowns. And her fiancé—"

"Harper Pierce."

"Yes. Harper seemed just as eager to have a big wedding as his mother-in-law. He kept talking about social contacts and publicity and expectations of the family name."

"And Miss Austin didn't want any part of that?"

"My job is to listen to the bride—to help make *her* dream come true. I tried to stand up for her, but I'm not terribly persuasive." Perhaps seeing the damage she'd done to the hat, or just needing a break, she returned it to a box of tissue paper on the counter. "Bailey threatened to call off the whole wedding. They argued about it all the way out into the parking lot."

"Where our perp probably heard the commotion that drew his attention to Miss Austin."

Hope's posture visibly wilted before she faced Spencer Montgomery again. "I was locking up the shop and turning out the lights before going to my apartment upstairs when I saw her walking past the front window. I should have gone after her."

"Did you see any vehicles following her?"

Hope moved her head from side to side in disbelief. "Harper and Mrs. Austin-Mayweather pulled out of the parking lot and turned that direction. I thought they were going after her. Why wouldn't they give her a ride?"

"She probably refused if she was angry."

"I should have invited her back into the shop. I could have saved her."

Maggie stepped out of the background at the woman's growing distress. "Don't blame yourself. Once a guy like that sets his mind on a target, he won't stop until he gets what he wants. He saw someone who was vulnerable and alone, and he went after her. Chances are if you'd gone out there and gotten in his way, you might have become the victim instead."

"Me?"

"Now you're just scaring her." Brian Elliott was back on his feet. He slipped an arm around Hope's shoulders. His protective paternal look included Maggie as well as the detectives. "I think it's time for you to leave."

Spencer pointed to the small cameras placed inside both the front door and the side entrance to the parking lot. "I don't suppose you have security cameras installed *outside* your building and this shop where we might have captured a picture of the man following Miss Austin?"

Brian Elliott never took his eyes off the detective who'd challenged him. He merely tightened his arm around Hope's shoulders and pointed to his assistant. "Reggie, make a note to get exterior cameras installed tomorrow. I want Hope to feel safe here."

"Yes, sir."

Spencer Montgomery had heard enough. Reaching inside his jacket, he pulled out a business card and handed it to Hope. "Miss Lockhart, thank you for your time. If you think of anything else, or you see any other suspicious activity in the neighborhood, please give me a call."

She squeezed the card in her hand. "I will."

Nick was already opening the front door as Spencer acknowledged the others in the shop. "Mr. Elliott. Ma'am. Have a good meeting."

On her way out the door, Maggie's phone vibrated on her belt. When she saw Annie Hermann's number, she apologized for delaying the two detectives. "I need to take this. It's the crime lab—about that break-in I had at my place."

"Go ahead." Nick waited for a young professional couple bending over the same smartphone to pass by on the sidewalk before pulling back the front of his leather jacket and stretching his shoulders and neck. "I want to do some checking around the outside of this place, see what kind of vantage point our guy had to have if he spotted his vic in the parking lot."

Detective Montgomery was less affable. "Are you kidding me?" But Maggie saw that his irritation was directed at the dark-haired reporter lounging outside his SUV across the street. Gabriel Knight nodded to the two young women carrying their cups of coffee into the nearby office building before pulling off his sunglasses and turning toward the three of them. "What do you suppose he wants?"

"Besides the scoop on breaking our case?" Nick teased. "Or taking another potshot at us in the morning edition?"

Spencer waved Nick off before checking pedestrians and traffic and stepping into the street. "You two take care of your business. I want to make sure Knight doesn't hassle Miss Lockhart—or any other witnesses around here we need to talk to."

Hanging back on the sidewalk while the two men went to work, Maggie answered her phone. "Hey, Annie, sorry about that. We were finishing up at the bridal shop. Did you find anything on Danny?"

Annie's sigh gave Maggie the answer she didn't want to hear. "Sorry. The only prints we found in your storage locker were yours and Joe Standage's."

Maggie released a frustrated breath of her own. "Joe helped me move stuff down there this winter. What about outside the locker or on the news clippings themselves?"

"Nothing. I went over everything myself. Your guy was wearing gloves. Forensically, we can't prove it was Danny Wheeler who broke in there."

The man was smart, which only made him more dangerous. "Okay, thanks."

"No problem. Hey, we're on the same team, right? Anything I can help you with, you let me know."

"Same here. Thanks."

After putting away her phone, Maggie looked up and down the street, wondering how these busy blocks had looked at night to Bailey Austin, when the shops and offices had closed. It looked like a nice enough neighborhood on the surface—maybe not as cosmopolitan as it had been in its original heyday. But it was no longer the run-down, homeless crime lane it had once been either. Much of the historical architecture had been restored. There were new businesses going in, thriving shops, a café, apartment living on the upper floors.

Just how truly alone had Bailey Austin been that she jumped out as a target to the Rose Red Rapist? It was hard to picture it now, with the clear blue afternoon sunlight, and the bustle of activity on the streets and sidewalks.

Had someone been inside one of those doors or windows who might have seen something? A custodian cleaning an office perhaps? Or someone else who lived above his or her business like Hope Lockhart did? There were several night spots within a couple of blocks in either direction. Had there been no overflow parking on this street? No couple strolling hand in hand on a date?

What made Bailey Austin the rapist's target? There were so many women here who fit the same general description.

A camera flash of understanding went off in her head. Maggie's gaze shrank from the big picture she'd been contemplating down to the individual faces of each woman on the street.

"Nick?" She spun around, looking for the burly detective. "Nick!" She jogged down to the entrance to the Fairy Tale Bridal Shop parking lot to catch him before he disappeared around the corner. "I just realized something."

"What's that?"

She pointed to the people in their cars and walking past on the street. "Look at the women here. They're all professionals." Some were younger, perhaps newly out of college and chasing after a new career. Others were older, well-established by the look of their BMW or designer bags. They had different ethnicities and looks, but they were all a certain type. "Detective Montgomery talked about Rose Red having a hunting ground. All the victims have been career women. They've all had money and class, or were well on their way to having both."

Nick nodded, seeming to find merit in her assessment. "Women with self-confidence, authority. Women who are going places."

"Upset or not, he picked up Bailey Austin here because she was the right type of woman."

"And he knew he could find that type in this neighborhood."

A little rush of excitement buzzed through Maggie's blood. They were onto something here. At least they might be able to narrow down their search area for where the serial rapist might strike next. "That's why our guy has gone after blondes and brunettes and different racial types. It's not a look he's targeting, like most serial rapists. He has a thing for women who have power. Strong women. He didn't go after Bailey Austin because she was upset and vulnerable. He went after her because she was strong enough to stand up for herself against her fiancé and mother. In public."

"I'm telling Spence to get his butt back over here. You okay to get back to the station on your own? He can drive me in his car." She nodded as he pulled out his phone to text a message. After hitting Send he held out his arm to give her a congratulatory fist bump. "Good profiling, Wheeler. How come you never made detective before?"

"I didn't have the college degree."

"What took you so long to get it?"

She held up her wrist and pointed to the time. "Because I have a ten-year-old who's playing a baseball game in an hour. I've been kind of busy raising him."

"He any good?"

"He will be. Apparently he has a good eye for catching pop flies. Now if we can just get him to step into the pitch when he swings the bat."

"Sounds like my kind of evening." He groaned as if he knew he'd be spending his evening doing something much less enjoyable. "Get out of here and enjoy the game. I'll mention what you said to Spence."

"Thanks." She headed for her truck down the street.

"And Wheeler?"

"Yes?"

Nick Fensom grinned. "File the promotion paperwork. You'll make a damn fine detective."

A damn fine detective.

Nick's praise and her own sense of success buoyed her

spirits in a way she hadn't felt for weeks now. Her life wasn't perfect, but things were definitely heading in the right direction. Both personally and professionally, she'd made some choices that just might pay off if she kept working hard at them.

She was waiting in traffic at the intersection where Bailey Austin had been attacked, looking forward to Travis's game and seeing John and getting a good report with Chief Taylor, when the light changed and her mood sank like a popped balloon.

Parked at the corner was a white van, with a bug and rat and Boyle's Extermination logo painted on the side. And behind the steering wheel sat Danny Wheeler.

Watching her.

JOHN PATTED TRAVIS'S left leg. "This one here." He covered the boy's hands with his own around the handle of the bat and swung it with him. "Go forward. Don't step out. You're losing the amount of space over the plate that your bat can cover, so you have less chance of hitting anything. And remember, keep your eye on the ball all the way to the bat, or to the catcher's mitt if you decide to take the pitch."

"Keep my eye on the ball. Right." Travis nodded. The boy stooped down to smear his hands in the dirt, spit on them and rub them together. He knocked twice on his helmet before gripping the bat and aligning his stance the way John had shown him. "Like this?"

John grinned at the theatrics as he stood back and watched Travis take a couple of swings on his own. It felt like forever since he'd been that young and eager to imitate the big leaguers he'd watched on TV and at Kaufmann Stadium. "With a little less fanfare that's it. You'll get more power moving into the ball like that, too."

"How's that swing coming?" John looked up to see the

copper-haired police officer walking toward them with a sports drink and bag of sunflower seeds in her hands.

"Hi, Mom." Travis ran over to the fence to pick up his game supplies and accept a casual, just-an-arm-around-the-shoulder hug from Maggie. "I'm gonna get a hit tonight. John showed me how."

"Fantastic."

A shout from Coach Hernandez summoned all the boys to end their warm-ups and join him in the dugout.

"Thanks, Mom!"

"Have a great game. Do your best." Maggie cheered him as he ran across the diamond.

John scooped up a couple of practice balls on his way to the fence. Now that Travis was gone and the field lights were coming on, a glance at Maggie's pale skin and the time on his watch made him suspicious of the smile on her face. "You're late. Everything okay?"

She followed him down to the gate on her side of the fence. "There are four games going on here tonight. I had to park clear at the far end of the lot and walk a quarter of a mile."

"Hey, Mom!" They both turned at Travis's shout. "Don't yell my name, okay?"

"Okay." Maggie flashed her son a thumbs-up. "Go get 'em." Her eyes were on the concrete path before them when he joined her at the base of the bleachers. "Thanks for getting him to the game."

"We got some practice in." She still hadn't made eye contact with him. Instead, she was eyeing the parents and grandparents in the stands, and looking beyond them to the people lined up at the concession stand and still milling in the parking lot. He had to concentrate for a moment on where he was placing his false foot as they climbed the open stands, but he didn't have a good feeling about this. "Sarge, what is it?"

She slid between two rows of metal seats and sat. "How about here? Are we too far up?"

Uh-uh, she wasn't getting off that easily. He sat down beside her. "I've had warmer greetings from enemy troops. What's wrong?"

He silently dared her to say *nothing* and take them several steps backward in this tentative relationship. But there was a reason he admired her courage. Her darting gaze finally landed on him. "I saw Danny this afternoon."

"But his restraining order—"

"He was far enough away that I couldn't cite him for anything. But he was close enough that he could watch me. We were out around the city, conducting interviews. I don't know how long he was following me." John's blood heated with protective anger and he, too, started scanning the perimeter of the ball fields and park, searching for the enemy. "I took the scenic route to get here, and lost him. But he already knows where Danny plays, so he could show up again."

"You want to go home?"

Her cheeks flooded with a healthier color. "I'm not taking Travis away from his game."

"Good. I'd rather see you ticked off than afraid. Danny Wheeler doesn't get to control your life. Not anymore." For John, it was a personal vow. That bastard was never going to hurt Maggie or rob her of that genuine smile again. Not on his watch. And he wasn't planning on going anywhere anytime soon. "Let's sit here and enjoy the game," he suggested. "And Danny can just hide in the dark and miss out on what really matters in life."

"Family and friends?"

John turned toward the field. "Baseball."

She laughed out loud, as he'd hoped. But she surprised him by capturing his jaw and pulling him closer to press a kiss against his cheek. "Thank you."

It was brave and spontaneous and perfect.

He smiled and leaned in farther to kiss her squarely on that beautiful mouth. "I like that even better than being ticked off."

Yeah, that was the smile he wanted to see. And he had no problem when Maggie laced her fingers together with his and leaned her shoulder against him. John held on tight, enjoying the game, Travis and the woman who was becoming more and more vital to him with every passing second.

He'd come a long way from that roadside bomb in Afghanistan. Maybe, just maybe, this was what finally coming home was supposed to feel like.

And no coward watching from the darkness was going to steal it away from him.

"That was my first double."

John lined up the darkened park entrance in the beam of his headlights and turned into the empty parking lot as the victory celebration that had been going on since he offered to take Travis and Maggie out for ice cream after the game continued. "I think we've pretty much figured out that if we can get you on base, buddy, you're a fast runner. Is that the first time you've scored a run this year?"

"Yep." He heard a crunch from the backseat of his truck. "Dat's da foost time I 'tole a base, too."

Maggie turned in the passenger seat to lay down the mom law. "Not even ice cream stops your chatter. Now you finish that cone before it melts all over John's truck. Leaving a mess isn't a very nice way to thank him."

John wasn't worried. "It washes off."

She passed a paper napkin back to Travis and faced the

front again. "I'll have to wash him and his uniform off, too. Once the sugar and excitement wear off that boy's going to crash."

"It was a great night, wasn't it?" John reached across the seat to touch his fingers to Maggie's, sending the message that he was talking about more than just a baseball game.

She shifted her hand to link them together palm to palm, letting him know she got the subtle message, even though she answered, "That was the Tigers' first win of the season. Awesome job, Trav."

"Uh-hmm."

While Travis stuffed the last of his chocolate ice cream into his mouth to continue discussing his exploits, Maggie pointed to the dark pickup in the shadows at the far end of the lot. "That's me."

John slowed to pull up beside the truck. "If you want to leave him buckled up and his gear in the back, I can just follow you home." He turned on his brights to give her a clear, safe path to her driver's side door and stomped on the brakes. There was nothing *safe* about what he saw. "Sarge."

"Oh, my God." Maggie was out the door before John could stop her. "Stay back."

Like hell.

"Maggie!" He glanced into the rearview mirror. "Stay in the truck, buddy," John ordered. He killed the engine and climbed out, leaving the lights on to illuminate the atrocity parked before him. Grabbing Travis's baseball bat from the bed of the truck, he armed himself before hurrying after Maggie.

She flinched when he caught her by the arm to pull her back but refused to let her go.

"Do you think they can find some evidence now?" he

growled, wishing she'd let him turn her away from the vandalized truck.

There wasn't a window that hadn't been bashed in or splintered by dozens of hard blows. The headlights were toast, the hood and fenders dented in by something long and narrow—like the bat he held.

And that devastation wasn't the worst of it. The front tires had been punctured and all manner of vile things had been carved into the paint by a very angry hand. *Mine. Liar. Bitch.*

If he hadn't been so alarmed by the unblinking pallor of Maggie's expression, he would have heard the footsteps a moment sooner.

"Mom, what's a 'who-ree'?"

"Travis!" Responding like a fierce mama bear when she wouldn't protect herself, Maggie grabbed her son, hugging him tight to her chest and turning him from the graphic image of what Danny Wheeler had wanted to do to her. "Don't look, sweetie. It's not a nice word. None of it's nice. Don't look."

"Mom?"

"Let's get him out of here." John hated the tremor he heard in Travis's voice. He hated that either one of them had to ever see something like this. He wound his left arm around Maggie's waist, shielding both mother and child in his embrace. He moved them out of the light from his truck, making them harder targets to spot.

"Is this when we go to a safe place and call the police?" Travis asked.

"Yes." Maggie's voice was stronger now. She was moving with a purpose. "Yes, sweetie, that's exactly what we need to do right now."

John urged them both back to his truck, all the while scanning the ball diamonds and parking lot and street beyond for any sign of movement, any vehicle that didn't belong. He briefly wondered if it was worth leaving their side to break into the maintenance booth and turn on all the ballpark lights again. He opened the door and Maggie helped Travis scramble up into the backseat before climbing into the passenger seat and pulling out her phone. "Lock it. Call for backup. Get a BOLO out for Danny Wheeler."

Maggie nodded and punched in a number. He was going for the lights. But almost as soon as John turned away, the truck started behind him and he whirled around to see Maggie lowering the automatic window. "Where are you going?"

John spun the ball bat in his fist and peered into the darkness. Evil was lurking out there in the shadows. Of that, he had no doubt. "I'm gonna find that bastard, or at least some sign of where he went."

She unsnapped the holster on her belt and pulled out her GLOCK. She pushed it out the open window, butt first. "Then take this."

He pushed it right back. "No, you keep it. Wheeler's the kind of man who beats up women and empty trucks. He doesn't have the guts to come after me. If he shows his face before I get back, shoot him."

LIKE A COCKROACH CLINGING to the dark places of the world, Danny Wheeler had refused to show himself and face John's protective wrath. But he'd left a trail that even a private on his first sortie could follow.

With the park lights now casting daylight over the nearest ball field and parking lot, John knelt next to a pair of skid marks on the concrete pavement. The stripes of black rubber beneath the paint chips and shattered glass indicated a quick stop and speedy retreat.

The suited-up detective with the light red hair who'd introduced himself as Spencer Montgomery and taken charge of the scene nodded his agreement. "Something big stopped here."

Maggie followed right behind the detective. "Like a white van?"

"That'd be about the right dimension to match this wheel base." John pointed out the bits of displaced gravel around Maggie's truck. "And those are definitely man-sized footprints."

John braced his knee and pushed to his feet as Detective Montgomery nodded. "I've already put out an APB on the bug van and Wheeler. We'll find him, Maggie."

An outburst of laughter from the back of John's truck, where Montgomery's partner, Nick Fensom, was playing some kind of game with Travis to keep the boy's attention off the disturbing scene, turned Maggie's head. But only for a moment. John could tell that something had changed inside her, something had hardened knowing that Travis had seen this. Whatever bond of fear Danny held over her had finally been burned out by pure, white-hot anger. She wasn't the skittish, paranoid woman John had first met on the elevator that day. Knowing that her innocent son, who'd never known his father, had finally gotten a glimpse of the unspeakable things he'd done had finally enabled her to seize the courage and strength she possessed.

"Nick's good with kids." She pointed out the obvious.

"Probably because he's the oldest of six brothers and sisters."

Maggie still worried like a mom, but she was thinking like a cop now—not a battered spouse who lived in constant fear of her ex's return. She went to stand by John and face the detective. "How did Danny get out of jail so quickly?"

Montgomery shrugged his apology. "We tried to hold him, but his boss, Lawrence Boyle, posted bail. He's a free man until his assault hearing, unless we can pin this or something else on him. Then I doubt he'll ever be a free man again."

John wanted a better answer. "Can't you arrest him on suspicion or take him in for questioning and lose the key to his cell? Who else would do something like this to Maggie?"

"We have to find him first," the detective pointed out. "But we will. Doing something like this seems like suicide for a man who wants to stay out of prison. But because he's so keen on going back, I'm happy to put together a case and oblige him."

John liked the cool, methodical thoroughness he saw in Montgomery's documentation of the crime scene and questions he'd asked Maggie. If there was evidence to be found and a case to put together, this guy would get the job done.

He slipped his hand to the middle of Maggie's back. There was nothing more he could do here—Wheeler was smart enough to be long gone. "Is it okay if I take Maggie and Travis home? It's getting late and he's got school in the morning."

The detective nodded. "Sure. Let us work on this. I'll order an extra patrol unit to keep an eye on your building."

"Thank you." Maggie leaned back against John's hand, no doubt feeling the emotional fatigue of the day.

Montgomery may have noticed it, too, because he reached out to give Maggie's shoulder a supportive squeeze. "I need you to focus on the Rose Red case, and that talent you have for getting the victims and witnesses to open up and talk. You don't need to be dealing with this sick…" The tension in his voice faded away to silence. "I guess that's why you relate so well to the victims."

"Call me if you find out anything," Maggie said, turning toward her son.

"I'll see you at work tomorrow." John paused, a step behind her when Montgomery put up his hand. "Are you military?" he asked.

"United States Marine Corps, sir."

"Are you staying with her and the boy?"

Maggie came back, making a polite argument that John wouldn't hear. "John lives next door. I wouldn't ask—"

He'd answered the call of duty more than once in his life. He'd answer it again.

"Yes. They won't be alone."

Chapter Eleven

"We'd better put these away." Maggie slipped the navy blue Marine Corps jacket from beneath Travis's limp hand and tucked his arm beneath the blanket and sheet. She swept the shock of chestnut hair off his forehead and leaned over the bed to kiss his sweet, unfurled brow. "I don't want anything to get wrinkled or broken."

As stressed out by the clear threat against her as he'd been excited about the ball game, Travis had been too wired to sleep. But John had had the brainstorm of bringing over his uniform and medals and sidearm to reassure her son that he was someone who could keep him well and truly safe.

The gun had quickly been stored away alongside Maggie's, but the ploy worked. Soon enough, Travis's natural curiosity kicked in and he'd begun to ask questions. Maggie had sat on the bed beside Travis while John patiently answered each one, sharing the meaning of the USMC logo and the brass buttons. Why he had captain's bars and what a major, colonel and general's brass would look like.

And then he'd brought out his boxes of medals and Travis's face had lit up with real awe. Maggie listened, too, tearing up with heartbreaking sadness as John glossed over the more gruesome details of a routine patrol cut short by a roadside bomb, and the selfless sense of duty it took for a man with a shattered leg to crawl back and forth between a bunker and the burning vehicle to retrieve his wounded and deceased friends.

For once, Travis had been silent, hanging on to every word of John's story. "You never gave up, did you, John?"

"No, son. A marine never gives up."

Tears burned along Maggie's cheeks and dripped into her lap at John's matter-of-fact account of the tragedy that had earned him his Silver Star. And even though Travis might not have fully comprehended the magnitude of John's sacrifice, he understood enough to know that with this man, he would be cared for and safe.

"Oops." Just as Maggie reached for the felt box in Travis's other hand, he rolled over in his sleep, hugging John's Purple Heart medal as close to his chest as he'd held his ball glove the night before.

"Let him keep it." John picked up the other medals from the bedside table. "If it helps him sleep." He cupped his hand over the crown of Travis's hair. She could see the impulse to lean in before he stopped and asked, "Do you mind?"

Maggie smiled her permission. "He'd love it." She could easily understand how safe and assured Travis felt when the tall, muscular marine bent down and gave her sleeping son a gentle goodnight kiss, as well. "You're his hero. Mine, too."

"I was just doing my job."

She swiped the dampness from her cheeks at the humble comment and closed the door to Travis's bedroom before following John out to the living room.

"Don't tell me you're all heroed-out. The man I saw tonight—" she paused to turn on a lamp and summon the courage to say what was in her heart "—the man I've seen every day since I met you is a hero." She shook out the folds in his jacket and held it out for him to put on. "May I?" When he reached out to take it from her, she pulled back a step and tilted her face up to his. "Please? I'd love to see you in it. I have a feeling you're stunning in your dress blues."

"Stunning?"

Okay, maybe not the word a marine wanted to hear. But when she refused to let go, he relented and turned his back to her so she could help him slide his uniform jacket on over his T-shirt.

"There you go." He held his arms out to either side and turned. *"Semper Fi."*

When he faced her again, Maggie saw the man she knew him to be inside, the same man she wished he could see. She supposed she should come up with a different word to describe the man she was looking at right now—hot, impressive, noble, sexy, patriotic, proud, powerful, handsome.

"Well?" he prodded, waiting for her opinion.

"Stunning."

John grinned, shook his head and started to shrug out of the jacket.

"Wait." Maggie picked up the box with his Silver Star and opened it.

"Sarge…"

"It's not complete yet." She pulled out the prestigious medal and unhooked the clasp.

His hands settled at either side of her waist and he tried to look stern with her. "Maggie…"

"Shh. Let me."

He touched his fingertip to the corner of her eye and traced the salty track of a tear down her cheek. "Will it make these go away?"

She nodded.

"Then do it."

Humbled and honored by the permission bestowed on her, Maggie slipped her fingers inside the front of his uniform to protect his heart as she pinned the medal above the pocket. She felt his chest heave against the back of her hand as some deeply hidden emotion surfaced. His fingers slid beneath her blouse and massaged the skin above the waistband of her jeans, as though holding still for her was almost more than he could endure. She pulled the pin back through the material and sealed the clasp. John leaned in to rest his forehead against hers.

Maggie outlined the ribbon with her finger and touched each shiny point of the star. Then she rested her hand over the medal, over his heart, and smiled. She tilted her eyes to look up into the unblinking intensity of his. "Your character, your commitment, your caring—those are the things that make you a hero, John. Not this medal." She slid her hands higher, framing the stubbled warmth of his jaw between them. "But maybe every now and then, if you look at this or your Purple Heart, you'll remember the men whose lives you saved. And the ones who helped save yours." She stroked her thumb across his lips and felt him shudder beneath her touch. "And maybe you'll remember what makes you a hero to my son. And to me."

She stretched up on tiptoe to replace her thumb with her mouth. She kissed him gently, felt his hands nip into her waist. She kissed him again, more firmly this time, and his lips chased after hers when she pulled away. Green-gold eyes locked onto hers. And then John's arms snaked behind her back, drawing her tight against his chest and lifting her so he could claim her mouth in a fierce, passionate kiss.

Maggie wound her arms around his neck and held on as

the emotions she'd unleashed poured out of him with every kiss and caress. She met each foray—taste for taste, touch for touch, need for need. He squeezed her almost painfully tight, imprinting brass buttons against her breast and stomach. His hands slid inside her blouse, dipped inside her jeans, stroking her skin, sending shivers along her spine even as she grew feverishly hot.

"John," she whispered, brushing her lips across his cheekbone, nibbling at his jaw. As much as she loved seeing him in uniform, she was beginning to think he needed to take it off. She wanted to touch the heat of his skin. She wanted to learn the supple movements of his body beneath her hands. She wanted to feel his thudding heart beating against hers.

His mouth opened warm and hot over the bundle of nerves beneath her ear and she gasped at the instant response in the tips of her breasts and deeper inside. With blind impatience, she pushed at the collar of his jacket and he quickly shrugged out of it and tossed it onto the couch. His lips moved from her throat down into the V of her blouse. He slipped one button free and rasped his tongue against the open spot.

"Your skin is so soft."

Another button opened and he dipped his tongue into the cleavage between her breasts.

"So pretty, so hot."

Her blouse fell open to her waist and John fit his big hands to her breasts, gently kneading, squeezing. His thumbs teased the proud tips straining against the confinements of satin and lace.

Each touch was a torment, every kiss a call that beckoned her to answer. She ached to feel his skin on hers, to feel his hardness against her curves. She wanted to feel the weight of him on top of her, inside her. It had been so long since she'd wanted. And she'd never wanted like this.

She tugged at the hem of his shirt and pushed it up beneath his arms to take the same liberties he had. She touched. His smooth muscles quivered beneath her hands. She closed her lips around his flat nipple and coaxed it to attention, tasting the musky flavor of his skin.

He groaned in response and slipped his hands down to cup her bottom and drag her up against the hard evidence of his desire. "Maggie, I want… I need… Can you? Will you?"

"Yes." Her answer was too breathy, too unsure. *Say it louder.* "Yes," she repeated. *Make this right, Maggie. Do it.* She pulled his mouth back up to hers and whispered against his lips. "Yes."

Seconds later, they were in her bedroom with the door closed behind them, tumbling onto the bed. Her blouse was gone, her jeans MIA. Maggie reached for the snap of his jeans and eased the zipper over his erection. But she got no further before his hands closed over hers and pulled them away. "Wait a second. Slow down."

"I don't need slow right now, John. I just need…" Oh, no. Had she done something wrong? Been too bold? Danny had never even asked her what she wanted, much less encouraged her to take the lead. Scrambling up onto her knees beside him, she grabbed a pillow from the head board and hugged it over her chest, feeling suddenly unsure. "I'm sorry. What should I—"

John sat up and pressed a finger to her tender lips, silencing her. "Whatever you're thinking right now, stop it. And you don't need this." He plucked the pillow from her grasp and tossed it to the floor. "I want to see every beautiful inch of you."

Maggie followed him to the edge of the bed where he swung his legs over the side. "Then what's wrong?"

"There's not a damn thing wrong with you—with this." He combed his fingers through the loose waves of her hair and draped the ends over the swell of her breast, stroking her with the backs of his knuckles and raising chill bumps there. "I know my timing sucks, but…" He released her hair and raised his hips off the bed to tug his jeans down to his knees. "I need to take my leg off. It'll get tangled in the covers or it might knock against your shins or hit the bedpost if I'm not thinking about what I'm doing with it, and I don't want to bruise you or spoil the moment."

The self-conscious cloud cleared and Maggie knelt on the floor in front of him to help him pull off his shoes and jeans. When he was naked and vulnerable in front of her— his desire for her as obvious as the worry shining from his eyes—she bent forward to press a kiss to the elastic brace encircling his knee. She gently touched the strong, surprisingly lightweight post that extended down to his false foot. Tears scratched beneath her eyelids. "Oh, John. How you must have hurt."

"Actually, the burns killed most of my nerve endings." A tear spilled over at the suffering he'd endured. He cupped her cheek and brushed away the tear. "Hey, I thought these were going away."

If he could come to terms with his past and focus on this moment together, then so could she. With a brave smile, she sniffed away her sorrow and began peeling back the elastic band that covered the joint between his real and artificial leg. "Show me how."

"Ah, Sarge." She'd exposed the joint itself, revealing the miraculous testament to medical genius and the human will. "You don't have to do this."

"I want to." With gentle, reverent touches—and fingers

that were more sure than she'd expected—she followed his instructions and removed the prosthetic. She pushed his hand aside and took over the job herself when he massaged the rounded stump. "I'm not scared of this, John. It's a badge of honor, even more than your medals. I'm scared of…"

"Of what?" He pulled her up and fell back across the bed with her. He propped himself up on his elbow beside her and flattened his palm at the center of her stomach. "Maggie, what scares you?"

She was obliquely aware of the shorter leg falling on top of hers. Yet it wasn't the handicap she noticed, but the erotic differences between his crisp, masculine hair and her smoothly shaven thigh. She was aware of the corded strength in his leg, the arousal nudging against her hip. She was aware of the desire shading his hazel eyes and knew he was a powerful, potent man.

Maggie splayed her fingers over John's and looked down at them, embarrassed to speak the truth. "I haven't had sex in ten years, and I was never great at it, even before the rape."

For several awkward moments, John said nothing. And then he pulled his hand from beneath hers. "I'm not having sex with you, Maggie Wheeler."

Shocked at how easily he'd changed his mind, her eyes darted up to his. Embarrassed, heartsick, she tried to scoot away. "You don't have to do me any favors. If you think you're being noble or you're worried I'll freak out or—"

John rolled his body half on top of her, caught her chin in his hand and silenced her protest with a kiss. She went completely still except for the rapid rise and fall of her chest beneath his, and the needy, inevitable response his lips triggered in hers.

He finally pulled back when she was clutching at his

shoulders and shamelessly giving whatever he asked for in that kiss. She lay back on the bed, trapped in his eyes and confused by the delicious promise of his embrace. "I don't understand."

"I don't know what kind of garbage Danny put into your head, but we're not having sex." He pushed a bra strap off one shoulder and then the other. "I'm making love to you. Slow, wonderful, make-you-cry-out-my-name love to you."

The vow in those words made her blush. She felt the heat of them sinking into her blood and shimmering throughout her body. John dipped his head to kiss the rosy stain of heat on her breast. He kissed her again, pulling away the satin covering and tonguing the puckered nub of the nipple that sprang forth to meet him. Beneath his tender, thorough seduction, she moaned with helpless need. "Neither one of us is perfect. But together, I think we just might be."

It was an intoxicating promise. Maggie framed his face between her hands, drew his mouth back to hers and nodded.

"Yes, what?" he whispered against her swollen, tender lips.

"You're a good talker, John Murdock. Now show me perfect."

Soon, she was just as naked, just as needy, just as sure that being with John was what they both wanted. With her body on fire in ways it had never been before, she willingly climbed into John's lap as he sat up and pulled her onto his thighs. He entered her in a slow, patient stroke that finally bound them together as one. There was no need for words as they fell into a rhythm that took him deeper, faster, completely inside her.

She wanted to feel, to fly, to know the joy of loving a man who wouldn't hurt, who wouldn't take, who wouldn't force. She wanted to be with John Murdock tonight as much as she'd ever wanted anything in her life. He held her close, chest to chest, as the tiny tremors inside her quaked and grew.

And when he thrust up inside her, groaning with his release, and waves of sensation cascaded down all around him, Maggie buried her face in his neck because she did, indeed, cry out John's name.

LATER IN THE NIGHT, John awoke to the clinging blanket of the sleeping woman wrapped in his arms. Maggie's freckled skin was somehow both pale and warm in the dusky moonlight filtering through the blinds at her window. For all her height and strength and courage, she seemed fragile and vulnerable and oh, so feminine draped against his side, her bare breasts pillowed against him, the even rhythm of her breathing fluttering across his skin.

Humbled by the gifts of her passion and trust, he pressed a kiss to the soft jut of her shoulder. Then he extricated himself from her bed as gently as he could and pulled the covers up over her.

Dressing in nothing but his boxer shorts, he made a quick trip to the john to freshen up. Hopping on one leg, bracing his hand against a wall or door frame when he needed some balance, he made his way throughout the apartment, double-checking the locks on the front door, securing each window and making sure the answering machine was clear of any vile messages from Danny before he went into Travis's room.

The ten-year-old was sprawled out in sleep, covers kicked to the floor. John removed the medal box and set it on the lamp table beside the boy's ball glove before tucking the covers around him again and heading back to Maggie's bedroom.

"Is everything okay?" she asked in a warm, drowsy voice that made him want her all over again.

"We're safe. Travis is asleep and the placed is locked up tight. Everything's perfect." He climbed beneath the covers with her and gathered her into his arms. She might have been asking about her son or building security, but he was talking about her, this—Travis, too—all of it.

"John?"

"Yeah, Sarge?"

She walked her fingers across his chest and rose up in the bed beside him. "Is Travis hard asleep?"

"I think so."

"Then can we… Again?"

The covers had fallen to her waist and his thoughts zeroed in on her peachy breasts and how the cool, air-conditioned air excited them. His body responded with an instant heat at her shy request. "Oh, yeah."

He raised his head to capture a tempting breast in his mouth. She was so responsive, so giving, so beautiful. Without any words about hang-ups or handicaps, he pulled her down and rolled her beneath him, taking his sweet time to reacquaint himself with her body. He let her explore his as well until he was too hard and too needy to resist her mewling cries of pleasure any longer. She wound those long legs around his hips and welcomed him deep inside her feminine heat.

And when they were both sated and spent, he spooned himself behind her and they drifted off to sleep. Once upon a time, he'd gone to war because he couldn't forget a woman he could never have. Now his heart was so full of Maggie Wheeler and how much he loved her that he couldn't even remember any other woman's name. And he wasn't going anywhere.

John brushed her hair away from her face and kissed

the back of her neck. He nuzzled his nose in the scent of her there, finally understanding that of all the things he'd lost in his life, nothing could destroy him like losing this woman could.

"ARE YOU OKAY?"

Maggie smiled into her phone, wondering if she'd ever get used to having a man like John be interested in her welfare. "I'm fine. Really." She turned and waved to the uniformed officer who'd driven her straight to The Corsican's front doors after her shift at KCPD and a trip to the grocery store. "I'm home now. Someone was with me all day today and I'm about to knock on Joe's door to let him know I'm here."

Following their agreed-upon checklist of safety precautions, Maggie had called to report her location.

"I still wish you would have let me pick you up," John groused.

Maggie walked up to the building supervisor's door. She couldn't really do anything more unless she set down her bags of groceries or ended the call. "Your shift doesn't end until four, and because you're picking up Travis at school, it doesn't make sense for you to leave the station to bring me home, then go all the way back to his school and here again."

"I'd do it."

"I know you would, John." And even though she loved how he wanted to protect her, as a cop, she knew a thing or two about the protection business herself. Besides, "Knowing that you'll be there to get Travis home is a huge relief for me. I can watch out for myself. But when I'm worried about his safety, I tend to get distracted."

"Don't be distracted. Travis will be safe with me," he reassured her.

"I know."

"You call again as soon as you're in the apartment. And lock everything behind you," he reminded her unnecessarily.

"I will. I'll see you for dinner, then?"

"Sarge?"

"Yes?" She waited expectantly for him to continue. She knew they'd promised to move their relationship along slowly. But at what point did a man and woman declare their love for each other? When was it so soon that she'd scare him away? When was it too long that he'd lose interest in her?

And did she really need to hear the words from John? Danny had always been quick to tell her he loved her, even after the rape. From him, the words had meant nothing. From John, could she trust that they meant more?

But John said nothing further beyond, "I'll be there. Nobody goes in that apartment except Travis and me. Understood?"

Her disappointment rushed out in a soft sigh. She still had a lot to learn about a healthy relationship apparently. "Understood."

Once Maggie had ended the call and clipped her cell phone back on her uniform belt, she knocked on Joe Standage's door. The super had agreed to "clock her in" whenever she entered the building. But there was no answer at his door. Maggie knocked again and leaned her ear closer to his apartment door. There was no indication of movement inside. Had Joe been called to an emergency elsewhere in the building? Or was he not even going to get the simple request of being there to say hello right?

By the third knock with no answer, Maggie had already decided to head up to her own apartment. If she waited any longer than five or six minutes—ten minutes, tops—

to check in with John again, she had a feeling he would be calling her. Or even more worrisomely, skipping his promise to pick up Travis and heading straight here to make sure she was okay. So she punched the elevator call button and dialed Mr. Standage on his cell.

It went straight to voice mail. For a brief moment, Maggie considered trying his door again. But she hadn't heard another phone ring. If he was in there asleep or in trouble, surely she would have heard the ring. "Hey, Joe. Maggie Wheeler here. I just knocked on your door to let you know I'm home. Why don't you call me back when you get this message. Thanks."

The elevator dinged and the doors opened. She peeked inside to make sure it was empty, then swallowed her fear and stepped across the threshold. She clipped the phone back to her belt and punched in number 7.

Her breath caught in her chest as the doors slid shut and the car jerked, before beginning its slow rise up the shaft. *I should have taken the stairs.* But the groceries were heavy, she was a grown woman wearing Kevlar and carrying a gun, and John really would worry if she didn't call him soon.

When the elevator jerked a second time, Maggie gasped and grabbed on to the railing. Apartment, house, RV or tent—whatever her next home might be—she vowed that it would be located on the ground floor.

The 5 lit up over the doors and the elevator slowed its ascent. A scuffling sound on the outside of the car above her startled her. She glanced up at the fluorescent lights and decorative plastic grate on the ceiling. She trusted her eyes and willed her apprehension to dissipate. The light for the sixth floor lit up and she heard a thump. She glanced up again, a riot of goose bumps pricking across her arms

and neck. Something was malfunctioning in the pulleys
and machinery above her.

"Oh, God."

Some*one* was up there. The nightmare was happening
again.

Maggie dropped her bags before the elevator jerked to
an unnatural stop. She unholstered her gun before the service door opened. She flattened her back against the wall
before the lights shattered and the ceiling crashed in and
Danny Wheeler jumped down into the elevator with her.

"Hello, Mags." She raised her gun and he grinned. "At
last we're together."

Chapter Twelve

Shock or terror or the adrenaline roaring through her blood created a moment's hesitation, giving Danny a split second of time to slam his arm down over her wrists as she pulled the trigger. The shot deflected off the ancient carpet and sparked against the steel wall. In the same follow-through of his swing he clamped his hand around her throat and pinned her against the railing.

Maggie kicked at his shins, shoved at his throat.

He snagged her wrist as she brought the gun to bear again and he slammed it into the wall beside her. One smack stung her knuckles. With a second blow her fingers went numb. With the third her grip popped open and the gun crashed to the floor.

Danny kicked it away before she could even gurgle a cry through the choke hold on her throat.

"Danny," she growled, "you're going to prison."

"I don't care." Picking her up by her throat and wrist, he hurled her across the elevator.

That was his first mistake.

She was closer to the gun now. Maggie pushed forward with her knees, stretched, reached.

"I saw you kiss another man." He kicked the gun away. He whirled around and kicked out again, his foot catching her in the abdomen below her vest and robbing her of breath. "You kissed him!"

Curling up into a protective ball, Maggie fought off the bruising pain and the flashback to another time and another blow.

"You were with him last night, weren't you?" He made the healing beauty of her time with John sound like a damning curse.

Truth or lie, there was no need for her to answer. He wouldn't listen.

"You promised to love me forever." Danny picked up her gun and pressed it against her belly. Maggie held herself still against the bruising poke of the barrel as Danny grabbed her phone and handcuffs off her belt. She inhaled a deep breath when he pulled away, then bit down on a fearful curse as he slipped the cuffs and gun into the pockets of his sweaty, grimy coveralls. Wherever he'd been hiding for the past twenty-four hours, soap and clean water hadn't been a part of it. "And now you're bangin' some other man?"

"Danny, don't." That one plea sneaked out as she watched him drop her cell phone into the empty hole where the elevator's emergency phone was supposed to be.

He reached up behind the panel and did something to the wires. The lights of the panel blinked on again. The machinery above her hummed to life as he pulled out his arm and straightened. He punched the *G* for the parking garage and the elevator began to descend. Maggie's heart sank with it.

"I made that same promise. I love you. I have always loved you. I always will."

His promise had ceased to have meaning long ago. "You have to let me go, Danny," she wheezed through the pain in her gut. "This is kidnapping."

He smoothed his fingers over his bald head, his hand coming away from his skin in a fist. She made the mistake of watching the fist when she should have been watching the boot.

"Shut up!" She rolled up at the last minute, deflecting his kick to a glancing blow off her vest. He kicked her again. "Nobody…" And again. "Tells me…" And again. She was saving herself from broken ribs, but the blows were robbing her of breath. "What to do! You're mine, understand? He can't have you!"

No, she argued with herself. *You're a different woman—stronger, braver.* She was smarter now than she'd been ten years ago. She had a son to live for, fight for. She had John Murdock in her life. She had hope for something better. Maggie knew how to fight back now. She wanted to fight back. She had to fight back. *Do it!*

With a primal scream, Maggie kicked out with her own feet, catching Danny's leg on the next blow and knocking him flat on his back. And then she was up on her knees, attacking him for all she was worth. She put her fists together and hit him square in the gut, stopping his cursing by stealing *his* breath.

She pushed to her feet, staggered to the control panel and pushed every button, ensuring a quicker stop. She sensed Danny rising behind her, smelled him closing in and rammed straight back with her elbow. His grunt of pain told her she may have cracked an unguarded rib. When he lunged for her again, she kicked straight for the groin and doubled him over.

"Help me!" She turned and pounded on the door. "Joe! Anybody! Call 9-1-1! Help!"

She had to get her gun. She had to stop the damn elevator.

"Why aren't we stopping?" she shouted.

"Because I'm smarter than you, bitch."

Too late, she felt the hand in her hair. She whirled around, kicked, punched. But Danny had her now. He slammed her head down against the railing and pain splintered through her skull.

Maggie dropped to her knees as the design in the carpet swirled into a blur and she felt like she might throw up.

She was going to die. She had a son to raise, a job to do and a man to love. And she was going to die.

She heard the click of the handcuffs and felt the pinch at her wrists. And then Danny was hauling her to her feet, capturing her, limp and woozy, against his side.

"I rigged the elevator, Mags. Just like I've rigged it before." He sounded triumphant as the *G* lit up and the elevator slowed to a stop. Blood was warm and sticky where it dripped into one eye, half-blinding her to the gun he pulled from his pocket. "You may be too stupid to learn that. But know this." He pressed a kiss to her temple and she nearly retched. "We love each other, Mags. And you will never be with any man but me."

Maggie heard a ringing in her head. It sounded like her phone, only there was no phone to answer. *Think, Maggie.* But the ache in her head was throbbing so badly that she could barely stand, much less keep a coherent thought in her brain.

When the doors opened, the instinct to run tried to clear her foggy senses, but her feet were like lead. Danny's arm anchored at her waist was the only thing that moved her forward, and when he stopped abruptly, she would have pitched to the concrete floor if he hadn't pinned her to him.

"Boyle, what the hell are you doing here?" Danny's seething anger prompted Maggie to lift her bound wrists to try to wipe her vision clear.

She blinked Lawrence Boyle's bleached-blond hair into

focus. "You said you were going to hide out at the shop," Lawrence explained calmly. "But you left. I knew you were coming to see Maggie."

Danny waved the gun at his friend. "Are you trying to get me arrested? Get that thing out of here." He pulled Maggie forward as he pointed to the extermination company's white van. "That thing's like a beacon for everyone in KCPD who's looking for me. What the hell were you thinking?"

Instead of replying to that, Boyle planted himself in their path, forcing Danny to stop. The bruises might not show up for a few hours yet, but there was no mistaking the blood on Maggie's face. "Did you hurt her?"

Maggie held out her hands, beseeching her only ally. "Help me. Please."

The dark bug eyes darted over to her. Boyle didn't look away until Danny spoke again.

"She's my wife. How I straighten her out is my business." Danny pointed the gun toward the van. "Now if you really want to help an old friend, you'll drive that thing away from here and take the heat off me."

"I'll help. Come with me."

As her deflated hope struggled to think of a way to outsmart two abductors instead of one, Danny dragged her to the back of the open van with Boyle. The burning stench of open chemical containers stung her sinuses and cleared her head like a whiff of smelling salts.

"What are you doin' with all this stuff, man?" Danny was as dumbfounded by the mess as she.

But Danny was only confused. She was instantly on alert.

The containers were empty.

"Oh, my God." She exhaled her fear on a soft breath, then ducked as Lawrence Boyle grabbed a wrench from the back of his van and swung it at Danny's head. The blow knocked him to the ground. Maggie staggered after the gun that slid beneath the van's rear tire, but Boyle beat her to it.

Before she could utter a warning, he pointed the gun at Danny's head and fired.

Maggie jumped at the sharp report that echoed throughout the garage. She tore her shocked gaze away from the pool of blood forming beneath Danny's head and looked up into the cool, emotionless expression on Lawrence Boyle's round face.

"Give me my gun, Lawrence," Maggie ordered, knowing her world had just taken a wild turn into Crazy Land. The relief she might have felt at Danny finally being purged from her life never came. This was something new to fear, something far less predictable than a violent ex. "Give me my gun."

Boyle looked at the handcuffs on her outstretched wrists, but made no comment or move to free her. He looked up into her eyes and smiled. "I took care of the problem for you, Maggie. Danny will never hurt you again."

"Thank you, Lawrence." Did she move in closer to try to reach the gun? Or should she retreat? Maybe it was enough just to keep him talking. "When the police come, I'll explain what happened. It was clearly self-defense. You were assisting an officer."

"I did that for you, Maggie. Danny was a bad man. I came to save you."

Maggie nodded. She tried to keep her focus on Boyle while scanning the garage for any sign of movement or sound. Two gunshots had been fired in the past ten minutes. The elevator had stopped and reversed course. A man was dead on the garage floor and no one was responding?

Her phone rang from inside the elevator again. John!

Please let one person notice that things were not right in her world.

Frustration screamed inside Maggie's head but she kept her voice calm. "Do you have a phone, Lawrence? We need to find my phone and call 9-1-1." She needed to get him to talk, like when she interviewed a victim or witness. It might mean the difference between living and dying today. "I'm worried about the chemicals you may have spilled." She glanced into the back of his van. "Where are all the poisons you killed the ants with?"

"You need to come with me." Maggie wondered if she was the one who was mad when he closed his beefy paw around one of her bound hands and led her toward the door to the storage lockers. "I wasn't sure how I was going to make this happen until Danny tried to take you away from me today. When he left the shop with his tools, I knew he was going to hurt you. I had to be here to stop him. He can't take you from me."

"Lawrence, no." *Please, no.*

He opened the door and led her inside. Once she crossed the threshold, the stink of chemicals—formaldehyde, permethrin, who knew what else?—was so heavy in the air that her eyes watered and she felt woozy again.

The door closed behind her, trapping her in the close space with only a sealed window at the end of the walkway. "What are you doing, Lawrence? How are you helping me?"

He stopped in front of her storage locker. The crime lab had taken all the newspaper clippings and left a black dusty mess of fingerprint powder over most of her things. Boyle pulled a ring of keys from his pocket and reached for the padlock on her door.

The lab had taken Danny's lock and replaced it with a

new one, but Lawrence jabbed his key at the lock as though he expected it to open.

Not Danny's lock.

The shrine, the pictures of her life, the clippings taped to the wall—they hadn't come from Danny. Danny hadn't gone through her things.

Maggie backed silently toward the door while Lawrence tried another key on his ring. The chemicals in the air, soaked into the wood and belongings all around her, were getting dense enough, toxic enough to make the open gash in her hairline burn.

When the keys didn't work, another man might have cursed. But Lawrence, with the strength of an ox and a chilly lack of outward feeling, leaned his shoulder into the wooden frame and barreled into it.

While wood splintered and chicken wire was pulled from the staples that held it in place, Maggie lengthened her silent steps toward the exit. The door was in reach now. She could turn, twist the knob...

"Don't leave me." She heard a small snap of sound behind her.

Maggie's blood froze in her veins. She slowly faced Lawrence again, expecting to see the gun pointed at her face.

Instead, he held a burning cigarette lighter.

"Don't do this, Lawrence." If he dropped that lighter... "You don't want to hurt me. Danny wanted to hurt me." She wondered how thick the fumes had to be before the air itself caught fire. "He ruined my truck and said terrible things to me. But you wouldn't do that." She gestured over her shoulder toward the garage. "You just saved my life. Danny wanted to kill me. But you saved me. You have to save me again."

"I love you, Maggie." His bulgy round eyes glistened

with tears. From the volatile chemicals? Or from the emotion that cracked his voice? "Not the way Danny did. My love is pure and true. My feelings for you have sustained me for a long time now. I've loved you from the moment Danny first mentioned you."

"In prison?" *Get him to talk. Distract him. Stop him.* "Did Danny talk about me when you shared a cell with him?"

"Every night. Your picture was so pretty." He glanced toward the empty wall of the storage locker. "I have more pictures of you in here. I come here to look at you, where I can be closer to you."

"You saved all those pictures of me?"

The lighter snuffed out, but he clicked it on again. "You look so strong, but Danny said you needed to be taken care of. I'm good at taking care of people."

"Yes, you are." She forced herself to focus on his eyes and not the flame. "A lot of people are going to die if you set this room on fire, Lawrence. The whole building will burn. Help me again. Please. Let me go warn the people upstairs."

He climbed over the broken frame of her locker and pulled out her winter coat. He hugged it to his nose and sniffed deeply, smiling as he pulled it away.

Maggie watched in horror as he held the lighter to the hem of the coat and it burst into flame. "Boyle!"

It was unnatural the way it caught fire so quickly. He'd doused it in the chemicals from his van. How many other things in here would turn to ash that quickly? Or would they simply run out of oxygen first?

"I tried to take care of you in little ways," he murmured as he watched the coat burn. Maggie glanced up to spot the sprinklers on the ceiling, then wrily despaired that they were probably broken and that Joe Standage hadn't gotten them fixed yet either. "I sent you your favorite flower at work. I followed you to make sure you were safe. I kept Danny away as much as I could."

She'd backed all the way to the door. If she wasn't cuffed, she could hide her hands behind her and open the door. Maybe she could even get it closed again before he fired off a shot.

"You were nice to me, Maggie." She was? When? "That day at the police station—after Danny tried to hurt you— you reached out to me. You touched me again that night I came to help Joe with the ants." She'd grabbed him to stop him from contaminating a crime scene. He thought that meant she cared? "Danny let the bugs out in the building, you know. He wanted a reason to come in and see you. But he won't do anything like that again."

"Let me go, Lawrence," she begged, watching the coat shrivel as it burned. "I have a child to raise. If you truly love me, you'll let me go."

"I do love you, Maggie." The bug eyes blinked and turned. "This is the only way I can keep you from ever being hurt again. This is the only way we can be together."

He dropped the coat into a puddle on the floor and the pool of chemicals exploded into toxic white-and-orange flames.

"No!" Maggie screamed and spun toward the door, but the fire raced along the floor behind her. In mere seconds, the entire door was a wall of burning wood and chemicals.

She was trapped between a killer and certain death.

"ANSWER YOUR PHONE, damn it!"

John raced through the city—his siren blaring, the lights on his truck flashing.

Twenty-four minutes without hearing a word from

Maggie. She should have called him in ten. He'd tried her cell and the apartment. Nothing.

He swung through an intersection, screeching as he careened onto the street that would take him to The Corsican. He'd already put a call in to Spencer Montgomery to warn him that Maggie might be in danger. He'd left two messages with Joe Standage, one asking when Maggie had checked in with him and another demanding that he get off his sorry butt and go find her.

Three blocks away.

He tossed the phone onto the seat beside him and gripped the wheel tighter. Driving his modified truck with his left foot was getting easier, but at this speed, even a man with control over two good feet had to be careful.

He could see The Corsican's brown facade rising above the buildings and trees.

Two blocks away. One.

"I'm comin', Sarge." *Be alive. Be strong.* "I'm comin'."

He'd promised to keep her safe. He'd promised himself.

John stomped on the brake and fishtailed around the corner, crashing through the parking garage's security gate that thus far hadn't kept out any threat to Maggie. He skidded to a stop at the base of the entrance ramp. The entire level was filled with smoke.

"Hell." He lowered his window half an inch to take a sniff of the swirling black fumes. "Ah, hell." He picked up the phone beside him and punched in 9-1-1. "This is John Murdock out of Station 23." He wheeled the truck around and sped back up the ramp to clear the entrance. "I'm reporting a fire at 11387 Mediterranean Drive—The Corsican. The basement level is engulfed with smoke. From the smell of things, it's a chemical fire. I'll begin evac."

He drove his truck around to the front of the building

and jumped out. Why the hell weren't the building alarms ringing? "Maggie!"

He grabbed a mask and helmet from the kit in the back of his truck and charged up the stairs. Inside the first-floor doors he could see the smoke, along with a toxic cloud of chemical gases, puffing up through vents and cracks. The fire had to be downstairs. Good. That meant relative containment if KCFD got here fast enough. Bad if enough air got to the source and flashover occurred. Then the whole building could light up in a matter of minutes.

If whatever chemicals those were didn't blow the place to smithereens first.

The businesslike assessment was done. His emotions were as under control as they were going to get. Time to move.

Step One—hit the alarm. Thank God. The ear-piercing honk of sound should wake even the tenants with hearing aids.

"Maggie!" Step Two—beat down Joe Standage's door and determine the worthless charmer wasn't home.

Step Three? John slipped the oxygen tank over his shoulders and shoved open the stairwell door. He was a few years and a few injuries gone from being able to sprint up the stairs like a young stud like Dean Murphy. But he intended to be at Maggie's door in a matter of seconds.

FIVE MINUTES LATER, John was working his way down from the tenth floor.

Maggie was gone. Missing. She'd never even made it to her apartment after reaching the building. He tried not to let the fear make him crazy, but this was so wrong that his heart was breaking with the thought that he was going to lose another comrade in arms. And there was no medal, no therapy that could ever heal the wound of losing the woman he loved.

Ladder trucks and hoses were positioning themselves outside. Reinforcements were already in the building, clearing tenants from the lower floors. Because he was already on the upper floors, he'd agreed to go door to door to check for elderly residents who might still be in their apartments. He intended to open every damn door in the building to find the one Maggie was hidden behind.

The Wongs were on their way down the stairs. He'd just gotten Mr. Cutlass and his cat out of their apartment. Now he was pounding on Miss Applebaum's door. He could hear the sounds of a television inside.

"Miss Applebaum!" She had about ten seconds before he busted down the door. "John Murdock here. There's a fire in the building. You have to evacuate."

Five. Four. Three. Two…

The door swung open to Joe Standage struggling to pull his pants up over his briefs. "Come on, Frances. We have to go."

John glanced beyond the half-dressed super to see his elderly neighbor pulling a bathrobe on over her nightgown. These two were in flagrante delicto? "Seriously?"

Miss Applebaum buttoned her robe right up to the neck as she stepped into the hallway. "Joe was just fixing my faucet."

Right. So all the breakdowns and seeming incompetence that required so many repairs was just a cover for an affair? So no one had really been watching over the building. No one had taken responsibility for keeping Maggie and Travis safe. Not until the day he'd moved in.

John might have laughed if the situation wasn't so dire. He grabbed the older man by the arm on his way past him. "Did you see Maggie? Did she get home all right?"

But he already knew Joe's answer. "I've been up here most of the afternoon. But I never heard anything across the hall. The elevator was having fits, though. I was gettin' set to go check it when it started running again. Went all the way down to the basement and stopped as far as I could tell. I'm gonna have to call the repair company again."

The elevator. Maggie's worst nightmare.

John hurried the older man along to the stairs with him, then passed him by. "Get Miss Applebaum outside to safety. There should be firefighters coming up the stairs to meet you."

"Where are you going?" Joe hollered after him.

Into the heart of the fire.

One way or another, he was going to find her.

He just prayed it was the right way.

MAGGIE DROPPED THE BALL bat she'd knocked Lawrence Boyle over the head with and got onto her knees beside him. Thank God her son had been a fan all his life and she'd been too sentimental to get rid of any of his equipment.

The dwindling oxygen in the storage space had made her kidnapper light-headed and disoriented anyway. So sneaking into the storage unit behind him had been more about keeping her own senses awake and sharp than about out-muscling the bug man.

She dug into the pockets of his coveralls, searching for her gun. The key to her handcuffs was still in Danny's pocket on the other side of the fire, so it was awkward to pull her battered body along the floor toward the area's lone window.

She put her nose right next to the concrete and tried to catch a breath. The flames had burned through Boyle's chemicals, but they'd burned long enough that the wood-framed doors of each unit were now burning. The ceiling was charred and black with the flames from the walls.

Maggie was roasting like a marshmallow over an open flame. The heat was cooking her skin. The smoke was stealing the breath from her lungs. The toxins in the air were stealing the life from her body.

She'd been a victim of violent love, of obsessive love. But she wasn't done with love yet. If Travis was her heart, then John Murdock was her soul. The fates couldn't be so cruel as to deny her the chance at happiness she'd so recently discovered. Her own will wouldn't allow love to be taken from her now that she'd finally found it.

Maggie dragged the gun along the concrete floor. She thought she could hear a siren outside. She'd even imagined she heard someone shouting her name. But she was so tired. Her lungs ached.

Breathe, Maggie. Fight. Live. Love John.

"Some things are worth fighting for." She whispered the mantra against the floor and then summoned the strength to push up to her knees. "*I'm* worth fighting for."

She raised the gun into the smoke and fired blindly toward the window. Her shots pinged and crashed off wood and concrete. And then she heard the explosion of shattering glass.

Oxygen rushed in as the flames licked across the ceiling. She had to get out. She had to crawl, move. Now. Before that escape route was blocked, as well.

"Maggie!"

She hadn't imagined her name.

"John?" she croaked. Her throat was so sore, her lungs so full. She coughed and stumbled to the floor.

More glass shattered. "Maggie!"

She pushed to her feet and lurched against the wall. "John?"

"Come on, Sarge. I've got you. Reach!"

Maggie clawed her way up the wall, extended her hand. "John?"

Big, gloved hands reached in through the broken window and latched on to her wrist. The hands pulled her outside and lifted her into strong arms.

"Sarge?" Definitely John's voice. "I need a medic over here! She's bleeding!" And then she was lying down on the ground. Fingers stroked across her cheek. Someone cursed. "Sarge, sweetheart, talk to me. Medic!"

Maggie faded out for a few seconds until urgent hands put a mask over her face and cool, pure oxygen streamed into her nose and mouth. She blinked her eyes open to see The Corsican's dull brown bulk towering in the distance. Bright yellow-and-white flames danced back and forth with the shower of water shooting up from the ground. Lights on bright yellow fire engines flashed on and off in her peripheral vision.

And she saw beautiful green-gold eyes watching over her with such intensity that it made her smile.

"That's it, Sarge." She was aware of the hand holding hers now, and of other hands, packing a bandage over the wound in her head. "You stay with me."

Despite the protests of the paramedic working on her, Maggie reached up to pull her oxygen mask down to her chin. "Travis?" she asked.

"He's safe," John assured her. "Detective Fensom picked him up and is driving him here now. Danny?" he asked.

"Dead. Lawrence Boyle, too, I expect."

"Boyle? The bug guy?"

"It's a long story. But not all the things that have happened were Danny's doing." She touched the bump on her forehead and winced. "Although he did do this to me."

"He's lucky he's dead, then."

She wondered if she would ever regret that Danny had been murdered. She didn't yet. "Boyle shot Danny to *save* me. Seems all of Danny's talk about me over the years got Lawrence to thinking I was some kind of ideal woman he wanted to take care of. He started the fire because he loved me."

"How is that taking care of you? That fire damn near got you killed. Forget it. Just tell it to the cops when they get here."

She nodded, happy, for now, to save enough strength so that she could turn her hand inside John's and lace their fingers together in that way that had always made her feel close to him. "And John?"

"Yeah?"

"I've decided to move out of this death trap. I can't live here. I can't be your neighbor anymore." There had to be a safer, happier, friendlier place to live somewhere in Kansas City.

The paramedic mentioned something about stitches, but John shooed him away for a few minutes. "How about moving in with me? I'm dumping this place, too. It tried to take you from me too many times—in too many ways. I'm thinking about buying a house, investing in something more permanent."

Maggie's heart jumped at the idea of being with John. But she'd acted impulsively with her heart once before and had paid dearly for it. She needed to think about this step. She pushed herself up to a sitting position on the blanket where she'd been lying. She could see now that John was wearing a firefighter's coat, and that his skin was as smudged and dirty as she suspected her own face was. He'd come for her the moment she hadn't called. He'd been there for her just like he'd promised. He'd saved her.

"I have Travis. I can't just move in with you."

He scooted closer so that his damaged leg was propped up behind her back, supporting her. "I don't like having even a thin bedroom wall between us. I want a family. I want a future. I want you. I love you."

She'd thought about it long enough.

Maggie's heart thumped loudly in her chest. She reached inside John's coat to splay her fingers over his heart and feel its strength beating in time with hers. "I love you."

Tunneling his fingers into the loose hair at her nape, John dipped his head and covered her mouth in a deep, thorough kiss. Maggie wound her arm around his neck, pulling him close and answering with all her heart.

A ten-year-old's honest voice intruded. "Eeuw."

With a laugh, John pulled Travis onto his knees beside them. "This is what you wanted, wasn't it? The three of us together as a family? Isn't that why you called me at the fire station that night?"

"I guess." Nick Fensom politely faded into the crowd and let the reunion unfold. Travis squinched up his face as Maggie pulled him into her lap and John swallowed both of them up in a hug. "I really just wanted you to teach me how to hit a home run."

John's green-gold eyes looked downright mischievous as he leaned in to give Maggie another kiss. "That will be the second thing on my list."

Epilogue

The man rubbed the hand sanitizer along every finger, from knuckle to tip.

The newspaper article by Gabriel Knight in the *Journal*'s weekend edition mentioned that one of the task force members out to catch the Rose Red Rapist had nearly died in a fire in her apartment building. There'd been two other casualties, as well. Two deaths that were of no importance to him tonight.

He massaged the sanitizing gel into his cuticles and beneath his nails and watched the lights go out inside Robin's Nest Floral Shop.

Even after reading through the article twice, he'd found no mention of any new developments on the task force's investigation, although the *No comment at this time* by lead detective Spencer Montgomery made him suspicious. Perhaps KCPD did have some kind of lead that they didn't want him to know about yet.

The voice in his head chimed in, just as he'd expected it would. *That's exactly why you need to turn this vehicle around and go home. It's too soon for this. It isn't safe.*

But he wanted, he hungered.

The young woman with short black hair, styled in those sculpted waves that meant she had enough money to go to a salon on a regular basis, came outside and locked the door. She glanced up and down the sidewalk, no doubt concerned for her safety at this time of night. She pulled down the security bars over the front window and doors and locked it, as well.

And then she looked again. Not for lurking danger. She was looking for someone in particular. Someone who hadn't shown up when they were supposed to.

The man stowed the sanitizer in his pocket and sat up behind the wheel, suddenly interested in the young shop-keeper's plight.

It's too soon. You'd be smarter to wait.

She'd made him wait. And then she'd humiliated him. They were all laughing at him.

He needed her to pay. He needed the laughter to stop.

The dark-haired woman was on her phone now, lam-basting someone as she marched up the street. Good money said the person who'd just stood her up was get-ting an earful.

Was she heading home? Going to the bar around the corner? Meeting someone else?

Whatever her destination, he could guess it wasn't to meet the missing friend. No, this one was too independent to go home and cry or miss out on the fun just because she was alone.

After slipping on a pair of latex gloves from his bag, he fingered the red rose he'd bought earlier today. The rose he'd bought from her at that very shop.

Don't do it. You have nothing left to prove.

Oh, but he did.

With the voice silenced and the decision made, he started the engine and pulled onto the street, following her into the night.

* * * * *

So you think you can write?

Mills & Boon® and Harlequin® have joined forces in a global search for new authors.

It's our biggest contest yet—with the prize of being published by the world's leader in romance fiction.

Look for more information on our website:
www.soyouthinkyoucanwrite.com

So you think you can write?
Show us!

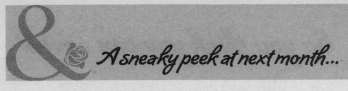

INTRIGUE...

BREATHTAKING ROMANTIC SUSPENSE

My wish list for next month's titles...

In stores from 17th August 2012:

☐ Mercenary's Perfect Mission – Carla Cassidy

& Cowboy Conspiracy – Joanna Wayne

☐ Soldier's Pregnancy Protocol – Beth Cornelison

& In the Enemy's Arms – Marilyn Pappano

☐ The Widow's Protector – Rachel Lee

& Death of a Beauty Queen – Mallory Kane

☐ Cowboy Under Siege – Gail Barrett

In stores from 7th September 2012:

☐ Trace of Fever – Lori Foster

Available at WHSmith, Tesco, Asda, Eason, Amazon and Apple

Just can't wait?

MILLS & BOON® Book Club

2 Free Books!

Get your free books now at
www.millsandboon.co.uk/freebookoffer

Or fill in the form below and post it back to us

THE MILLS & BOON® BOOK CLUB™—HERE'S HOW IT WORKS: Accepting your free books places you under no obligation to buy anything. You may keep the books and return the despatch note marked 'Cancel'. If we do not hear from you, about a month later we'll send you 5 brand-new stories from the Intrigue series, including two 2-in-1 books priced at £5.49 each and a single book priced at £3.49*. There is no extra charge for post and packaging. You may cancel at any time, otherwise we will send you 5 stories a month which you may purchase or return to us—the choice is yours. *Terms and prices subject to change without notice. Offer valid in UK only. Applicants must be 18 or over. Offer expires 31st Janaury 2013. **For full terms and conditions, please go to www.millsandboon.co.uk/freebookoffer**

Mrs/Miss/Ms/Mr (please circle)

First Name

Surname

Address

Postcode

E-mail

Send this completed page to: Mills & Boon Book Club, Free Book Offer, FREEPOST NAT 10298, Richmond, Surrey, TW9 1BR

Find out more at
www.millsandboon.co.uk/freebookoffer

Visit us Online

0712/I2YEA

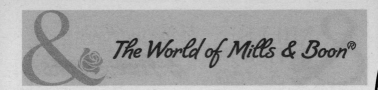

The World of Mills & Boon®

There's a Mills & Boon® series that's perfect for you. We publish ten series and, with new titles every month, you never have to wait long for your favourite to come along.

Blaze®

Scorching hot, sexy reads
4 new stories every month

By Request

Relive the romance with the best of the best
9 new stories every month

Cherish™

Romance to melt the heart every time
12 new stories every month

Desire™

Passionate and dramatic love stories
8 new stories every month

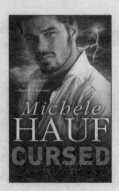